DYING BY DEGREES

*Also by Judith Cutler
and featuring Sophie Rivers*

Dying to Fall
Dying to Write
Dying on Principle
Dying for Millions
Dying for Power
Dying to Score

DYING BY DEGREES

Judith Cutler

HEADLINE

First published in 2000 by
HEADLINE BOOK PUBLISHING

10 9 8 7 6 5 4 3 2 1

British Library Cataloguing in Publication Data

Cutler, Judith
Dying by degrees
1. Detective and mystery stories
I. Title
823.9'14 [F]

ISBN 0 7472 2338 6

Typeset by Palimpsest Book Production Limited,
Polmont, Stirlingshire
Printed and bound in Great Britain by
Clays Ltd, St Ives plc

HEADLINE BOOK PUBLISHING
A division of the Hodder Headline Group
338 Euston Road
London NW1 3BH
www.headline.co.uk
www.hodderheadline.com

For Janet

ACKNOWLEDGEMENTS

I would like to thank the following for their invaluable assistance: Dr Carol Miller, University of Birmingham; Robert Kornreich, University of Central England; Dr Dorothy Rowe; administrative staff of Warwickshire County Cricket Club; Angela Lloyd.

The men and women of Piddock Road Police Station, Smethwick, have been consistently helpful and kind, but none is to be found in the pages of this book. The University of the West Midlands is entirely fictitious, though some of its problems may not be.

Chapter One

Let's face it, there were very few males I'd have let into my house to keep an eye on me while Mike was in Australia, doing his best – sometimes, I thought, single-handedly – to retrieve the Ashes for England. But Ivo was one of them. He sat – young, elegant, handsome, radiating maleness – on my kitchen table. He selected a peanut, hitched himself into a more comfortable position, and regarded me with his big brown eyes while he listened to my woes. It was a miserable November day – I don't think it had ever got light before it started to get dark. And I was finding a Master's course in Education at the University of the West Midlands far less satisfying than I'd hoped. Which was tough, as I'd taken a year's sabbatical from lecturing at William Murdock College of Further Education to put myself through it.

'I don't know whether my expectations were too high,' I said. 'Maybe the teaching's not all that good. I can't even follow the books. Either they aren't very clear or more likely I'm out of practice at reading academic material. Oh, Ivo, why am I stuck in Birmingham while Mike's out there in Australia?'

Ivo finished the peanut and started on another.

His silence said, quite clearly, that if he was a substitute for Mike, then I was also a substitute for the man in his life. Who was, as it happens, Dave, one of Mike's England colleagues. Dave was a fast bowler: a man with shoulders that wouldn't

1

disgrace a carthorse, a fascinating capacity for beer and a tender spot for small mammals. I'd been sworn to secrecy: on no account must I let anyone know that Ivo was living with me. It wouldn't have done Dave's street cred any good at all if anyone had known about that. No one had bothered to work out what effect it might have on mine, should I still have any, after announcing to my nearest and dearest that I was preparing to abandon the world of singletons to marry Mike. Not that there were many near or dear to announce it to. Most of my family had popped their clogs, and my absentee father was too busy playing the field in the naffest corner of Spain's Costa Geriatrica to give a damn either way. Three people – plus the spouses of two of them – were in on the secret: Aggie, my next-door neighbour, who uttered occasional Cassandra-like moans when I was least expecting them; Shahida, a fellow William Murdock College lecturer; and a man who fancied he might have been an old flame, Afzal. Others might have suspected, not least my policeman friend, Superintendent Chris Groom, battling with the accents and his limited budgets in the fastnesses of Black Country Smethwick. I'm sure Ian Dale guessed too. He'd once been Chris's closest colleague, but had now left the force, and was currently pursuing ways of augmenting his police pension.

I twirled the big emerald on the ring finger of my right hand. 'Not the left, you see, Ivo. I'm not announcing my impending change of status to my fellow students. Don't get me wrong. It's not that I want a farewell fling. Absolutely not. But can you imagine what the press would make of it? Here's the team in the midst of another series of débâcles and the papers would love to blame it on – well, love. Oh, I know Mike's not failing. Any more than your guy is. But the others . . . In any case, we've agreed that one day, when we feel like it, we'll simply go and get married. OK, a party afterwards. But in the meantime, shtoom. What d'you think?'

Ivo Baggins agreed. He was the latest, Dave had said, in a

long line of gerbils called Baggins. There'd been Bilbo and there'd been Frodo, named after other creatures who liked to live in round holes in the depths of the earth and who definitely preferred two breakfasts. I wondered how many more names there were ending in 'O'. There was always Tommo, the nickname of one of the most distinguished Australian fast bowlers, but I didn't, in the circumstances, see that ever being used.

Ivo agreed that I deserved a swig of something celebratory now my ticket for Australia lay in my hand. I was going to join Mike for Christmas before we slotted back into our respective struggles, mine for an M.Ed., his for the Ashes.

After the swig, I'd better return to my books: there was another assignment coming up all too quickly.

I laid my ticket on the table and fished a half-bottle of champagne from the fridge. OK, it was an extravagance when I wasn't earning a salary this year, but what was a ticket to Australia if not an extravagance? And at least my sabbatical from William Murdock College had so far proved stress-free enough to give my perennially dodgy tum time to heal: it no longer exploded when I downed fizzy acid.

But it did now! I leapt across the kitchen with more speed than was wise, given the amount of bubbly still left in my glass: Ivo had abandoned the nutrition of his peanut for the roughage of my airline ticket. There was already an inch semi-circle gone from the top copy.

He was so engrossed that he didn't notice my hands, ready to scoop him up. Fortunately. While not being the most venturesome of explorers – something, according to his owner, to do with trying to nibble the pilot light of a central heating boiler when he was young – he emphatically did not like being returned to his residence. No, not a cage. Ivo lived in an aquarium, half-full of a mixture of peat and sawdust, through which he excavated labyrinthine tunnels. At one end hung his water bottle. At the other lay a little dish in which I was supposed to tip his food, but which he regularly filled with peat, so vigorous was his digging. But he sustained himself on little nibbles found in his tunnels, some of them already sprouting. If an animal had to live in captivity, this was surely the kindest of environments – even if he did try to escape from it the moment I left the wire-mesh lid even slightly loose. I adjusted the label Dave had written in perfect italic script: *IVO BAGGINS*. And left him to it.

There was a tiny new safe in my airing cupboard: Mike liked to give me jewellery but he also liked to know it was hidden away from Burglar Bill. I stowed the tickets in that. No doubt when I presented them someone would think I'd got bored and hungry in the check-in queue.

It was a good job I hadn't sunk all that champagne. I was just settling down to work when Steph – my long-lost son – phoned me, and suggested we meet up for one of our occasional baltis. He tended to assume I could always drop everything the moment he phoned; the problem was, given the state of my social life and the enthusiasm I felt for my course, I usually could. And did. So there I was, eyeing up the most enormous naan I'd ever tackled. Steph didn't think it merited more than a twitch of an eyebrow, and tore in.

I hoped he'd invited me to tell me that he'd told his adoptive parents that he'd gone hunting for his birth mother and found her – me, that is. But he seemed perfectly happy to sit in silence munching the naan and plunging it into a balti hotter than the incandescent bowl it was served in. I'm not of the purgatorial school of curry-eaters, and dipped more circumspectly into a milder dish that for some inexplicable reason contained not only bananas but also glacé cherries.

It was never easy to find something we could really talk about. College education should have been a possible: he was halfway through a course. But he never wanted to talk about it. Perhaps he was skiving. But if I tried to press, his jaw tightened.

On bad days, he'd flounce off. On good ones, like today, he'd deflect the conversation by asking about mine.

'It's not very exciting,' I admitted. 'They suggested developing some project work I did for the city colleges a couple of years back. But the whole thing's a lot tougher. You need proper theoretical bases and better research methods . . .' I shook my head, longing for someone to listen with interest and to ask the right questions.

His eyes were glazing. 'What about money?' he asked. That was one thing he was always interested in. To look at him, swathed in onion-like layers of T-shirts, most of them tatty, you'd never guess his adoptive parents were rolling in money and made him what sounded to me like an incredibly generous allowance. I presumed a fair proportion went on pot. A faint aroma always hung around him, though he'd never smoked in front of me. And from the stains on his fingers and the smell of his breath he didn't just confine himself to spliffs. Oh dear. Smoking that heavily at his age . . . Why didn't his parents do something?

Except who could do anything with teenagers? I'd seen enough of them to know they went their own ways.

'Money? Oh, that's better than I thought it would be.'

He didn't quite sigh with relief – for an awful moment he must have been afraid he'd have to pay for himself.

'My tutor—'

'That's the new one, right? While the other one's pregnant?'

'Right. He discovered that I can teach English to overseas students, so he's roped me into that—'

'English! How come they need English lessons? They're supposed to be university students!'

'Oh, they are. Just because their English isn't brilliant doesn't mean they're not very bright indeed. They've just never had to speak or write English except in school. Or at university overseas. So they're not used to hearing it spoken

5

under normal conditions.' I inserted quotation marks with my fingers.

'And not with a West Bromwich accent, either,' Steph agreed. He spoke Estuary English, which irritated me, and must have his posh Sutton Coldfield parents pulling their hair out.

'Quite. So they have to practise – preferably before their course starts. But there are always some students who join late, and others who need an extra bit of help.'

'So you're being paid for this.'

'Absolutely.' At much better rates than I'd have got for similar work at William Murdock. 'And they've also asked me to be personal tutor to some of them, even when they've embarked on their courses – for continuity.' And an even better hourly rate than the English teaching. 'Which means,' I started, for some reason embarrassed at my new-found affluence, 'I've decided to fly out to see Mike for Christmas.' Oh, I should be with him in a matter of weeks!

'Great,' he said absently, removing a couple of layers of T-shirt in deference to the heat of the curry.

'The thing is,' I said, paying exaggerated attention to an errant piece of chicken, 'Mike and I have decided to get married.' Why I should be overcome with maidenly coyness goodness knows, but I was, every time I told anyone. And, of course, the complication here was that Steph knew Mike wasn't his father but didn't know who the real one was. Nor, strangely enough, had he ever asked. All in all, he was dealing with our relationship far more phlegmatically than I was.

'Wicked!' he said. The highest praise. And then the grin slipped off his face. 'Hey, you won't be needing me to make any speeches or anything?'

'Not unless you want to,' I said as lightly as anyone chomping naan rather tougher than it looked could hope for. Not that I felt as insouciant as I hoped I sounded. He could scarcely play such a prominent role without telling his parents first. Could he?

'Nah,' he said, looking hopefully at the vegetable curry we were supposed to be sharing. 'Not if it means monkey suits and that.'

I shook my head firmly. 'Mike and I are just going to have a couple of witnesses for the actual marriage.' I pushed the vegetables across to him.

He dug deep. 'No monkey suits?' He peeled off another T-shirt.

'No monkey suits. But we're going to have a wild party a bit later.' What if he'd consent to be a witness? That would be wonderful. But I didn't know whether he'd feel overwhelmed if I suggested that now. And asking him would upset a lot of people who'd known and loved me for years. Hell, this new relationship was making me go through all sorts of manoeuvres I wasn't sure of. Well, both these new relationships, to be honest. And to pussyfoot over things I'd normally have asked outright. Perhaps it was doing the same to Steph. But I felt too shy to ask.

'Wild? With your mates there!' He grinned derisively.

'Mike's too,' I pointed out. 'So there'll be a few people without Zimmer frames.'

'Not if they're England cricketers,' he said. 'D'you see the latest score?'

I nodded glumly. Not only did I listen to as much of the overnight Radio Four commentary as I could, I also looked at the report on Ceefax. I'd always thought only sad people without lives read Ceefax. And here I was glued to it every day.

'I suppose you'll have to have that policeman who looks as if he's got a lemon in his mouth. Or up his backside.'

'Chris? As a witness? No. I don't think he'd like that. On the other hand, he'd probably prefer the high seriousness of a wedding ceremony to any amount of revelry,' I observed, parodying Chris-speak.

Steph rolled his eyes in appreciation. 'Tell you what, I could fix the music for you – got this mate who's a DJ.'

'Sounds good. I suppose he can organise the St Bernard's Waltz and the veleta?'

Steph's mouth twitched. 'No probs. And what about the Gay Gordons? Or would Chris prefer them straight?'

Chapter Two

'I hear a rumour,' Tom Bowen said, as he pushed back from his desk and returned the thick file to me, 'that you're a very fine cook.'

This was scarcely the response I'd been expecting from my new tutor to the detailed outline of my dissertation proposal. But then, a great deal about the University of the West Midlands had been surprising. The location, for a start. True, I hadn't been hoping for the architectural merit and charming location of an Oxbridge college. But my memories of Leeds, where I'd taken my first degree some fifteen years ago, hadn't quite prepared me for this university. The department in which I was based was housed in what looked like a converted factory – no, not a chic eighties warehouse conversion involving recycled bricks, but a sixties job, with fading coloured panels, uniformly ill-fitting windows and stained concrete. It nestled between an architecturally preferable factory pumping out phenol into the atmosphere as if there were no such thing as pollution control, and a first-division soccer stadium. Such academic peace as the bare corridors allowed was shattered every time West Bromwich Albion scored a goal. I knew from bitter experience that further education – as exemplified by William Murdock College – was underfunded to the point of desperation. But I'd heard that higher education was better off. Even if this were true, it didn't apply to UWM. Not this part of the university, anyway. This was clearly a Cinderella, horribly similar to poor William Murdock in its design, tatty equipment, overlarge classes and underfunded library. But as at William Murdock, there were bonuses. I'd expected the staff to be like the remote gods of my undergraduate days, preferring on the whole not to have too much to do with students. These turned out to be hard-working career teachers. True, some had fancy titles. Like Bowen, for example. Assistant Dean of this faculty, and my tutor. On whom my future – or, more specifically, the future of my M.Ed. dissertation – depended.

'Is it OK? The dissertation?' I asked. 'Really? You see, I did all that work with the city-wide computer-based education project a couple of years ago, but the conclusions other people have come to are different from mine . . . And there's a problem with my research methods—'

'That's what a review of literature should show up. Didn't Anna Whatshername tell you that?'

Anna Wade had been my original tutor, until she'd started on her maternity leave. Bowen had inherited me, with, I presume, ill grace. And I suppose it was quite late in the course for him to have to take on someone else.

'Yes. And I'd already outlined some of my problems in the research proposal. There are some ethical problems too—'

'Don't worry about that. Work your way through them, then. So you'll have a proper basis for your dissertation. You've got plenty of time, after all. You don't have to submit for another year at least. And then you can get an extension if you need it. I'll see you for your next session – let's see – in February.'

February! And this was November! 'But I need to see you before that! I told you I had to submit the dissertation in July.'

'Oh, come off it! No one submits in July. Oh, I know it says you do in the regulations, but no one takes any notice of them. Everyone asks for an extension. Everyone.'

'But I don't want an extension. I want to do the course in a single year. I know once I'm back on the William Murdock treadmill, I won't have time for anything extra.'

'To hear you teachers talk you'd think no one else ever did any work.'

Had I sounded as if I was whinging? I hadn't meant to. But I did want to drive home to him the urgency of the situation. 'Dr Bowen—'

'Come on, Sophie, you clearly know more about the subject than I do. And I'd say you can do joined up writing. I'm sure you can do joined up brainwork too. Just get on with it: you'll be OK. I'll see you in February.'

I shook my head. What sort of tutor was this, who couldn't make time to see his tutee? Who couldn't even remember a colleague's name? 'I need to see you before then. As soon as the new term starts.' To my fury, my chest started to tighten: the last thing I wanted was to wheeze all over the man, so I grabbed my asthma spray and had a quick, single burst. Ideally it should be two, but I didn't want to invite him to get all sympathetic – and forgetful.

'OK. When the new term starts.' He scribbled a note on a scrap of paper.

I had a nasty suspicion he was the sort of man who'd promise something just to shut one up. I'd have to keep on at him until we had a firm date.

'Now, about your cooking – you did the catering for a party I went to the other day. Right?'

'They were friends of mine. I helped them out.' I'd not socialised at the party, so I hadn't seen him there. Not that I wouldn't have been welcome. Instead I'd retired – with the hosts' permission – to listen to the Radio Four cricket commentators bringing Mike's century to life in their spare room. Where my presence had, incidentally, embarrassed a pair of would-be bonkers for whom the terms maiden over and Test Match might have had another meaning.

'But money changed hands. Heavens, woman, I'm not about to shop you to the tax man. I want you to cook a meal for me!'

Bowen looked like a man who cared for his food. Possibly rather too much, given his reddening complexion and the way his stomach overflowed his trousers. Though that could have been too much beer, too little exercise. Whatever it was, he must have been carrying at least two stone he didn't need, risky for a man in his late-ish forties.

'I don't want to mess up my work schedules,' I said. Even to my ears, I sounded horribly prissy.

'Haven't I just told you you're well ahead of the game!' He produced a Father Christmas smile. 'And I know you post grads are always looking for ways of augmenting your income – that's why I put that teaching your way. I mean, the course fees don't come cheap, and I presume the mortgage and other bills don't just go away. Come on, Sophie: if you can produce food for a hundred of that quality, I'd like to see what you can do for an intimate dinner. For twenty, say.'

Intimate! And presumably he had a dining table big enough to seat them, and a room big enough for the said table. He was on something bigger than a further education lecturer's salary, then.

'I can see you're the sort of woman who likes a challenge,' he said. 'In fact, I'd say you were busy working out a menu right now.'

A hit. A palpable hit. I pushed away projects for individual portions of poached salmon and fished out my diary. 'When were you planning this feast?' I almost hoped for a date I couldn't manage. Goodness knows why. Provided he didn't want fiddly canapés to welcome his guests, a dinner party wasn't a major problem and I could certainly do with the money. I'd have preferred twelve to twenty, especially as I hadn't seen his kitchen, and I didn't know how far I'd have to ferry stuff from my house in Harborne.

He named a Friday a couple of weeks away. My diary was singularly blank on the day on question, and the one before. It should be a doddle. A profitable doddle.

'I'd better let you have some sample menus and a scale of charges,' I said.

He looked briefly taken aback. He didn't assume I was doing this for love, did he? And I wasn't happy with his smile. 'I guess there'll be a discount, won't there? I mean, we're both teachers.'

If not quite the same kind of teacher. Oh, of course he'd get a discount – when I'd jacked up the prices first. I smiled duplicitously back.

The walk back to the post-graduate work-room – yes, despite the obvious financial pressures on the university, they'd set aside a room for us furnished with filing drawers and computers – was marred by all sorts of unpleasant suspicions. Surely the man wasn't suggesting that my grade could be affected by what I'd thought of as a business deal? And wasn't it rather dodgy of him to have asked a student of his anyway? I'd never have approached any of my students in that way, even in the remote event that one had been in a position to do anything for me. But perhaps, I told myself, in the adult world of HE things were different. After all, none of us was a minor, in need of protection from predatory grown-ups. And if things like that hadn't happened at Leeds, well, maybe it was because there was a whole new university climate these days – and I wasn't thinking of the phenol which was especially pungent today. In a few moments I was due at a seminar – and it wouldn't be the intimate eight or ten of my undergraduate days. Twenty-five, more like, crammed into a room with inadequate ventilation for so many, broken blinds, and an overhead projector with a cracked lens. Home from home for ex-William Murdock students, then, one or two of whom I bumped into from time to time. They were clearly bemused that such an elderly person as me should be creeping round. But there were plenty of other people whom they probably saw as wrinklies here – people topping up their teaching qualifications, or students who'd done access courses in their thirties and forties and were now doing their first degrees. Not that I was a wrinkly. Thirty-seven was no age, I told myself as I slogged up the stairs. Not if I eschewed the lifts, got out my bike, and reminded myself about jogging again. Somehow, without Mike to urge me on, I'd lost motivation. I'd better find it again, pretty fast. When at last we were reunited, he'd be in peak condition and nicely sun-tanned: I might have to turn up pale – there was no way I'd use a tanning bed – but at least I should be sleek too. And maybe the profits from Bowen's dinner party would fund some of that expensive wrinkle-prevention cream I'd seen the other day . . . Imagine my coming to this!

I dumped my stuff in my lockable drawer – we'd all been given one though most people left stuff lying around on a wide shelf which was supposed to constitute our work stations. I'd put too much effort into the work to want to mislay it. And I always feared losing what I didn't use. Like my leg muscles, come to think of it.

As I left the seminar room after the class, I fell into step with Carla, the lecturer who'd been leading the group. She'd worked very hard with us. We were all experienced teachers but you would never have guessed from the level of participation. Perhaps they were all on something? Not speed, though.

As we split up to go our separate ways, she said, 'Thanks for your contribution, er . . .'

'Sophie,' I said. 'Sophie Rivers.'

'Of course. I get more and more hopeless with names the older I get.'

She might have been in her early fifties. It was difficult to tell with her short-cropped red hair and skin to die for. But her bright, brown eyes twinkled over the half-moon glasses, a style that always signalled middle years.

My contributions had been less hostile than those of the other

14

main participant. This was a tall, thin man, probably thirty-five or so, who thought that a beard that bristled with contempt made up for a follicly challenged cranium. He was actually quite good-looking, if you liked men with bones very near the surface of their faces and a blue intensity about the eyes. Pity his teeth hadn't seen an orthodontist when he was younger. He was of the school of thought which considered that a question should be less concerned with eliciting an answer than with showing off the learning of the questioner. He'd given Carla a tedious time this morning.

Carla and I both seemed to be heading for the refectory. Although there was an area reserved for staff, this was closed more often than not, so we saw quite a lot of them slumming with us.

We both asked for decaf, and she reached for the biscuits and choc bars. She took a couple, looking at me.

'No, thanks. They're my favourite but—' I hesitated. I was about to go into prig mode again. 'They've been taken over by that firm involved in the Third World baby-milk scandal. I'm on this one-woman campaign to bankrupt them.'

She put them both back. 'You'd better tell me about this,' she said, paying for my coffee too and heading for a table.

It was a story she could have read in any of the quality broadsheets. A major Swiss company had broken World Health Organisation guidelines on exporting baby-milk to people who hadn't the literacy or the clean water supplies or the sterilising facilities essential for bottle-feeding. Instead of home-grown mother's milk, babies were getting expensive doses of bacteria. I'd seen the results first-hand, in a hospital funded by my cousin Andy in Africa. I'd done a stint or two out there in the past during some of the long summer holidays.

'Andy Rivers?' she repeated. 'The pop star? But you seem to be such a decent woman! Oops!'

'Andy's decent too,' I said. 'Don't believe everything you

see in the red-topped tabloids. He's become a roving ambassa-
dor for UNICEF. And he's set up a trust fund for this hospital
of his, which takes a huge amount of his income.'

'Which is enormous,' Carla reminded me. 'Squandered
millions on booze and drugs and—'

'That was then. He hit success too young. OK, he did all
the stupid things kids do when they've got too much money
and too little self-discipline. But he's reformed.'

'That's what they all say!'

'That's what I know. He lives a remarkably normal, indeed
frugal, life and—'

'"Frugal"?' she persisted.

'And–' Oh dear, if I'd been priggish before, what was I
now? '–he's recently married a headmistress.'

And, oddly, that worked. I wonder how she'd have reacted if
I'd announced something I'd yet to announce to Andy himself
– that he was the father of my son. Andy was Stephan's dad.
He'd been out of his skull on a cocktail of drugs, and raped
me when we were both teenagers. I'd kept my pregnancy
secret – Leeds was a long way from my home – and had
my son adopted. If he was still too scared to tell his parents
about me, I was still too anxious to tell Andy about him.

Carla drained her cup, saying apologetically, 'There, I spend
all my life teaching students not to believe what the media say,
and I've gone and believed something myself.'

'A lot of people have.' Including, in all probability, Steph.
'Anyway, he's truly Mr Squeaky-Clean, these days.' Which
might make him even less attractive to Steph, come to think
of it. 'Another coffee?'

'No, thanks. They say that decaf's worse for you than the real
stuff – Alzheimer's and all that. And the one thing I'm really
scared of is losing it like that. I mean, aphasia's bad enough.
But imagine your mind packing up altogether. Ugh. Horrible.
It's not the dying frightens me, it's the soggy brain before you
go. Losing your identity, your knowledge of who you are.'

Which was unanswerable, particularly as it sounded a very personal fear. Had someone close to her gone that way? I gave her a look that was meant to tell her I'd listen if she wanted to talk, but she smiled slightly, shook her head as if to clear away dark thoughts and started to gather her things together. But she stopped, and leant towards me. 'Now: how's that assignment of yours going? Any problems so far . . . ?'

Chapter Three

If I was afraid I was showing my age there was no doubt that my old sparring partner Superintendent Chris Groom was showing his.

We were having what was supposed to be a quiet meal in a tiny newly opened trattoria, not far from his home in Edgbaston. Unfortunately our meal coincided with the arrival of a bunch of red-braced yobs, with loud public school brays and endlessly yelling mobile phones, who completely overwhelmed the waiters and destroyed the whole ambience.

Chris's face was sinking into ever deeper lines of disapproval, and he called for the bill as soon as the forks were finally down on our main course plates. He declined the offer of sweet or coffee in tones so terse as to border rudeness, left the most perfunctory of tips and strode out. I followed, wishing my legs could produce a decent stride, but fearing that all they were managing was a scuttle. That's what happens when you never make it above five foot one.

Chris was unlocking his car before I was halfway to the parking lot.

'Coffee at my place or yours?' he flung over the car roof.

'Mine. It'll save you the double journey, won't it?' I said sunnily. In other words, I wouldn't be forking out for a taxi home from his place. To be fair, Chris was always abstemious whether he was driving or not. On the rare occasions he hadn't been, he'd slept the night on my sofa on to which he'd keeled.

19

Not that he'd ever blacked out: he was always so near the limit of fatigue that it only took a limp whisky to push him into sleep.

There had, of course, been a short period when he'd spent the night in my bed, or I in his, but neither of us ever mentioned that these days. We'd always functioned well as friends, but edgily, indeed abrasively, as lovers. And – with the exception of one or two significant issues, not least my son – we were back in friendship mode again. He seemed to have accepted I was with Mike, and had proved to himself that he could fall in love again, even if his choice had been singularly unfortunate. To the best of my knowledge he'd not visited the woman in question in her new accommodation, courtesy of HM Prison Service.

'There's another thing,' I added, as he set off, as smoothly as if he were driving a hearse – Chris never took driving risks, no matter how angry. 'Ivo's on the loose. I want to run him to earth before he chews through the mains cable and blows himself to kingdom come.' Or, worse still, stopped me videoing the late-night Test highlights. I'd left little piles of digestive biscuit crumbs at salient points, plus a couple of toilet roll inners, which always brought him infinite satisfaction. He'd crawl through them, balance on top of them, and, when he'd exhausted all the possibilities that occurred to him – apparently he'd never been to primary school or watched *Blue Peter* – he'd set to and gnaw them to confetti.

'It shouldn't take a Scene of Crime officer to tell me where he's been,' I added.

'But they don't always tell you where the perpetrator's going,' he said, his voice suddenly light with amusement.

Chris was back into grim mode by the time we'd spent thirty-five fruitless minutes hunting for Ivo, who'd refused all the blandishments I'd left scattered.

'What you should have done,' he said, with his penchant

for stating the obvious, 'was construct a trap for him – a deep tin with biscuits in the bottom, a ramp up with crumbs at enticing intervals . . .' At least he revived at the sight of my new malt collection. I'd always been a Jameson woman, but several liquor purveyors had taken an interest in Mike's ability to transform a dull innings into a sparking one – hence the champagne I popped from time to time. Hence too the row of esoteric bottles which completely occupied a shelf in my glory hole hitherto devoted to spare light bulbs and shoe-cleaning materials.

Chris opted as conservatively as I'd have predicted, with half a finger of Laphroaig. I plumped for the remains of a bottle of wine tucked into the fridge.

He raised his eyebrows.

'Before it goes off. I've got one of those suction pump things that gets the air out, but even so the wine doesn't last for ever.'

'Not that it would have to with you around.'

'*A glass of wine for your stomach's sake*,' I quoted. A sanctimonious voice in my head was about to point out I was as careful as Chris when it came to drinking on my own. I stifled it. There was no point in needling Chris these days. No fun, either. Though someone would have to do something about his joyless life. Another woman, that was what he needed. A friend if not a lover. I'd have to organise something. Even if I'd hated it when people tried to organise me into relationships in pre-Mike days.

'So how's life at Piddock Road Police Station, Superintendent Groom?' I asked. What little conversation we'd been able to sustain in the trat had been devoted to mutual friends. We always left business till last.

'I can sum it up in one word,' he said. 'Budgets.'

I nodded. The ground bass of all discussions on the public sector. He might add a tenor line about cost centres, I a soprano one about my poor old college, William Murdock

21

– not to mention UWM! Nice harmony: shame about the theme.

'I had this WPC in tears in my room today,' he said, rolling the whisky thoughtfully round his glass. 'Pregnant.'

'What's that to do with budgets? Apart from hers?'

'Who does her work while she's away? More to the point, what work does she do when she's too big to go out on patrol?'

'There must be lots of work you can do from a desk. Not to mention community liaison, crime prevention work—'

'They're specialised areas, Sophie. You can't fish people out and slot people in – not just like that.' He snapped his fingers. 'Thing is, I want to be quite sensitive. It seems at her last nick, during her first pregnancy, some clown had the idea of getting her to work through a whole lot of files about paedophilia and child abuse and enter all the salient details on to the computer. She's afraid we shall do something like that to her.'

'I wondered why she'd gone straight to the top,' I said. Chris was what was these days referred to as an Operational Commander, and thus cock of the whole dung-hill. 'It wouldn't normally be your bag, would it?'

'You know my open-door policy,' he said.

I did. And approved of it. Even if Chris was chronically tired, he seemed to be enjoying his job these days. His new secretary, Bridget, might be partly responsible. I'd only met her a couple of times, and been embraced the second like a long-lost cousin. When Chris mentioned her, it was always with affection as well as respect. She was motherly, efficient, humorous, and not above telling off anyone she thought deserved it. Her only trouble, as far as Chris, a not-quite lapsed Catholic, and I, a deeply lapsed Baptist, were concerned, was her devotion to the Sacred Heart and her habit of entrusting all her problems to it.

Nose deep in the glass, he inhaled. Then just the tiniest sip. He set the glass down on the floor beside him. He was waiting for something, wasn't he?

'So how are things apart from budgets?' I obliged.

'Don't ask. We've had an attempted sexual assault in Sheepwash Urban Park. And another in Greets Green Park.'

'Any connection?'

'It's almost axiomatic that sexual offenders move from a comparatively minor crime to bigger ones. I'd like to get hold of him before he turns his attention to rape. If it is one man, of course. The incidents took place tennish at night, so none of the victims got a good view of his face. Nothing we could start putting together as a description, let alone a photofit. Crazy, women walking in open spaces at that time of night!'

'You're not suggesting they're asking to be attacked,' I asked, keeping my voice under maximum control.

'No.' He raised his hands in a pacifying gesture. 'Absolutely not. But there are certain precautions everyone has to take. And I wouldn't fancy prowling round a park alone at night. Would you?'

'I'd like to think I could if I wanted to. But no, not these days. I even lock myself in the car when I drive through certain parts of Brum.'

'So I should bloody hope. So, to go back to your original question, I'd bet they are connected.'

I tried to imagine a page from my *A–Z*. 'There is another link, isn't there? Don't both parks link up to cuts?'

'And neither is all that far from the Oldbury Road, either. Easy to get away by car.' His voice tailed away, as if he was thinking hard. Then he gave a grim snort of laughter. 'Funny thing, though, we have got one incident in the canal system.'

'The cut,' I corrected him.

'OK, the cut. Anyway – sorry, any road up!' he corrected himself, using the Black Country phraseology. 'Any road up, one of our cuts had a body in it the other day. Nicely decomposed. A woman. With the pathologist at the moment. Seems there's something he wants to check on before he

23

gives his final report. Such as: cause of death. And, more interesting, race.'

'Not some citizen of your fair patch?'

'Hard to tell. From what was left of her. She'd been there . . . some time.'

I swigged my wine. A jab in my stomach told me that might have been foolish. 'I thought bodies . . . bodies floated up to the surface. Eventually,' I added.

'Not if their left wrist was trapped in an old bed-spring,' he said. 'Some bloke got something tangled up in his propeller and – you don't want to hear the rest of this, not with your dodgy tum.'

'Superintendent Groom, you must know that the cuts are my birth-right,' I declared, grandiloquently. I made a wide sweep with my wine-glass. It was either that or throw the wine over him: I thought by now I'd trained him not to try and protect me.

'OK. But don't say I didn't warn you. This old geezer's chugging along the cut – or is there any Black Country term for chugging?'

I shook my head. 'Not to my knowledge.'

'His propeller fouls on something. He has a look, expecting – oh, whatever you find in cuts – an old hosepipe, a Sainsbury's trolley, whatever. And he finds he's got what looks horribly like a human thigh bone.'

'How would he know that?'

'TV programmes.' He got back under way. 'So he reaches for his traditional navigational aid, the mobile phone, and calls for assistance. The poor sods of the Police Diving Team retrieve the rest of the skeleton, its wrist, as I said, stuck firmly in the springs of this cast-iron bed frame.'

'Lovely.' I took another, smaller swig. 'And have your colleagues found anyone to help them with their enquiries?'

'Neither literally nor euphemistically.' His grin invited me to trump that.

I declined.

'So what about this course of yours?' he asked, changing the subject with a crash of gears.

It was easier to plunge in, telling him about my new tutor, and his reaction to my plea for help.

He nodded sadly. 'The thing is, Sophie, you went in with such high expectations, some disappointment was inevitable. And I'm not sure it was a good idea to use that research project you did at Muntz as the basis for this new qualification. I know everyone thought it was the best thing since sliced bread, and that you were proud of it – quite right: don't get me wrong! But you can come over a bit cocky, you know. Maybe you set this geezer's back up, and he's having a subtle bit of revenge. In any case, I'm sure you can make an appointment to see him sooner.'

Anyone else tell me I'm cocky, and I'd yell. But Chris was clearly trying to help. And who knows, perhaps, in my anxiety to conceal my nervousness, I might have been brash?

'If I *was* cocky—'

Chris grinned.

'—he seems to have forgiven me. He's put some work my way, teaching, that is. And now – Chris, you are not hearing this! – he wants me to cater for some dinner party.'

'So I won't ask questions about health and safety inspections of your premises, your public liability insurance or your tax declaration.'

'I pay tax on all the teaching I do. At least, I shall when I get paid. It seems they only pay visiting teachers like me every high day, holiday and bonfire night.'

'It must be tough after all those years of a regular salary – even an inadequate one like yours,' he said, straight-faced enough for me to believe he meant it. Certainly, compared with his, mine was a pittance, though I was way up the scale and many of my colleagues considered me a veritable Croesus.

I nodded. I didn't want to tell him that the very few rows

I'd had with Mike had been over money – his desire to slosh dollops of dosh my way at every opportunity, when I battled to retain some semblance of independence. I gave my ring a surreptitious twiddle.

'I shall survive,' I said. 'So long as Ivo doesn't eat me out of house and home.'

'How on earth did you come to be landed with a *gerbil*, of all things? I know you got on quite well with that rat—'

'Do you mean the human or the rodent sort?' I asked. It was a measure of how far we'd come: at one point Chris had fancied himself a rival to a two-timing poet, a period neither of us had ever alluded to. Ever.

He shrugged. 'But choosing to have one . . .'

'Looking after him for a tender-hearted friend,' I said, comparing with some amusement my adjective with those Dave preferred to apply to himself. Fearsome, tempestuous, vicious? Something that went with snarls and war-paint – oh yes, his histrionics would have put Branagh's Henry V to shame. Even Olivier's, come to think of it.

And at that point I became aware of a movement. I said nothing. But the movement was heading purposefully towards Chris. And towards Chris's immaculate trousers.

I couldn't, could I? I couldn't let those needle-sharp incisors sink themselves into those Aquascutum turn-ups! But if I warned Chris, he'd naturally whip them away as fast as he could. And poor Ivo would take fright.

I waited. Chris was recounting some conversation with Bridget. In went the incisors. On my knees in a nanosecond, I pounced. And the incisors sank into what I trust was a succulent part of my thumb. When I shook the little bleeder off, he dropped, straight as a stone. Into Chris's glass.

It speaks volumes for the poverty of Ivo's taste that he made frantic efforts to escape. So frantic it took me several moments to grab him by the base of his tail and fish him out.

I whizzed him at arm's length – did whisky spots stain

carpets? – to the kitchen and his residence. And came back to find Chris on his feet, dourly regarding the whisky he'd just been about to drink. In the expensive liquid floated a small but indisputable turd.

I'd been so busy soothing Chris – clearly, simply washing the glass was inadequate, so I'd found another crystal tumbler in a household more accustomed to your average Woolworth's – that I'd left Ivo to his own devices. It was only when I realised that these included licking the offending liquid from his fur that I had to move. He was woozy enough to make a sitting target. I had ways of sobering him up.

'I never knew they could swim,' Chris said, watching without sympathy poor Ivo's frantic attempts to haul himself from my washbasin.

I glared. I'd asked him to hold the poor inebriated creature while I gently showered him. His refusal had been curter and more pungent than I'd expected.

At last, after a couple of changes of water, I deemed Ivo clean. Now it was my turn to glare: Chris was about to wrap him in my new bath sheet. A clear case of overkill, but also rampant temptation – all that lovely fluffy cotton to chew. I found an old hand towel scheduled for the duster box: efficient and, yes, chewable. Ivo was in heaven. He might even tolerate the hair dryer.

'Hair dryer! Sophie, for goodness' sake. It's an animal. You don't need a hair dryer!'

'Would you prefer the tumble dryer? I know he's an animal, but he's not my animal and I want him to be a live animal when his person gets back.'

By the time everyone's ruffled fur was smoothed to their satisfaction – though Ivo's could really have used some of my John Frieda Restructuring Serum – Chris had had far too much malt to risk his licence. He looked disdainfully at the sofa. Yes, I knew it would give him backache.

'The spare bed's made up,' I said. If my voice didn't ring with enthusiasm it was at the thought of what Aggie – who never missed a trick and certainly not one as large as Chris's car – would say when I next saw her.

Chapter Four

It had been a long time since I'd sat at the kitchen table, my head down on my arms, crying at three o'clock in the morning. Ivo, out for some bonus exercise, paused from time to time in his exploration of the area and watched me. Probably he had his eye on the little heap of tissues I was rendering soggy and unchewable. I pushed a dry one across to him. He sat on his haunches and shredded it with enthusiasm. I usually reserved that sort of shredding – in my case metaphorical – for a weak essay by a good student. Funny thing, being a teacher. I'd have given a weak student producing the same essay a veritable bouquet of praise. But I'd have given both the same mark.

I'd certainly got weak students now. They were some of the overseas batch whose English Bowen had asked me to bring up to standard so they could benefit from the courses they were taking. Most of them had been steaming ahead – nothing much to do with my efforts: they were so intelligent, highly motivated and enthusiastic almost any halfway decent teacher could have got results. But there was a group of about twelve who I was absolutely unable to help. The clever teaching methods I was supposed to be basing my dissertation on were proving useless. Which suggested, very forcibly, that neither my methods nor my dissertation had much value. Or that the methods were only useful to young people like those at Murdock and at Muntz, who'd been born in this country to non-English speaking parents. Come to think of it, why had I ever assumed that speech patterns of people from Mirpur should be anything like those from the Pacific Rim, where this group seemed to have come from? Yes, I was a failure.

Ivo transferred his attention from the tissue to the chocolate biscuits in which I'd decided to seek consolation.

It would have been unkind – and indeed foolhardy – to try to separate him from the piece he was currently attacking, but I'd had the strongest of warnings. Sweet biscuits would damage not only his teeth but also his digestive system and probably his kidneys. Wholemeal might be given in moderation: chocolate wholemeal were *verboten*.

And, come to think of it, I was supposed to be looking after my teeth, etc., etc., with the important addition of my figure. So why I was indulging myself like this goodness knows. Particularly as my patent cure for insomnia – cupboard cleaning – had always been very successful. The principle was that any self-respecting brain would much rather be tucked up asleep than padding round a cold kitchen cleaning out cupboards. If you treated yourself with milky drinks and a good book, your brain would think that this was a good idea and get into the habit of waking you for the next little feast.

I explained all this to Ivo as I scooped him, and his fragment of forbidden food, back into his aquarium. He was so impressed he promptly disappeared into the large jam jar he used as his bedroom and buried himself in shredded tissue.

There was nothing left for me but to do the human equivalent.

The logical thing to do – as the cold light of the following morning showed clearly – was to go and talk to my tutor. How many hours had I spent with tutees who were unhappy, inadequate or simply in need of a friendly shoulder? But despite his outward cuddliness, I suspected Tom Bowen's shoulders would not welcome a tearful student, especially after our last encounter. What I'd better do was talk to him about his proposed dinner party – venue, menu, prices – and slip my problems in as an aside when he felt more mellow. Except that that would be to mix two parts of our professional relationship best kept apart.

I spent ten minutes at the computer adjusting upwards the prices of my dinner-party menus. None of these was fixed; I always discussed them in detail with the host or hostess. I'd want to see what facilities they could offer for cooking at their house. After all, the less of my own gas and electricity I used, the lower my prices would be. I'd certainly rather use their china – there was always more incentive for them to be careful with it. Glasses ditto.

There. Ready for me to show Bowen. Teachers' discount indeed!

If I found it hard to adjust to the large seminars, I couldn't believe the sight of all the students pouring out of the lecture theatre this morning. These weren't on the M.Ed. course; to join this you had to have some experience as a teacher. These were on the Post-graduate Certificate in Education. In other words, they'd just graduated and were now being trained as new teachers. All these young lemmings hurtling into teaching. And in such numbers! In my undergraduate days, your absence was literally conspicuous, and a responsible lecturer would buttonhole you to demand why you'd skipped the session on irregular Anglo-Saxon verbs, or whatever. One particular woman always followed up the previous week's work with a nasty little test, much to our horror in those laid-back days. But we didn't miss many of her classes. Nor many of the others, to be honest. In retrospect, at least.

I fell into step with the student who'd given Carla the hard time at yesterday's seminar. He flashed his teeth at me, reminding me for a moment of Ivo.

31

'It may be tough at my place,' he said, 'but at least we don't have to teach fifty of them at a time.'

I nodded, sighing. Perhaps for their misplaced idealism; perhaps for the loss of mine. Or perhaps because we'd got a three-hour session scheduled for this evening. There were so few of us taking this full-time M.Ed. course we had to be fitted in with people brave enough to try to study part time and teach full time. And what were we doing this evening? A compulsory module: Managing the Curriculum.

'Ah, yes. With Hoffman, isn't it?' Bald-head said. 'He's not bad, I suppose. A bit intense. Talks too much, of course.'

That was Bald-head speak for controlling the class discussion so that no one person – such as Bald-head – dominated it. 'All to good purpose,' I said. 'He divides the time well.' Like I did with such enormously long classes. 'And I do like an allusive teacher—'

'Showing off, if you ask me. But he's better than that stupid American woman.'

'American?'

'Carla Pentowski or whatever she calls herself. All icing and no cake.'

I'm supposed to be observant and I'd never noticed that Carla was anything other than English. She had all the right rhythms for a native English speaker, accentuated words and sentences in the right places and – yes, I'd have marked her down as Home Counties, overlaid by Oxbridge or good redbrick. 'American?' I repeated. With someone like this guy, there'd be no point in asking if he was sure. He would be. Absolutely positive.

'There's no doubt about it,' he said. 'Those "t" sounds come out much closer to "d", every time. You listen. You'll see.'

'Or hear,' I couldn't stop myself amending. 'I thought she tried very hard yesterday. It was the students that were the problem. It must have been like wading through custard.'

'Isn't a good teacher supposed to overcome that sort of

problem? And if they're teaching us, who are supposed to be good, experienced teachers, shouldn't they be excellent teachers? After all, they're supposed to be giving us the benefit of their experience, not the other way round.'

I came to a standstill by the refectory door and stared at him. And smiled. Of course! From nowhere came the idea how I could check up on these problem students of mine! Their application forms!

I'm told – by one who knows, but might still be biased – that when I smile my face lights up like a Hallowe'en lantern. So my fellow student got the full benefit. He responded with a beam of his own. 'You'll join me for coffee?' he asked, his voice modulating a couple of notes lower.

That smile had let me in for a chatting up, hadn't it? I'd have to cool the conversation considerably. 'OK,' I said, reaching for my purse. 'Actually, a penny just dropped while you were speaking. I've got this group of new South-East Asian students whose English doesn't seem to be getting anywhere at all. I'm supposed to be preparing them for this course, and was wondering why I was doing so badly.'

'Those dim women?' he flung over his shoulder as he reached for a muesli bar.

'I can't communicate with them well enough to tell if they're dim,' I snapped. 'And that's what's been worrying me – still is! Do you remember the application form we all had to fill in? There was a section there asking what English language qualifications overseas applicants were offering.'

'I suppose the place was low on numbers.' Perhaps he didn't intend to be as dismissive as he sounded. 'Doesn't your college ever bend the rules when you're a few students light? I know my last one did. Not this one, though. Francis Asbury.'

At least I knew better than to shake his hand and call him Francis.

He continued, 'I always wanted to break the rules at Asbury

– considering we're named after such a pious old gent. You know, the Methodist born in Great Barr.'

I nodded. I did indeed, and wasn't sorry to forestall him. 'The first American Methodist Bishop, wasn't he?'

Sandwell – which was the artificial name for a conglomeration of good old Black Country towns such as Smethwick and West Bromwich – had seen fit to commemorate him with a further education college, managed with such imagination and commitment I'd always been green with envy. Asbury had been born and lived in the area and had seen the Methodist light in the 1760s, eventually emigrating to preach the word over there. Perhaps naming a college after him was some sort of reparation for the riotous way earlier denizens of the area had dealt with Asbury's mentor, John Wesley.

It would actually have been nice to know my fellow student's name without having to do the obvious thing, which was of course to ask him. But we'd seemed, thanks to my banana grin, to have moved on to an altogether too intimate footing for me to want to encourage him. And here he was, insisting on paying for my coffee, and pulling back a chair for me, as if we were in some up-market wine bar. I nodded my thanks. No way would I utter the fatal words, *I'll pay for the next one, then.* With a bit of luck he wouldn't know my name either, so we could do a straight exchange, preferably initiated by him. If the worst came to the worst I'd have to resort to peering at his files in case he was public-spirited – or brash – enough to bruit his name to the world.

He soon returned to the attack on Carla Pentowski. Unlike me, he didn't consider she'd prepared enough. Probably she wasn't well enough grounded in her subject. Here he launched into a scathing attack on the standards of American universities.

'Oh, yes,' he was saying, 'I did some research there for my Master's – just after my first degree. Their Master's was just about the same level as my first degree.'

'Is it still the case?' I asked, thinking about the huge expansion of the student population of British universities and general rumours about dumbing down.

He shrugged. So this was a man who preferred not to clutter his prejudices with facts.

'What are you doing now?' he asked, teeth in evidence. He turned on a twinkle in his rather cold blue eyes.

My smile didn't attempt to get past the end of my nose. 'Some work.'

His smile changed the twinkle to a dazzle. 'Why don't we meet up for some lunch?'

I knew it. But he was spared a put-down by the appearance of Tom Bowen, who strode up to the table and addressed me as if I were on my own.

'Could we sort out that dinner?' he asked.

I was so irritated by his rudeness that I ended up apologising to Anon for the swiftness of my exit. But I made no reference to lunch.

Bowen's interest had been grabbed by the information on my estimate that cooking at his house would reduce the costs, and he insisted on taking me there immediately. He drove a newish Saab, fast and rather fussily. But then, I'd been spoilt by several years of Chris's driving, and then by all too few journeys with Mike. Sometimes – like this moment – I missed him so much tears would come to my eyes.

Bowen parked with a flourish outside a big 1930s house in Handsworth Wood. Everyone knows about the urban decay and consequent racial tension that afflicted Handsworth. Except they didn't, of course: they afflicted Lozells, an even more deprived district, only for some reason no one ever remembers that. Anyway, Handsworth Wood is an altogether more affluent neighbourhood than Handsworth. Very couth.

So was Bowen's house. He had to tackle two locks to admit us, but to my surprise hadn't bothered to use his burglar alarm

system. If I ever warmed to him enough, I could pass on
the advice of one of Chris's colleagues – that no lock was
impenetrable and it was a good idea to deter casual burglars
with a lot of noise. There were also a couple of windows open
upstairs.

I stepped into the hall. A staircase rose on my left, ran in
the form of a landing straight ahead, and carried onto a second
floor on my right. The remarkable effect was topped by a
pyramidal skylight, the base possibly six feet square. The rest
of the house hadn't been small to start with, but some tasteful
extensions at the rear provided an inevitable conservatory and
a huge and well-planned kitchen. I had to stuff my hands into
my pockets to stop myself rubbing them in glee. Yes, a good
triangular working pattern, everything at the right height, a
wonderful range of implements, from le Creuset casseroles to
Sabatier knives, plus everything in between. A food processor
and an old-fashioned Kenwood Chef jostled a tower double
oven, separate hob and versatile microwave. So why wasn't
the person who'd chosen all these delights going to use them
on Friday?

The dining room was dominated by a long Victorian multi-
leaved table, eight chairs each side.

'Are all the leaves in?' I asked, probably failing to sound
casual.

'I can add another couple.'

All the chairs except the carvers matched. And they matched
each other. Sets of old chairs are expensive, and the price goes
up exponentially, so eight chairs cost more than twice as much
as four, and sixteen far more than four times as much.

'Would that mean bringing in different chairs?'

'I've another couple of pairs tucked away.'

I paced the room. I gestured the space I'd need for the heated
trolley I preferred to bring with me – and then noticed he had
a larger model ready in place.

'It might be a bit tight for serving if you have more than

this number of covers,' I said, enjoying a tiny bit of jargon. 'Which reminds me—'

'Don't worry. You won't have to serve. Or get anywhere near the washing-up. You do the skilled work. I'll sort out the unskilled.'

I raised an eyebrow.

'OK, so serving's skilled. I'll make sure they can do that. A couple of students,' he added casually.

'You'll recruit them?' It was best in this job to tie up every possible loose end.

'I said that, didn't I?'

If I was surprised by his vehemence, I wouldn't let it faze me. 'So all I have to do is buy the food and cook it.' I ticked off items in my notepad. 'Now, as I told you, the menu is up to you. You can either have one of the menus I've suggested—' I tapped the folder I'd given him – 'or you can tell me what you want and if I can cook it I will.'

'Pork,' he said promptly. 'I want pork. Good old-fashioned roast pork.'

'Stuffed with apricots?'

He shook his head. 'I ate at this *auberge* once.' His face softened in a reminiscent smile. 'At this long table, cheek by jowl with all these French peasants. And they served roast pork with some sort of mashed potato. Only it wasn't, if you see what I mean.'

I nodded. 'Probably *pommes boulangère* – cooked with herbs and onions and stock.' And a real bonus for a busy cook, as it took very little preparation and looked after itself. I knew just the sort of roast pork to go with it.

'And some veges. Now, I'm a soup man. So none of your fiddly little starters. Oh, except some canapés would be nice. With the drinks.'

'That'd bump up the price a bit,' I pointed out.

He shrugged. 'How are you on wine?'

'Some hosts leave it to me, some prefer to deal with that themselves.'

'So you don't get a cut! Do you charge corkage if I use my own?'

'I'm a caterer, Dr Bowen, not a restaurant. Now, I usually use organic ingredients wherever possible. You may find this raises the prices slightly but I'm sure you'll agree the quality is reflected in the flavour.'

'I—'

There was a slight noise from somewhere upstairs.

'Right, Sophie,' he said, 'that's settled then. Work out your costs and let me have the details tomorrow. And remember that staff discount, eh?' He pulled back his cuff ostentatiously. 'Time we were getting back to the treadmill. I assume you'd like a lift?'

I was out of the front door before I realised, and he was double-locking it again. But still he didn't set that alarm.

Chapter Five

If I was hoping to discuss my academic problems with Bowen on the return journey I was disappointed. As soon as he was in the car, he'd flicked on the radio: the tail end of the lunchtime news, followed by one of those Radio Four general knowledge quizzes. He fired off answers to most of the questions well before the contestants. Correctly, as it happens. When I tried to join in, it was clear he preferred centre stage, so I shut up and thought about his dinner party. Because he'd decided on a very traditional menu, the major expenditure would be on top-class ingredients, not labour. I'd floated the idea of trendy, palate-clearing sorbets, but he was adamant: canapés with the drinks, a hot – and no doubt filling – soup, the roast pork and potatoes we'd already discussed, with appropriate vegetables, and a decent pudding. Maybe two puddings: one impenetrably stodgy; another for the more faint-hearted – fruit salad of some sort. Oh, and some cheese to round the whole thing off. I was to buy appropriate wines. He didn't like the idea of paying for the time I'd have to take choosing them, so I'd do what I'd done to other tight-fisted customers: bury it in the overall bill. I really preferred to be more experimental in my menus, but I was, after all, running a business and not entertaining like-minded friends. I just hoped any potential clients wouldn't be put off. Perhaps I could sock it to them with some really original canapés.

He parked, and turned to me. 'How soon can you give me the quote?'

'Tomorrow morning at nine,' I said promptly.

'Excellent.' He unclipped his seat belt.

'Would it be possible to talk to you then about my dissertation? I've hit a megasnag.'

'Surely we've agreed a time for your next supervision.' He was getting out of the car.

I got out too. 'That was if all was going well,' I said, across the car roof. 'As I said, it isn't. And remember, I have to complete by the end of the summer. Have to.'

He shrugged and patted his jacket elaborately. It was clear he was going to announce he hadn't got his diary on him.

I didn't move. 'We'll fix that tomorrow morning too, then,' I said. My smile was as businesslike as if I were the tutor, he the importunate student. He was not going to get away with this any longer. Particularly as I had something he needed: my cooking skills.

His smile acknowledged the fact.

I don't think either of us especially wanted to have to make small talk on the way back to the front entrance, so I was delighted when I recognised a figure emerging from another car. It was the trade union's regional officer. I excused myself and hung back to greet him.

'Seb! What industrial strife brings you here?'

'The union doesn't always deal with strife, Sophie,' he said, giving me a whiskery kiss and a hug. 'You OK? And Mike?'

I nodded.

Seb was a solid, indeed bulky, man who in my last year at William Murdock had provided me with invaluable support. In the process his office had been fire-bombed. But he was not a man to bear grudges, and had been heard to claim that the fire had dealt so effectively with his filing that it should become an annual event.

'No, I'm here for a meeting,' he added. 'Another bloody

meeting. I wouldn't mind if they always got somewhere. Sorry,' he corrected himself, 'had outcomes.'

'You mean, *achieved appropriate and satisfactory outcomes*. Got time for a coffee?'

He shifted the armful of files he was carrying to check his watch. 'Maybe afterwards. Where are you based?'

I told him. 'But I'll probably be in what passes for a library.'

'Come on, it's not as bad as all that! And after William Murdock, anything with more than half a dozen books should be absolute paradise.'

'It would be if someone hadn't sliced a lot of pages from the books I need. Underscoring in ink's irritating enough but when a whole chapter's gone walkies I want to kill.'

'I thought you usually left that to the others, Sophie,' he said, smiling, and holding the door open for me.

Before I could get on with my own work, I had to teach one of the intensive language sessions that was causing me so much grief. I faced myself in the loo mirror and told myself that I was an experienced teacher, that I could handle most things in the classroom and I could certainly get this lot speaking adequate English – well, *any* English in some cases – using a bit of expertise and a lot of initiative. OK, maybe not that all-singing, all-dancing system I'd designed with some colleagues in what seemed a long-ago research project. But somehow. Even if I had to raid every library in the West Midlands conurbation to do it. And talk to every expert I could find. The students were forking out so much money, for goodness' sake, it made my own investment look quite pitiful. And they were human beings who deserved the best I could do.

Except this afternoon's batch of human beings seemed different from the last. All these impassive, polite faces sat staring at me. There's that terrible racist remark, isn't there, that they all look the same – African-Caribbeans, Indians,

Greeks – whatever group you want to denigrate. I'd tried hard to combat this attitude, but not always succeeded. But so many of these young women, all lowered eyes and neutral, self-effacing behaviour, seemed to be striving to match their sisters, as if they wanted to be clones. It might have been my hesitant delivery as I called the register, which failed to distinguish first from family names, that made them respond hesitantly. And yet I'd have sworn – if not in a court of law – that one or two of the brief smiles illuminated different faces from those I'd seen last time. And that they had responded to names that were not their own.

Dismissing this speculation as post-lunch fantasy, I embarked on my class.

'You look whacked,' a voice said, as I leaned against the narrow shelf in the ladies' loo.

I used the mirror to smile at the speaker: Carla, the lecturer I'd liked but whom my still anonymous colleague criticised.

'If you were wading through custard the other day, I've been pushing my way through thick, sticky porridge. It's this remedial language group.'

'Remedial! That's not a term I associate with higher education! Have you checked their qualifications? They should be on a print-out somewhere – all the staff had one. And a print-out of their initial tests when they started the course.' She started to flick through a pile of papers as if hoping to produce the relevant sheet there and then.

'They've all sat the tests?'

'If they're not from countries in the European Union, they have to – before they're admitted on to the course. Central Admissions have to check each student's got an appropriate qualification before they pass the paperwork that enables the student to get a study visa. Then, as a fail-safe, really, each student has further tests – written, aural and oral – before the start of the first semester.' She abandoned the pile of papers, parking them precariously on the shelf designed, possibly, for make-up bags. 'And for monitoring purposes every teacher has a print-out of the results.'

'"Monitoring"?'

'To compare students' progress on the course – results in assignments, that is – with their entry qualifications.'

'Isn't that racist?'

'We have an Equal Opportunities Committee to ensure it isn't! No, you can't take all those thousands of pounds off people if their English isn't up to the course. We may need to build even more language support into the system.'

'So if I'm teaching them, I should have a list of results too?'

Carla pulled a face. 'Well, you're in this funny position, aren't you – both student and teacher? Someone somewhere may have decided it was inappropriate for you to have confidential information about people you're sitting next to in the lecture room.'

'I'll take it up with Tom Bowen. After all, it was he who suggested I teach them.' I would have liked to mention my anxiety about the apparent changes in personnel, but since the first rule of teaching is get to know which name attaches to which face I felt too embarrassed. Especially as a student from the group in question – a permanent member! – ducked into the space behind us, managing an extremely clear, 'Good afternoon, Sophie,' before disappearing into a cubicle.

Carla smiled, and gestured me out into the corridor. 'She one of yours? Well, then: nothing to worry about, surely.'

I shook my head doubtfully.

'Come on, you're being too conscientious. Why don't you come along to my room now and I'll see if I can find my print-out?'

It occurred to me as she rooted through piles on her floor, desk and coffee table, that the staff offices themselves weren't in bad nick, at least compared with the student facilities.

The chairs for both the desk and the computer table looked ergonomically sound – in fact, the one by the computer was the twin of mine at home, so I knew roughly how much it had cost: quite a lot, even with educational discount. The walls and woodwork were newly painted, and the carpet wasn't pure institutional gunge.

A foot-high pile of files slithered slowly but inexorably from the coffee table to the floor.

'I need a secretary,' she said.

I nodded. 'I've often thought a wife would be nice,' I admitted. 'Someone to clean, collect the dry-cleaning and get the washing in—'

'And put it away! Bliss!'

'My partner's not bad . . .' I had this dreadful longing just to say his name. But careless talk – even to someone as kind as Carla – could still find its way to media sources. 'In fact, he's quite domesticated. But we're still running our own houses. And his working hours are peculiar. And he's away a lot.'

'So I'll bet you end up getting *his* washing in and dashing to Sainsbury's when *he* runs out of sugar. Come on, admit it!'

'Well, I will confess that at the moment – he's out of the country, you see – I make a point of nipping round to water his plants. And I've been doing some pruning for him.'

'And you run the vac and duster round – just to make it look lived in . . . Oh, Sophie, as a sister you're a failure.'

I hung my head in mock humility.

'Tell you what,' she continued, 'if you're on your own at the moment, why don't you come round for supper one night?'

'Love to!'

We fished out diaries, mine from my bag, hers from under a pile of phone directories. We fixed a date – Friday of the following week.

'If you're doing the food, I'll bring the booze,' I said.

She shook her head. 'Just enough for you.' She hesitated. 'I'm an alcoholic. I've tried drinking just a little. It didn't work. Not when you lose it like I do. Alcoholism isn't something you get over. Once an alkie, always an alkie.'

'I'm sorry . . .'

'My problem, not yours. Nor is it a problem for me if you want to drink. No, really.'

But it might be. Impressed by her honesty, I resolved to make it a dry night. After all, I'd be driving. And although I never had more than one glass if I was at the wheel, none was distinctly better than one.

'Now,' she said, 'I'll give you a little map for you to find my place. I'm between streets, not on one. I live on a narrow boat, you see. Cue for that old joke—'

'I live on the cut: do drop in one day!'

'That's the one. Anyway, I'll give you a little sketch so you can't miss me.'

'I'm a Black Country woman,' I said. 'Born and bred. I'm used to cuts. But not, come to think of it, of cuts with habitable moorings.'

'A nice new initiative, thanks, I guess, to European money. But, Sophie, you don't have the accent!'

'I have *an* accent. An Oldbury one. OK, I disguise it most days of the week, but it pops up when I talk to another native. Which I'd say you're not?'

'No,' she said.

Before I could pursue Anon's theory about her origins, another pile started to slither to the floor and I judged it best to leave her to it.

I was just on my way to the library for another bash at some of those densely written texts when I ran into Seb.

'Barely quorate,' he said tersely. 'So we got a lot done.' He grinned. 'Coffee?'

I nodded and led the way to the refectory.

As he tipped the third packet of sugar into his coffee, he

45

asked, 'How are you enjoying being a student? After all that time on the teaching treadmill?'

I wrinkled my nose.

'I'll take that as something of a negative, shall I? Come on, I've got broad shoulders – pour it all out.'

'Apart from missing Mike—'

'Poor old Sophie. Still, the course of true love . . .' He stopped. 'Sorry. You *are* missing him, aren't you!' He pushed the corners of my mouth into a grin. 'That's better. Now, what's wrong with the student life?'

'Things I'm not at home with. Perhaps that's the best way of putting it. Take accommodation, now. *Si monumentum requiris, circumspice!*' There weren't all that many people I knew who'd have responded to that, but Seb was definitely one of them.

'OK, so it's not exactly Christopher Wren, but what would you expect of an old local authority commercial college promoted beyond its means?'

'I wouldn't have expected the classrooms to be quite so tatty. But then, some of the staff accommodation's pretty good.'

'So I should hope. Not everyone has to live in the sort of tip you William Murdock people inhabited.'

'And the staff are pretty . . . uneven in their response to their teaching role.'

'Sophie: get real! Universities are graded – and funded! – less for their teaching than for their research! Some top academics don't ever have to venture into a lecture room. They're paid to sit and think great thoughts; their job is to turn out good quality publications. So if you want to entice staff in, you've got to give them pleasant surroundings.'

'And I suppose they do have to use them for tutorials,' I conceded. 'That's if they bother to give tutorials. Oh, I suppose I'm jealous. All these fat cats in their plush rooms—'

'Fat cats? Wherever did you get that idea from? They're on

the same scale as you, love, and probably most of them are a lot worse paid.'

I goggled.

'Tell you what, I'll send you a copy of the pay scales. How about another cup, and you can tell me about your plans for Christmas . . . ?'

Chapter Six

When you teach a three-hour evening class you're so full of adrenalin at the end of it that you could go on and teach till dawn. When you're taught for three hours, it's a different story, and I staggered out, reeling after learning the theory of managing the curriculum.

Anon was there beside me before I could even yawn, suggesting a drink.

It was clearly time to establish myself as the sort of oddball he wouldn't want to be seen with.

'Not tonight, thanks. It's the first day of the Second Test Match.' I added sunnily, 'In Australia. So I shall be glued to the radio till I fall asleep.'

His eyebrows disappeared into what would have been his hairline, and the rest of his face clearly told me I was an imbecile to throw up the chance of spending time with him, but he said nothing. In his position I should have thought it a pretty weak excuse but of course I didn't want to use Mike as an explanation. It was an irritating situation anyway. I'd have thought my general body language would have indicated my complete lack of interest in him. If I said I was in a relationship with someone else, he could say he'd never wanted a sexual relationship with me. If I didn't, he could say I was misleading him. And there was the distinct possibility that knowing I was with someone else would enhance my value in his eyes and he'd pursue me even more. If it was pursuit.

49

I didn't want to go for a drink with Anon anyway. He struck me as the sort of man who'd want to make a conquest of any woman he was with and who wouldn't take kindly to outright rejection.

I set off.

'You really mean it, don't you? That you're going to listen to the radio!'

'Yes. Good night.'

I got home to a whole set of messages on my answerphone. Ian Dale, the ex-police sergeant, wanted to know how I was. I could discuss wine for Tom Bowen's dinner with him when I returned the call. Then there was my law-lecturer friend, Shahida, always good for a gossip about either William Murdock or her family. Steph, just after saying hi, like. And the one I wanted most: a few expensive words from Mike, telling me the letter I'd sent him on cassette had arrived safely, and one or two other things I wanted to hear.

Then to the radio. The Australians were batting – in for a good total, if the omens were anything to go by – and since Mike had never bowled a Test Match ball yet, I headed for bed. Not before I'd given Ivo a scrap of biscuit just to celebrate my happiness.

There I was, bright-eyed and bushy-tailed as I ever manage to be at nine o'clock in the morning, outside Tom Bowen's room, clutching a detailed estimate for his dinner party in one hand and my diary in the other. It was just like being a schoolgirl again, knocking, and waiting for the favour of a reply. I waited, fuming – yes, nine o'clock had been the time we'd agreed. Definitely.

At last, I shoved under his door the doctored estimate and a Post-it reminding Bowen I needed to see him. I stomped off to the library. Nine thirty already!

I'd done less than an hour's work when Anon presented himself at my side.

'There,' he said, pointing with a long, rather elegant finger at what turned out to be our course handbook. 'I told you she wasn't English.' He laid it on the pile of books on the table I'd commandeered.

I peered. Yes, there was a photo of Carla, and a short biography. Born and primary education in Canada; secondary education and first degree in New Zealand; doctorate in Australia: *Levels of Meaning in the Multi-Cultural Primary Classroom.*

I nodded as noncommittally as I could manage. 'But I don't see any problems,' I said. 'No one's ever said anything particularly nasty about Australian education, have they? Except their further education colleges imposed all sorts of draconian conditions on their staff—'

'And by their example ruined FE over here,' he concluded for me, loudly enough to raise a librarian's head.

Yes, it was wrong to talk in here. And he stood over me as if he had a lot to say. 'Tom was saying this morning,' he began.

Tom was saying when this morning? How had Anon managed to get hold of him when I was supposed to have an appointment? Exercising a little control, however, I touched my lips, gathered up my file and bag, and headed for the door. He was already there to hold it open for me. Yes, I'd have to ask his name – if only to be able to use it to tell him to get lost.

Sunlight streaming into the foyer told me it was a glorious winter morning; the outside world called imperiously. I wanted to shout, 'Hang UWM!'

'Bowen was saying what?' I prompted him.

He looked round, hunching his shoulders. 'I suppose it's a bit confidential. How about an early half at that pub down the road?'

I shook my head. 'I've got plans for lunch,' I lied. I

51

could, however, always make some. I set off briskly for the car park.

He fell into step with me. We walked in silence. Damn it, if he wanted to gossip he could open the conversation himself.

Which he did. 'I have a feeling you're avoiding me,' he said.

I wasn't about to accept or deny that one. 'Why should you think that?'

'Because every time I suggest a drink or whatever you say you're busy. I mean, last night! Whoever wants to listen to a cricket commentary, for God's sake!'

'Me.'

'No one likes cricket that much.' Not enough to skip the chance of being with him!

I flicked an eyebrow up: take it or leave it.

'You're quite an enigma,' he said.

Oh God, and he wanted to crack the code, didn't he? 'You were saying something about Bowen,' I said at last.

He stared. 'Oh, yes. Aren't we lucky to have him? I mean, a research record like that . . . He's been head-hunted by other places, of course.'

'I wonder why he's still here, then.'

'Loyalty,' he said.

I nodded. It would have to be a very good offer to prise me away from a house like that. And he probably wouldn't want to uproot children from their schools, his wife from her job . . . 'What was he saying that was confidential?' I asked, despite myself. I had a feeling it might be something derogatory about Pentowski.

The sun was warmer than it ought to be for late November. I wanted to bask and dream of Mike. Perhaps the thought of him allowed a smile to form. Foolish Sophie: Anon took it as encouragement. 'Oh, that she's gone down the woman's career path – too busy wasting time teaching to get stuck into research and publication. She'll never make it to the top. Mind you, she's too old, I'd have thought. Have to be there before you're forty, don't you? That's why I'm here, after all. And you,' he added with less certainty.

I reflected: if I didn't enjoy managing the curriculum in theory from six thirty till nine thirty in the evening, I didn't see me enjoying it much in practice during the working day. However Hoffman, the lecturer teaching the course, might interpret it, the very word *managing* sent a warning shiver down my back. It was the teaching I liked. The students. Not the managing. Not the admin. Perhaps I was having a road-to-Damascus experience in a Sandwell car park. If I was, I needed time to think.

'Look,' I said, 'I really do have to be on my way.'

He looked offended. Good. 'OK. If you ever have a spare moment, leave me a note.'

'I would if I knew your name.' Damn, it was out at last. I'd meant it as a put-down, but he could have heard it as a tease.

He did. 'James.' He added, with a would-be devastating smile, 'But my friends call me Jago. Jago Calvin.'

'And I'm—' I began, determined to betray by not so much as a twitch how appropriate I found his surname. Or how pretentious his first.

'Oh,' he said, smiling down at me, 'I know who you are. You're Sophie Rivers.'

My route home took me through Smethwick. On impulse, not far from Rolfe Street Station I parked the car and headed for the cut. Hanging round on towpaths had been absolutely forbidden when I was a kid – the dangers of drowning, of being spirited away by person or persons unknown and, most realistically, I suppose, of being attacked by the vicious dogs which accompanied narrow-boat families everywhere. But this, unlike the cuts of my childhood, just down the road in Oldbury, was a heritage site. I could explore this, surely.

Then I looked at the lonely stretch – not a soul in sight – and did something sensible. I fished out the mobile phone I carry but so rarely use – I didn't want it to be frying tonight for my brain, not having once seen what microwaves can do in the wrong place – and rang Chris Groom.

'Have you had lunch yet?'

'Not yet, but—'

'It's a lovely day and I need some sane company.'

'I won't suggest our canteen, then.'

'No. Tell you what. Get some sarnies and we'll find a bench in the sun on one of the towpaths in Galton Valley. I'm parked on Great Arthur Street.'

I was so absorbed in my thoughts that I jumped when he tapped on the window, some ten minutes later.

'Old Main Line or New Main Line?' he asked, with no preamble.

Funny that they should give cuts names that seemed more appropriate for railways.

'Old's closer. And the New's in such a steep gully there won't be any sun at this time of year.'

'Old it is. *Avanti!*'

We headed briskly down the ramp, and along the high-level canal. There was sufficient undergrowth to give the pretence of countryside, and there was a constant coming and going of birds hunting for late seeds and berries. Not to mention the constant roar of traffic and industry. We found a bench and stared at the ivy climbing up a huge blue-brick wall.

The advantage of being with an old friend was that you didn't have constantly to be worrying about silences like this. If either of us wanted to talk, we could. Or we could sit and watch the wind ruffling the surface of the cut, not everywhere, but in patches selected apparently at random.

He was halfway through a tuna sandwich when he nod-ded at the water. 'All very calm and peaceful, isn't it? Noise apart.'

His sigh reminded me that the murky waters could hide tragedy.

'Any news of your corpse? The one stuck in the cut?' I asked.

'A young woman. They can't tell much; there wasn't much left to go on. She'd been in there too long.'

'How long?'

'Six or eight months, maybe. She wasn't European or from the Indian continent. Almost certainly Malayan, something like that.'

'Malaysian,' I corrected him.

'No, Malayan. Specifically from the Malay bit of Malaysia,' he said. 'About five-one. No sign of any injuries. We don't even know whether she was alive when she went into the canal. Cut.'

'I suppose getting tangled in the propeller didn't do the corpse any good?' I was glad my sandwich was cheese. *Malay!*

'Nope. But the pathologist reckons she might have dislocated her wrist herself – so she could have drowned in there.'

'Here?' My voice shot up an octave.

'No. Along the Engine Arm canal. Near the old malthouse.'

'Not very easy to get to. There's no way through from Rabone Lane, is there?'

'No. She'd have had to get on the towpath back at Engine Bridge.'

The afternoon sun seemed distinctly weaker. A walk, a run, a dash along the towpath? From where? From whom? A young woman like those I was trying to teach!

Chris was not a man for histrionics. I must ask a sensible question. 'Does she fit anyone on the Missing Persons register?'

'No. No one her age, her build, what I'm told I should refer to as her ethnicity reported missing in the period that would be appropriate. Maybe she's what one or two of my colleagues will insist on calling "an illegal".' Chris's voice was unusually expressive. 'We're working on it. Or rather, Peter Kirby is. He and Harvinder Mann. They make a good team,' he added.

'Nice cop, nasty cop,' I agreed.

Whatever he was going to say was drowned by the roar of a passenger train. 'Ironic,' I said, when we could hear each other speak again, 'that by the time the third canal modification had been made – Telford's—'

'That's the New Main Line?'

'Yes. By the time Telford's was ready for use, the age of the train was already beginning.' Oh dear. Always the pedagogue. But local history was one of Mike's passions, and he'd begun to infect me.

Chris pulled a face. 'If my recent trips on the railways have been anything to go by, it's time we had another train age. Or, perhaps, a return to the canals.' He stood up. His lunch break, all twenty minutes, was clearly at an end. And it was certainly too cold to sit still for long.

At least I'd got him out of his office into what passes in Smethwick for fresh air. And while I didn't have to dash anywhere myself, I turned back to walk up the ramp to Brasshouse Lane with him. While I was in the area, I might as well take a stroll along the High Street and lay in a supply of fresh coriander and methi. Maybe a few of those wonderful sweets. Then I remembered my resolution: no sweets, then.

'Aren't you going to go for one of your walks?' he asked, as we crossed the road.

I stuck out a foot. 'Not in these shoes. And not alone. Not unless you've found your flasher.'

'Alas, no.'

'So I'm just being sensible. Don't worry, your sad little story hasn't freaked me out, even if it does puzzle me . . . No, I'd rather come sensibly shod and with a bit of company.'

'You must be getting old, Sophie,' he said, the affection in his smile turning to something else. 'Tell you what, would my company do, another lunchtime?'

'None better,' I said. But my heart sank. Oh, Chris, not again.

Clutching aromatic bags of fresh herbs, and another bulging with splendid glossy aubergines, I paused on my way back to look along the Old Main Line towards the locks, the work of Brindley and Smeaton. This must be where Carla lived: a neat row of gaily painted narrow boats – if that isn't tautology – moored along the approach to the locks. Ship's cats were basking in the sun, and late geraniums still flowed from hanging baskets, but a more fitting reminder of the time of year was the little plumes of smoke rising from narrow chimneys. In the distance I could pick out a solitary figure, running with more speed than sense along the towpath. He'd have to slow down by all those ropes or risk hurting himself – badly: the path was cinder-covered and he was only wearing a singlet and shorts. He had a very good body: it looked as if he worked with weights, as well as running.

He dodged the ropes successfully and picked up speed. He was so close now I could have waved to him. But for whatever reason, I wouldn't have wanted Jago to know that I'd seen him on his run.

Chapter Seven

I would leave the answerphone messages till I'd had a quick tidy in the garden. Not that there was much to do. At the start of a William Murdock year I'd have had no time to venture anywhere near the dahlias so much as to dead-head them. So to have not just lifted but also dried them in the hope that they'd overwinter in my garage was a minor triumph. The fuchsias I always tried to rescue looked somewhat affronted at having to share their accommodation. The garden itself was extremely tidy. Unnaturally tidy. Another reason I'd spent so much time in it was because Mike had never really made it his territory; I missed him more when I was in the kitchen. I missed him at his house too, of course, painfully, but Carla Pentowski had been right: yes, his garden was looking pretty good too.

I did wish that line from the Louis MacNeice poem about the sunlight on the garden hadn't kept coming into my head. I wanted to cage all those minutes with Mike. It was the minutes that were golden, not the cage, surely.

At last, I'd done enough and it was getting dark and very cold. Maybe there'd be a frost tonight. What was the temperature supposed to be in Perth now? Forty plus? No, best to think about switching the heating on, dealing with the stuff I'd bought in Smethwick, and taking the calls on the machine.

Call. Just the one. From an apologetic, indeed grovelling Tom Bowen, who told me my estimates were brilliant, that he was sure I was undercharging, and that he'd be in his office all Monday morning if I still needed that help. 'But I'm sure you're underestimating yourself, Sophie! Now—'

But the machine had had enough and cut him off.

Shahida phoned just as I was getting some supper, full of doom about William Murdock. The new Principal and the new Head of Department, replacing those currently in custody awaiting a major trial, had been imposed on them by the Further Education Funding Council, the arm of government responsible for colleges.

'And they're both tartars,' she wailed. 'There's talk of imposing a new contract on us. Goodness knows what that will be like. The rumour is it'll be thirty-eight hours in college every week, twenty-seven hours' teaching every week, and no more than twenty-eight days' holiday.'

I reflected silently on the easier ways at UWM.

'And it's check this, list that, record the other. You can't take a breath without filling in a form. Nor can the students. Even one absence and they're chased. They've got this idea we should phone every morning to make sure they're coming in. God knows when we're supposed to do it. Not now there's a diktat saying we mustn't leave our teaching rooms during classes on pain of death.'

I gasped. There was no need to say anything.

'I tell you, Sophie, I'm looking for another job. So is everyone else.'

'So when I come back—'

'*If* you come back. That was what I phoned for. There's talk of a major reorganisation – merging a lot of jobs and getting rid of half the senior staff. All you senior and principal lecturers will be made redundant and made to apply for your own jobs. That's the rumour.'

'My God!' How could any of us work any harder? Perhaps for a year or so – well, I was having a break to recharge my batteries, wasn't I? – but more than that . . . ? And there was no escaping to another FE college – they were all under the same pressures, if not directly under the FEFC thumb.

'I almost feel tempted to have another baby. The maternity leave would be nice,' Shahida continued.

'But imagine trying to cope with two children with those working conditions,' I said.

'Hmm.' She didn't sound convinced. Then, as I feared, she changed tack. 'Hey, when are you and Mike—'

'We're not even married yet,' I said.

'That doesn't worry most people these days.'

'It would worry me,' I said firmly, indeed pompously. 'I think kids need two parents. If at all possible.'

'Well, don't leave it too long. Maria's already . . .' And she gave me a long account of my quasi-goddaughter's latest achievements. It was only when that young lady fell over – I could hear the yells – that Shahida put down the phone.

No, I'd said nothing about Steph. Nor would I until he'd got round to telling his parents. And I'd got round to telling his father.

I'd just finished a very sober supper when Ian Dale phoned again.

'I was thinking, Sophie, we've got this satellite stuff, now, and if your young man's batting, you might like to come and watch him here. Have a jar or two. Val says to bring your nightie – the bed's aired.' For 'jar' read not a pint of bitter, but the taste of at least two different wines, both no doubt excellent.

'That'd be magic!' And extremely convenient, given I wanted his advice. But mostly magic.

'Come on, then. Whenever you're ready.'

Ian had videoed Mike's innings in the First Test for me. I'd been tempted to get my own satellite system, but Mike had been horrified by the idea, given the tiny amount of TV either of us watched. 'It's only my job,' he'd said. 'Come on, you'll be with me at Christmas for the Fourth Test. And with a bit of luck we'll be flying home together.'

I'd shaken my head. 'You'll be a dead cert for the One Day series.' And on current form he would be. Nor would I wish it otherwise. After all, England needed at least one man they could rely on to stay put and score runs. But then the days between my return and his, mid-February, would be very bleak.

'I've picked up a bit of gossip,' Ian said, as he opened his front door.

'Oh, let the poor girl get in the house before you talk shop.' Val's voice came from the kitchen. 'The first bit of winter we get and you want to stand there letting it into the house as fast as you can.'

It took time, not to mention affectionate hugs and friendly cups of tea, before Ian could settle us all in the huge squashy three-piece suite in front of the screen. Also in front of the TV were a couple of bottles of Australian red. No, we weren't to get tipsy, we were to taste. But I knew Val's invitation to stay over was as much to do with Ian's horror of drink-driving as with the cricket.

'So the word is, things are worse at your old place than they thought,' Ian said, pouring half an inch into a large glass and swirling it. 'Those two managed to stash away more than we realised.' Anyone else would have referred to them as two bastards. In my book very few words would be bad enough for the ex-Principal and ex-Head of Department, but Ian hated bad language, especially in front of women.

'How much?' I swirled and sniffed. 'Yes! This is wonderful. All those blackberries . . .'

'How about four million?'

'Four million pounds?' Val and I yelled as one.

'They've called Fraud in,' Ian said, in Eeyore mode. 'A

slow business, of course. Fraud always take their time. All that paperwork . . . Oh dear, look at that.'

And the first England batsman trailed dismally back to the pavilion.

Saying it was late, Ian and Val crept off to bed. But I had a horrible feeling that they were trying to be as tactful as if Mike and I wanted to do a spot of canoodling in their front room.

Funny how weekends are designed for couples. It had never hit me before, when I wasn't part of one. Working on the principle that if I didn't have any time to spare I wouldn't miss him so much, I shopped, ran, washed, ironed, worked on an assignment and read two Sunday papers. All that so I could retire to bed with Mike – via the radio this time.

Bleary though I might be – and if Mike hadn't been run out on fifty-five by the cretin at the other end wanting to take a run that wasn't there, I'd have been a lot blearier – I turned up at UWM at a reasonable hour. But not so reasonable that Bowen wasn't in. He was just unpacking his briefcase.

If I'd expected him to be as jolly as he'd been on the phone, I was to be disappointed. Perhaps he wasn't a man for early – or even a mid – morning meetings.

'I gather from Pentowski that you're not happy with those students I put your way.'

'On the contrary, I think they're delightful. I'm just aware that they've got different language problems from students I've taught before. Hence the problems with my dissertation. And I wondered what language qualifications they came in with and how they'd got on in their assessment tests. She mentioned a print-out.'

'I'll bet she couldn't find one.' He mimed a frantic Ivo-like dig through mounds of paper.

I risked a complicitous grin. Face back in Father Christmas mode, he returned it, patting the significantly smaller piles on his own desk. 'Tell you what, I'll find mine and put it in your pigeonhole: how about that? Now, these problems with your dissertation. If you want, I could see you early next week. Monday, let's say. About this time. Let me have all the notes you've done so far on Friday, so I'll know exactly where you're at. Oh, and the overall plan. And a brief summary of the problems you've got. OK?' He sat down, smiling.

'Great.' I felt better already. Perhaps this degree would be what I needed to save my job at William Murdock. Or indeed, get me one somewhere else. 'Just one more thing,' I added. 'Is there a system for reporting absences?'

'Why do you ask?' The smile swept from his face.

'It's just that they're very hot on it where I work. We have to submit all these forms to the office.'

'No need for that here!' he said, breezy again. 'Just tell the tutor. In their case, me. And for God's sake don't bother if they miss the odd session – they are adults, after all, and they're paying their own fees. Just if a pattern emerges.'

'Just like the old days at William Murdock, in other words.'

He nodded. 'Before things got so bad in FE a student can't scratch his arse without someone having to record it. Jesus, a friend of mine was saying the other day . . .'

He certainly kept abreast of the current further education disasters, I had to give him that. And his coffee was good. It sorted out my cricket hangover. Which brought us, if somewhat circuitously, to the wine we'd drunk at Ian's, and my suggestions for his dinner party.

'Pretty obscure, isn't it? I mean, not one of your great names.'

'Nor one of your great prices,' I pointed out. 'A famous label, and you'd be paying twice that. Trust me.'

'Yes,' he said, 'I think perhaps I will.'

Chapter Eight

'Sophie!' A familiar voice stopped me in my tracks. 'Sophie Rivers! How are you?'

It took me half a second to place the speaker, since she was so out of context. It was one of our administrators at William Murdock, one of the most reliable and teacher-friendly ones.

'Kathryn! What are you doing here?'

'Didn't you hear the splash as I hit the water?' she asked. 'I'm just another rat hopping over the side.'

Yet another cup of coffee, and yet more William Murdock misery later, I left Kathryn to her administrative challenges and returned to the post-grad work-room. Jago was there, presenting his better profile as he used the pay phone. He might have been back in his own college staffroom, fending off importunate students.

'Of course, her time is very much occupied . . . Original research . . . Very time-consuming, yes . . . The library, of course . . . No, of course not. Yes, I'll pass on the message . . . Oh, of course.' He replaced the phone, wrote down 'Chris Groom' in big letters on his pad and, absorbed in his task, shoved the paper under his files, oblivious to my presence. Now, how long would it take Jago to pass on whatever message Chris had charged him with? It wouldn't surprise me if he 'forgot' altogether. A subtle bit of revenge, for my not fancying him, perhaps. What interested me was how long he'd maintain the absence of mind, and how much amusement I could derive from finally catching him out.

'Morning,' I called brightly from behind him. 'Another lovely day.' I busied myself in my drawer.

'Yes, indeed. Sophie, someone was looking for you. Lola. The lovely Lola.'

She was actually quite lovely: a statuesque Ghanaian with a voice pitched right down there – a delight to listen to even if what she said belonged to another, more formal, age. She sported either what she dismissed as 'just tribal stuff' on warmer days, or the most elegant European couture when it was chilly. I wondered if today would find her in après-ski.

'Any message?' Or better still, *messages*.

'Oh, that she'd try again after lunch. Which I was hoping you'd take with me today. Cricket permitting, that is?' His voice dripped irony.

I supposed I had to award him marks for persistence or for thick skin. I wasn't sure which. In any case, I would make certain he didn't enjoy his lunch enough to repeat the offer.

'So long as it's funeral baked meats: did you see the overnight score?' I arranged everything to my satisfaction and straightened to look at him.

'I'm a baseball man,' he said loftily.

I knew that Chris would never phone me at work without having something important to say, but I dearly wanted to play the point out as long as I could. If he ever did get round to mentioning it, damn it, I'd put a fiver in the next Oxfam tin I saw. I could always phone Chris anyway. But not yet. Here was Lola again, and it was clear she meant to speak to me now.

'Me? Help you?' I asked, getting up to adjust the vertical blind. We were in the small room I used for my tutorials, the sort of general purpose interview room I'd always craved at William Murdock, where some of my most sensitive counselling had

had to take place in the ladies' loo. Despite the privacy I was unnerved. I was just a student, a colleague. The fact I taught a little oral English didn't put me on the staff. The students weren't assessed on work in my class and, knowing it could have put me in a very difficult situation if I'd had to fail anyone, I wouldn't have taken it on if they were.

'Exactly. And as I said, it's entirely confidential. What's worrying me has actually nothing to do with me at all,' Lola said. 'But if it's not my problem, it's certainly not my job to broadcast it. I'm worried about one of my colleagues.'

'*Our* colleagues.'

'I could have talked to my tutor, but – you know,' she smiled, 'I always prefer to talk to a woman about other women. And when I tried to see Dr Pentowski, she was evidently busy.'

Everyone seemed to want to criticise Carla. Resisting the urge to ask how she manifested her busyness, I sat down again. 'You must know I've no authority in this place. I'm a student, just as you are.'

'Neither flesh nor fowl,' she acknowledged, 'nor good red herring. But probably a good teacher in your own college. Conscientious enough here. And those students in your English classes appreciate your efforts. At least, they say you're kind; you don't make them feel like this.' She held her thumb and forefinger half an inch apart.

I waited.

'I think one of my colleagues,' she continued, 'may be getting herself into trouble with the Law. Shoplifting.'

Oh God! African students shoplifting was surely a media myth! 'Surely not,' I said. 'Not one of us!'

'It's not a matter of shoplifting fine clothes from big stores and smuggling them back to wherever. But shoplifting food. Food's not a luxury item, Sophie. But stealing it might be a deportation offence.'

'I can't even speak to her about it – and I notice you haven't given me her name – until there's some sort of evidence,' I said, fending off the moment I knew I would say, 'Which I guess you have?'

'I'm sure you could see for yourself this very lunchtime. I know the sandwiches in the canteen aren't that wonderful but they're cheap and possibly nutritious. So why does she sneak into the furthest corner and eat top-of-the-range Marks and Spencer? I mean, smoked salmon!'

'Don't some of the big stores donate end-dated food to the homeless?'

'Is she homeless? If she is, don't tell the Home Office! And this "end-dated" food?'

'All food has a sell-by date stamped on the packaging.'

'Of course. So you'll check the packaging when she's discarded it.'

'I will. But not this lunchtime.'

'Oh, the handsome Jago's managed to win you over at last. We've been taking bets, one or two of us.'

'How kind of him to make me the object of gossip!' Her sentence patterns were catching, weren't they? 'I've been trying to let his poor ego down gently, Lola. But I'm afraid this lunchtime he'll have to have it straight between the eyes.'

'He won't enjoy that experience. Are you sure it's wise to confront him tactlessly?'

'Any other man would have taken the hint days ago. I shall simply tell him I'm in a relationship.'

'Pistols at dawn! When he wants something, that sort of man, he usually makes sure he gets it.'

'Not from this woman he won't.'

'I fear he might find it even more exciting to see off a rival.'

'But he won't see him off. No, Lola, ten minutes with a broken heart, and he'll be after you.'

'No,' she said seriously, 'I'm too tall. A man like that likes to be able to look down at the top of his companion's head.'

'So he wouldn't fancy me if I were taller! Lola, you've

destroyed me. More to the point,' I added, 'what are we going
to do about this colleague of ours?'

'You could really insult Jago by standing him up?' She
laughed. 'OK, I'll try to see myself whether the sandwiches
are fresh. And if the freshly squeezed orange juice lives up to
its name.'

'If it does, if the sandwiches are fresh, does that prove
anything anyway?'

'The woman does not wear tights in this weather because
she can't afford them, and she chooses the most expensive way
of feeding herself?'

I pulled a face. 'Lots of people don't get their priorities
right. Tell me, how good is her English? Would she realise
if she were paying over the odds?'

She squinted at the colloquialism: I was amazed she didn't
know it.

'Paying too much for something she could get much
cheaper.'

She seemed to be registering it for future use. 'Who can
say?' she asked at last. 'She's in one of your groups. But
since my sense of honour forbids me to reveal her identity
until I have some evidence, I can scarcely ask you how well
she's doing! Oh, Sophie, how complicated we make our lives:
me by not telling you this woman's name, you by not telling
Jago where to put his lust.' Before I could respond, she added,
her face serious, 'But it occurs to me how close the name Jago
is to Iago. Take care, Sophie, take care.'

Jago was waiting, jacket ready to button, when I got back to
the work-room.

'I've got to be back by one thirty,' he said. 'I want to talk
to Pentowski about her Ph.D. paper. There may be something
in there I can use.'

Despise her and pick her brains. Fair enough, I suppose.
That was the lot of all teachers, wasn't it?

He set off at a brisk pace through the car park. Maybe he hoped I'd have to scuttle to keep up with him, but he was no Chris and I'd enlivened the last few mornings with the intensive Canadian Airforce exercises which had for years kept me fit. So, if not step for step, I could still keep up with him, without so much as a pant. Fortunately he didn't test whether I had enough breath for conversation, though I was sure, after seeing him run yesterday, he wouldn't be stretched by such a trivial thing as a fast walk.

I remembered the pub from my teens: the Queen's Head or something. Now it had a fancy new name – the Chalk and Talk – and fancy new décor. The menu matched, but my mouth refused to water. I had no evidence to substantiate my suspicion that every enticing item was cooked elsewhere, frozen, and merely reheated by the high-hatted chef, but my taste buds insisted it was so.

'Mineral water,' I said firmly when Jago asked me what I wanted.

'Oh, surely you could make it a spritzer.'

I shook my head. 'I like wine and I like water but I prefer to keep them separate. I also prefer to be credited with knowing my own mind.' I looked him straight in the eye. 'So when I say I'm buying myself a tuna salad, it means I don't want you to try to buy it – or anything else – for me.'

If he'd dared mention moods or times of the month, he'd have had the water in his face. And I think, from his expression, he knew it.

We sat warily opposite each other at a table I chose: it was too big to permit the accidental rubbing of knees.

'If I'm eking out my existence by teaching,' I began, 'how are you keeping body and financial soul together? After all, we're the only full-time UK students on the M.Ed. course. All the others do the course part time over a longer period so they can still work.'

70

'Yes, it's the overseas – oh, I mean, the *international* – students who have money, these days, isn't it?'

If he hoped to lure me into a digression castigating new politically correct terms, he was to be disappointed.

'So how do you survive?' When he didn't answer, I said gaily, 'Oh, I suppose you're one of those lucky people with a partner back home to support them. What does your wife do? Is she a teacher too?'

He flushed, but the arrival of our salads prevented him from snarling. 'Alison works for a building society, actually,' he said.

I thought about cheap mortgages and other benefits Alison might bring. 'How do your children cope with Daddy having to do homework?' Apart from probably having to sit in total silence, that is.

'They – I – Alison—' He looked at my hand, and made a valiant effort. 'You're not married yourself?'

I thought I'd scored enough points to be able to let him off now. I shook my head, smiling. 'But I'm in a very strong relationship. With a professional sportsman.' I hoped the term would conjure precisely the sort of thick-necked, bone-skulled sportsman Mike wasn't, and hoped Mike would forgive me.

But Jago had a quicker mind than I'd credited him with. 'Ah! The Australian interest. The cricket at midnight.' His smile might have conceded sexual defeat. Then he turned the subject swiftly to how he used to run for his county. No, he hadn't quite given me up; but whenever had I fancied someone simply because of an athletic body?

I realised, as I set off for my class, he hadn't passed on Chris's message. And I hadn't remembered to phone. I must be as off form as the England team.

Chapter Nine

So what titbit did Chris have for me that Jago had tried to deny me? It might be nothing much – news is the currency of friendship, after all, and there were times when we'd had to work hard to keep ours solvent. The work-room empty, I reached for the pay phone.

There are two ways of phoning an individual policeman. If you are lucky you know their direct dial number, otherwise you have to go through the general police phone system, which can take forever. Chris's number was engaged, as was Bridget's. Since Piddock Road and its Victorian police station were almost on my route home, I decided to pop in and see him. By some miracle, there was a parking spot only ten yards from the impressive front portico. But the heavy doors were shut, and a sign directed me a few yards further to an entrance, all automatic doors and clean lines. Why Chris had never seen fit to mention such a dramatic change, goodness knows. Perhaps because he never used that entrance anyway. The man on reception was the same as ever. He greeted me with an amused smile, and gestured me to a new blue plastic seat, a far cry from the nasty, sagging Rexine-covered ones I knew but didn't love. They'd even brought in some new posters to decorate the walls, in both the public and the police area. Through the screen separating the two, I could see a hand-written notice: 'Keys to hearse'. I was still considering that when Chris's head popped round the door, and I was whizzing, not through Victorian corridors I was used to, across a yard that at this time of the year was always gusty, but through a glass tunnel to the part of the station that was his domain.

Bridget was just emerging from the loo. 'Ah, now you'll be wanting a cup of tea,' she announced as she saw me.

Chris didn't argue: I doubted if he'd dare.

He'd barely had time to do more than sit opposite me and wipe his hands over his face when Bridget pushed open the door and deposited the tea-tray on the table between us. Did she keep the kettle perpetually on the boil, for goodness' sake? The handles of the pot and the milk jug pointed in my direction. Grimacing, I played mother. The china cups I poured into were some of a set I'd given Chris to replace those Helena, his previous secretary, had smashed.

Just as he was about to draw breath to speak, the door flew open again, and a plate appeared between us. Not much sign of the plate, actually. Too much cake and soda bread for that. Butter, in a separate little dish, materialised as well.

And Bridget was gone.

'All home-made, still?' I asked.

'Could you even dream otherwise? This is what I have every day. And she won't accept a penny from me. But I've found a way of making some recompense,' he said. 'Ian found me this article saying whisky was good for you. So I gave her a copy, and a bottle of Jameson. Purely medicinal.' He gave his schoolboy grin. 'One day soon I'll have to ask after her health and find another bottle – maybe Bushmills, this time.'

'I didn't know such women still existed.'

'Well, she's not far off retirement age, of course. I don't know if there'll be another generation to follow. I mean, you may see her as a stereotypical mother figure, but her typing's fast and accurate and her filing's miraculous. Meanwhile, I never was one to check up on gift horses. Though perhaps it's time I learnt.' He looked at me. 'Helena's started to write to me. She wants me to intercede for her.'

I passed him his tea. 'And will you?'

Chris had started to fall in love with her before he discovered what she was up to. Which was something nasty.

'How can I?' His voice was controlled. But his knuckles, as he put down his cup, were white. He got up and leant on the windowsill, back towards me. The sun had disappeared entirely. It was undeniably winter. 'Anyway,' he said, turning back to me, 'the good news is the budget's found enough money to get me a proper table and decent chairs. And a really pukka chair for me. So I don't get back problems – in work time that is.' He grinned, his face younger by ten years. He strode back to his desk and sat down. He looked good in his uniform, and had got rid of his habit of easing a finger round the tight uniform collar. 'And if I get stressed, by spring I shall be able to sit in a garden – of remembrance,' he added, the last two words devoid of the cynicism of the earlier ones. 'They're constructing it in memory of the officers who've died . . . I hope you're impressed by the front door,' he continued, an ironic gleam returning to his eye. 'Civic reception and media and everything, that involved.'

All this was very interesting, but nothing to do with a phone call to me which had sounded urgent. And I had an assignment to complete.

'I'm sorry I didn't ring back this lunchtime,' I said. 'I've got this megaprick – or do I mean miniprick? – of a colleague who "forgets" to pass on messages.'

'How did you know I phoned, then?' His eyes twinkled and disappeared into a maze of crow's feet.

'Saw him write your name.'

'Why didn't you grab the phone in your usual subtle way?'

'I wanted to test him.'

'Would he pass the message on? That sort of thing?'

'And would he have passed it on if you'd been a woman? Anyway, I've sorted all that out now. Over lunch. I don't somehow think he'll ask me out again. If he does, I shall set Ian on him.'

'Ian?'

'Ian doesn't approve of married men with children trying to have a bit on the side.'

'No more he does. Anyway, the reason I phoned was to ask if you'd fancy a chamber music concert at the Barber Institute on Wednesday evening. Someone offered me a couple of tickets. Schubert and Brahms. Just your handwriting, I'd have thought.'

'Absolutely. Yes, please.'

He unlocked a drawer and fished out his wallet.

'Chris, this is a police station! Aren't people working here supposed to be honest?'

'In general. But don't you remember,' he said, looking me in the eye, 'the sort of thing that can happen in a police station? And did? In this very station? Here: have your ticket in case anything holds me up and I have to miss the start.' He shoved the wallet back and turned the key with an authoritative click. He pocketed the key. 'By the way, we've got another body. By rights, it's the Transport Police who've got another body. But it's my patch and I'm interested because – guess what? It's another young woman.'

I waited. What had this to do with me?

'First reports suggests she was from the Pacific Rim. Another Malay.'

Ah! Like the one they'd found in the cut. 'You never did believe overmuch in coincidence, did you?'

'No more than you did, Sophie.' He smiled. But then he was serious again. 'The pathologist couldn't find any signs of violence from other people, but what she inflicted on herself was profound. She lay down on the railway line about a hundred yards from where we had our lunch yesterday. And waited for a train.'

It was always easier to ask questions than to dwell on the

horror, wasn't it? 'I suppose there's no chance of it having been an accident?'

He shook his head. 'The evidence we have at the moment suggests she laid her neck precisely where the train wheels would sever it.' He let that sink in and added, 'It also suggests she was holding a Koran when . . .'

'My God.' Again it was easier to ask questions: 'Any ID yet?'

He shook his head.

'No match with any Missing Person?'

'I gather Harvinder and Peter are busy scouring every Oriental restaurant in the entire conurbation.'

'Are you sure that isn't a bit racist?'

He had the grace to look sheepish.

'It isn't just restaurants that employ young women from the Pacific Rim,' I continued. 'There's my new dentist, for a start. There are computer companies and – hell, there are a lot of Malaysian women students! I mean, there are all the universities in the area—'

He ticked them off on his fingers. 'Aston, Birmingham, University of Central England and UWM . . .'

'You forgot Wolverhampton. There are a load of Malaysian and Singaporean students on the course I'm on, for instance.'

'And you're teaching some of them, aren't you?'

'Trying to. Failing to.' And getting confused as to the identity of some of them, suspecting some of answering to other people's names when I called the register. Was I simply confused? Or was something else going on? It was the first time I'd allowed the thought to form in full.

'What sort of age?'

'Oddly enough,' I said, 'considering some parts of the course cater specifically for experienced teachers, some are quite young. Mid-twenties. Of course, many people do get an M.Ed. before they start; helps them get a better job. Or a job full stop.'

He nodded, writing. Chris never jotted, never scribbled furiously: he wrote. I'd never seen his handwriting anything other than clear and elegant. 'How's your stomach?' he asked at last.

I stared.

'I mean, you're over that gastritis, aren't you?'

'More or less. Why?'

'This is the longest of long shots, Sophie, but – if you wouldn't mind . . .'

I knew the way his mind was running. 'Photo of head or actual head?' I asked, maybe too brightly.

He shook his head. 'Don't worry – just a photo. At this stage anyway,' he added, laughing that sort of grim laugh I associate with serving officers doing unpleasant work.

The CID room was its usual bustling self.

'Haven't you set up an incident room?' I asked.

'Not for one suicide,' he said. 'Or even two. I'd have thought you'd know that by now.'

'But as you yourself so sapiently observed, neither of us believes strongly in coincidence.'

'I need more than my nasty suspicious nature – and yours, Sophie – to start a major inquiry at this stage. Ah! Peter, there you are!'

Peter Kirby paused in the act of hanging his coat up, started to come over, and thought better of it, returning to sling his coat and a brightly coloured scarf on to a hook.

'I see you get not just your mugs but also your clothes courtesy of your nephew,' Chris observed. 'You remember Sophie, don't you, Peter?'

Stupid question, really: after a series of spats, we'd drunk tea together out of the vivid mugs Chris was referring to.

'Once encountered, never forgotten,' Peter said. But his smile and friendly handshake took any sting from his words. 'Your bloke's doing pretty well,' he continued. 'How come you're not out down under with him?'

'I'm on this course at UWM,' I said.

'But he's the only one doing any good. Apart from Hussain, I suppose.'

'And one or two others.'

'But not with his consistency. So what's taken you to UWM and the excitements of West Bromwich?'

'A teaching course. Tell your wife I may be about to be made redundant,' I said.

She too was an FE lecturer.

There was a little pause before he said, 'So this course will make you more employable?'

I nodded. Then shrugged. 'But the important thing at the moment is that there are a lot of Pacific Rim students at UWM. Singaporean, Chinese, Malay. And Chris has this charming idea—'

'Just the photos, Peter,' he said, before Peter could do more than open his eyes wide.

'Walk this way,' Peter said. And started a John Cleese lope.

Relations between the two had clearly improved.

'The trouble is, whatever you do to a stiff to make it look alive, it ends up deader than ever,' Chris said. 'Does this do anything for you, Sophie?'

Apart from making my stomach heave, which I certainly wouldn't admit? I peered closer. 'Not so much,' I temporised – was it really someone I knew? – 'as to make me want to rush to the morgue to have a look at the real thing!'

'But . . . ?'

Damn! He'd spotted my hesitation.

'I don't want to give you this "all look the same" twaddle,' I said. 'But there's nothing especially distinctive, except that little mark there. Is it a speck of dust on the lens or a tiny scar?'

Both men peered. Both shook their heads.

'If it is a scar?' Peter asked.

I spread my hands. 'Oh, I don't know, I really don't. Tell you what, sometimes it's easier to compare a photo with a photo. I could go through the student records at UWM . . .'

'Are you looking for anyone specific?'

'I think – no, let me check my register and the photos. And if she's in class tomorrow morning, I won't even have to bother doing that. Fair enough?'

Despite the by now miserable cold, which he refused to acknowledge by so much as a quiver in his immaculate white shirtsleeves, Chris walked with me to the car. He touched the windscreen experimentally, but what misted it was condensation, not frost.

'So you'll call me as soon as you know whether this woman's in your class tomorrow?'

'Of course. Here, what's Bridget's number? So I can get through to her if you're engaged. And, Chris, don't expect anything. It's too long a shot, too much of a coincidence.'

He nodded. 'But at least it's moved us on a bit. Peter and Harvinder have now got all the educational establishments in the West Midlands to check.'

'Not necessarily all of them. There used to be a lot in FE colleges until the Thatcher government gave the fees an enormous hike. But they still consider British unis prestigious enough to apply to.'

'They'll be on to everywhere possible,' he said.

I unlocked my door and got in. He grasped the top of it, leaning into the car. If he'd meant to say anything, he didn't. At last, he passed me my seat belt.

'One thing, Sophie. You will take care this time, won't you? And keep that out of anything that isn't your business.' He touched the tip of my nose.

And still not so much as a shiver as I shut the door on him and drove away.

I rubbed at my nose. He'd sounded so damned meaningful!

All I was doing was checking a student, for goodness' sake. As it happens, I wasn't into risk-taking at the moment. Not for my sake so much as for Mike's. He'd not been keen on my taking risks to clear his name last summer; he'd be very unhappy if he thought I was putting myself in any danger quite disinterestedly. Just as I would if I thought he was being foolish. Not that there was any sort of risk involved with checking if there was the remotest chance that it was a UWM student who'd topped herself. None at all.

But I was glad I'd stopped off at Safeway on the way home. Amongst the other trolley-pushers were an ill-assorted-looking couple. He was in his fifties, with the sort of roughened skin and bulky muscle that suggested a life of hard work in the open; she was a tiny, fragile-looking girl barely out of her teens. No matter how curtly he spoke to her, she beamed back at him. At one point he lifted a thick finger to touch her cheek, just as one might touch a favourite cat. I'd read about agencies which arranged marriages between British men and subservient Asian women. Yes, Malaysians, like this girl. Now what if Chris's suicide had been a girl in an arranged marriage which didn't even have the casual affection of this one? I grinned to myself: now that should give poor Peter and Harvinder even more hours' fun.

Chapter Ten

There in my Tuesday morning class, of course, large as life, was the girl with the scar, Rokiah Binti Ahmed. She gave a modest smile and waited, eyes lowered, while I called the other names. I drew a couple of blanks there, and noticed they'd already missed two classes, something they could ill afford to do if their English was as dodgy as I remembered. Some of the group, however, wrote the language a good deal better than they spoke or heard it: perhaps Ruksahna Kamarrudin and Mahsuri Mushtaq had left the group because they felt they didn't need it – or me.

I phoned Chris, reached Bridget as his substitute, and left the news, plus the suggestion that Peter and Harvinder could extend their search to international marriage agencies. That should cheer them no end. Then I popped down to the admin staff's offices, and Kathryn.

'You remember William Murdock's system of reporting absences,' I said. Surely there must be one here. If I drew official attention to my students' absences, indeed disappearances, my conscience would be clearer. And perhaps some action would be taken – they might even trail back.

She shuddered: 'One form after one absence in one subject. And the mandatory phone call if the student skipped classes in more than one subject. And then there was all that to-do when that girl didn't want to marry that guy and slipped off to the police safe house and the family threatened to sue us for not phoning the minute she didn't come into college so they'd have had a chance of catching her.' She grabbed a breath. 'Happy days.'

'But at least we kept track of people,' I said, 'much as we all hated the system. And I gather from Shahida it's getting worse . . .'

Kathryn raised her eyes heavenwards and sighed. 'But it sort of worked,' she agreed. 'Unlike this shambolic affair here. And while it doesn't matter if adult home or European students skive, so long as they get good marks in their assignments, of course, it certainly matters if non-European students on study visas do. Here . . .' She fished in a concertina file and came up with a sheaf of Home Office enquiries. 'How can I deal with them if people aren't properly registered and if you people don't complete the forms?'

She paused for breath long enough for me to ask, 'What forms?'

'Sophie! You of all people . . . ! Here.' She thrust a sheet of turquoise paper at me.

I stared.

'Don't tell me you never saw one of those before. OK, not this colour: that was my idea – different colours for each course. The PGCE course has these orange ones.'

I held out my hand with the air of one doing reluctant duty: there was no point in making loud objections that someone should have told me the system. Kathryn had probably had her fill of messenger-shooting; staff sounding off at her as if she were solely responsible for the load of admin coming their way.

We agreed to have a drink together in the near future – 'More like a wake for poor William Murdock, if you ask me,' Kathryn observed – and I nipped back to the work-room to salve my administrative conscience. Yes, I was happier with a few official forms to complete – my William Murdock habit was craving a quick fix. Perhaps it was a sense of being back in a routine, however low and loathsome, that made me check my pigeonhole. Nothing but a crumpled Coke can and an empty Benson and Hedges packet. Thank you.

But there was an envelope pinned to our work-room door. Jago was just about to remove it, no doubt to lay it on my bit of the work area. No doubt. Perhaps the flourish with which he handed it to me suggested some sort of guilt.

'Thanks. I'm glad some messages get through.' I tried to look him in the eye but he was busying himself with his briefcase. 'The police were trying to get hold of me yesterday and someone failed to leave a note.'

'Police?' Whatever he was looking for must have been right at the bottom of his case.

'Hmm. Quite an important message, I'd have said. Nasty thing, not passing messages on. Or worse: obstructing the course of justice. Wasting police time.' I was quite enjoying this flow of spurious accusations. The poor man couldn't argue back, or he'd be admitting guilt. Eventually he found what he'd been looking for – a large apple – and sank his teeth into it.

This morning's communication was from Tom Bowen: a note thanking me for my notes and the list of entry qualifications and UWM pre-course test results he'd promised me. He'd scrawled across the top: 'GOODNESS KNOWS HOW SOME OF THESE PEOPLE MANAGED TO GET THEIR ENGLISH QUALIFICATIONS!'

The test results highlighted particular weaknesses: most students, predictably, were much stronger in the written tests than the oral and aural ones. Well, I can cope perfectly with written French, but trying to have a French conversation with a native speaker's another matter altogether. I shoved the list into a new folder, and stowed it in my drawer. OK, if Chris could lock his desk drawers, I could lock this, however unnatural it felt. And so to the assignment due in on Friday.

*   *   *

85

Whether by accident or design Jago fell into step with me as I headed off to the refectory for a sandwich.

'What was that missing message about?' he asked. Just like that.

'Someone's death,' I said repressively, infusing enough gloom into my voice to suggest that there might be a personal connection.

'Anyone – close?' Yes, he was chastened. And he also sounded concerned.

'No, as it turns out. Nothing to do with me. Except in the John Donne island sense.'

The refectory was unusually crowded, but there were a few seats available. Two were at a table occupied by Bowen and Pentowski who were deep in what seemed to be irate conversation. I'd have left them to it – what teacher, after all, wants to share a lunch table with a student? – but Jago pushed his way over, and Carla smiled warmly enough in my direction to make me feel I wouldn't be entirely unwelcome.

But it was Jago who grabbed the conversation. His dissertation was on much the same area as Carla's, it seemed, and he wanted to pick her brain.

'I really could do with seeing your references – and other research materials. I mean, I'd love to see the whole thesis. I'm sure it would be invaluable.' He followed up with a wonderful smile.

'It might well be,' she said. Her smile was grim. 'But – you know I live on a narrow boat, Sophie – I had this house fire. Everything went. All my books, papers, clothes. The computer. Everything.'

'My God! How dreadful!' I'd had my house done over by criminals once, and still missed some of the things they'd smashed, however much I told myself one shouldn't become attached to material possessions. I didn't want to interrupt her by telling my story, however.

'It was bad,' she said, making clear that the adjective was

an understatement. 'Bad. An involuntary sloughing off of all my history.'

'A violation of identity,' Bowen suggested.

'Inasmuch as identity comes through the things one acquires, collects . . .'

And remembers. No wonder she was so terrified of Alzheimer's.

Jago asked: 'Were you insured?'

'Underinsured, they reckoned. And the fabric, too.'

'So why did you choose to live on a boat?' he pursued.

'There's not much space,' she said. 'So you learn to live without accumulating. You have to become what you are, not what your trappings say you are. Having said that, I must admit that I like living on the boat. It feels very safe – rocked on the bosom of the deep, or something.'

'"Deep"?' I repeated. 'A cut?'

'OK. Not much risk of drowning unless your feet hit the mud at the bottom and you're held down,' she agreed. 'But – goodness know what a Freudian would make of this – being rocked gently, the sound of water lapping at the side of the boat . . . yes, all very comforting. And if that loses its charm, there's always the TV and a good video.'

We laughed obligingly.

'All mod cons, then,' said Bowen.

'All mod cons. Just small mod cons. And there are times I yearn for a soak in a big, deep, hot tub.'

'My tub is your tub,' Bowen said, getting up and producing an extravagant bow. 'And now, if you'll forgive me, I must be on my way. Sixty essays from the PGCE course to finish by Thursday teatime. Now, are you still all right for next Monday, Sophie?'

Jago and Carla carried on talking while Tom and I sorted an exact appointment time. Jago had raised again the issue of Carla's doctorate. Tom was just leaving when I heard her say, 'No, the only copy's back in Oz, I'm afraid. Lodged in the uni library. Now, if you'll excuse me . . .' She gathered her bag. 'Sophie – I've found that print-out!' she yelled, and was off. So what had made her take to her heels like that?

It left Jago and me. I was on my feet in a flash but no faster than he.

'Imagine,' he said, gesturing me through the doors, 'losing everything.'

'I can't. My place was ransacked once and that was bad enough.' How irritating that the memory insisted on forcing its way out at last, and to Jago of all people. 'They smashed a lot of my stuff, but I still had my clothes, my books . . .'

'My God, that's terrible! Such a violation of your territory!' He spoke with as much sincerity as if Bowen hadn't said almost the same words a matter of minutes before. 'Oh, Sophie, I'm so sorry. You poor—'

'These things happen,' I said, not wanting to be his poor anything, particularly not a poor dear. But, slightly more in charity with him, I continued, 'Do you know which uni Carla went to? Because, as you'll recall, my partner's touring down under. They don't get much free time, but I'm sure if he was in the relevant city he wouldn't mind nipping into the library and photocopying the pages you need. And he could fax them back.'

'Sophie, that'd be wonderful! Absolutely wonderful. Except . . . I mean, university libraries—'

'I know, they're hardly the place you'd expect to see a professional crickcter. Unless he happens to have a degree rather better than mine.' I grinned to soften the put-down. 'Tell me— Oh, sorry!' We'd cannoned into Bowen and a student.

'Melbourne Uni, I think. Yes, I'm sure it was Melbourne.' We'd slowed down, the better, I suspected, for Jago to eye up a student, a young Asian woman in her twenties, about my height and with a figure to die for.

'Well,' I said, 'he's in Perth at the moment. Then they're

off to Melbourne later this week. They may even have one rest day. It'd be a shame to waste that. I'll e-mail him.'

'Promise me one thing,' he said, peeling his eyes off the girl. 'You'll tell me of any costs incurred. I mean, this would be so useful – invaluable. I hope Carla won't mind.'

'Surely not! It's an honour to be consulted, isn't it? Anyway, theses are as good as published once they're accepted. Public property. I'll get on to it.'

'You will make sure he bills me!' By now Jago was backing down the corridor, in pursuit of the beautiful student. 'Jenny!' Jenny Lee: one of the brightest on the course with no need at all of my skills.

Tom Bowen watched the little charade and turned to me, as if ready to commiserate with me for being rejected for so young a woman. 'And didn't I hear you make him an offer to die for? To help him with his research? No manners, these young men.'

'No.' I looked at the sheet of crow-black hair, the jeans that looked as though they'd been sprayed on. And now she was turning, so we saw her fresh skin and bright eyes. 'No, but impeccable taste.'

'Sophie, if I fell for every pair of bright oriental eyes, I'd never get an hour's work done. Though I admit she'd look wonderful in a cheongsam.'

We stood and watched the preliminaries of the courtship dance.

'I suppose he's married?' Bowen asked sadly. 'I've seen it so often. Happily married young men thrown into a student milieu again and they want to repeat the amorous adventures they had first time round. Except they forget the wife and the fact her full-time job pays the mortgage – and indeed his fees.'

This was a new side to Tom. 'I suppose the young women in similar circumstances want their bit of the action too?'

'You tell me!' He laughed.

I shook my head. 'My relationship's still so shiny and new I don't want anyone else.'

'Not even poor Jago? He's a handsome enough man, though, isn't he?'

'I suppose so. It's just that I prefer a bit of loyalty from my aspiring suitors. Or a bit of discretion.'

We could hear the two voices raised in laughter.

'Why,' I added, 'it seems only yesterday he was after me.'

'Oh, I know, I know. He was telling me how attractive he found you. And I, of course, was applauding his taste. If you'll forgive an old man for saying so.'

'Tom, if you were an old man, I would.'

Simultaneously we looked at our watches and discovered a pressing need to be elsewhere. A gentle flirtation we might have had – and I'd certainly discovered a Tom Bowen that I hadn't met before – but I still suspected that he really liked me no more than I liked him.

Shrugging mentally, I headed off to the library. He was renewing – with increased vigour – his argument with Carla, whom he'd overtaken as she emerged from the loo, almost dragging her into his room.

Chapter Eleven

The post-graduate students' work-room was deserted that afternoon, and it made eminent good sense to stay and drive on with the assignment. I didn't have to rush – Friday was the due date – but every day spent on it was a day away from the all-important dissertation. So I promised myself that if I finished it today I'd treat myself to something expensive and luxurious.

It was coming together so well that I decided to grab a snack from the refectory and work on into the evening. It was quiet but not creepy: most of the courses run in this building were for part-time students, many of whom found it more convenient to come to evening classes like the one I had to go to on Thursdays. And I found the peace helpful: by nine I knew I'd done as well as I could. Knew? Still anxious – after all, writing assignments is a far cry from setting and marking them for other people – I homed in on the print icon.

And when it ticked busily from the ink-jet printer, blow me if it didn't look just as good on paper as on screen. But I'd always been a woman for second thoughts. What if . . . No, I resolutely gathered it up and slipped it into the plastic folder I'd bought. Not the cheap three-sided ones my students favour – they're difficult to remove the paper from and impossible to get the paper back into after marking. My colleagues and I refer to them without affection as literary condoms. No, mine was a pukka affair, folded A3 with a removable plastic spine for easy reading. The equivalent of an apple for teacher. There. It looked really good now.

I'd deliver it straight away – push it under Carla's door.

I squatted, supporting myself with a hand against the door. In mid-crouch, the door flew open. Just like that. On my hands and knees, scrabbling for a remnant of dignity, I saw only darkness. Carla had got as far as switching off the lights, but hadn't locked the door. Not even shut it properly. Even at William Murdock we were more security-conscious than that. Here, however, as if on cue, came security in the form of a solidly built guard. He regarded me, as well he might, with suspicion, an emotion that looked as if it had permanently shaped his middle-aged features.

Still on my knees, I explained. He raised an overgrown eyebrow, but switched on the light. 'You can put it on her desk,' he said. It was quite clear he would stand and watch.

My name caught my eye as I put my assignment in Carla's in-tray. In her out-tray was what I presumed was the test results print-out, with 'SOPHY RIVERS' scrawled on the top.

'This is for me,' I said, reaching for it. One day I'd gently remind her about the spelling. 'She promised she'd leave it in my pigeonhole.'

'But it isn't in your pigeonhole, is it?'

That was unanswerable.

'You can see it's meant for me.' I dug for my ID card. 'Here. And here's my name on this essay.' Except it wasn't. All that work and I'd forgotten my name!

He acknowledged the ID with a curt nod, but didn't rise to a smile when I explained about the essay.

'OK,' I said, 'I'll have to take this away and re-do the front page. But this time I'll try not to fall flat on my face when I deliver it.'

'I'm locking up now,' he said. 'So it looks as if you'll have to wait till tomorrow.'

I was torn: to do the job properly or simply scribble my name? I scribbled.

He locked up behind me, ostentatiously bored, heaving weary, indeed exasperated sighs. I tried the Hallowe'en lantern smile, but it singularly failed to lighten his darkness.

Back home, I treated myself to something extravagant. Two things, actually. A fresh bottle of wine and a phone call to Mike. We talked several expensive and satisfying minutes, during which the tactics of the England captain and the successes and failures of the rest of the England team did not feature prominently. He was quite happy to toddle off to the university and promised the reference list and anything else he could photocopy. But it might not be for a couple of days.

'We're got these morale-building sessions, you see.'

I could quite understand why the rest of the team should need them, but Mike was after all scoring consistently and, moreover, holding his catches. Still, it would no doubt reduce team morale to the pits if he declined to join in – and Mike wasn't that sort of man, anyway.

'What you must do is to tell everyone the secret of your success,' I suggested. Suggestively.

He laughed, the warm, lazy laugh that we shared in bed. 'What? And have the entire squad trying to score with you?' We'd joked about knights and battles and their ladies' favours. But I wasn't quite prepared to believe it was simply our relationship that drove him to such heights. Maybe there was a lot of hard work and an enormous amount of skill involved too.

The conversation degenerated into tender bawdy, to which Ivo listened with embarrassing attention. And, although they can presumably close them against sand when they're burrowing, gerbils have remarkably alert-looking ears for their size.

I awoke – late – to the sound of driving rain, and in no haste to go into UWM, all things considered. Not after my exertions of the evening before, my call to Mike, and the night spent tossing and turning over whether I'd done the right thing to hand my assignment in without a beautifully printed name on the front cover. Clearly I'd have to print another front cover, complete with name, and ask Carla to substitute it for the first. And clearly I was going off my head, if I really thought such things mattered. All those years of marking the scruffy offerings of others – I'd be lucky to get an essay at all from most students – and now I lost sleep over a mere title page.

I'd stay at home long enough to pick up my post. And that would mean the rush-hour jams had dissolved. Parking might be a pig, however. Hmm. In the end I settled for an early lunch at home before setting out.

I was not the only late arrival. Tom Bowen was locking his car and flapped a hand – his arms were occupied by sheaves of paper. It looked horribly like marking to me. I caught up with him.

'Tom, I wonder if I could have five more minutes in your kitchen before I make the final arrangements next week.'

He looked surprised but said nothing.

'The cooker,' I said. 'I need to know how it works. There was one dreadful occasion, you see, when I was using the host's oven, only to find that it had stuck on the timer programme and no one had the least idea how to unstick it.'

'If I know the make and have a manual and guarantee it's not in timer mode, then there's no need for another visit?'

'That's right.'

'Better see what I can find. I'm disappearing under this lot at the moment. Time's at a bit of a premium.'

'Fair enough. Only I'd hate to give you raw pork. I suppose I could always do a mega stir-fry, but that's not quite your traditional French meal.'

'How's your assignment going?'

'Gone. Wrapped it up last night.'

His eyebrows shot up. 'But it's *de rigueur* for mature students to demand extensions for everything – even though they rarely get them.'

'And younger students, believe me. It's just that with Mike in Australia, I have fewer diversions than usual.'

'Mike? Ah, your partner? Will he be away long?'

Awarding him another brownie point for the right terminology – I might well have to deduce that he was much nicer than I'd first thought – I smiled. I didn't want to go into all the ins and outs of his possible selection for the One Day series, so I just said, 'It's not definite yet.'

'So you're all on your ownio!'

The unpleasant experiences of the last few years must have left their mark. 'Not quite,' I said. 'I've got a friend staying with me.' I didn't even cross my fingers behind my back. Ivo and I were – surely – friends? We whiffled noses at each other whenever we chanced to meet. 'Ivo,' I added.

'Good. It always worries me, in these violent days, to hear of a woman living on her own, unprotected. And you've got a burglar alarm and use it?'

Considering his cavalier attitude with his own! I grinned. 'Of course.' A state-of-the-art system, in fact. 'But it shouldn't be "do as I say", Tom. You locked your house beautifully the other day but didn't set the alarm.'

'Didn't you hear the noises off? I've got this hyperactive cat, and haven't quite learnt how to set the alarm's protection zones. I've got a manual thicker than the one for the cooker, but if you're over twelve you can't understand it. Makes your average video pensioner's play.'

I cackled: so did he. No, he wasn't was bad as I'd thought. But we didn't dawdle any longer. The rain was heavier now, and by the look of the sky it was setting in for the duration.

When I went to drop by the new title page for my assignment Carla's door was still locked, so I slid the work under her door.

This time I stood up to find Lola's shadow over me. 'Tutorial room?' she said.

I nodded, following.

'It is not as we hoped,' she said, as soon as I'd shut the door. 'The food our colleague eats is not past its sell-by date.'

Lola was not the sort of woman to make mistakes about things like that. I flung my hands in the air. 'But what can we do? Other than trail her to M&S and grab her ourselves before the store detective does?'

'You could talk to her.'

'Me? I'm only a student, like the rest of you. I'm not really on the staff here—'

'You are a visiting teacher and this woman's tutor.'

'I'm not convinced that with adult students the pastoral function extends to accusing them of shoplifting.'

'It must surely extend to preventing them committing a crime which could result in their losing their visa.' Head teacher to raw recruit, that was her manner.

I bristled. 'And how do you suggest I go about this? Given that the English of most of my group isn't up to asking more than the time of day, let alone responding to such sensitive questions. If she can even understand the questions.'

Lola reached for the door handle. 'I expected more kindness from you, Sophie.'

'You can have all the kindness you want. It's the practicalities I can't manage. Like who I'm supposed to be talking to. And how I'm to communicate with her. And what I'm to say – let's not forget that.' What had happened to turn Sophie, the people's friend, into this defensive, uncooperative woman? It wasn't as if what Lola wanted me to do involved any risks. Just a certain amount of trouble. 'Do you know anyone who could translate?' I asked at last.

It occurred to me later, however, that there was more than one way of skinning a cat. Why not change the order of English lessons set out in the syllabus and get my group to talk about shopping and food when we met the next day? Then I could talk obliquely about the perils of shoplifting, the need to buy cheap and nutritious food and the hazards of overloading credit cards. Lola thought the idea good, but perhaps oversubtle, as we discussed it in the women's loo.

'I like subtlety,' I said. 'And I always encourage students with problems to stay back afterwards. So perhaps that will elicit a response from her. Better than going at the whole thing bull-headed, anyway.'

'Bull-headed?'

Lola did not look as if she liked the implicit criticism. She was about to press me when Kathryn came in, pointing, as soon as she saw me, an accusing finger.

'Those absence reporting forms I gave you,' she said.

Lola raised her eyes heavenwards. 'In the schools in which I've taught we do not have to report absences,' she said grandly.

'Oh, do you have those clever computer terminals all connected to a main office system?' Kathryn asked.

'We don't have absences.' Lola left the small space with a big flourish.

'What would you expect from the daughter of a cabinet minister?' Kathryn asked.

I blinked.

'I'm getting everyone's details up-dated on the computer,' she said blithely. 'Which is why, Sophie, I need your returns. Yesterday.'

'Might as well be back at William Murdock,' I grumbled.

'Always assuming there's a William Murdock to go back to,' she said, heading for a cubicle.

Dredging my memory for a quotation from a Latin A level set book about many-headed rumour – it was certainly active at the moment – I trailed sadly back to the work-room. The room was abuzz with chatter this afternoon, and I was hard put to stop myself remarking out loud that it would make more sense to apply one's efforts to the assignment than to sit there belly-aching about doing it.

The last thing I wanted to do was show any lack of comradely angst, however. I couldn't imagine that the news that I'd finished and delivered mine would be greeted with universal congratulations. So I gathered up my registers and Kathryn's vivid forms and headed for the quiet of a tutorial room. Just for the record, I decided to do something about correlating the entrance grades of my students with their current achievement: Kathryn would soon be asking for those statistics, too, no doubt. I was right. This time my pigeonhole contained not just a large sheaf of forms but also a computer print-out of all international students' entrance test results. I took my own advice and got stuck in. At least I had Schubert and Brahms to look forward to.

Chapter Twelve

Chris was already at the Barber Institute when I arrived, a circumstance to which he drew my attention by an ostentatious flick of his wristwatch.

'I thought you might have been upstairs in the galleries looking at the pictures,' he said, 'but clearly . . .' He looked me up and down.

'I meant to. But I got held up at UWM and you know how rain nourishes rush-hour traffic—'

'Not that it's rush-hour now.' He looked at his watch again. So the first glance was to establish that I was late, the second actually to see the time.

'—and I had to drive way over to the car park by the Muirhead Tower,' I concluded.

'I left my coat on a couple of seats,' he said. 'Maybe you'd better hang that one up. You're very wet.'

'Didn't you notice the rain?'

We were in the foyer of an art gallery attached to the University of Birmingham, endowed so generously by one Lady Barber that it houses a small but wide-ranging collection of world-class paintings and sculptures. We were heading for the integral concert hall, the ideal size for a chamber concert such as tonight's.

When I got back from the loo, he was buying programmes from a young oriental woman, just the sort of student whose death his colleagues were even now investigating. She was fluttering otherwise demure eyelids at him, and he was beaming down at her. Yes, age was suiting him. The baldness that had struck him prematurely sat well with the authority now written strongly on his forty-year-old face. He was responding to her delicate flirtation with a boyish, even impish smile, his eyes twinkling amid his crow's-feet. Soon it would be time to bring him down to earth with a face the mirror had confirmed as very gloomy indeed.

I managed a smile as he turned to me, but it was perfunctory, as he was quick to spot.

'I thought you'd left all your problems behind at William Murdock,' he said, ushering me into the auditorium. 'Not that it hasn't enough problems of its own, according to Fraud. You're sure you want to go back there?'

'Always assuming it's there for me to go back to,' I said, echoing Kathryn. Whom I would have to see first thing the following morning. About the print-out she'd left me.

'I suppose you could always move in with Mike and start a family.' He started to sidle along a row towards his coat, right in the middle. Trust Chris to pick the best two places in the house.

'You been talking to Shahida?' I asked dourly, inching in his wake. Other than that I would not bite. I wouldn't point out that the vast majority of women worked, partners, children or not, and that I would be one of them. Wouldn't I?

We settled down. He handed me a programme, fishing out his reading glasses and flicking open the second. Just as I thought he was absorbed in its contents, he turned: 'So what's the problem? You look as if you've lost a bob and found a rusty button.'

I hid a grin: whether he liked it or not, Smethwick was educating him.

'I've found—'

But my neighbour shushed me. The musicians were coming on to the stage.

*　　*　　*

However much anyone else might have been diverted by free wine and loud, middleclass discussion of the first part of the programme – Schubert's Quintet, the one including two cellos, which was one of my favourites – I knew Chris would return sooner or later to whatever might be worrying me.

'It's the register of my English language class at UWM,' I said, with no more preamble than a gesture with my glass of orange juice.

'You usually allow yourself one glass of wine,' he said, staring first at the juice then at me. 'Sophie, you skipped an evening meal, didn't you? Don't you realise how foolish that is, with your stomach? You'll be getting your gastritis back before you know it. And you know it's easier to get it than to get rid of it.'

'I was tied up. With this register.'

He steered us to the edge of the crowd. 'Well?'

I took a deep breath. 'There are several students who don't appear to have been registered at UWM. At least, they haven't according to one print-out, supplied to me by Kathryn, our new administrator, which records the results of their initial language tests, but have on another apparently identical print-out supplied by—'

He held up a hand. 'Slow down. How can the two forms be identical?'

'They both purport to be form IS9909. But they don't have quite the same names on them.'

'Computer hitch? No: you think it's more serious than that, don't you?'

'They come from different sources. The one without the names in my group, from Kathryn—'

'Kathryn – don't I know . . . ?'

He probably did. She'd been in post when he was working on a case there. 'Ex-William Murdock.'

'Ah! Very bright, very efficient. Nice-looking, too. And

she's abandoned ship, has she?' He shook his head, but not in doubt. 'Well, it'll be easy enough to check with her, won't it, that you've got the latest edition? Come on, you're always moaning about students who don't get it together sufficiently to start a course on time: perhaps no one's got round to inputting these latecomers on the computer.'

The Barber doesn't have anything as vulgar as a bell. Some sort of osmosis takes place between the concert organisers and the audience, who herd themselves back in as neatly as if propelled by a sheepdog or two. We were self-herding now.

'OK,' he said. 'I can tell there's something else on your mind. But just try and forget it during the Brahms. I don't think you heard a note of the Schubert.'

The second of the Brahms Sextets is the music I would choose to die to – if one has a choice in these matters. And it received a good performance. So I battened down my anxiety, telling it not to think about starting up again till after the music. Maybe I could talk it through with Chris over a light meal. Mistake! At the thought of food my stomach embarked on a symphonic rumbling.

Any hopes I might have had about its inaudibility to all but me were promptly dashed.

'Where shall we eat?' Chris demanded, still clapping enthusiastically. 'And why doesn't someone do something about that crazy door?'

The musicians, none less than five foot ten, and two of them sporting cellos, of course, all had to duck through a door in the wings that would have even me stooping, each time they came on to the stage and off it again.

'Don't know. It's always been like that, hasn't it?'

'All the more time, then, for someone to take a saw to it. How about a takeaway from that excellent place on the High Street? Tell me what you want and I'll meet you at your place.'

Gentleman Chris indubitably was, but he wasn't going to

volunteer to escort me through the still torrential rain when my car was four hundred yards away. Not when his was only thirty from the Institute.

I shoved the central heating on high for a while, hung my coat and brolly to dry, and opened a bottle of wine I happened to have in the fridge. Not, to be honest, that I ever didn't have one in the fridge. No, I didn't think I was going down Carla's road; I often went several days without even noticing I hadn't had a drink. It was just that when I did want a drink I wanted it to be at the right temperature.

'Long queue,' he said briefly, dispensing foil boxes from a carrier. We'd eat at the kitchen table.

As usual, we kept the talk to gossip while we ate. He'd seen me when my tum had been at its worst – and, of course, I'd *been* me when my tum was at its worst. So between us we tried not to irritate it. We'd helped ourselves to fruit from the glass bowl between us before either of us mentioned work. No, there was no news of the sex attacker: no more incidents, in fact. Then he broached the topic of UWM.

Full of food and wine, I was able to shrug. 'Probably you were right earlier – that Kathryn has supplied me with an old print-out whereas the one Tom Bowen's given me – he's my tutor—'

'Since that woman went on maternity leave, right?'

'Right. And Tom asked me to do some teaching: English for overseas students who are on my course and on the PGCE.'

'Unusual? And it must put you in an awkward situation.'

'Sometimes it does,' I said, thinking of conversations about shoplifting I would have to have tomorrow. 'But it's not all that rare, especially as the work I did when I was on secondment to William Muntz College is relevant.'

'Anyway, this tutor fixed up for you to teach a group and gave you a list of names?'

'The register, yes.'

'And another list of names with all overseas students' results on them? Which doesn't tally with the one that Kathryn gave you.'

'The results do. But there are some students on Bowen's list that don't appear on Kathryn's.' No, I wasn't getting less anxious at hearing Chris spell it out. I was getting more anxious.

He narrowed his eyes. 'And you're sure this teaching is kosher?'

'Why shouldn't it be? Anyway, I had an official contract, duly signed by the powers that be. It's upstairs in my office,' I added, not quite irrelevantly.

He nodded. 'Go on.'

When Chris used that tone, when his face shifted into those planes, it was hard to resist his compelling mix of kindness and authority.

I drained my coffee and put down the empty cup. 'For a couple of weeks now I've had the strangest suspicion that some of the students in the group aren't the ones I started out with. But they still answer to the same names. Eventually.'

'It takes time to sink in that they're supposed to be using that name?'

'Put like that it sounds pretty damning, doesn't it?' My smile was apologetic. 'I hope I'm not about to open another can of worms, Chris.'

'Let's just look at that contract of yours,' he said.

It didn't take me long to lay my hands on what the office always referred to as self-carbonated sheets. My little acquaintance with carbonated things makes me expect them to fizz – but then, my experience is very limited.

'Well, your filing must have improved,' Chris said, setting down the glass of whisky he'd poured himself. 'I expected it to take you at least ten minutes to find it.'

Whisky! On top of all that wine? That meant Aggie would be finding his car outside again tomorrow!

'Where money's concerned my filing's spot on,' I said. 'Look, this is my part of the contract. I handed the other one back, signed. And this is what I have to give in when I've finished the term's classes.'

'Hmm. Both standard printed forms. Both with the classes you're teaching filled in by hand. Not computer-printed?'

'I presume that's standard practice.'

'I presume you'll be asking the fair Kathryn tomorrow.'

'You presume right. And you can also presume that I shall be asking her for the latest print-out.'

'What's the betting all three are different? And what about getting an ID on all your students.'

'I've already photocopied the register so I can ask them to sign beside their name. That way I can compare the signatures with those on their application forms.'

'Assuming you can find the application forms. I take it Kathryn is a new addition to the staff?'

I nodded.

'So it won't be a matter of great surprise if you find in the UWM office the sort of chaos that reigned until Kathryn's arrival at William Murdock?' He groaned, presumably at the memory of trying some years ago to verify student details.

I shook my head.

'Oh, Sophie,' he said, shaking his head sadly, 'I suspect you're going to start shoving your nose into things again, aren't you?'

I nodded.

'But you will be careful, won't you?'

This time I broke the pattern by nodding again.

Chapter Thirteen

Thursday dawned – if you can call seven thirty in early December dawn – grey and bleak. I scraped myself out of bed and over to the window. By the look of the carrier bags flapping in the trees like pale vultures, there was a lazy wind – one that would slice through you rather than bother to go round. It was a day for cowering inside, with a good book and central heating. If you had to go out, then an early return, cheered by hot soup, was the order of the day. Except this was my evening class night, three hours of the theory of Managing the Curriculum. All those worries about doing it in practice were still unresolved. After his flash of light, Saul of Tarsus hadn't hung around like I was doing. But then, he hadn't had his vision in a car park, and I hadn't been struck blind. I suppose my record on persecuting other people was better than his, too. The evidence was, in the past at least, that *they* had been after *me*.

At least very few of them would be after me while Chris's car was parked immaculately outside my house. This year's model, it made assertions about power without anyone needing to look up the price. Not that it would be there long, parked under its guardian streetlight: Chris was already in the bathroom – he was rather late this morning, come to think of it – and would set off immediately to have his breakfast in the police station canteen. Good for Piddock Road morale, I suppose. And much better for my reputation, the fewer people who saw he'd spent the night here. Aggie had always regarded him as a sort of favourite grandson, and however much she let Mike charm her, she made it quite clear to me whenever I saw her that I'd made a terrible mistake not marrying Chris. Not, of course, that he'd ever asked me. And not, of course, that I would have done if he had, even before Mike burst on to the scene.

It occurred to me, as I retreated back to bed and the duvet, that Mike hadn't come back to me about Carla's thesis. Or anything else. The tour team morale-building must be taking a lot of time. Well, with the team's results so far, that wasn't surprising. All the same, I felt like a child learning Christmas had been postponed, I wanted so much to hear his voice. Or even see what he'd put on fax. Or whatever.

Ah, there was Chris going downstairs now. He'd relock the Chubb and drop the key though the letter box. As if in the half-hour or so he fancied I'd be lingering in bed anyone would come and penetrate the Yale.

In one sense it was nice to have someone looking after me; in another it was quite unnerving.

That was the front door closing. And that the thud of the key. Any moment now the gentle shutting of the car door – slam it? In a residential area! And then the engine would start.

And I would get up.

I lay. And waited.

And heard feet sprinting back up my drive, and the sound of an irate bell.

Grabbing my dressing gown and shoving my feet into my shoes – that doorbell was far too irate to wait for me to look for slippers, except from the sound of it the batteries were expiring fast – I hurtled down the stairs.

'Did you hear anything last night?' He stepped inside and reached for my phone. Always anxious about frying his brain on his mobile, Chris. 'Vandalism,' he threw over his shoulder. He punched the numbers with the air of one shoving a finger into offending eyes. Looking back at me he took in my outfit. 'Have a look.'

Despite Mike's eruption into my life, my dressing gown was a neck-to-ankle affair, tightly belted and so modest not even Ian Dale turned a hair. Decent it might be, but Puffa-jacket it wasn't. So I only looked at the two nearest cars – his and mine. Someone had thrown paint stripper over both bonnets. Huddling back into the house, I collided with him coming out.

'Ours and at least three others,' he snapped. 'You'd better get dressed. Someone's on his way from Rose Road.'

I needed a shower hot enough to thaw the worst of the frostbite. And would take one. Surely the police didn't bother with that sort of petty damage these days. And certainly not with any urgency.

In fact I'd hardly got dressed when a pair of uniformed kids presented themselves at the front door. Presumably Chris still carried enough clout at his old nick to make things happen briskly. The elder lad, who looked about fifteen, introduced himself as Constable Aherne, and asked me to report the criminal damage to my vehicle. As soon as I'd done so, they'd go and break the good news to my neighbours.

I suppose there was always the consolation that though They were definitely persecuting me, They were also having a go at a few others.

The garage I always favoured was a side street but eminently respectable one in Selly Oak, not so far, as it happened, from Mike's place. I stopped off for an estimate and some sympathetic tooth-sucking. I'd have to go round scar-faced for a couple of days, Martin said. And hadn't I better get an insurance estimate from somewhere else? But if they got the job, they'd make sure it was serviced and got through its MOT while it was in their care. Meanwhile, yes, it was drivable, if not pretty.

'Let's just make sure, shall we?' Paul said, sauntering up. 'There's nothing on the ramps at the moment. Never hurts to have a quick look, does it?' Wiping his hands on his overalls, he slid a polythene cover over the driving seat and had it into the service bay before you could say car-ringing.

The expression on his face as he peered up at those parts of a car best not seen told me the news would be expensive.

Martin and I joined him.

'Lot of wear on those brake hoses, wouldn't you say?' Paul pointed.

'A suspicious amount. In fact, I'd call it damage, not wear,' Martin said. 'I'm not touting for business, Sophie – in fact, we couldn't start on it till next week – but I'd say it would be better not to drive it too far.'

'I'll get the insurance assessor to call here,' I said crisply. 'But he may not be the only one to call. I've got a policeman friend who might want to have a look, seeing that his car had similar treatment this morning. And several neighbours, come to think of it. Jesus, what a night's work!'

'It wasn't just you, then?' Martin asked.

I shook my head.

He patted the rear wing as the car descended. 'Good. Only I was thinking – it's had quite a tough life, this little thing, hasn't it?'

I'd had to take a taxi from Selly Oak to West Bromwich, and just made my class on time, having dropped my coat and gathered up the register folder in one hasty movement. And then a scrabble for the folder of work I'd prepared. And another scrabble for the homework folder. Thank goodness for the single drawer which forced me to be systematic.

This time calling the register wouldn't be the usual per-functory technicality. I wanted finally to assure myself that the person responding and the name I called were one and the same. I also got them to sign a sheet this morning, with

110

their name in blocks alongside. Some of them looked at me strangely, as well they might. And at the end of the class I'd go and check with signatures and the photos on the application forms somewhere in Kathryn's files.

Meanwhile, we had to practise the vocabulary of food and of shopping. And I had to hammer home the message that cheap could be just as nutritious as expensive, and that everything had to be paid for. Had I had a fistful of shares in Marks and Sparks at risk from light-fingered activities, I could not have been more persuasive. Nor more emphatic.

But my fine words caused no flushes of embarrassment, and any fidgets were probably irritation that I was hammering on at such length.

I'd have to wait till the following day to see if anyone might have heeded what I was saying, of course. Today's lunch break might at least give me the opportunity to see who exactly it was who was indulging in expensive sandwiches.

Meanwhile I headed off to Kathryn's empire to look at mug shots. And found her door locked. This was a training day, a glum secretary told me. Everyone except her was off having an away-day with nice lunch.

Perhaps that's what Lola's student was doing: there was no sign of her in the canteen, Lola said.

'You should have grasped the nettle at the time, Sophie, and not pussyfooted around.' She paused, presumably for me to applaud her idioms.

'Perhaps you should have trusted me with her identity,' I said ungenerously. 'Anyway, there was a full house in the English class this morning. Everyone should now be able to go shopping and pay and not run up big bills on their plastic. And no doubt the proof of the pudding will be in the eating. We'll check it out tomorrow – yes? – and if she's still eating top-of-the-range sandwiches—'

'You can tackle her. I'm going up to town tomorrow.' Something in her intonation suggested she wasn't going to

111

paint Birmingham red. 'My father's coming over to meet your Foreign Secretary, and I shall be hosting a reception for him on Saturday.'

'So there it is,' Chris said, swallowing a yawn and sliding our halves of mild on to beer mats. We'd chosen a pub that was quiet enough now, though trendy kids would no doubt be taking it over later. 'A whole street full of vandalised cars, but yours is – as far as they can see – the only one with more than superficial damage. Funny thing, that. Who've you annoyed this time, Sophie?'

I gestured my thanks with the glass and took a mouthful before I answered. 'As far as I know I'm everyone's best friend. Maybe whoever got busy with the paint stripper got interrupted before he could attack all the other brakes, too.'

'Maybe.' Chris did not sound convinced. 'I suppose yours was one end of the line. Good job Paul was so conscientious.'

I nodded. 'He did say it would have been a slow leak, one I'd probably have noticed, not one that would have put me at immediate risk.'

'Enough risk for him to get you off the road. OK, they'll be pursuing all lines of inquiry, of course, I should imagine.'

'It's at times like this you'd like to leap from behind your desk and start solving crime, isn't it? You've got that wistful expression,' I explained.

'The consolation is that the better I do my job, the better others can do theirs. And as DCI I'd never have been involved in simple criminal damage – not unless it proved to be something more serious,' he added meaningfully. He yawned again.

But he wasn't going to get another invitation to stay at my place. It was not to become a habit.

I was tired too. And miserable. Still no news from Mike. Tonight I'd phone him to see what was going on, even if it did look like checking up. After all, I needed to sound him out about using his sponsored team car while mine was off the road. I knew what he'd say, of course, that there was no point in my hiring a car when there was a perfectly good one sitting in his garage. I, on the other hand, was not so sure I wanted to make his sponsored car a target for whoever might – or might not – be after me. Perhaps if I made a point of garaging it every night?

'What are you going to do about transport?' Chris asked.

I blinked. I did wish our minds wouldn't do that. 'Borrow Mike's car?'

'With all those logos all over it? You must be off your head. And no talk about cycling, either.'

'Buses take all day,' I grumbled. 'And though it was very kind of you to pick me up tonight, Chris, we've both got too many commitments for me to rely on that.'

'Does your insurance policy allow you to hire a car?'

I shook my head. 'When I was at William Murdock I could always cycle or use buses: there was no need to rely on four wheels.'

'Can you afford to hire one?' His tone was remarkably delicate.

'I can't afford not to,' I said, dodging the issue.

'Get something small and unremarkable.' He looked at his watch.

I drained my glass. 'Could you drop me off on your way home?' I asked.

If he'd hoped to use my spare bed, he didn't show any disappointment. In any case, perhaps he didn't wish to test my theory about the brake hoses by leaving his car anywhere near my house.

So now I could relish my conversation with Mike in private. He'd left a message on my machine, asking me to call him back.

To hell with the expense: I wanted a natter. I poured out my troubles one by one, aware even as I did so that they were nothing compared with the ill-fortune of Mike's team. From his sympathy you'd never have guessed it, however.

'What I can't understand,' he said at last, 'is this business of Malaysian students not having much English. When I've stopped over there, I've always found their ability to communicate embarrassingly good. The same with Singaporeans. And, believe me, Singaporeans don't go in for petty theft unless they're absolutely desperate; not with their legal system.'

So what was going on? Was Lola imagining things, after all? But it was too expensive to speculate, so I asked what he'd been up to. Apart, I hoped, from missing me.

'I've checked all three universities in Melbourne,' he announced, 'and can't find any record of a thesis by Carla Pentowski. More to the point, when I asked at the registries, they had no record of any Carla Pentowski ever having attended.'

'But—'

'I even got them,' he continued, anticipating my question, 'to search their computer records simply for Carlas, just in case she's simply changed her surname, and, guess what? There are no Carlas who could possibly have a background appropriate to the thesis she's supposed to have written.'

'Not at any of them?'

'I checked them all. There's no thesis of that title at any of them, either. What do you suppose that means, Sophie?'

Chapter Fourteen

Friday morning saw me peering out at the world with an inexplicable apprehension. And yet, come to think of it, it was quite explicable. OK, I didn't have a vulnerable car sitting waiting to be vandalised, not this morning. But the very fact that it was confined to a garage with that sort of damage made me shiver. I thought when I parted company with William Murdock I would have a year free not just from student and management hassle, but from all the other irritations that had come my way in recent years. Now UWM seemed to be bringing other problems. And someone had attacked my car. One of a row it might have been, but that didn't stop me feeling paranoid.

This was the evening I was due to have supper with Carla, and her thesis, or rather, the lack of her thesis, hardly seemed the sort of topic to introduce over the coffee.

I told myself, as I picked up a dark blue Fiesta from the nearest hire centre, that Carla's thesis was none of my business anyway. None. I'd do far better to worry about adjusting seats and sorting out gear positions than to worry about how and when I should tackle her.

And I couldn't possibly tackle her anyway, not until I'd seen with my own eyes her claim that she'd been at university in Melbourne. After all, any one of us could have misremembered, or there could have been a slip-up when the course booklet was put together. And perhaps Mike hadn't located them all: they'd probably proliferated like UK ones.

Kathryn: she was the *open sesame* to everything. The students' files with their photos, definitely, and the staff files, with their CVs, possibly. Or should I talk to Carla first?

Round and round it went.

Halfway down Bearwood Road, I had a quick rush of common sense to the brain. Mike and I were the only people who knew. And maybe there was just an outside chance that I might be on safer ground if someone else knew: yes, the seven o'clock paranoia was back. What if there were something fishy? The obvious person to share my fears with was, of course, Chris. And there was no reason why I shouldn't briefly divert down to Piddock Road nick to leave him a message. I didn't even need to name any names. Did I? Grim experience had taught me in the past that if people had something hidden, they sometimes went to unreasonable lengths to keep it that way.

The young woman on the reception desk might have raised overplucked eyebrows when I trundled in and asked for writing paper and an envelope, but she found both quite quickly when DS Harvinder Mann came in.

'What's up with you, Sophie?' he began.

'Been sticking her nose into something,' came Peter Kirby's voice, over Harvinder's shoulder.

Though it was clear they'd been about to leave the building, they turned round with me and I found myself sitting in Kirby's room. I scribbled the note to Chris in the time it took Harvinder to brew herbal tea all round.

'Any progress on your Pacific Rim deaths?' I asked, since presumably that was what they wanted to discuss.

Peter shook his head. 'It's just that I never like coincidences,' he said.

'Particularly unidentified coincidences,' Harvinder agreed.

I had to admit that I didn't either. Then I took a deep breath. 'I've got another coincidence here. Nothing to do with the Pacific Rim, but a strange coincidence. That's what this note

116

to Chris is about.' Pulling it from the envelope I shoved it at Peter. He came as near to blushing as I'd ever seen.

'But I mean – isn't it – private?'

'See for yourself.' Hell. Yet another person putting Chris and me together and making a relationship. 'Strictly business. It's just I'm supposed to be going to supper with this woman tonight and I'd rather – if I happened to end up trapped by my wrists in the cut – that someone knew why.' Now it came out in words, it sounded so bloody melodramatic!

The men stood side by side to read the note. 'Looks like a specialist fraud job,' Harvinder said, tapping it.

'You leave Fraud out of this,' Peter said. 'Or we'll all disappear forever in their bloody paperwork.'

'Of course,' I said, back-tracking, 'it may be a simple case of changed names or a misprint at work. Let's leave it at that till I've checked the records. We don't really want Fraud diving in, do we?'

Kathryn greeted my arrival in her office without apparent enthusiasm. When I told her I wanted to see the students' files, she flung her hands in horror.

'They're in this locked store,' she said. 'And while you're quite entitled to see them, I have to remain with you for security. And don't play the innocent with me, Sophie: I've heard it all before. "I just want to check on X. Y's gone missing and I want to tell his parents. And it's not worth your while staying here, Kathryn. I'll lock up carefully and give you the key!" Oh, yes. Really locked up they'd be, then.' Her voice dripped disbelief. 'And not even for you am I going to break the rules.'

'It sounds as if you're already broken them for someone else and regretted it.'

She looked at me but said nothing. At last she said, 'The earliest I can help you is Monday afternoon. A great pile of stuff came in yesterday while I was on that training course—'

'Was the lunch any good?'

'Even worse than the course.' She sat down and picked up a pile of forms.

I didn't take the hint. 'What if I wanted to look at my own file – check out the form I filled in when they asked me to take that language class? Not my application form to join the course.'

'Oh yes, you're entitled to see that. No problems. Except staff records are kept in the main building. Oldbury Campus.' Her smiled failed to convey sympathy. 'And,' she added, 'I think you'll find they're catching up with yesterday's work, too. What they might do is fax you a copy through to here.'

That didn't suit me at all. After all, it wasn't a record beginning with R I wanted to check but one beginning with P. I just wanted to let my fingers stray a little and fish out Pentowski's file entirely by mistake.

'The problem is, Kathryn,' I said, sighing heavily, 'that – oh dear, this makes me sound really racist, and perhaps I am . . . You see, I can't tell my students apart. They all look alike! No, of course they don't, but—'

'You never had a problem with students back at William Murdock.'

'Easy there. You got to know the troublemakers' and the good students' names straight away and filled in the rest as you went along. But there aren't any handles like that here. They're uniformly polite and hard-working and—'

'Wearing those Muslim headscarf things,' she supplied.

'No! No, they're not! But they've all got Muslim names!'

'Well, they would, if they're Malays. OK,' she flicked up her hands in a gesture I hoped was surrender, 'how about three this afternoon?'

'Two?'

'Two thirty's the earliest I can manage. You can photocopy the front pages and scarper.' She bent to her paperwork. She looked up again. 'Oh, Sophie, now what is it?'

I also wanted another copy of her list of test results, didn't I? But now was clearly not the time to ask. 'I'll talk to Carla about it,' I said. 'See you at two thirty.'

Carla's door was locked. There was nothing pinned to her door to indicate where she might be, as there was on Tom Bowen's. He informed the world that he had disappeared under a pile of marking but could be contacted by e-mail if the emergency were truly dire. So what was I to do about supper tonight? Simply turn up? And how did one gain admittance to a boat? Knock? Or stand on the towpath and holler, hoping that she'd pop up out of her boat – after all, I didn't know which one it was! – and holler back.

Given the pressure I'd already put on Kathryn, I was reluctant to pester her for further help. I'd try the front-desk receptionist, who'd always struck me as suitably approachable, even if I'd never had to approach her before.

I knew from both her name tag and the name block that sat on her desk that she was called Kulvinder. I'd also heard her talking to other people, with, to everyone's obvious surprise, a thick Devon burr. At the moment she was talking at the phone, but she smiled as I hove into view, pointing apologetically at the handset and then at her watch.

I listened while she extricated herself from a long-winded caller. Her calendar was up-to-date, her filing tray was neat. And she was strikingly attractive by anyone's standards. I wondered how long it would be before someone lured her to more profitable pastures. And then I thought of Chris, and Bridget's retirement . . . No, I must stamp firmly on any such ideas before they became even embryonic.

Putting down the phone, she beamed at me.

I introduced myself and explained I was supposed to be having supper with Carla. 'And I don't know whether the invitation's still open, and if it is, exactly where she lives,' I concluded. 'What I was wondering was if you'd be kind

enough to call her and pass back any message. Or ask her to
phone me. Whatever.'

The expression on her face had passed through concerned
to firm to amused.

'I thought you were going to ask me for her number,'
she said.

'Against all the rules I've ever worked under.'

'That doesn't stop people.' She brought a list of names
forward on her computer. Had she not run her finger along the
line I'd never have been able to distinguish Carla's number. I
scribbled it on to my palm even as Kulvinder dialled for me.

'Answerphone,' she mouthed.

'Ask her to ring me on my home number – I've got
an answerphone too. Here.' I wrote it down on her message pad. 'And this is my name. Oh, and here's my e-mail
address, too.'

Now for my lunchtime detective work. The more I thought
about it, the more reluctant I was to do it. Why should I,
who tended to keep myself to myself, suddenly bother to
schmooze up to a group of students who only knew me from
the class or tutorial room and start asking one of them about
her eating habits?

Because I wanted to save her from detection and possible
deportation, that's why. Come on, Sophie, where's your milk
of human kindness?

Into the refectory then, and a bright determined smile as I
looked around.

Grabbing a tuna mayo baked potato, I headed for the knot
of Singaporean and Malaysian students gathered in their usual
corner. There were polite if puzzled smiles from most of them,
and they made room for me. Most but not all of my group were
there; all were tucking into warm food like mine. Not an M
and S wrapper in sight. Blast Lola and her sense of honour!
How can you help someone if you don't know whom to help?

If indeed there was anyone in trouble: maybe Lola was making what she might call a mountain out of a molehill.

After a few minutes' conversation – friendly but stilted – I excused myself and headed back to the work-room.

I did some perfunctory reading but couldn't engage myself properly. So I gave up and headed off to Kulvinder again. Perhaps she'd have Lola's phone numbers including the one at the Embassy or High Commission or whatever. This time I was unlucky: she had no access to student phone numbers. She only had the staff ones, she explained, so she could phone through when visitors arrived for them. I'd have to get hold of it from Kathryn, if she were still on speaking terms with me when I'd taken her time. No point in bowling off to Oldbury in the interim. And then it struck me: UWM no doubt had a Website with all the information the heart could desire. And a bit more. My heart leapt. Details of staff and their publications should be on there!

The computers were down this afternoon.

'Sophie? Are you all right?'

Jago!

'Miles away,' I said, stating the obvious. 'Oh, no news yet from Melbourne, I'm afraid.'

'Your bloke too busy pulling Australian Sheilas, no doubt.'

Just the sort of joke I'd find really amusing. I produced a bland smile. And my chest tightened. What a moment to have to huff an asthma spray. I needn't have worried: he didn't seem to connect his words with my deed.

'And bloody Pentowski's taken it into her head to do some research! At this stage! I ask you!'

'Research?'

'According to the note on her door. The academic equivalent of "Gone Fishing", I suppose.'

Note! It hadn't been there half an hour ago. Drat. Carla must have popped in while I was busy pestering Kulvinder to leave an answerphone message.

'Does it say she'll be back in half an hour?' I asked hopefully.

'Just gives her e-mail number – like Bowen's does. Whatever did they do in the old days?'

'Phone? Fax? Carrier pigeon? Or simply assume students were such a low form of life they didn't need to know.' Why had the usually thoughtful Carla left it so late to put the note on her door? It would certainly have been better for us to know right at the start of her absence.

'Hmph.' He started to sit, but thought better of it. 'I've been trying to get hold of the woman since Wednesday. No professionalism. Damn it, they're paid to teach us.'

I trotted out what Seb had said, as if the wisdom were my own. I even dug in my drawer for the photocopied sheet of salary scales he'd sent me and waved it under Jago's nose. 'Whatever they're supposed to do, they aren't paid all that much to do it.'

He took the paper, running a figure down the depressing columns. His eyes widened. 'Well, I had thought of applying for a job somewhere like this – oh, a bit more prestigious, maybe – but not for that sort of money. I'd do better to go back into a school—'

'And battle with OFSTED and National Curriculum?'

'Oh, it's all right for *you*! I suppose when your man gets back you'll be giving up work and settling down to raise a family. Before the biological clock stops. Mind you, I wouldn't blame you.'

'I'm very glad to hear that. Because it would be none of your business what I did!' Better to add more rationally, however: 'For God's sake, Jago, get real! What year are we in? Because attitudes like that went out thirty years ago. At least. I'm in the same employment situation as you.'

'Worse, I suppose,' he agreed, sitting down at last. 'Because the word is that your old place is going bust.'

'What?' I was on my feet. It was one thing to know the

worst in your unspeaking bones, quite another to have the information tossed across like that.

'Just a rumour – it's in the lunchtime edition of the *Evening Mail*. But you must know about it. They're making all the senior staff redundant, it says. I suppose that means you too.'

I reached for the pay phone. Not surprising, perhaps, that all William Murdock's lines were engaged.

Defeated, ready to retreat to the loo so he wouldn't see the tears in my eyes, I remembered I was supposed to be checking student faces against photos. Keep Kathryn waiting? Not on your life! I shot off.

'There is just one more thing, Kathryn,' I said, as I shoved the last of the application forms back into the filing cabinet. I'd photocopied not just the front pages of the forms but the back ones too: I was after those signatures. 'Could I have another print-out of their test results on entry?'

'Don't say you've lost the one I gave you!' She looked at her watch ostentatiously.

'Would I dare? No, it's just that it differs from the one someone else gave me. There are some names that aren't on yours.'

'It was the latest version,' she said.

'I suppose there could be some late enrolments still in an in-tray somewhere?'

'To get their ID, they have to be in computer. To get through the door, they need an ID.'

'So how come Bowen's list is different from yours?'

'Just to shut you up, I'll give you the absolutely latest version. On Monday.'

'Kathryn – just one more thing?'

She turned, arms akimbo. 'No!'

'Tell me, what time does the Oldbury Campus shut down?'

Chapter Fifteen

By the time we'd got from West Bromwich to Oldbury together, dealing with aplomb with the tangle round Savacentre, and once I'd accepted that the pre-set radio was a total and probably enduring mystery, the Fiesta and I were firm friends. I was wondering about developing a relationship with one of its top-of-the-range cousins when I was back at William Murdock. Except—

Putting the rumours firmly to the back of my mind, I concentrated on finding a parking spot. There were very few, despite the fact that, according to Kathryn, the admin. side of the campus closed down at four fifteen. Presumably academic staff and students went on past that. Well, Black Country people had always had a reputation for working hard and for long hours, men and women alike. And while I didn't see myself quite in the light of a latter-day nail-maker, there was no doubt that any trip round the area had my roots twitching.

The buildings on the Oldbury site were no more appealing from the outside than ours, but inside was another matter. Someone with imagination had been at work: whatever limited amount of money they'd had had been well spent. The lighting was good, the plants were well tended, and there was an air of bustle and purpose that wasn't entirely to do with going home on time.

The receptionist who greeted, rather then intercepted me, pointed me in the direction of Personnel, which was, to anyone used to William Murdock's discreet ways, surprisingly well signposted.

Again I came up against a receptionist, but as I started to speak, a door opened.

'Sophie! By all that's wonderful!'

My hand was seized and my arm pumped up and down as if to produce water.

'Luke!' I gasped. This was luck indeed, far too great for me to worry about possible wear and tear to my various joints. 'What are you doing here? I thought you'd moved to Wolverhampton. After that little problem I caused you with that railway trip.' In fact, I knew he had. I'd been at the party to bid him a warm farewell from William Murdock.

'I did.' His smile was forgiving.

My answering smile didn't forgive me. It was my careless talk that had resulted in him being badly beaten by hired thugs who'd got on a train with him.

'Water under the bridge, Sophie. I told you that when I left. And Wolverhampton was a nice little promotion, remember. Teenage daughter! Such expense!' He gave an enormous Jewish shrug, worrying his hands in anxiety. 'If you don't have a child, you don't know what it's like, oy vey!' He dropped the self-parody and looked hard at me. 'Sophie?'

I smiled: I was happy to trust Luke with this. 'But I have. He turned up last summer. Grown up already.'

'Already already!' Then his face became as serious and kind as anyone could wish. 'Is it OK?'

'Not so OK I tell everyone. Not yet. It's his family. He – he doesn't want to upset them. So if I phone him I have to pretend I'm someone from college.'

'He hasn't told them yet?' He put out his arms and hugged me.

'So what are you doing here?' I asked at last.

'Another promotion. And the travelling was too much. And I need to see Mother. I had to let her go into a home, Sophie, and though I can't flatter myself she needs me – even knows me – I need to see her.'

'She's bad?' She was in the early stages of Alzheimer's when I last saw him.

'Mind's—' He made a slicing gesture. 'All those memories . . .'

I touched his arm. If her memory had gone, it took with it not just her life but the life of a whole family. All their relatives had been destroyed in the Holocaust. His mother had survived Auschwitz.

He nodded, although I hadn't spoken. 'What Naomi's losing . . .' He produced a brave smile. 'Now, how can I help you?'

I looked around. 'Somewhere private?'

'Am I going to enjoy this conversation?' he asked, tapping numbers into a security lock and opening a door. He gestured into a carpeted corridor, shutting the door behind us. Then he opened another door, into what appeared to be his office.

'It isn't meant to put you in any danger this time,' I said. 'Not that last time's was meant to.'

'I won't leave any unguarded messages this time with untrustworthy people. Come on, don't look so serious. I got a load of compensation. All the bruises are healed. I don't have any problems travelling by train. I'm not troubled by nightmares. *Always look on the bright side of life!*' he sang.

I looked at him sideways. He hadn't always been so lively.

'Love!' he announced in a dramatic whisper, tiptoeing back – his walk was suddenly Pink Panther's – to check the door. It was firmly closed. 'I've got a lovely new woman in my life. At my age! That's why,' he added in his normal voice, 'I don't want to take any risks, even for you, Sophie.'

And did I want to take any risks, with Mike out there?

'No risks,' I said firmly. 'For either of us. Anything that we find wrong will be dealt with through official channels.'

'And what,' he asked, 'are you expecting to find wrong?'

'Just a detail in someone's CV.'

'A detail? What kind of detail?'

'A detail like their Ph.D.'

'Yes? For God's sake, woman, get on with it!'

Despite myself I looked around. He spread his hands, eyes skyward.

'Someone saying they've got one when they haven't.'

Round-eyed, he gave a low whistle. 'Who'd do a thing like that?'

'Carla Pentowski.'

'But she's a lovely woman. Look at what the students say about her in their reviews.'

'We get to criticise our lecturers? Jesus!'

'Oh yes, you shove your oar in your lecturers' appraisals. Why not?'

'And my students' in mine?'

'You shouldn't have a problem there, Sophie: you always had such a good reputation back at William Murdock. By the way, have you heard the latest? Several million adrift, I heard.'

I nodded. 'Be that as it may – and don't forget my job's at risk if it is – William Murdock isn't this afternoon's *mouton.*'

'You realise I can't let you see her file?'

'You can tell me what it says her Ph.D.'s about. And where she got it. If not in Melbourne.'

His eyebrows disappeared into what would have been his hairline. Saying nothing, he fished a bunch of keys from the top drawer of his desk. 'OK. Make us some tea while you wait.'

In his absence, I had a chance to look round the office. It had been painted recently enough for a distant smell of emulsion to linger. The furniture wasn't flash new management stuff, but oldish wood, with years of good service left in it. An array of geranium cuttings basked on the windowsill, and some healthy-looking spider plants dominated the tops of his filing cabinets. On the wall opposite his desk, apart from the regulation wall chart, hung one of those photo frames holding a set of family portraits: his mother, his late wife, several of his daughter and one of a blonde woman in her forties or fifties – good eyes, good nose, shame about the chins. The new love, no doubt.

On the wall to the right of the door was a clock big enough to have graced a station. OK, a small station. It was clearly a lot older than the room. Perhaps it had been someone's idea of an appropriate gift when Luke had left Wolverhampton. The minute hand moved with a curious two steps forward and one back click – very loud. It would have driven me crazy in ten minutes flat. In fact, it was likely to do so. Luke had been gone nine minutes. And it was already four twenty-five. What on earth could be keeping him?

I made tea. He seemed to be hooked on the sort of herbal brews Harvinder favoured. One day I'd have to point out to them the list of additives gracing this particular so-called pure brew. The sad thing was, whatever the teas smelt of – wild strawberries or whatever – they never quite seemed to taste of it. Like instant coffee, I suppose.

The clock had clunked past four thirty when he reappeared, running fingers through his remaining hair. I didn't need to ask, did I?

'Gone, gone, and never called me mother,' he announced, taking the mug. Was the wretched man never serious for two minutes in a row? But he was jiggling the tea-bag string sharply enough to slosh some of the brew on to the carpet. 'The whole file.' He slung the bag into the bin. 'Shit, shit and thrice shit!'

'Any others missing?'

'There may be. They seem to have got out of true alphabetical order. But there's no real problem. The computer ones will be OK.'

I could have screamed. Why hadn't he looked at those first? Before I could ask, however, he said, 'We hope the system will be back up on Monday. Alas and lackaday, the programme went bananas yesterday. Not the whole system. Just the bit we need. Splat.' He smashed his fist into the other palm, with what I took to be mock ferocity.

'What a coincidence,' I said drily.

'Oh, these things happen. It's not a system I'd have gone for myself but there you are.' His face changed. 'You think there's something sinister, don't you?'

I shrugged. 'Whatever I think, this must stay between the two of us. Don't ask anyone about that missing file. If you even think about it, think—'

'Think yobs with knuckle-dusters,' he concluded. 'I suppose a general enquiry about who might have been rooting through the files . . . ?'

'If you're happy, it's up to you. But keep my name out of it. My – my young man likes my face the way it is.'

'"Young man", eh? Oh, I wish there was a proper term for all this. At our age – OK, I know I can give you ten years, but you know what I mean – boyfriend or girl-friend's entirely the wrong word. "Partner" is a bit committed, "lady-friend" makes Elsa and me both sound about eighty and coy with it! But you've got a young man. Tell me all about him.'

'Now?' I pointed at the clock.

'Oh, my ears and whiskers, I must be off, you're quite right. Friday night is here again!' He sang the phrase to the tune of 'Happy days are here again'. 'And are you spending it with the love of your bosom?'

I wish! 'I would that I were.' I felt it behoved me to respond in kind. 'But he's in Australia—' To my horror, I felt the tears spring to my eyes. Perhaps because I heard Jago's voice: *pulling Australian Sheilas.* What if he was?

'And you're missing him. Look, why don't you come round and share our Shabbat? I know you're a lapsed Baptist but that doesn't put you beyond our pale. I'd like you to meet Elsa. And Naomi will be there.'

'I'd love to. But I'm supposed to be having supper with someone else.'

'Anyone I know?'

'Carla. The woman whose file's gone missing.' I'd meant it as an exit line – Luke was putting on his coat, after all, and gathering his case. But he stopped, one arm still free, and put down his case.

'Are you sure that's a good idea?'

'No reason why not,' I said, his tension making my airy assertion sound hollow.

'Maybe. Once bitten, twice shy, Sophie. Like I said, I don't take risks these days. Do an old man a favour: phone her first.'

'I will. I don't even know if she's still expecting me.'

'Well, I'll be expecting you on Monday. Hang on. There's a meeting on the West Brom campus in the afternoon, I think. Why don't I up-date you then? How about over lunch? One fifteen?'

'At the pub? The Chalk and Talk?' I didn't need to spell out why I'd prefer it to the refectory. Hang looking for that sandwich-eating student. I couldn't talk to Luke and counsel her anyway, not both at the same time.

'Fine. And next week you share our Shabbat? Come on, you know I'm not orthodox, but I just like to keep the traditions alive.'

'Lovely.' I checked in my diary. 'How about the following week? Next week I cook for another UWM missing person – oh, he's just taking time off to mark! Tom Bowen. You know I do this cooking scam?' I explained as we walked together to the car park.

'Just make sure it isn't your goose you cook. Ah! These clichés!' After another enormous self-parodying shrug he let himself into his car and drove off.

I waved him out of sight. And found myself walking backwards into the huge bumper of a Saab. No lights, so I didn't catch the number. In any case, there was no harm done to either of us. And so to my Fiesta. If only I could remember its number.

There were no messages at all in any medium when I got home. So what should I do about Carla's invitation? I'd better try phoning her myself.

I got through to her answerphone. Should I bother leaving a message? Perhaps, just on the off chance. I waited and waited for the little bleeps to give way to the big one. A lot of messages today. Or perhaps it had been some time since she'd checked them. I added to them.

I find Fridays the most dispiriting night to be on my own. I always have, ever since university days, when everyone else would be in the bar hoping to meet someone to go with to the Saturday disco and I was in my bedsit with my bulge. So, even if it were the longest of shots, I'd head for Smethwick, clutching a bottle of Perrier. If I had to come home, tail between my legs, no one could say I hadn't done my best.

Chapter Sixteen

Smethwick's canal basin hadn't yet been prettified like that off Gas Street, in Birmingham's city centre. All it had was moorings for half a dozen boats – or at least, only half a dozen boats were moored there. Across the spread of tarmac was a place for disposing of chemical waste, known to you and me as the contents of portable loos, a source of fresh water, and a lot of tarpaulin wrapped round what the contractor's boards promised would be a newly refurbished pub – completion date the forthcoming April. Then, no doubt, the picnic tables – the sort with benches attached – on the grass at the far end of the moorings would be heaving with life. The lighting over the whole site was good streetlight quality with lower lights to mark the start of the grass. The narrow boat residents could come and go in safety. Most of the boats were firmly closed up, no sound or light escaping. Maybe they were shutting out the Smethwick noise, which rumbled on even at this hour.

I prowled up and down the row, dodging mooring ropes and turds that might have come from a small elephant. They or something else, perhaps that loo-emptying point, smelt rank. I fought a heave of nausea.

Maybe I should give up now and go home. But the smoke curling from the chimneys of two of them, the gleams of light reflected on the water . . . yes, they were attractive in a *Wind in the Willows* way, and like Mole, I fancied being part of it, for the duration of a meal, at least.

'And what might you be wanting, pet?' demanded a man's voice with a Geordie accent. I nearly jumped into the cut. He'd padded down across the grass without my noticing.

Not knowing even the name of Carla's boat, I felt myself at some disadvantage.

'Well?' He wasn't drunk but he'd had enough to sound truculent.

'I'm looking for Carla Pentowski,' I said.

'Way, mon, I've not seen her these few days. There you are: *Laughing Jackass*. That's hers. Doesn't look like there's anyone at home, does it, now?' Without my asking, he reached across the stern and jangled a brass bell. Further along the row of boats a dog barked, basso profundo. It sounded big enough to have produced the mammoth doggy-does. 'Shut up, Sadie, pet, you daft bugger!'

No sound from this boat, however.

'You'd best be off, flower. My Sadie, now, she's a lovely dog and she'll be wanting her wee and her crap. But she doesn't like performing in front of strangers.' He stood, arms akimbo.

No point in hanging around. If a gytrash – oh yes, I knew my *Jane Eyre* – wanted its Lebensraum, who was I to object?

I retreated to the car, ready to give up. The car headlights spotlit a dog as big as I'd feared. Whether it was they that prevented her relieving herself I couldn't say. She was clearly more interested in something in the water near Carla's boat, baying with all her huge being at it. Eventually my Geordie friend cuffed her back on to his boat – how on earth did she even turn round in it – and quiet was restored.

I had to, didn't I? I had to cut the engine, leaving the lights on despite the protesting electronic whine when I opened the door. I had to walk back to the water. Whatever it was that the dog had barked at was the source of the smell. And – as my stomach emptied itself in the oily waters – I had a very good idea what it was.

* * *

It looked like hair. It looked like pallid skin. But I couldn't see the face. Not without touching and turning – no, I couldn't do it. Instead I checked my watch: the police might want details like that. Seven forty-five. I ran back to the car: it was just possible that Chris was still at Piddock Road. If he wasn't, calling in to the station would in any case probably produce quicker results than dialling nine nine nine. Quicker? When the body had been there long enough to smell, and no one – Sadie apart – had taken any notice.

In fact Chris's scarred Audi was nosing its way out of the car park as I pulled up by the barrier – I wasn't prepared to mess with street parking now. Obviously he wouldn't recognise my anonymous Fiesta, so I leapt out, waving frantically. The driver's window opened.

'Yes?' And then he recognised me. 'What on earth . . . ?'

I bent to his level. 'I think I've found a body. And – oh, Chris – it could be Carla.' Before I'd finished I was stepping backwards to avoid the car door. 'It may not be her. Just something else—' I made it to the gutter.

'Dead and stinking.'

'Not stinking. Just that sweet smell.'

'Where?'

A hapless patrol car driver hooted, as well he might, with Chris half in, half out of the car park and me occupying most of the road. Chris fixed him with a look, but we moved the cars anyway. Now both were on the road. The officer pulled in, parking badly when he found a space. 'Sorry, Gaffer, I—'

'Forget it, Gary. Good night.' His tone was easier, more relaxed than I'd known it. 'Care to show me?' He got into his car but didn't open the passenger door. The message was plain. If it was Carla in the cut, the police team wouldn't want to have to bother ferrying me back to my car.

The scene at the basin was exactly as it had been when I'd

first arrived. Illuminated now by two sets of headlights and Chris's torch, powerful for its size, there were the narrow boats, backed up to the bank. I pressed a tissue to my face and led the way. Chris glanced at me before directing his torch where I pointed. Then, gesturing me back – not that I wanted to go forward – he strode to the edge, squatting down. Within seconds, he was back on his feet, turning away with a surprisingly graceful movement. Then the movement became a clumsy scurry. I held his forehead while he lost whatever Bridget had given him for afternoon tea.

He took the tissues I proffered. 'Must be out of practice dealing with stiffs,' he said, reaching for his radio. 'Do you feel well enough to drive back to your place? As soon as there's anything to tell you, you'll know.'

I nodded. I'd only be in the way. 'We weren't particular friends,' I said, to save him having to ask. 'Teacher and student. But she seemed a nice woman. Understanding.' I turned to go. 'But there is something I think you should know.'

He looked at me sharply. 'Will it wait till I've finished here?'

I nodded. 'That's her boat, by the way.' I pointed to the brightly painted hull that kept jostling the red hairs. '*Laughing Jackass*. And there's a man along there who says she hasn't been around for a few days. Watch where you put your feet, by the way: he lets his dog use the whole area and doesn't clean up. I thought that was the origin of the smell at first.'

'Hoped, more like. Once smelt, never forgotten. Now, I'm going to bring in whichever cavalry it's supposed to be and leave them to it. I'll be with you by nine fifteen, with a bit of luck. Look, with your stomach you'll have to eat, whether you want to or not. I'll bring in some fish and chips, shall I?'

'Not fish.'

'Just chips. You can cook up some chicken. Keep your mind off things.'

Could I indeed? But he was already talking into his radio.

* * *

Just as I was beginning to dither and feel sorry for myself, the phone went. Mike! He'd got five minutes before play started in the Melbourne Test. I chatted animatedly about his prospects for the game – he'd scored fifty-odd in both innings in the match just over! – and how he thought the team would fare.

'It's no good,' he said at last. 'I can tell there's something the matter.'

'I didn't want to tell you in case it disturbed your concentration. You know that woman you were looking up? I've just found her body. In the cut. By her boat.'

'Just get on a plane and come out here,' he said.

Over the top his reaction might be, but it was music to my ears. If only . . . 'I'll be needed at the inquest,' I made my mouth say. 'And there's Ivo to worry about.' Not to mention the money.

'Give the little bugger to Chris. They should get on like a house on fire. Oh, I know you can't just drop everything. But, if you can swap your ticket for an earlier flight, you will, won't you? And if you can't and you need to come, just tell me. Please.'

There's this wonderful Nigel Slater recipe for chicken involving lemon, garlic, basil and white wine. The only vegetable you need is some green leaves – lettuce, rocket, whatever. Because you leave the skin on, there's a lot of rich juice. It's best mopped with bread. But since Chris had offered chips, I wasn't about to argue. Comfort food, that was what we both needed, after all that nausea. Until it came I wouldn't even try any wine. I'd stick to a remedy even Aggie would favour: tea.

And it was her voice I heard when I dabbed a belated finger on the answerphone.

'Only there was this man sniffing round, and I thought I ought to tell you. Says he's from this garage. Only – you know what? – I don't reckon he is. No oil. Do you want a description?' Her voice was hopeful.

I called back. 'I'll be round as soon as I can,' I said. 'I'm expecting Chris any moment.'

'Ah, I noticed you were back together,' she said.

'No, we're not.'

'Well, what was his car doing there all the other night, that's what I want to know? Don't tell me it wasn't his. I heard his voice when he was walking up the drive. And I heard him in the morning.'

'He'd drunk too much to drive. So I made up my spare bed.'

'Ah, that's what they all say.' Which one of us she was referring to, I had no way of telling. Since Chris was such a favourite of hers, I wouldn't have placed bets either way.

Chris was later than he'd predicted but earlier than I'd expected. The chicken was almost ready. I sloshed some wine on to the pan juices and reduced it all fiercely while he tipped the chips on to the plates and helped us both to some of the rest of the wine. I relayed Aggie's message deadpan. And word for word. There was no way I was having him stay over tonight. If I was – occasionally – worried that Mike might be tempted by Australian beauty, he certainly didn't need the news that Chris and I were close again. He'd been very tolerant, but there was no doubt he preferred Chris's room to his company. And the media would certainly relish a love-triangle story involving one of the few England batsmen who was having any success.

He shrugged. 'Nosy old bat.' Not the sort of comment I'd have expected of him.

'If she noticed, other people might have done too. Chris, I love you dearly, but we're much better as we are. And Mike's got a lot on his plate. The England team aren't exactly conquering heroes. We're thousands of miles apart. And our relationship is – forgive me – even more important than your driving licence.'

'I suppose I could always kip on Aggie's floor.'

'That's not the point, is it? Unless you leave a large notice on that car of yours saying "SLEEPING AT AGGIE'S, NOT WITH SOPHIE." And I don't reckon too many people would buy that.'

'OK.' He sounded resigned, even irritated, rather than depressed. 'Now, suppose we get outside that chicken while there's still some gravy left.'

'Then we must go round to Aggie's. She keeps early hours.'

Aggie's tea was thick brown no-nonsense stuff, inadequately diluted with sterilised milk. Chris's way of dealing with it was to spoon in what no doubt constituted his week's intake of sugar. Mine was to have a few delicate sips and forget to finish.

'Any road up,' Aggie began, 'this man was ringing and ringing your bell, and then started sniffing round the side of your house. He'd been making enough noise for me to think it was my bell, hadn't he? So I popped my head outside. That soon stopped his snooping. "Good afternoon," he said, "I wonder if Ms Rivers lives here." So I said yes, you did and I was expecting you back any minute, which I wasn't, but he wasn't to know, was he, and I knew you'd have left your alarm on. So I asked him what he wanted and he said he wanted to talk to you about your car. I thought he might be from your insurance or something, so I asked him for his card. And there he'd gone and forgotten them. So I asked him point-blank where he was from, and he said her garage.'

'Could have been some sort of manager,' Chris said.

'Where I take mine, they all get their hands mucky,' I said. 'Any of them would have oil under their nails, even smelt of it.'

139

'No oil. Now, my son – my youngest, God rest him – worked in a garage. And no matter how hard he tried to clean up, he always smelt of oil. Or that Swarfega stuff. Always. But the only thing this man smelt of was – no, I don't know.'

Chris lifted a finger. As if I needed warning to keep quiet! My glare was lost on him: his eyes were locked on Aggie's face. He smiled encouragingly at her.

'It's no good, me love. Maybe it'll come. But when you get to my age, your memory starts to go, you know.'

'It's just that you remember different things,' Chris said, patting her hand. 'Now, how old would you reckon he was?'

'Not old, not young. Not much older than you, young Chris, but carrying a bit more weight.'

'What about hair?'

She peered. Perhaps, I realised with a pang, her eyes weren't as good as they had been, either. 'Hard to tell. It never seems to get light, these days. Maybe a bit more than you, me love.'

'How tall was he?'

'Middling. Oh, I reckon he might have come in that big car. A bit like yours. Actually, he had a nice smile, I'll say that. Friendly. Spoke nicely, too. If you hadn't dinned it into me never to let people in, I might have given him a cup of tea. Nice young men like that don't often come my way.' She cackled.

'I'm glad someone takes some notice of me,' Chris said. 'Now, shall I check you're all locked up for the night? And would it help if I gave you an arm up those stairs?'

'Creep,' I hissed, as he deadlocked her front door and dropped the key through the letter box.

'I never had a gran,' he said.

'I did, and she was nothing like Aggie.' I killed the burglar alarm. Yes, we'd only been gone a few minutes, but unlike Bowen I always used it. 'OK. Let's talk.'

I steered him to the living room and produced a bottle of Perrier. 'I need to flush Aggie's brew,' I said.

140

'My dad used to make it like that. Railwayman's tea. When he was a kid he used to put bacon on to the stoking shovel and sizzle it. Wonderful stuff. But he preferred diesels, when it came down to it.'

What had brought on that little burst of reminiscence? He sat staring into the pseudo-coal gas fire.

'What makes you think of him?' I asked gently.

'His hatred of those fires! Now, you tell me all about Pentowski's life and I'll tell you all about her death.'

I obliged: everything I knew, from her kindness and competence as a teacher to Mike's strange inability to find her thesis – or indeed, any trace of her – in Melbourne.

'But you say she was a good teacher?' he summed up.

I nodded. 'An unqualified success, you might say,' discovering why the police went in for such black humour at times like this.

Chris gave an appropriate grimace. 'And Luke will check out everything on Monday?'

'No one must know we're talking to him. Remember last time: my big mouth.'

'His naiveté too. OK. Monday lunchtime. And you'll get straight back to Peter Kirby with the info. Or maybe he should.'

'The lower Luke's profile the better, I should say. The only reason I agreed to have lunch with him was I thought nothing could be more natural than two refugees from William Murdock meeting up for a chinwag.'

He didn't look convinced. Any more than I felt it.

'OK. Your turn. What about Carla's death?'

'I'd say,' he began, draining his Perrier, 'that we have a death-by-misadventure verdict looking us in the eye. What you've said only encourages the belief. We have a woman apparently claiming qualifications she doesn't have and upon which, presumably, her appointment depended. This mysterious fire. Was she living a lie and afraid that student – Jago, did you call him? Sounds like a character from those Mazo de la Roche books I used to bring my mum from the library! – might be about to uncover the lie? Let's take that as a scenario. She takes refuge in the bottle, is too pissed to judge the distance between boat and shore, and plunges in. The high wind does the rest, crushing her between the hull and the bank. Quick, but not especially pleasant. And as she sinks, for good measure her skull gets crushed too. Poor woman.'

I'd never known Chris so full of creative intuition! I said, 'Only one problem. She didn't drink.'

'Lots of evidence in the boat to suggest she did. And that Geordie bloke swears she liked her booze.'

'She told me she didn't touch the stuff. Ever. She was a reformed alcoholic.'

He shook his head. 'Alcoholism means addiction to drink. Addiction means the temptations are enormous – especially when pressures start to build in your life.'

'You won't just assume all this, will you? You'll keep an open mind?'

'Of course. We always do.' Something in his voice suggested that impressive though all this might be he was thinking about something else. 'Do you know of anyone who might have wanted her dead?'

'Not offhand, but—'

'Any reason, then, for me to divert resources from my everyday police problems to some spurious investigation?' Ah! Management-speak. I wish Aggie could have seen soft, cuddly Chris as hard as this!

'You mean problems like parking and speeding—'

'And drugs and domestic violence and that body in the cut.'

'OK. Point taken.' There was no point in arguing just for argument's sake. 'Did you stay back at the moorings long enough to talk to the police surgeon?'

He nodded.

'How long did he – it is a he, is it? – reckon she'd been in the water?'

'Two or three days. The PM should give a more definite timescale.'

'Right. How come, then, she managed to leave a message on her office door saying she was going to be away doing some research? At least a day after she was dead?'

He frowned. 'She was going on a bender and wanted to put people off the scent? Phoned in? Left a message someone didn't prioritise?'

'Possible. But I'd say Kulvinder was pretty on the ball; I'd be surprised if she forgot anything. Ever.'

His face took on the stubborn-little-boy expression that always made me want to smack him.

'Would it do any harm to get a Scene of Crime person to look at the boat?'

'My dear Sophie, they'll check the scene as a matter of course. Not tonight, before you ask. Probably tomorrow, if Peter and I can agree the overtime. And don't you go sniffing round there!'

'I wouldn't want to contaminate the scene,' I snarled. 'Would I?' If I was anyone's dear Sophie, I certainly wasn't Chris's.

'Of course not,' he said, leaning forward to refill our glasses. 'Any ideas about this soi-disant mechanic of Aggie's?'

'I think she's getting glaucoma or cataracts or something,' I said, aware I wasn't answering his question. 'Have you noticed the way she looks in your direction, but not always quite at you?'

'Time she was thinking of heading to her granddaughter's, perhaps,' he said. 'You'd better talk to her about it.'

Funny how I got all the good jobs.

'She'll leave a big hole in your life, Sophie.'

'And new neighbours to run in,' I agreed.

We sipped in silence for a minute.

'Well?'

'She didn't give us much to go on. I know several middle-aged men who might fit that description. We didn't even get hair colour, did we? Or build?'

'I wanted her to remember, not say something to please me.' He drained his glass. 'No ideas then?'

'I do have quite a number of male acquaintances.'

'Come off it. Male acquaintances wouldn't be sniffing round. Men connected with—' He gave up, gesturing vaguely. 'Men you might have annoyed. Like whoever had dealings with your car.'

'You mean someone's got a contract out on me!' I rolled my eyes and clasped my hands to my chest. 'Joke, Chris!'

'No joking matter. OK. It could be someone you've annoyed in the past. But what about someone in the present? At UWM, for instance?'

'The only men there I've had any real dealings with are Jago and Tom Bowen, my tutor. They're much of a height, but Jago's stringy and Tom's cuddly. Or not, as the case may be. Jago's found solace in the arms of another student, by the way.'

'You don't think his *amour propre* would be sufficiently dented by your rejection to prompt him to damage your car?'

I pulled a face. 'Not to paint-strip a whole row. And surely not to tamper with my brakes.'

'Bowen?'

'The only way I could have offended him is my request for a tutorial. No, he's OK. In any case, he needs me in one piece to cook for him. Next Friday. And he knows I'd need wheels to do the job.'

'Not everyone takes food as seriously as you do, Sophie.' He shifted in the chair. 'There's always the remote chance it could have been one of the guys from your garage?'

'Surely not. They'd phone, not come round in a big car.

But, just to rule them out, I'll ring them first thing tomorrow. Which it almost is.' I got to my feet.

Less speedily, Chris got to his.

I didn't quite push him out. But he got little more than a flap of the hand before I shut and locked the door. And pressed the downstairs zone of the alarm system. Just in case.

Chapter Seventeen

Saturday morning was so fine and sunny I wanted an excuse to be outdoors. First of all, however, I had to phone the garage, which didn't wake up till about nine fifteen. When I finally got through, Paul could scarcely restrain a guffaw at the idea of such a small outfit making home visits, especially when the car in question was on their premises.

'The good news, though,' he said, 'is that the insurance inspector came yesterday afternoon, and he's given the go-ahead for all the repair work. We convinced him – and he didn't take much convincing – that the brake-pipe had been vandalised, not worn out. So she's up on the ramps now. All systems going.'

'How much more active life would you say she's got before she starts costing me money?'

'Well, your clutch seems a bit notchy. And I'd like to get the timing chain changed soon – just to be on the safe side. One of the dampers – oh, nothing urgent. Why do you ask?'

If I bought a new car – one with a warranty, one that wouldn't need frequent repairs – it would reduce his business, wouldn't it?

'I could have fallen in love,' I said, 'with my hired Fiesta.'

'Come and talk to us before you commit yourself to any particular make,' he said immediately. 'And be sure to test-drive everything going. Even the less obvious ones.'

I promised I would. Knowing Paul's absolute loathing of

answerphones, I gave him my number at UWM, wished him a quiet weekend, and rang off.

The next thing on my list was to phone Chris: answerphone at home, of course, and no reply from his Smethwick extension. I tried the general switchboard without too many expectations, none of which would have been fulfilled anyway. At least I'd left a message.

Now for the rest of my day. An obvious thing to do was to cycle to the butcher's to sort out the meat for the following Friday evening. After all, I'd spent a long night thinking about the menu – anything, I suppose, to keep the thoughts of poor Carla at bay. My answerphone was switched on: if Peter Kirby or Harvinder Mann wanted to reach me, they could leave a message.

Yes, it was a wonderful day; shame about the wind which must have come straight from Siberia. When I was a kid, I listened open-mouthed to local lore that if you stood on a particular Black Country hill – the one nearest to our house, as it happened – the next high outcrop would be the Urals. I've never checked it out, not even to see how high the Urals are, but it's certainly true that the West Midlands plateau suffers in an east wind and we feel a peculiar pride that it's come all the way from Russia. As I locked my bike outside Roger Brown's I heard teeth being sucked. Shrewd eyes scanned the sky: 'Too cold for snow,' people were saying – and this was Harborne, remember, suburb of cosmopolitan Birmingham, not some Thomas Hardy village.

The meat order quickly and easily dealt with, I had to endure some ribbing from Roger and his lads about the performance of the English team – another overnight collapse, with even Mike managing no more than twenty-nine. I couldn't resist buying some steak and chicken for this weekend. Then to the shop next door – like Roger's, organic – to order vegetables, and thence to the deli to organise cheese. At both I found myself buying enough for the weekend as well as Tom Bowen's dinner party. Next to the florist's, where I agreed to trust Malcolm's judgement as to the best value flowers when Friday dawned. But I was unable to resist some long-stemmed hot-house anemones, despite my strictures to myself about personal spending and waste of world resources.

Now what? Home, via the newsagent's to pick up the *Guardian*. Since the *Birmingham Post*'s front page carried a paragraph about Carla's death, I bought that too. The brevity of the item confirmed what I suspected – the police would be as cagey as possible. Nothing on the answerphone. No point in even thinking about the garden with a frost this hard. And so it dawned on me. The only displacement activity possible this weekend was the dreaded housework.

I was just dusting the first windowsill when I noticed Aggie struggling to hang out her washing. I was outside before you could say peg.

'What do you think you're doing?' I yelled. 'And without a coat too.'

She looked sheepish. 'Only it seemed a lovely day for my whites. But I reckon they're freezing in the basket.'

'Go and let me in: I'll do them for you.'

She obeyed with surprising – indeed, alarming – docility. The hand I squeezed as I went through her door was icy.

'Why don't you make us a cup of tea?' I said.

Outside, I was glad of the jacket I'd slipped on. My hands too were blue when I'd finished. I'd had to repeg some of the towels: either her eyes or her grip weren't up to it. I bit my lip; the thought of Aggie becoming really old, not just the kind old lady who'd kept an eye on me ever since I'd moved in, was appalling. Hell, she was the nearest I'd got to a family. Steph wasn't really part of my life and my father absolutely not part of it.

'You all right, me love?' she demanded when I dived back into the warmth of her kitchen.

'This wind,' I said. 'It whips the tears from your eyes.' I scrubbed my cheeks.

She nodded. 'They was saying on the radio that this here wind-chill factor would make it more like minus five this morning. And goodness knows what it'll be down to tonight. I thought I'd better put the paraffin light on in my shed tonight. Don't want to lose all my fuchsias, now.'

'You knock on the wall to remind me and I'll come and do it. Come on, Aggie. Imagine if that hip of yours let you down outside in that sort of temperature.'

'Wouldn't last five minutes, would I?' She sounded remarkably cheerful about it. 'They say as you just feel very tired and your heart slows down and—'

'And all this time you're in excruciating pain from that hip.' I edged to her living room and sat down. Often I had to make my excuses and dash, but there was no way I'd budge today. But how was I to be tactful? I didn't want to sound as if I wanted to be rid of her.

The heat enveloped me. 'Oh, you've got it nice and cosy in here.' I slipped off my jacket. The jumper would come off next.

'Nice and cosy. That's it.' She sat opposite me, on her favourite chair. 'My granddaughter always says it's baking hot, and how she can't breathe. And her place – she likes the windows open all the time. Even in winter. All them draughts!' She shuddered. Her place was virtually hermetically sealed, with secure secondary glazing fitted by the friend who'd transformed my home into Fortress Sophie. Then she leant closer, as if there were unkind ears to hear. 'Trouble is, the heating bills. The government's supposed to give us all this extra money if it's cold, aren't they? But they always seem to wriggle out of it. I suppose . . .' She plucked at the crocheted blanket which made a nest of her chair. 'I suppose you and Chris couldn't move my bed down here, could you? Only it'd save having to heat upstairs all night. I could use my little gasfire.'

Her gasfire was a museum piece.

'When did you last have it checked?' I asked dubiously.

'This gas isn't poisonous, not like the old sort.'

'No, but carbon monoxide can poison you. If the flue's not working properly.' I took a deep breath. 'You wouldn't have any of these problems in a nice bungalow, would you? And you always talked of going into a sheltered home. Down near your granddaughters.'

'Move to Evesham? But when all's said and done, this is my home. All my stuff . . .' She gestured.

'You could take most of it. The things that really matter. Come on, you'd have a grand old time sorting it out.'

There was a long silence. Had I gone too far?

'I'd have to have some new glasses for that,' she said at last. 'And that new young man, the one that took over from that nice Mr Plumley, he's not a scrap of good. He says these are as strong as he can give me, and I can't even read my paper with them.'

'Did he think you might need some drops or something?'

'What do you know about my eyes?'

I'd better be straight with her. 'When you were talking about that man who came looking for me, you told me about his smell, nothing else.'

She shifted in her chair. 'I don't want no operation, Sophie, and that's the truth. Them lasers – they're what they use to kill people, aren't they?'

'And to cure them. Didn't they use one to fix Mrs Thatcher's retina?'

She cackled. 'See, I told you as they were killers!'

I didn't point out that Thatcher was still alive.

She chewed her lip. 'You reckon I ought to go and see them at the eye clinic?'

'I'll take you myself if I'm free. Or talk Chris into it if I'm not.'

'No, he'll be too busy. There's always that nice Ian, the one who had me to his retirement party.'

151

There was indeed. And I suspected there was a certain cachet about being escorted by a personable male, albeit one in his fifties.

She smacked her hand on her thigh. 'That's who he reminded me of. That man. He reminded me of young Ian.'

Who was thickening about the waist, but still maintained, despite its visible retreat, a reasonable head of hair.

'Except his voice: that was more like Chris or you.'

Not much Brummie accent then. You could still just detect a note of Scotland in Chris's, if you listened hard enough.

'If only I could see better.' She rubbed the offending eyes. 'You really think I should go, don't you?'

'I said, I'll take you.'

'No, into a little flat. With a warder.'

'You know as well as I do it's a warden.' I leant over and squeezed her hand. 'I'd like to say no, Aggie, because I love you and you're better than any gran in the world to me. But if I were you, I'd want to choose where I was going to live, not have someone else do it for me. Why don't I give your granddaughters a buzz and get them to fix an appointment for you to go round one?'

'There are two lots I could try. One bungalows, one flats.'

'Maybe you could stay down there a couple of nights.'

She nodded. 'So long as you tell them to shut the windows. I don't want no draughts, remember.'

This time there were a couple of calls waiting for me. The first was from Ian, offering me his satellite and his spare bed, just in case there was an Australian collapse and Mike should be batting again. I accepted for Sunday and promised to fill him in on Aggie: he'd always liked her and would no doubt do everything he could. The other was from Harvinder Mann. My business with him would have to wait till I'd spoken to Lucy, Aggie's favourite granddaughter.

'I'm on duty tomorrow morning,' she said. 'And I've got

something booked for the evening. But if you could pack a case for her, I could make a flying visit after lunch and collect her. She could stay here while we looked for a more permanent place. That is,' she added, 'if she doesn't want to live here. Oh, Sophie, I'd no idea things were so bad. Why didn't she tell me?'

'Why didn't she tell any of us? I only found out by chance. And when she started talking about having her bed brought downstairs, I was really worried, believe me. The thing is, Lucy, I don't think she wants to do more than visit you: I really think she'd be happier in her own place.'

'So she can build up a nice thick fug,' she laughed. 'I bet she told you to tell me to keep all the windows closed! Yes, she'd be better off somewhere warden-controlled with emergency buttons and things. After all, I couldn't give up work to look after her.'

'Can you imagine her letting you? Oh, I shall really miss her, you know . . .'

When I got round to it, it wasn't easy to return Harvinder's call. He wasn't on his direct-call extension, and when I tried to penetrate the general switchboard to leave a message I was tempted to give up in despair. At last my phone started its little double chirrup. Someone was hearing this BT voice telling them she was trying to connect them and that I knew they were waiting. A live caller beat a dead switchboard any day.

It took me a second to place the caller: I never heard the tiny Asian sing-song in Harvinder's voice when he was face to face.

'Hey! What a coincidence! I was just trying to phone you back!'

He sounded stressed. 'Really – look, I hope I'm not interrupting your lunch?'

Was it that time already?

'Not even thought about it yet,' I said.

153

'I wonder, then, if you could spare time to join me in a quick pub lunch? We could meet halfway between here and Smethwick? I'm afraid there aren't too many places of gastronomic excellence round here.'

'Don't believe all Chris tells you about me and food,' I said. 'You name the pub and I'll be there. Oh, and not too close to the Hawthorns – I think the Albion are playing at home this afternoon.'

We settled on the Pheasant, a thirties place opposite Warley Woods, largely because despite the cold I fancied a brisk after-lunch walk in an open space with plenty of folk within yelling distance. The sandwiches were fresh and the mild good. Harvinder was quiet and anxious.

I munched and waited. He'd asked me, after all, and perhaps he was having second thoughts.

'It's these coincidences,' he said, chasing a fragment of someone else's crisp round a beer mat. 'I don't like coincidences.' He looked up at me and grinned. 'Even when it's just a matter of people trying to phone each other at the same time.'

I laughed. And waited.

'Three canal deaths,' he said. 'Well, one was near enough. Peter says it's all nonsense. No connection between the two Asian deaths; no connection between the two canal deaths. Just coincidence. But . . .' He shook his head and sipped his bitter. 'And the budget's so tight, Sophie: they want us to fight crime with no resources. All this fuss about people being falsely imprisoned! What about those guilty ones still roaming the streets free to kill again?'

I didn't think the word fuss appropriate if you'd been banged up for years for a crime you hadn't committed. But the important thing was the cases now in hand. Carla's especially.

'Are you involved in the investigations into Carla's death?'

'I want to be. I went along to her long boat yesterday.'

'Narrow boat,' I said. Funny how I can never resist making

154

factual corrections. 'Long boats are what the Norse invaders came in.'

He looked puzzled. 'But I thought the canals were nineteenth century?'

'Eighteenth, anyway.'

His expression, hitherto one of gloom to the point of depression, suddenly lightened. 'Are you sure? Wouldn't it explain a lot if these Norse invaders had had to pull their sails down to get through the tunnels – a sort of getting-a-ship-into-a-bottle routine?'

'In that case, the horns on the invaders' helmets must have struck sparks from the tunnel roofs and set fire to the sails! That must be the true explanation for the funeral pyre ships!'

He didn't look convinced. 'But perhaps that's why they did all that raping and looting: because their sails caught fire.'

'That's right! Really pissed off they'd be – coming all this way only to lose their sails!' I was laughing so much my sides hurt.

He was wiping his eyes. 'Oh, if only history at school could have been like this. I might have remembered some of it. We had all this project work for GCSE and I know a great deal about a very little. Oh dear.' One last giggle and he was serious again.

Reluctantly, I took my cue from him. 'But to get back to our narrow boat. Chris says there was evidence to suggest Carla was a heavy drinker. And this Geordie neighbour says the same.'

'With due respect to Chris, the Geordie neighbour – Eric . . . er, Eric—'

'Eric Bloodaxe!' I started to giggle again and choked on my mild.

'Or Eric the Red!'

'Discovering America!'

'A bit late. And it'd have to land on him, not him on it, the way he is!' He slapped me on the back, before saying, with a great effort at seriousness, 'Eric *Conrad* says it sounded as if she was having a great party—' he looked at me with concern '—one night this week. Tuesday or Wednesday. He can't quite remember which.'

I coughed hard and managed to ask, 'Too pissed himself?'

'Probably. And probably in denial: he claims half the bottles in the bin were hers. But if we got Fingerprints on to them we'd probably find otherwise. In any case, there were plenty of bottles on her boat. All tidied up into a kitchen bin, as it happens.'

'It might be interesting to fingerprint them. Resources permitting,' I added primly.

'What might you expect to find?' His eyes started to twinkle in response.

I shrugged. 'Someone else's. God knows whose. Just some-one else's.'

'You still cling to what she said about not drinking.'

'She specifically said she was an alcoholic and didn't touch the stuff. Ever. The bottle of Perrier I took to her boat – she'd said I could take booze but it didn't seem fair – is still in the car. Just Perrier. No flowers, no chocs. A rather ungracious guest.'

'Did you expect her not to be there?'

I took him through an account of my attempts to run her to earth.

'So you weren't really hopeful of seeing her?'

'Some time on Friday, a word-processed note appeared on her door, telling us students that she was unavailable because she was doing research. The funny thing is, her research record doesn't appear to be very . . . strong.' I told him what Mike had found. Or not found.

'Another of these strange coincidences. Sophie, you know Chris well. What do I have to do to persuade him to change his mind? To let me have resources . . . manpower?'

Was this what he'd been wanting to ask, all through lunch?

156

It could be. He'd offered no other explanation. I'd give him an honest answer. 'Easy,' I said. 'Find something the SOCOs may come up with. Hard evidence. By the way, if you see him, tell him there's a message for him on his answerphone at home. Aggie – did you ever meet my neighbour? – intercepted a visitor yesterday. He said he'd come from my garage. He hadn't.'

He was just setting down his empty glass. 'Do we have another coincidence here?'

'You tell me.'

He shook his head, looking at his watch. 'I don't know, either. I must be getting back, I'm afraid.'

We stood up, and headed for the door. As we stepped into the bitter wind, he pulled his collar round his ears. 'What are you doing this afternoon, Sophie?'

'I had planned to go for a walk through the woods.'

'Well, just remember,' he said, kissing my cheek, 'if you don't want a big surprise, you'd better go in disguise.'

Chapter Eighteen

There was no doubt about it, Aggie knew her departure from Harborne, no matter how temporary, for the watershed it was. It signalled the start of a new era, one that ultimately could have only one end. But I tried to be as upbeat about her packing as I could, and sat and shared her lunch. At least I knew that as long as she had any sight left she'd feed herself properly. She was always extremely precise in her shopping lists for me, and demanded the best ingredients she could afford. Roger Brown was terrified of her: he topped up her freezer from time to time and woe betide him if any of the meat were below par. Today's certainly wasn't: we tucked into a Sunday-lunch casserole that wouldn't have disgraced Elizabeth David: shin of beef melting into a gravy that I personally wouldn't have thickened but was none the less delicious. Her pastry – as in apple pie – beat mine into a cocked hat.

And then the phone rang.

'You answer it, me love,' she said, wide-eyed. 'Don't know who'd be phoning me at this time.'

It was Lucy. Her exhaust had blown and—

'Don't worry,' I said. 'I'll bring her. It's a lovely day for a drive. It'll do me as much good as it'll do her.'

Aggie heard the change of plan with apparent equanimity. 'At least now you'll know the way when you come to visit me,' she said, drying her hands and hanging up the towel. The washing-up was done, and the plates gleamed on the drying

159

rack. 'You're sure you don't mind coming in here to check up on things for me?'

'Have you ever complained about doing the same for me?'

'But you're at work.'

'I'm a student now,' I said. I added, though I was sure she wouldn't notice the irony, 'And look what carefree lives they have.'

Whoever had been peering through my windows – and, yes, Aggie's – while I'd been taking Aggie to Lucy's had left footprints in the flowerbeds that edged both bays. I photographed them, a ruler alongside to show the scale, and then did a really weird thing. I zapped into town, just making it into Boots' dispensary before it shut, and bought plaster of Paris. Our twin intruder lights and the streetlamp should provide enough light for me to play Girl Guides and make a few casts. Just in case. I didn't do them all: I couldn't get the consistency right. As I pulled up what seemed like half the garden I could have cried. It wasn't just my house I was looking after, though, was it? Aggie's, though far more burglar-proof than the average, was now my responsibility.

I'd have to do what I hadn't wanted to do: call Chris.

'You know,' he said, 'I really enjoyed that. Nice to know my old skills haven't deserted me.' He held a perfect cast up to my intruder light. 'Not that I'm at all sure why I'm doing it.'

'Of course, it was a genuine old friend, wondering why I wasn't in! Or Aggie, of course.' I removed my tongue from my cheek. 'No note, no message on the machine. And don't say "no paper, no change for the phone" or I shall scream.'

'Could be a symptom of paranoia, screaming.'

'Just because you're paranoid that doesn't mean they're not out to get you,' I observed, probably not for the first time. 'And get that mud off your shoes before you even think about coming in. I did my housework this weekend.' My voice oozed virtue.

'Wasn't there anything in the Sundays, then?' He scraped assiduously. And then slipped his shoes off anyway.

'Saving them for tonight.' I shut the door. 'For Ian's. He's invited me round to watch the Test Match. I shall read them if rain stops play.'

He stopped halfway through stripping off his Barbour and turned to face me. 'You're just like a schoolgirl with a crush,' he said. 'Watching this guy on TV all the time. Scanning the sports pages. Don't think I haven't seen that little pile of newspaper cuttings.'

'You forget, Chris, that I've always liked cricket. And that I love Mike. That's why I'm . . .' Hell! I was only about to throw at him in a fight the news that Mike and I proposed to marry. 'That's why I'm going to Australia this Christmas.' He wouldn't like that news particularly, but it would prepare him for when the other bit came.

'I thought you were supposed to be hard up,' he said, with the heady superiority of someone on £50,000 a year.

'There are some things worth being hard up for.'

If only Lola had been there. She could have articulated the proverb Chris was all too clearly biting back: *a fool and his money are soon parted.*

By now I was too angry to offer Chris the simple courtesy of a cup of tea, not that he'd have been keen to drink it. He slammed the cast down on the kitchen table, so hard I feared for its safety, and rinsed his hands, in an unusually perfunctory way. No towel, of course. It was flapping on the line in my back garden, with the others, and I'd have to go out there in the dark to collect it. I wasn't usually afraid of the dark.

In silence I passed Chris the kitchen roll. In silence he ripped a couple of sheets free, scrumpling them into the bin as soon as his hands were dry. I was glad he hadn't left that lot on a nice clean towel. I'd have to bear that in mind when, chilly and anxious, looking over my shoulder for nothing, I gathered the frozen towels from the line.

* * *

'You mean you still haven't taken any action?' Lola's contralto filled the women's loos. 'My dear Sophie—'

I wasn't her dear, either. 'Allow me to point out, Lola, that were it not for what I consider your entirely spurious sense of honour, I would have known which student had the problem and would have been able to deal with the situation accordingly.'

OK, it might be *lèse-majesté* to speak thus to a future Ghanaian Minister of Education, but I had gone to some trouble to do the impossible, which wasn't, of course, my job anyway. She was so shocked at being interrupted I could continue. 'If you point her out to me today, I will speak to her. But with reluctance. I am no more responsible than you are.'

It wasn't as if I hadn't enough to do. Oh, my schedule was nothing compared with the amount of work I shifted at William Murdock, but it felt tight, crammed with irritating little things. I hadn't checked my class's faces or signatures against the photocopies Kathryn had let me take on Friday. There was the small matter of my appointment with Tom Bowen, too, to discuss the dissertation. And, of course, a new assignment to prepare – this one for the dreaded Managing the Curriculum. It was a long time since I'd swept out of anywhere, but believe me, I swept out of that loo.

Pity there wasn't a more appreciative audience than one single student: Jenny, the beautiful Malaysian woman that Jago had been chatting up. Since the loo door was on a slow spring, she might not have noticed how I'd slammed it. Though I did wonder what she might have heard.

Tom was just letting himself out of his room as I came down the corridor.

'Thank goodness you've caught me,' he said, flapping a shred of paper under my nose before shoving it into his pocket. 'I was going to leave a note. There's this meeting – three-line whip – about quality. Leave me a note about your free time this week and I promise to come back to you. Hell, we need to make final arrangements for Friday.' He fumbled in another pocket, producing a bubble-pack of antacid tablets – the solid form of the medicine which had seen me through some painful times at William Murdock. Funny, I wouldn't have seen him as a man to suffer stress indigestion. It must have been how a cavalier tutor responds to the idea of being pinned down for inspection.

'I'll be at your house by two on Friday,' I said. 'All you have to do is let me in. If you're going to be out during the afternoon, you'll need to leave me a key, just in case. And, of course,' I added drily, 'your burglar alarm code.'

He laughed. 'Only when I've tamed the cats. But I'll see you before then, Sophie – promise.' With a flap of the hand he was gone. So what was all this cats in the plural stuff? He'd only mentioned the one when we were at his house.

A little window of opportunity, then, to return a pile of books to the library and to catch a stronger than usual coffee. Mike had been in slow but stubborn form, following an early collapse in the batting, and had kept me up till five till he'd amassed fifty diligent runs.

By now the news of Carla's death was official: a black-framed notice was pinned to her door. Maybe whoever had done it had simply screwed up the original note and slung it into a nearby bin. Feeling next thing to a bag lady, I burrowed, coming up sticky with Coke – why did people never empty their cans before slinging them? – but empty-handed. On to one further down the corridor in the direction of Tom Bowen's room. This time I was triumphant. Carrying it by the extreme edge, I took it back to the work-room, hoping I'd encounter no one who might feel entitled to an explanation as I shoved it into an envelope and thence into my drawer. Which I locked.

There were too many people buzzing around for me to deal with the signature and photo business. There was an air of shocked disbelief: but the commiserations were largely with Jago, who had clearly informed all and sundry how much he needed Carla's references. I wondered how many he'd told about my part in the search for it. And when he'd ask me for the results of Mike's activities. I wasn't quite sure what I'd tell him, but it certainly wouldn't be the truth.

'Not just quality, but Quality Assurance Agency,' Luke said, putting a glass of white wine on the beer mat in front of me. 'Big time. It's the university equivalent of OFSTED. The people who reduce school teachers to gibbering wrecks. But it should be seen as an opportunity to prove that we're doing things right, not some massive club to punish us for failure. You get so much notice – they're not coming for another eighteen months – you can polish the systems you've got and initiate any you need.' All that and not a single one of his corny jokes or snatches of song. But then, Luke had always taken quality seriously, even before it acquired a capital Q.

'So that was the meeting you had to come over for? I thought you said it was this afternoon.'

'It is! The university-wide one, that is.' He hunched and darted his eyes from right to left, touching his lips. 'Word on the street is the meeting's here because this site is going to need the most work doing.'

'But Tom Bowen said he was off to a meeting this morning.'

'He may well have been. Each faculty had to come up with an action plan by two. Maybe Education's a bit slow.'

Or maybe Tom hadn't prepared for our session.

A waitress was touting round two cheese salads. They came decorated with slivers of smoked bacon.

Luke covered his eyes extravagantly. 'Oy vey, I only eat kosher bacon.'

I passed the plate back to the waitress who rather too clearly did not appreciate his joke and went off muttering about bloody

Muslims. I didn't want to catch his eye. I'm sure we both had a strong suspicion that in the kitchen the bacon bits would be simply shaken off and the original salad returned to him. An Orthodox Jew would have acted on the suspicion – but then, I didn't see Luke as an orthodox anything.

'Right, how are the record folders?' I asked.

'I haven't been able to fix them, but then, no one else has been in the drawers anyway. I hid the master key. As for the computerised records, there's this geek working away seeing why the program is being so unyielding.'

'Program? So it isn't the whole system that's down?'

'Told you it was the program on Friday. With the system here, everyone has access to certain levels of information. All the tutors can record assignment and exam marks direct on to students' records. The timetable's there for all to see – or modify. A password will get you access to the more confidential parts of a student's record – references sent to us, those we're sending out. Then there's another password for staff. It's easy to reach their timetables but you need to get through a security system to access their personal details.'

I sighed. 'It was what we always wanted at poor William Murdock.'

Luke stopped eating and looked at me hard. 'You speak about it as if it's a person, not just a couple of buildings with people in them. As if it's an entity. With feelings.'

'Oh, the feelings are mine!'

'But I'd say you've got too many of them. People move on, Sophie. All the time. Till now, all your promotions have been at one place. You need to gain experience of a wider world.'

'That's why I'm here. To make myself more marketable. I thought it was to get a promotion; now I think it may be simply to get another job when I get made redundant.'

'With redundancy comes a redundancy package, Sophie. Don't forget that.' He raised a finger. 'When I was there you were still on the old contract. You still are? Good. Because that gives you a far better deal than those on the new. Might I make so bold as to offer you some advice? If you get offered redundancy, demur a bit – just to raise the stakes – then grab it and run. Invest it wisely. Carry on with this cooking business. Do a bit of part-time teaching here and there, just to keep your hand in. Polish your CV. And then, when the right job comes up, go for it. That's my advice.'

I nodded. Luke was on the wise side of clever. He gave sound advice.

He started to eat again, briskly. The big clock on his office wall might have been in his head, so clearly did he signal that it was time for us to be on our way.

'How would you feel about police geeks trying to sort out your computer problem?' I asked as I gathered up my coat.

'Eh? Oh, we're back to that, are we? Well, if you really think her file contains anything absolutely essential, and if this geek can't fix it, we may have to bring in someone from outside.'

'You don't sound keen.'

'Not all policemen fill me with pleasure at the thought of seeing them.' He stared over my shoulder, as if distressed by some long ago policemen, perhaps wearing a different uniform.

I turned too. There were Jago and Jenny. Though they were probably too engrossed in each other to notice, I flapped a half-hearted hand. And repeated the gesture as we walked back to the building, and we encountered Tom Bowen striding back from the car park. So much for no one knowing Luke and I had ever met.

Chapter Nineteen

Although the work-room was now empty, the general bustle had convinced me that checking twenty pairs of minuscule signatures against another, each written with incredible neatness with a fine, fine pen, was beyond me. As for the photos, my eyes would hardly focus. Age. It must be age. I grabbed the web of flesh between thumb and index finger with the other thumb and index finger. If you pinched and it didn't spring back, wasn't that supposed to show how old you were getting? Or perhaps, since the skin zipped straight back to normal, it was some other part of the body? The triceps, they were where middle-aged flab really started. Without stripping off jumper and shirt, there was no way I could check. As for hips and thighs, I was proud to declare they didn't know the meaning of the word cellulite. Unless they'd learnt it this morning. And I wouldn't put it past them, the way the rest of me was going.

In any case, this was really a job I shouldn't be doing here. I could take it home, spread everything on my dining table, boost the central heating and have that new CD of the Brahms Serenades on while I worked. That sounded much more attractive. I stowed everything in my briefcase – Mike had got so irritated with my penchant for using supermarket carriers till they shredded that he'd bought it for me from an Oxfam shop – and gathered my coat.

I was struggling into it when the door was flung inwards:

Lola, magnificent in her anger, even if it seemed to be directed at me.

'She's gone! She hasn't been to college since last Thursday! They must have arrested her! It's all your fault. And you must go to the police to sort it out!'

A traffic policeman would have envied my stop gesture.

'Oh, come off it, Lola. She may have a thousand and one reasons not to come in.' I waved my hands around in airy irritation. 'There's a lot of flu around – she may have gone down with that. She may have broken her leg. Have you checked her digs?'

'Digs?'

'Flat, bedsit, whatever. Kulvinder, no, Kathryn will have the address. Ask her for it.' Although I still couldn't see any of this as in any way my responsibility, I wasn't very proud of myself for running that hare. I was quite sure neither of them would violate the confidentiality rules, not even for the formidable Lola, and they might get their ears chewed off by her for their pains. With a bit of luck, however, I'd be out of the building before she got back to fulminate against me even further.

Anyway, I had those photos and signatures to check.

I was halfway through the main doors when I thought of Harvinder and his coincidences. All those Pacific Rim girls whose lives were over. Not just Pacific Rim. Specifically Malay. Just coincidence? OK, Lola probably wouldn't get hold of the address, but I could certainly pull sufficient staff clout to persuade even Kathryn that I should. I was chasing one of my absentees, wasn't I? Resplendent in my aura of conscious virtue, I toddled off.

To draw a blank.

Kathryn was at that meeting, wasn't she? That all-singing, all-dancing quality assurance meeting. With Luke, Kulvinder and any other person with easy access to what I wanted. If only, of course, I'd had the student's name.

* * *

Luke hadn't exactly turned down my suggestion of using a police geek to sort out the computer system, and, of course, Piddock Road Police Station was pretty well on my route home. With a bit of luck Roger Taft, a detective I'd worked with earlier in the year, would be there. He was the nearest to a geek I knew, though he was inclined to be modest about his skills. He also had a reputation for living up to his first name. None the less, he was part of Peter Kirby's team, and with Peter in his office and Harvinder probably in the room I'd be safe enough. Safe! A woman my age worrying about young men! He'd probably be offering me his mum's knitting patterns, not a quick chat-up line.

Trying to be tactful, I asked at the police station reception desk for Peter or Harvinder. Harvinder appeared more quickly than I'd expected, and ushered me quickly into an interview room. Not one of the redecorated ones.

'You shouldn't be here. Chris Groom gave me the bollocking of my life when I dropped out that you'd had lunch with me.'

'When was this? The bollocking, not the lunch.'

'This morning.'

'Well, the bollocking was nothing to do with you.'

'But he tore a million strips off me for revealing confidential material.'

'Chris and I had a row last night,' I said simply. 'Tell me, Harvinder, do you have a wife or partner?'

He stared, his neck stiffening. What had I said?

'Neither,' he said at last.

'Well, until we can find a replacement for Helena—'

'He's got Bridget!'

'Helena as girlfriend. Until he's got a new love interest, Chris'll be fancying himself back in love with me again. And you know what unrequited love can do to a man.' The pun was unintended: I blushed from my stomach.

'Not this Mann,' he said, adding, after a moment's hesitation, 'In fact mine is not unrequited. I shall shortly be getting

169

married. An arranged marriage, before you ask. From time to time I get the coldest of feet. But it's time I was settling down, and all the years I've been on the loose I've never found the right woman. And a Mann must think of having children.' He grinned to emphasise the word.

I grinned back. 'I hope you'll have a very happy marriage and enjoy your children. Congratulations.' I reached to kiss his cheek.

He turned so he took it firmly on his lips. Oh dear. Nice enough to remind me of what I was missing.

'Now,' I said, 'about your coincidences. I've got a few more. I don't think I mentioned on Saturday that there was a glitch in the uni's computerised information retrieval system. And one or two of the paper files had gone walkabout. Chris knows but he may not have deigned to pass on the info.'

He shook his head. 'He truly doesn't think there's a case.'

'Don't you believe it. It's just that he's gone down with that dreadful terminal disease, managementitis. And complications have set in already: managing-a-tight-budgetitis.' Was that the disease I was afraid of catching? 'Anyway, I wondered if I could talk to Roger Taft; see if he could unglitch the system.'

'Gone,' he said. 'Moved off to – let me think – Bournville Lane.'

'But the man had a gift for the keyboard.' Alfred Brendel might have envied his ability.

'He's taken it with him, then. Decentralisation is the flavour of the month. Get rid of all the specialised units! Put all the work out to OCUs like this! I suppose we're all supposed to pick up each other's skills via some sort of osmosis. And they've flattened management structures so – oh, sometimes I feel like chucking it in and going into teaching or something.'

'Word of advice, Harvinder: don't.'

* * *

Even if Chris was being petty, that didn't mean I didn't need a geek. As a member of the public I couldn't wander round the place on my own, so Harvinder accompanied me – making himself as invisible as possible – to Bridget's office. I'd wait there till I found out if Chris was too busy to be interrupted. If he was, I could leave a note. Bridget wasn't there, but a plate of cheese scones to tempt angels waited on her desk. I sat on my hands. When she came bustling in, I could scarcely speak I was salivating so hard.

She pushed the plate at me. 'Go on. Help yourself. There's young Chris going down with some bug or other, I'm sure. Not so much as a peck at his food. And him no more flesh on his bones than . . . Not that you're fat yourself, are you now, but you know what I mean. Go on. Just the one won't hurt your figure.'

God, was my figure spreading already? It would be the gym for me every night this week.

'As soon as I hear him come in I'll be making him a nice pot of tea. And what would be nicer for him than to have you take it in?'

I could think of a lot of things. I didn't do waiting on men. Especially Chris. But Bridget would think I was off my head if I said so. It would be almost as incomprehensible as if I suggested that Chris should make his own scones in future. So I waited for the kettle to boil, heard the slam of his door – we raised sisterly eyebrows in disbelief: Chris was not a slammer of doors! – and I staggered through with the loaded tray.

He was tucking his gloves into his cap when I laid the tray on his new table – a blessedly sensible height, this one, for which my back gave thanks. I expected him to say something offhand but kind – he wouldn't take his petulance out on Bridget. Instead, he demanded sharply, 'What now? I gather you've been talking to Harvinder again.'

'You do indeed. I was hoping to rope young Roger Taft

into helping Luke and me retrieve the files that have gone walkabout.'

'Surely you've got your own experts. The Government's always saying how much money it's pumping into education. Our resources, on the other hand—'

'To see why Carla's files have disappeared, Chris. A matter of some interest to the police, I'd have thought.'

He grunted: the verbal equivalent of that door-slam. 'And another thing: how come you were in Smethwick on Friday anyway, supposedly having dinner with Carla? I thought Friday night was your choir night?'

'Spot on. They're touring the States at the moment. It was a choice between going with them—'

'And going to Australia.'

'I was going to say, getting on with my M.Ed. And money did come into it. It would have been nice to go. William Murdock's always prevented me going with them in the past. Maybe next year if I'm made redundant.'

He looked at me sternly. 'Throwing up a chance of something like that!'

'To take advantage of a different chance.' I passed him the plate of scones. He took one, absently. So did I.

'So what can't you get off the computer?'

'I told you. It's not me. It's Luke Schneider. Staff records.'

'I can't believe he hasn't got hard copies.'

'I told you on Friday: someone's mixed them all up.' I felt like some luckless witness under hostile interrogation. The difference was that Chris was supposed to be one of my closest friends. Or – wait a minute – maybe, just maybe, entirely straight-faced, he was leading me up a thistle-filled garden-path. I tried to suppress a smile. 'I don't suppose . . . no . . . Yes, could it be that the SOCOs have come up with something to persuade you that maybe she didn't top herself in despair?'

Very casually, he said, 'The post mortem may have done.

172

And the SOCOs are checking it now. Her ankle and her knees. A long narrow bruise across one ankle. Both knees bruised.' He drew lines across his immaculate trousers. Then he put his hands out, palms forward.

'As if she tripped over something thin and fell on to her knees?'

'And then went arse over tip into the cut, pissed out of her mind,' he said, in a fair imitation of a Smethwick accent.

Another one trying jokiness to deal with the macabre. 'Poor Carla. No marks on her hands?'

He shook his head. 'The theory is that she hit her knees on the bulwark and grabbed for something to hold that wasn't there. Straight into the cut.'

'Jesus.' I made an effort. 'It'd be nice if the Scene of Crime team found evidence that she wasn't drinking on her own.'

'It wouldn't. It would be too expensive.' He gave a short laugh. 'But that won't stop them. They've made it a sterile area already. Sterile apart from that dogshit, of course.'

To celebrate my clear victory without the tiniest crow, I poured the tea. Just like the mud-tea I made when I was a kid. I held up half a cup for inspection.

Chris grimaced. 'I wish she'd get it into her head that more isn't necessarily better, when it comes to spoonfuls of tea,' he said. 'You see that parlour palm. She can't understand why it's wilting.'

'Don't tell me – tea dregs!'

'If it does that to a plant imagine what it'd do to my insides.'

'I thought the police were renowned for liking strong brews.'

'Not in these days of accountability and budgets and—' He gave up. 'Imagine Ian trying to get that down him.'

'Poor parlour palm,' I observed, tipping. 'More tannin for you. Will you ask her for fresh or will I?'

'It's a man's job,' he said, smiling for the first time. 'A job

173

for a leader of men. But even I'd better have some more scone crumbs round my mouth before I risk it.'

When he came back in, I was checking those signatures, sitting at his desk – I wouldn't have dared use the Table – his executive light beaming down on them.

'What are you up to?' His tone wasn't entirely friendly. Surely he knew me better than to think I'd have a quick shuftie at anything I wasn't supposed to see.

I explained. And pointed. He fished out his reading glasses and joined me.

'Better pour that tea first,' I said.

He trotted obediently back to his fine new table – I'll swear I caught him giving it a quick stroke – and poured. The brew would still have alarmed Ian, but it should at least kick my brain back into action.

Half an hour and two separate checkings later, I called Chris over from the table where he was working on a speech to the local Neighbourhood Forum. He'd nobly pointed out that I needed better light than he, but it was the call of that table, I was sure.

'What do you think?' I vacated his executive chair – willingly, as it happened, since it was designed to support an altogether longer frame than mine; my feet dangled like a kid's on a bus.

He burrowed in a drawer and came up with an object I'd not seen him use before.

'I don't believe it. Chris, you're not seriously going to use a magnifying glass! Where's your meerschaum and your deerstalker?'

'Magnifying glasses make things bigger,' he said firmly, 'and we, my dear Watson, need these signatures made bigger.' He bent in concentration. At last he straightened. 'I'm no expert, but I'd say – well, probably what you'd say—'

'That at least five of those little squiggles on these register sheets don't match the little squiggles on the original thingies – the application forms.'

'I just love it when you talk technical,' he said. 'Let me get my head round this. We've got a sad crop of Malay women's deaths. These are Malaysian—'

'And Singaporean.'

'—students who are not who they are supposed to be. We think. I don't know if there's any connection but we ought to float it as a possibility.'

'What about your budget?'

'Bugger the budget!' He reached for the phone. 'Time we brought Peter and Harvinder in on this. The Malay women are their cases, not mine, much as they intrigue me. And I owe young Harvinder an apology for something too.'

'I may be jumping the gun,' I said. This was now a Meeting, albeit extremely unofficial, and the four of us were seated at the Table. 'After all, it's not unknown for students to skip classes and sign in for each other. But these are serious students, who've paid serious fees to be here. Why should they want to skive? And we also have,' I added, producing my list, 'this list of students who are in my class but are not recorded on the main computer. Now, Kathryn assures me that you can't even breathe the university's air without being on the computer. You can't get even a temporary ID.'

'What if you're a bona fide student and waiting for funds to come through?' Chris asked.

'No. According to Kathryn even those are computer-issued. Special code, or something.'

'But how often are the IDs checked?' Peter asked, tipping back on one of those new chairs.

Chris watched him anxiously, concerned, I thought, less for his senior officer's back than for the chair's.

I shrugged.

175

'Well, Sophie, how often have you been asked for yours?' Peter pursued.

'Only once. When I was in Carla's room, and she wasn't there. I wanted to leave her an essay. There was a computer printout on her desk for me. But the security guard wouldn't let me take it.'

'Security guards are supposed to stop people taking things that aren't theirs,' Chris observed.

'But this had my name on it. Wrongly spelt, as it happens. It's probably still there. And there I had to put Kathryn to all that trouble to give me a new one.'

'Issuing new copies to all and sundry isn't usual?' Harvinder asked.

'Full-time staff get them as a matter of course. Students wouldn't. But I teach an English Language group twice a week and I was so concerned about their lack of progress I wanted, I suppose, to justify to myself my lack of success with them.'

'Any reason why the list shouldn't be there?' Peter put in.

I wasn't sure I understood his question. 'Every reason why it should.'

'But it would be nice to check.' He wrote in his notebook.

'There's another Malay thing too,' I said, slapping my forehead in disgust. 'This may just be a coincidence—'

Harvinder's head shot up. 'Another?'

I nodded. 'One of the group was eating expensive food and has now disappeared.' I told them Lola's theory. 'There may just be something in it. Why buy from Marks and Sparks when the refectory food's cheap and good?'

This time Harvinder wrote. 'I'll make inquiries. I've a friend who's a security guard at M&S.'

'No! I don't want *them* warned. I want *her* warned – not to do it! She may not realise the seriousness of what she's doing.'

'You know what the fines are for dropping litter out there?

176

I'd reckon she'd know she wasn't supposed to nick sarnies.'
Harvinder's turn to rock back on his chair.

'The thing is, she ought to because I did this whole class
on the vocabulary of shopping, including all sorts of useful
words like "shop-lifting", "credit-card fraud", "magistrates'
court" and "deportation". What troubles me is that she hasn't
been back into uni since. Could be my fault – she could be
bored silly, I suppose!'

'Or scared. Let us know if she's still out tomorrow. And
Sophie, don't go zapping round to her place to warn her.'

'Couldn't even if I wanted to. Haven't got her name or her
address.' Yet.

Chris glowered: I must have sounded too innocent. He
pulled himself into summing-up mode. 'Now, I shall be at
that conference in Toulouse from tomorrow morning.'

Toulouse! He hadn't mentioned anything to me about leaving the country!

'I fly out at eleven tonight. I'm quite happy for Sophie to
keep a weather eye open for activity at the university which
seems out of tune – provided that she reports back to you two.
On the matter of Carla, I'm happy for you to keep her abreast
of matters on which she might be able to shed light – we've still
not come up with next of kin, I take it? – provided we have your
word, Sophie, that you'll maintain absolute confidentiality.'

'Business as usual, gaffer,' I said, as if I too were a junior
officer and enjoying his frisson of mock shock.

He looked at his watch. 'I have to go to a mayoral reception.
I'll see you all when I get back.' Dismissed – me as much as
the men – we left the room.

When he got back, eh? And when would that be? I couldn't
ask the others and betray my ignorance. And I was damned if
I was flitting back to him to ask. But I would have liked to
know. Weren't we supposed to be friends? And weren't friends
supposed to tell each other when they were going abroad?

Chapter Twenty

The only message on my machine was from Steph, pointing out we hadn't eaten for weeks, at least he hadn't, and since he was in the city centre we might as well eat there. Oh, and his bike was off the road, so he wouldn't mind a lift home. Which meant, of course, that I couldn't simply hop on the bus and drink myself silly; I had to stay within the limit, if not on the wagon altogether. Dancing to his tune I might be, but I was damned if I was going to eat to it. Since it would no doubt be my treat, I would take us to my favourite Italian place, where he could stuff himself silly if he wanted, but with what I knew would be good food. And my bank balance could still survive.

When he called back, he accepted the suggestion of Ciao Bella with the comment that it was 'wicked' – the highest of praise.

Focaccia is one of their speciality starters – the crisp bread of a pizza base, drenched in top-quality olive oil, with rosemary and garlic not so much sprinkled as snowed on top. But we didn't get to that until Abdul – OK, it may be unusual to have a Moroccan chef running an authentic Italian kitchen but the owners hail from Pakistan, so the whole place is unusual anyway – until Abdul had produced warm, sliced baguette to dip into olive oil, and a bowl of sliced black olives marinated in garlic and coriander. This is what I shall picnic on in the Elysian Fields, assuming I get there. Hell would be watching other people tucking in. I went easy on everything, running a surreptitious finger between waistband and tummy just to prove I still could. I went easy on the wine, too, all too aware that Abdul could emerge from the kitchen at any time and slurp a drop more into my glass.

Steph was too preoccupied with eating to say much. Or was he procrastinating?

Perhaps I'd made a mistake suggesting this place. The music – an Andrea Bocelli CD, I fancied – certainly wouldn't be to his taste. But he looked as though he was enjoying the food. Why was I too shy to ask? It wasn't as though I wasn't used to teenagers. I made a living dealing with teenagers. I could always natter to them. Always. So why not to him? Come on, woman. Just pretend he's one of your tutees. Why isn't he talking?

I waited until our main courses arrived: pasta for him, a chicken risotto rich with saffron and more coriander for me. Abdul produced with a flourish a plate of what he modestly called green salad but included avocado slices and artichoke hearts in the greenery. Then I fixed Steph with one of my more teacherly looks: the one that says, *OK, what's the problem?*

It worked!

He grinned, and had another swig of Coke, ostensibly to clear his throat, before he started.

'It's me mum, see. She gets these ideas, and like it's very hard to get rid of them. On and on she goes. And then – just to keep her happy, 'cause she's quite neat, really – you say OK. Well, Dad and I do.'

'So what have you said OK to?' My stomach clenched.

'To having you round to a meal one night. A dinner party she—'

'Hang on. You mean—' my mouth was smiling so much it could hardly form the words – 'you've . . . that they know . . .'

'Told them last week,' he said, spearing a bit of salad. It

turned out to be an asparagus tip, so he shook it back on to the plate and tried for cucumber instead.

'You might have told me,' I said. But I was laughing and waving my hands around so he didn't take it as more than the most gentle of rebukes.

Except he said, 'Well, it's not the sort of message you can leave on your machine, like, is it? Anyway, I told them about Mike being in Oz and you going out there and so you wouldn't be taking me away from the family at Christmas. Just, you know, so they could feel OK about that. So that's when they said you should come round for dinner. You know, the best plates and the lace tablecloth Grandma made for them.'

Oh God. A Family Occasion. I felt scared already. But I made myself grin and fish for my diary. 'Just tell me when.'

He wanted a lift, not, it transpired, to his parents', but to a friend's flat not far from the Chester Road. I reckoned I could smell pot even from the road, and embarked on my standard homily – low-key, but homily none the less. He took it with the vacuous grin of one who's heard it all before and I itched to box his ears.

'What if the police catch you with it?' God, I was getting old!

'It's in me socks, isn't it? They can make you turn out your pockets but not your socks, see.'

He was impatient to be off, and, after extracting a promise that he would indeed give his mother my firm assurance that I'd love to eat with the family, I let him go. Firm assurance indeed. There was nothing firm or assured about me at the moment. I was bloody terrified, and my hands were accordingly trembling on the wheel. My concentration level was so low I had difficulty remembering what to do when lights turned green, and I soon lost my way on an extensive diversion, ending up in a dead end in Lozells, a district I'd normally have preferred to avoid at that time of night. My arrival caused a little flurry amongst the perfunctorily dressed women there – how on earth did they keep warm between clients? – but when they realised I was a woman they returned to their previous postures. Most of them were black, aged about fourteen or fifteen at a guess, but there was one enormous older white woman with them. I'd have thought there was over twenty stone of her, none of it held in by underwear by the look of her horribly inadequate T-shirt. She looked like a great helpless duck surrounded by little black ducklings. And no doubt someone somewhere had a fetish longing for someone like her.

As I three-point turned, my eye was caught by the light of a massage parlour, Eastern Promise. It wasn't the Turkish delight sort of Eastern Promise. It offered the pleasures of much further east than that, and the sign crudely depicted a form young enough to be paedophile bait. Bastards, wanting to fuck kids who should be at home doing their homework.

The respectable Chinese families I'd come across at William Murdock had a far greater control over their children than comparable English ones. They would have committed wholesale suicide rather than let a child of theirs earn a living like that. So where did the kids come from?

What if they weren't Chinese? Maybe they came from further south and east. And I didn't mean London. Maybe, just ever so maybe, they could be Malaysian or Singaporean. I told myself I was off my head. Wasn't Thailand supposed to be the source of cheap flesh? But however much I argued with myself, I knew I had to mention it to my Piddock Road friends. For protocol's sake, I'd better tell Chris first. I'd phone him when I got in. Except he wouldn't be on the end of the phone, would he? He'd be flying to Toulouse after his mayoral reception. What on earth would he be doing in Toulouse, anyway? Not chasing up important connections between deaths, that was for sure.

I'd got to a set of traffic lights I knew by the time I realised how angry I was. Then this stupid kid roared up alongside me, fouling the night air with his music – so loud my car pulsed with his beat, even though as far as I could see his windows were shut, too. Stupid to try to see him off, of course. I could have had him carving me or tailgating me the whole way home. But I did see him off. Easily. And suddenly, I wasn't angry any more.

'Well, I can hardly go and check them out myself, can I?' I demanded, trying to jiggle the breakfast toast from the toaster as I held the phone. 'I mean, it's not a place I could go and not attract a bit of attention.'

'I suppose we could pull in a favour from Vice,' Peter said lugubriously. Justifiably. I'm a morning person and forget there might be people who don't like to be phoned well before eight. 'Or send a couple of WPCs. Probably not our patch anyway,' he said at last.

'I thought the whole of the city was your oyster,' I said unhelpfully, and put down the phone.

It rang again immediately. Peter. 'There was something *I* wanted to tell *you*! I think I may have found a geek, if you still need one. Give us a bell. Though why you can't have a go yourself I don't know. After all, your time would come cheaper.' His turn to drop the phone.

Cheaper to whom? Certainly not to me! I poked the redial button to tell him just how valuable my time was. But the number was engaged, and I still had my breakfast to sort out.

I regarded the jammed toast with disfavour: I had a horrible feeling it might be an omen.

But if it was, the postman might have brought me a good omen to counter it. A Jiffy bag smothered in Australian stamps. A cassette from Mike! He'd even typed the envelope to make sure the postman could read it.

He'd typed the address. Why should Mike type my address?

Very cold, shaking more than I knew was safe, I put it down with the utmost care on the kitchen table. Thinking calmly and carefully doesn't always come easily to me. Especially when what could be a letter bomb is sitting within blasting distance. But it had better come now. I could phone Peter, and have a bomb disposal team roaring round the suburbs doing high-tech things to make it safe – a euphemism for blowing it up. Or I could phone Mike. I phoned, watching with interest the way my hands were jigging round. But they were firm enough to dial correctly, and my voice firm enough to ask for him to be fetched. I'd phone back in the five minutes the voice at the other end suggested.

He was as breathless as me, and not pleased to be disturbed, even by me, though it was his voice, not his words that gave him away.

Trying hard to sound sweetly reasonable and reasonably assertive, I explained about once having had a letter bomb before. Now I had this unexplained parcel from Australia, with no familiar handwriting on it.

'It's not from me,' he said positively. 'Have a look at the postmark.'

'I already have. It's so blurred as to be indistinguishable.'

'Get the police,' he said, 'and get yourself down here the minute you can. OK?' If there was still anger in his voice it wasn't for me any longer, as his next few sentences made abundantly clear.

If I'd expected armoured cars, I was disappointed. In any case, what was the point, without Aggie to share the drama? But the whole operation, initiated by Peter, who was quick to recognise the terror in my voice and instigated everything, was conducted with friendly efficiency. A couple of rapid response cars had turned up, bearing, amongst others, a capable young woman who peered at the packet from a sensible distance. At last she called for a large black bin filled with what looked like polystyrene.

She slid the package into it, a sort of lethal bran tub. 'My

bomb box,' she said. 'Just in case it's a letter bomb.' She cast
a scathing look at the bloke who said she was probably about
to dispose of some black lacy undies my bloke had been too
embarrassed to admit to sending.

It was a hope I shared.

'What I want to do,' said Peter, carrying mugs of tradition-
ally hot, sweet tea into my living room, 'is to go quietly and
methodically through the people who know Mike's in Australia
and the people who might want to shut you up. Car vandalised;
now this – who've you offended? Hey, come on, Sophie: this
isn't like you!'

Nor was it. I don't normally shake uncontrollably. I can
usually deal with a bit of stress. I tried to drink the tea but
found it sloshing over my carpet and my skirt. I was furious
with myself for being like this, and on the way to being furious
with Peter for being so calm and efficient.

The phone rang. Mike, furious with me for not phoning
back to say what was going on. Calmly and efficiently I burst
into tears. They flooded down my nose, dripping off my
chin. Eventually Peter took the phone from me and explained
succinctly that all was well. 'All we know at the moment is
that it's a suspect package. That's all.'

I couldn't hear Mike's reply.

Peter said, with some of the authority I was used to in
Chris, 'I don't think she *can* just drop everything. Can you
imagine her giving up just now? Hang on, Mike – can you
really imagine her doing that?'

A rumble from Mike.

'Of course it's not sensible. It's foolhardy and brave and a lot
of other things. That's why you love the woman, isn't it?'

It appeared that it was. Back on the line, I told him to go
back to bed and stop worrying about me – he could take some
of those homeopathic sleeping pills I'd given him, couldn't he?
And I'd be with him the moment I could.

All this untoward activity had probably agitated Ivo, so I

fished him out, soothing his nice snuggly fur and treating him to biscuit. Peter watched without enthusiasm, and declined when I offered to let him hold him. Ivo took the rejection insouciantly enough, especially when consoled with a kitchen towel inner tube. He went down it outside, down it inside a couple of times, and finally, having exhausted its architectural possibilities, settled down for a good shred. That done, he made frantic but futile efforts to clamber into the fruit bowl: eventually, frustrated by the steepness of the glass sides, he sulked. I popped him back into his residence, adjusting his name label, and fed him a grape as consolation. He turned his back on it: he no doubt wanted a whole pear.

The tea had gone cold, but was altogether more stable in the mug.

It was an impossible task we had, of course. Who didn't know that Mike was in Oz?

'But how many people know you and Mike are together? He may be the media's blue-eyed boy, but even the *Sun* doesn't seem to have got on to you yet.'

'Only a matter of time,' I said dourly, 'after all that publicity last summer.'

'Half the papers probably still think you're having it off with that black guy.'

'The one that's young enough to be my son,' I agreed. 'Well, with a bit of luck, by the time Winston's experienced enough to be in the England team, Mike and I will be safely married.' I bit my lip. 'And you don't pass that on to Chris. He deserves to hear it from me.'

'Point taken,' Peter said, flipping his page imperturbably. 'Any road, as you people up here say, we've got a nice little list.'

'*They'll none of them be missed,*' I sang. But it seemed Peter wasn't into Gilbert and Sullivan.

He stood up. 'I know where I'd place my bets.'

'At UWM,' I said. 'Got to be, hasn't it? Which reminds me, Peter – God knows why I didn't think of this before – I did see someone I know jogging near Carla's narrow boat. About ten days ago. Friday, I think. I'd just had a sandwich lunch with Chris, as it happens, so he should be able to settle the date. I saw one of my fellow students. Jago. Jago Calvin.'

Chapter Twenty-one

I'd insisted on going into UWM to teach my English Language class, convincing Peter that I really was off my head. But I was afraid if I didn't go in, the impulse, growing every minute, to turn my back on the place and take up needlework, would overwhelm me. But I did accept Peter's offer of a lift in, and ultimately a lift back. It wasn't, as he said, far out of his way, and he liked the idea of regular up-dates. My first opinion of him, way back in the summer, was of a prickly, indeed hostile, man. Now he provided solid, kind support.

'This Calvin bloke: do you really think he could have had anything to do with Pentowski's death?'

'On the contrary, I'd have thought he had everything to gain from keeping her alive. She had information he wanted. Her thesis would have provided good source material, had Mike been able to find a copy.'

'Remind me: why did Mike need to be involved?'

I thought I'd been all over this once. 'Because she told us all the extant copies in England had been destroyed in a house fire that destroyed all her other possessions, too. Everything. So Mike – conveniently in Melbourne – checked out all three universities and found—'

'Nothing. Right. No doctoral thesis, nor evidence of her having been there. OK. And then she gets anxious that some-one's going to rumble her – assuming there's anything to rumble, not just a simple change of name. She takes to the

189

booze again – all too easy for an alcoholic – gets pissed and trips. Only SOCO find – and I'd have told you earlier, if we hadn't had all that kerfuffle – a mark on each side of the hull.'

'This has been worrying me. If someone tripped her with string or whatever, then what did they attach it to? There's no convenient bits of wood on that hull.'

'Quite. Strong adhesive tape. On the outside of the hull. Then pull it off and bingo, off comes a bit of rust. I'm afraid the whole thing needed a lick of paint. Hey, SOCO have finished now: you could come and have a quick shufty if you like.'

It would certainly put off the evil hour of going into UWM. But my brain was beginning to unfog a little.

'I've got my class! Plus there's something at UWM I want to give you. And something else I want you to check up on. In Carla's room.'

'That list of students' names,' he said.

If Peter had expected to see a couple of police cars gracing the car park, he didn't show it.

'Just hang on here,' he said, slamming the car door behind him and striding over to a WPC just getting into one of them. After a few moments, he strode back again. Chris would have been proud of that stride.

'Outbreak of vandalism. Some kids seem to have got in here last night and had the time of their lives. Fortunately Security heard something and stopped them.'

Not before they'd had a field day. There was spray paint all over the foyer, and scuff marks where bins had been kicked against walls.

'Have they attacked anywhere else?' I asked, my stomach already clenching against the reply I knew was coming.

'Some corridors. Several rooms. Apparently at random.'

'You believe that?'

190

'Perhaps they'd been left unlocked. Anyway, let's go see, shall we?'

We set off briskly.

'Hang on,' I said. 'This isn't a good idea. If I'm to be your snout, the less we're seen together the better.'

'Point taken. But you're not to go swanning round on buses trying to get home. Oh, Chris has told me all about you and your independence, love. When you want to go home, you give me a bell down at Piddock Road.'

'You've got work to do.'

'And you've got a skin to keep in one piece. And I'm answerable to Chris for that skin.'

Was he indeed! 'OK. I'll phone. And if I can't reach you then—'

'You'll hop in a minicab and come straight to Piddock Road. OK?'

'OK.'

The first person I ran into was Tom Bowen, looking distressed and dishevelled. 'Look at this, Sophie! Animals! Animals, pure and simple. You should see my room. Here, come and look.' He turned and led the way, stopping outside his door and leaning against the jamb, head against an upraised arm. He pushed the door open with his foot. 'They've cancelled all today's classes, so we can deal with our respective messes.'

It looked like the Blue Peter set while they were still at the experimental stage with their sticky-backed plastic: chairs tipped over, papers strewn everywhere and sticky-tape trailing like lianas. He picked up a flowerpot that had once held some of his geranium cuttings and dropped it again.

'Come on,' I said, 'at least we can rescue your pots.' I gathered and stacked half a dozen and thrust them into his hands. I shoved the cuttings themselves into couple of large envelopes. It wouldn't take him long to repot them, and they were too healthy to throw away. 'And provided we talk

191

dissertation, I'll give you a hand sorting out and refiling your papers. The cabinet's still usable, is it?'

He shook his head. 'I don't know. Oh, Sophie, a lifetime's work.'

'Who else have they done over?'

'Quite a few, I think. A couple of staff offices; the post-graduate work-room – haven't you seen it yet?'

'I've only just come in.'

He took in my coat and scarf for the first time.

'I had some car problems,' I said, not quite lying. Not if you took the story far enough back.

He nodded, uninterested, and bent to pick up a sheet of paper.

'I'd better go and look.' I might have lost things more recent than the 1988 exam papers under my left foot.

'I'll come with you.' He smiled kindly. 'I hope all your dissertation material was safe at home.'

Oddly enough it was, in duplicate, at least. But there was enough here for me to shake my head, as if afraid of what I was expecting. To my irritation, my chest was getting itchy inside: the vandals had stirred up the dust of ages, which was giving me an asthma attack. Still, if I breathed deeply and relaxed I should be all right.

We walked in silence along the corridor. A burst of red paint on the door told us to expect the worst, as did the sounds of anger and distress within. What I didn't expect was a strong smell of lemons. Jago had his back to us, his shoulders the picture of despair. When he turned to face us, I wondered if he'd actually been crying, so great was the chaos on the floor. 'It's all mixed up, everyone's stuff. And all this damned Sellotape everywhere.' His voice was little more than a whisper.

The vandals had done a good job. Someone had strewn computer disks over the floor. Like the others, I was on my knees scrabbling and bemoaning. But I managed to pull at my drawer. Locked. Still safely locked. Thank God for Chris and his paranoia.

A final wring of my hands and I got to my feet, clutching a selection of floppy disks. I laid them on the work surface. Lola was gently peeling tape from other people's papers.

'What about all our deadlines?' Jago demanded, peeling a throat pastille and balling the wrapper into a bin. 'What'll happen to our deadlines? We can't possibly meet them, not now!'

'We'll sort something out,' Tom said, patting him on the shoulder. 'I promise, we'll sort something out.'

I switched on a computer.

'Look,' rasped Jago, 'this is no time to be doing your own stuff. We're all supposed to be helping everyone else.' He thrust the waste-bin at me. 'Junk those and—'

'Why junk things that might be perfectly OK?' The wheezing no better, I turned my back on him to fish my salbutamol spray from my bag. Two good bursts and I'd be OK. I turned back. 'Look, both these disks are undamaged.' I carried on checking systematically. 'Lola, here are yours. Shall I test yours, Jago, or would you still rather bin them?'

'Sorry. It's this bloody bug.'

'Are you infectious?' Lola sprung up. 'Tonsillitis is the last thing we want now.'

'If it were tonsillitis, it wouldn't be catching,' Jago pointed out. 'But I'm afraid it must be some virus since I had my tonsils out years ago.'

'So when did the symptoms start?' she demanded.

'Thursday night, I think. Yes, I bought my first packet of throat tablets on the way in here on Friday.'

'Friday . . . Today's Tuesday . . . So you're probably not infectious any more,' Tom observed.

'Your disks are healthy enough, anyway,' I said, passing them over.

Jago took them and shoved them back in his drawer without locking it. 'Thanks.'

193

'There doesn't seem to be much of your stuff down here, Sophie,' Lola said.

I patted my drawer. 'It's what comes of working at a tough college,' I said, apologetically but disingenuously. Just to make sure, I unlocked it, checked the contents, and locked it again, pocketing the key.

And then it dawned on me, showing everyone where my stuff lived wasn't the most sensible thing I'd done this week.

Lola motioned me outside with a jerk of her head. 'I don't suppose,' she said, 'that you've managed to enquire about our missing student. No! Of course not! You white liberals make me sick: you pretend to be brothers and sisters to all yet you ignore a real cry for help! And you – I hoped for better things from you! But you're as racist as the lot of them. If it had been a white woman, you'd have been in there, advising her, protecting her. Not a Malaysian or a Singaporean woman. I dare say they all look the same to you!'

I tried not to wince, but hadn't I said almost exactly that to Kathryn – that I couldn't tell them apart? And there was that school of thought that said all white people were unconscious racists. But I didn't want to debate the issue now. This morning had taken more out of me than I liked to admit, and I was afraid I'd either lose my temper completely and say things about her class prejudice I'd almost certainly regret later or – and this was the more likely option – burst into tears.

'Right from the start I've denied any responsibility for this student. You have made things as hard as you could for me when I agreed to help by refusing to identify her. But if you give me the name and address I'll try now. You can come with me if you like.'

'I'm sure you're perfectly aware that as a mere student I am not authorised to receive such information. You sent *me* on a wild-goose chase.' There was no missing the stress on the personal pronoun.

'I'm by no means sure they'll give it to *me*. I couldn't get it yesterday, at any rate. I'll try again, though, shall I? *If* you're prepared to give me her name, that is.'

Shazia Nazir – how strange to be able to attach a name to her after all this time, even if I couldn't attach it to a face yet – lived in Church Lane, on the borders of Handsworth and Handsworth Wood, presumably in one of those huge old family homes now in multi-occupation. Not so far, but not within walking distance.

And I'd left the car at home, hadn't I?

'Sorry,' I said, catching up with Lola halfway through the afternoon. 'We're going to have to take a rain check. I'd forgotten I had a lift here this morning. No car. And I've neither the time nor the energy to wait for buses, not just at the moment.' Not after taking two hours to run Kathryn to earth.

Lola sniffed scornfully at what she didn't hesitate to say was yet another excuse.

'I'd take you out there myself only I have to finish an assignment,' she said. And then, taking me completely aback, she thrust a set of car keys at me. There was a Mercedes fob on the ring. 'Here.'

I goggled. I had to say something. Better ask a sensible question: 'Insurance?'

'Fully comprehensive. And, before you seek yet another excuse, there is some petrol in the tank.'

There weren't many Mercedes in the car park, and none juggling registration letters to form the nearest they could get to LOLA. It was a make of car I'd never driven before. I slid on to the driving seat. Hmm.

Oh, there was a lot to be said for being rich, wasn't there? Much as I liked the little Fiesta, it wasn't quite in this league.

Tempted as I was to take it a particularly circuitous route to

Handsworth Wood – via Barr Beacon, perhaps – I suspected Lola would have a very good idea how many miles were on the clock, particularly as there were so few, and confined myself to the task in hand.

Despite the big car, I didn't have the temerity to park on a double yellow. Church Lane is part of Birmingham's Outer Circle route, and the slightest obstruction quickly clots the traffic for miles in every direction. So I found a side road, and started hunting on foot.

There are times when I regret my tendency to act first and think second. This was one of them. What on earth was I doing, in the dying light of this cold and increasingly wet December afternoon wandering round on my own, without telling Peter where I was and what I was doing? And after receiving a possible letter bomb – after an all-too-definite attack on my own car?

Pulling my shoulders back, I told myself off. All I was doing was checking out a student and the reasons for her absence.

I was so busy arguing with myself, I walked past the house number I was looking for, and had to turn back. And then realised why I'd walked past it. Because it didn't have a number at all, at least not on the once impressive, stuccoed gateposts. What it did have, however, was a small brass plaque. Even with the drizzle now blurring everything, I didn't need reading glasses to see the words 'UNIVERSITY COLLEGE OF THE WEST MIDLANDS'.

Chapter Twenty-two

Now, I'd been teaching in Birmingham for – my God, was it really fourteen years? – and I'd been steering students into higher education for at least the last five or six. So I reckoned I knew most there was to know about higher education establishments in the area. I could probably do a *Mastermind* stint on them. Which universities wanted what grades. Which unis were best for what subjects. Which – yes, which existed. Anywhere in the country. Certainly anywhere in the West Midlands. I could even reel off phone numbers for most of them from memory.

So how come I didn't know anything about the University College of the West Midlands? Repeat, *anything*. Despite all the alarums and excursions of the day, despite the cold and the rain, this was something I'd have to have a look at.

The 'college' building was typical of the area: once grand, its stucco was now slightly the worse for wear, though it was by no means dilapidated. It stood foursquare, symmetrical, an Edwardian version of Regency. There was a shallow flight of stairs to the front door, recently painted, and a selection of plastic doorbells, suggesting that multi-occupation had been part of its history – might still be, in fact. In a brass surround set into the stone, what was probably the original bell, helpfully marked Press. I applied a thumb.

Nothing.

I peered at the individual plastic ones: most were anonymous, and no Shazia Nazir amongst the few that weren't. I pressed one at random.

Nothing.

I could always run up and down the whole lot, as if playing a scale. Controlling myself, and the vision of a dozen irate heads appearing from the windows, I tried one more. Then another.

Nothing.

The rain came on more heavily, somewhere a gutter dripped, and I headed for the warmth, and what I hoped was the safety, of the Merc. Locking myself in – paranoia or not – I set off back to UWM, thinking hard enough to miss a turning. So I was forced, absolutely forced, to take a circuitous route and enjoy the delectable vehicle for a few more minutes.

Being a lecturer was never going to make me rich. Perhaps redundancy was just the incentive I needed to make me seek my fortune in another way. Offhand, though, I couldn't imagine any career move that would bring in enough dosh for a car like this.

At last I parked in the space I'd vacated an hour ago. Lola had left her mobile phone on her passenger seat, stupid woman. Didn't she know the statistics for theft from cars in this area? Before I locked the car, I stowed it in the glove compartment.

There was no one in the spectacularly tidy work-room, so I picked up the pay phone. Peter answered first ring.

'I was just going to phone to find out what had happened to you,' he said, his voice sharp. 'Where are you?'

I explained. 'I'm fine. And I've got something to show you.'

'*I've* got something to show *you*,' he said. 'Stay where you are.' He cut the connection.

I'm sure he expected me to sit in the work-room and wait for him, but my stomach was now bleating quite pitifully that it hadn't had lunch and that it hurt. I sprinted off to the refectory to buy milk and chocolate biscuits, which I was consuming at my desk with an expression of beatific innocence when he thundered on the door.

To my surprise he took in the situation at a glance. 'Not surprising your tum's bad, after this morning.'

'I'll live,' I said, more in hope than expectation. Particularly when I still had to tell him how I'd spent the afternoon.

'What do you want to show me?' he asked, as if on cue.

'It'll wait. What about you?'

'Follow me.'

I did. To Carla's room.

'Not just locked, but police-sealed,' Peter said. 'And they still get in. That annoys me.' He nodded to a glum middle-aged constable and pushed open the door.

'I've a terrible feeling,' I said, peering over his arm, 'that trashing this was the object of the whole exercise.'

'What on earth do you mean?'

I shook my head, as if to settle the ideas into some sort of shape. 'Carla tells us she's got no past. Her records disappear from the paper files. The computer files become inaccessible. She dies, apparently by accident. Only it isn't. Her room is done over, apparently at random.'

'Only it isn't? Maybe. But why do everyone else's?'

'Cover?'

'For whom?'

'For whoever didn't want me to get hold of some information.'

'That list. The entry qualifications.'

'That's right,' I said. At least I wouldn't be sorting that chaos out. It'd be a job for some poor devil from SOCO, wouldn't it?

'Now, what have you got to show me?'

The notice that had originally been stuck on Carla's door. 'Follow me,' I said, hoping that my brave gesture to my locked drawer hadn't provoked someone into seeing how easily they could open it.

I heaved a sigh: it was still locked. But that didn't mean someone hadn't had a go at it. I pointed at the faint scratches, and let Peter have a look.

'Did they succeed?' was all he said.

I turned the key. The lock clicked sweetly enough, and out came the drawer, as I'd left it, even to the scrumpled note. Peter took it doubtfully. It smelt of oranges.

'Where did you find this?'

'I went fossicking in the bins,' I said.

'I suppose that's another of your Black Country words,' he said.

'I don't think so. Whatever it is, I've always used it. And you must admit, it's graphic.' I mimed a furtive dip and sift. 'There you are: to fossick.'

He nodded, already bored with the word and more interested in the paper.

'Why bother to "fossick" for this?'

'You know: this wretched nose of mine.' We both tactfully avoided mentioning the word 'smell'.

'Dare say it'll be covered in prints. The paper, not your nose.'

'Be more interesting if it weren't,' I said.

I saved my other find till we started off for home.

'You wouldn't mind going via Handsworth Wood, would you?' I asked.

He plainly did mind. It was gone six, he no doubt had a pile of paperwork still to complete, it was cold and wet and, as far as I knew, he hadn't had any lunch, either. His shoulders, his neck, the set of his jaw shouted in protest. He said nothing, however, but with the air of someone who wouldn't speak lest he lost his temper good and hard. He turned the car towards the city.

'Any particular part?'

'Outer Circle. And just keep on going.'

'Till you say when?'

'Till I say when.'

His windscreen hadn't had a proper clean for a couple of days: the wipers smeared road grease backwards and forwards. I was glad when I could tell him to stop.

'You see that big gateway? To your left? Just pull in there.'

He obeyed in the same tense silence. We got out of the car in silence. It was only when I walked away from the house, back to the gate pillar, that he uttered a tight, 'For crying out loud!'

But when I stopped and pointed he didn't moan any more. His, 'Well, well, well,' was full of interest.

We walked up to the front door together. This time there were lights on in a number of rooms. We could see unshaded light bulbs. The curtains, if drawn, looked skimpy, barely meeting in the middle.

'Does this look to you like a college?' he asked.

'Not the administration block,' I said, to be rewarded by a short laugh. 'Or even teaching rooms.'

'Hall of residence?' he pursued.

'Not exactly the Ritz. But then, student accommodation's never the Ritz.'

'No,' he said unexpectedly, 'but it's usually cheap conference standard. This is my second marriage. I've got twins at university. The universities need to rent their halls out to make money from Saga holidays – that sort of thing,' he added. 'Shall we see who's in?'

I gestured. 'After you, Claude.'

There was still no response from the original bell, but the first plastic one he tried produced, after a while, the sound of footsteps and the slow opening of the door.

One of my students. Definitely. A Chinese woman who had been there from week one. Christabel Ho.

'Hello, Christabel,' I said. 'Is Shazia Nazir in?'

201

'This no' her bell.' She leant round and pressed one. 'There. Tha' her bell.' She made to withdraw, but Peter stepped forward.

'Hang on, miss. Do you live here?'

She gave him the sort of look that any intelligent person might give someone asking a patently stupid question.

'I mean, do you live here or study here?'

'Live.'

'OK. So, who's your landlord?'

'The university, of course,' she said. 'Sophie, who is this man?'

'A friend of mine, Peter Kirby. We were looking for Shazia.'

'If she were in, she would have come down by now.'

Unanswerable.

'You mus' excuse mc. I'm in a hurry. I have to go ou'.' She withdrew, shutting the door in our faces.

We returned to the car.

'Not exactly thinking on our feet there, were we?' I said.

'What the hell's going on?' He slammed the door with more than necessary force. 'I mean, is it part of the university or not?'

'You mean, there's a misprint or whatever on the sign? Surely someone would have noticed.' I spared him my encyclopaedic knowledge of higher education in the area. For the moment, at least. 'Hang on a minute.' I got out of the car for one more look.

He waited.

I refrained from doing a jig. 'No,' I said, getting back in. 'No UWM logo. A coat of arms, though. Not unlike Birmingham University's,' I hinted.

'Fishy or what?'

'No, a mermaid.'

He looked blank. As well he might.

I explained, 'I'd say they'd lifted it from Birmingham

202

University's coat of arms. The other half's different. More like that man from Birmingham's coat of arms. Industrial Man. Almost looks as if someone's scanned images of both into a computer and produced a hybrid.'

'Now why should someone want to do that?' It was clearly a rhetorical question: he leant forward to start the car. 'Funny thing,' he said. 'For all your Christabel – where do these people get their names? – claimed she was in a hurry to go out, I haven't seen her leave the building, have you?'

'Nope. Unless there's a tradesman's entrance round the back.' That was a rhetorical suggestion, if such an oratorical device exists.

'Tell you what,' he said, 'my stomach's flapping against my backbone. Let's go and have a bite in the canteen and talk this lot through. I'll phone my wife to tell her I'll be a bit late.'

'I may have to make you later still. If we pass a chemist's that's still open, would you mind stopping? My stomach's being silly.'

He shot me a hard look, and headed, as if on some radar link, to a Lloyd's. It was easier to buy my usual antacid in tablet form – less efficient, but more portable.

'All right?' he asked.

I was pulling a face. 'It's just the flavour – I wasn't expecting lemon.'

'So long as it does you good.'

'So long as it does me good,' I agreed.

In the event he must have been much later than he told his wife. We were in the Piddock Road canteen tucking into a fry-up – OK, stupid, considering the state of my tum, but I always did like comfort food and Chris wasn't there to disapprove – when a young WPC hastened up to us.

'Gaffer,' she said, 'this may be nothing to do with you, but I thought you ought to know. There's a report of a suicide. No, not our patch—'

Peter was on his feet. 'But another young woman?'

'Right. Another Malay. Handsworth Wood.'

I was on mine. Please God, not Shazia Nazir. A deep breath told me I was being really silly to make such a deduction. I blamed all Lola's dark suspicions. 'Not at the University College of the West Midlands?' I asked, knowing I shouldn't.

The young woman looked from me to Peter.

He shrugged. 'Confidential, Sophie. And you won't hear the answer if I ask the question again, will you?'

I shook my head.

'Multi-occupied house—'

My God! I clutched my stomach.

But the address she gave was not Church Lane.

Peter looked at me with what might have been amusement. 'You and Harvinder and your coincidences! Even so, I think I'll talk to the investigating officer. Look, Carol, can you get Sophie a ride home?'

'I can take a taxi.'

'No way. Sort it, Carol, will you?'

'Gaffer.'

She ended up taking me herself, of course. We talked careers and bosses and lack of time to live our lives. She insisted on coming into my house to check there wasn't a man under the bed, fed Ivo a large crumb and went on her way.

Since I'd had no more than a quarter of my supper, it seemed sensible to top up. Sweet, I wanted a sweet. And one that wasn't too silly. I was just beating the batter for pancakes when the phone went.

No, I did not want double-glazing.

But the call drew my attention to the answerphone. One message. Aggie. Would I phone her.

Oh dear. I did hope things weren't going pear-shaped already. I gave the batter one final whack and left it to smooth itself out.

'I'm really enjoying myself,' she said. 'Luce's got this big-screen telly. Lovely. I shall have one myself when I get my new place. And I'm going round the flats tomorrow, and the bungalows on Thursday. Now, what I wanted to say was this. That smell. You know. That man.'

My Friday visitor.

'I told you he didn't smell right.'

'No oil?'

'Right. Now, I'll tell you what he did smell of. Lemons. How about that?'

'Lemons!'

'Like them lemon sherbets we used to have in the old days.'

I could feel my brain making connections. Lemons . . . antacid tablets . . . Tom Bowen.

'That's brilliant, Aggie,' I said. 'Thanks!' I wouldn't tell her about the footprints. Nor about today's post. 'Now, are you keeping warm?'

She dropped her voice to a conspiratorial wheeze. 'Only I've found where you change the temperature, see? And you know what, Luce hasn't noticed!'

I bet Lucy had – and wouldn't dare say anything. But I let it pass. I told her her house was still in one piece, assured her I was looking after myself, and returned to my pancakes. And the one thing I hadn't got in the house was a fresh lemon.

I was just going to bed when the phone rang. A woman identified herself as someone from Forensics.

I stiffened.

She must have picked it up from my voice. 'Would you like to have my number so you can phone me back? Or get Peter Kirby to? Only it's good news, and I thought you'd like to know before I did the official report.'

'You're still working at this time of night?'

'I wanted to get it sorted. But the report can wait till

tomorrow. Your bomb. Relatively harmless. Not explosive. A stink bomb. Unpleasant, but harmless unless you suffer from asthma or other respiratory troubles. It'd make your house a bit uninhabitable, of course.'

So, good news. Except, of course, given my lungs, it might be bad news. Apart from today, had I ever used my asthma spray at UWM? And if I had, who had seen me?

Chapter Twenty-three

'It's no good, is it, Ivo, all this pissing around?'

Holding his peanut at arm's length, he looked mildly offended by my language.

'This business needs more than one woman and a gerbil. It needs the resources of the West Midlands Police, properly co-ordinated, and not at the mercy of Chris and his hormones or even Chris and his budget.'

Ivo left the husk where it fell and looked hopefully for more. Since a kitchen table isn't a natural habitat for peanuts, he looked in vain. He turned his attention to the fruit bowl, then, once again defeated by the steep sides, stared at the apple I was eating.

'Wait for the core,' I said. 'And don't eat too much of that or you'll get bellyache.' To temper the words, I scooped him up and gave him a comforting nuzzle. He responded by first licking and then chewing my fingers. Apple juice. And blood. I shook him off, howling. And then wondered if I'd been too rough. I broke off a sliver of apple, but he turned his back on it and proceeded to wash parts of his anatomy best washed in decent privacy.

'What I really need to do is put all this down on paper,' I said. 'Brainstorm myself.'

'No, you don't,' he said, 'you need to put me back in my nice warm home, go to bed, and dream of Mike.'

Such powers of thought transference amazed me. Agreeing,

I scooped him back into his aquarium, made sure the lid was securely fastened, checked all the doors and windows, set the burglar alarm, and did as I was told. Except the dreams of Mike left me sad and lonely in what I'd come to regard as his half of my bed.

To my surprise, Peter Kirby appeared on my doorstep at 7.27 a.m. He was looking remarkably similar to how I felt. And saying much the same as I'd been saying to Ivo. That it was time for a co-ordinated attack on the whole business. Chris was due back at midday: he proposed to ask him to convene a meeting as soon as he'd got his head round returning to Smethwick. In the meantime, Peter'd get over to Forensics the notice that I'd retrieved from the bin near Carla's door, and he'd chase the SOCOs to see if that list of entry results was still in Carla's room. I forebore to ask why he hadn't already done both.

And then, halfway through his second round of toast, he put his head down on my kitchen table and wept. Just like that. I don't know how long I stood helplessly wishing there were something I could say or do. There'd been no emotional outburst – anger or anything else – to warn me. And – I still didn't quite see us as friends – I didn't know how to react.

Ivo paused in his destruction of a loo roll inner, looked at me as if he didn't know why I didn't do something, and then continued, his enthusiasm apparently unabated.

I poured coffee, grabbed kitchen roll which I thrust into Peter's free hand, and eventually did what I should have done in the first place, hugged him.

'She's locked me out. She's left me,' he said at last. 'Kaput. All over. Just like that. Says it was better living on her own knowing she was living on her own than living on her own thinking she was living with me. I'm never there, she says—'

God, and it was my fault he'd been home so late last night!

'—and when I am home I'm worrying about work. Or asleep. Never take her out. No sort of husband to her.'

On the briefest of acquaintances with his wife, I couldn't see why anyone would want to be with her in the first place, but I pushed such unsisterly thoughts away. If the man loved her, then spelling them out wouldn't do any good, would it?

With a great sigh, he pulled himself free from me.

'I'm sorry.'

'No problem. I'm just sorry this has happened to you.' Then, aware how painfully inadequate I was being, I said things about talking to Welfare – it sounded as if his police hours and responsibilities had been at least part of the problem – and getting time off to see if their relationship could be repaired.

'Repaired? She's changed the locks.'

He'd come, he said eventually, to offer me a lift. But today I was going in a different direction, heading for the Oldbury campus, where I was going to closet myself with Luke in an attempt to sort out the files business – if no one had sorted them already, that is. I had been known to hack, in my time, but that was then, and in quite different circumstances. I'd rather not do it again. But I would if I had to, just to have something positive to show Chris on his return. Something more solid, less ephemeral, than the smell of lemons.

Luke seemed pleased enough to see me, but, he told me, there was someone working on the computer even as we spoke. And he'd got a couple of work experience students to sift through all the paper files, putting them in order.

'If they know their alphabet, that is,' he said gloomily.

'This isn't what you're supposed to do with work experience students,' I protested, forgetting myself. 'You're supposed to give them experience of the real world of work. Asking them to do valid tasks and evaluating their performance. Then you discuss all this with their tutor.' Which once, a lifetime ago, I'd been for William Murdock students.

'This is the real world of work. This is an emergency. I spent twenty minutes working with them. It wouldn't hurt you to, would it? There are an awful lot of files to check! Unless you want to get under the geek's feet.'

'Luke, it's not my job to do either. But since I owe you one I'll help the geek. My days of playing with dusty files are over. Full stop.'

The geek wasn't the pasty-faced overweight nerd I'd expected. She was a business-suited woman not long out of university, fresh-complexioned and with an excellent figure that brought home to me my own recent lack of weight-training. She welcomed me affably enough, and gave me a rundown of her efforts so far. 'Whoever fixed this program knew their computers. It was a very sophisticated bit of work. I can't sort it.'

There was nothing I could add. 'So . . . ?'

'I'll take the computer back to the lab. At least they'll be able to use other computers on the system. It's just they won't be able to access those records.'

Feeling flat as ink, I went off in search of Luke, who was nowhere to be seen. I ran him to earth eventually, as I should have predicted, with the work experience students. The room was full of the sort of desks that I associated with exam rooms. Each had a letter of the alphabet on a sheet of paper and a large and unstable pile of brown card staff record folders. Luke was now checking that the files were in true alphabetical order, briefly inspecting the contents of each as he went.

'Thanks, kids,' he said. 'You go and get yourselves cleaned up—' they were indeed pretty dusty – 'and then get yourself something from the canteen.' He slipped them a couple of what looked like pound coins each. 'I thought you'd prefer me to say this in privacy,' he added after they'd gone. 'Carla Pentowski's gone as if she'd never existed. Someone's removed her from

210

the pay-roll program too. And her classes have disappeared from the timetable.'

'It happened to her once before,' I said. 'She had a house fire – lost everything.'

'That,' he said, 'was while she was alive. Doing it now, now she's dead!' His voice rang with a despair quite out of proportion to the case. 'Eliminating her, expunging her from the face of the earth!'

For the second time this morning, I was shocked by the force of a man's emotion. To me, Luke's was quite OTT. But then, I hadn't had all my family and all my family records destroyed. What could I say that was to the point? Very little. I sat down, waiting for his paroxysm to subside, and then said, as coolly as I could manage without sounding callous, 'It doesn't make sense, does it? If she'd wanted to disappear, it would have made eminent sense. If she'd been planning to do a bunk. If she had something major to hide. Say, she wanted to start a new life – as she says she once had to do before – then this might make sense. But if someone – if someone killed her, then it wouldn't make sense.' Bang went my promise to Chris of confidentiality.

Luke pulled a chair up and sat down not quite facing me. 'Did someone kill her?'

I hated telling Luke anything other than the whole truth. 'The possibility hasn't been dismissed, as far as I know,' I said, hiding behind police jargon.

He shrugged. 'Maybe we could use a coffee. If you want to clean up, the ladies' is just across the corridor from my room.'

'My advice to you,' said Luke, five minutes later, proffering biscuits to go with the excellent filtered coffee, 'would be to get on the next plane to Australia. The very next one. Go and get your bloke to rub sun tan oil on to your back. From what you say there's stuff going on in your life I wouldn't want to be involved in, I can tell you, if I could avoid it. Your car, your house, your notes.' He ticked them off on his fingers. 'What next? And now there's problems here. What if you're the next one to disappear? Your file, your teaching, your life! Just pack your bag and go!' He pushed away from his desk and prowled round the room. 'What's stopping you? Oh, I know what that chin means. It means you'll listen and nod, nod and listen, and then do exactly what you meant to do in the first place. Tell me, why stay if you're at risk?'

'It's a matter of . . . of honour, isn't it? Not letting go.'

'Pride!'

I shifted. 'Apart from anything else, I'm cooking a big supper for Tom Bowen on Friday. And my flight's only a few days after that. In fact, I've already got my cases out and there's a growing list of what I need right by my bed. Tickets. Passport. All I've got to do is arrange with Shahida when my lodger moves in with them.'

'You're not leaving him the run of the house then.'

'Certainly not! Now, Luke, I have to go. I'm missing classes and lectures all over the place. Somehow I don't think the university would see this as justifying an extension!'

'Get yourself a doctor's note – stress.'

I shook my head. 'I've got to complete the course this year. I couldn't afford another year off or another year's fees. Oh,' I added, 'you don't know what part-time teachers' contracts happen to look like, do you?'

'Know what they look like? My department *generates* them, Sophie.'

'How do you mean?'

He leant across to tap my temple with his knuckle. 'Hello? Anyone in there? Generate – we tell the computer what to print on them.'

'The computer prints them . . . ? I wonder why mine was hand-written.'

'Because some lecturer forgot there was a proper system

and that he or she should follow it. Happened all the time last year. I thought people would have got used to it by now.' He shrugged. 'Time to start worrying is if you don't get paid!'

It took more self-denial than I usually manage to drive past Piddock Road without checking to see if Chris's car was back in the car park. But I did. I even went along to the afternoon lecture and seminar as if nothing at all was bugging me. But I did commit that greatest of twentieth-century solecisms: as I left the work-room and its phone, I switched on my mobile phone on. Lecture room or not, if Chris wanted to talk to me, about my letter bomb or about anything else, this time I wasn't going to play hard to get.

Chapter Twenty-four

'My mate said it was just like in that book,' a young constable was saying. 'One we did at school. This big stain on the ceiling. Blood red.'

'And are we to suppose the stain was in the shape of the Ace of Hearts?' asked Chris. He'd phoned me – just *after* the seminar! – to invite me for a quick bite before I headed home. We were just on our way out when someone inside the CID room called him in. I followed, making myself invisible. Hearing this conversation, I wished myself elsewhere. OK, police officers had to find ways of dealing with the dreadful things they saw and had to deal with. But I had a feeling I wasn't going to enjoy the next few minutes.

'The President of the Immortals, sir. That was who was to blame in this book – *Tess*.'

I didn't rate this lad's chances. The Black Country is not known for its appreciation of the arts, not amongst its coppers, at any rate.

'Only in this case – which is, incidentally?' Chris prompted.

'That wench that topped herself, the foreign wench. Oh, not this patch, sir.'

'What a relief!'

'My mates Iqbal and Ted were the first ones on the scene, sir. A young lady like that, slitting her wrists. What a horrible way to go. Watching your own life ebb away.' The poor kid was near to tears.

'Not much fun for the poor bastard in the room underneath, watching his ceiling slowly change colour!' someone put in.

Oh dear, here it came.

'Must have thought it was the folk from that *Changing Rooms* programme on telly arriving without warning.'

'Might not have been them then, but they'll sure as hell need them now!'

'Unless they can get a few more wenches to top themselves to give it a nice uniform finish.'

'*Uniform!* Fucking hell . . .'

We'd left them to it soon after that. All the evidence, including a neatly written note, pointed to suicide, and, moreover, as the kid had pointed out, a suicide not on Chris's patch. I resolved to say nothing. Not unless I had to, at least. Perhaps I wouldn't need to. Chris turned back the way we had come. He stopped a couple of yards along the corridor. 'I suppose you and Harvinder would call that another of your coincidences.'

'It is a coincidence, that's indisputable,' I agreed.

He gave a short laugh. 'Which means you're convinced it's not. And – OK . . .'

So we made our way not to some convenient pub, or even the canteen, but back to Chris's room, where, as he'd predicted, Bridget had left enough food for an army. 'She doesn't think the French know anything about cooking,' he said, pushing a clingfilmed plate of sandwiches towards me. 'Do you fancy a cuppa?'

'Bridget would kill me if I let you make it.' I left my things in his room and pottered off. It didn't take me long to make a brew much more the puny strength I preferred. Returning with a tray, I shut the door with a shove of my bum.

The sandwiches looked excellent, well-filled with lots of cheese and what looked like home-made chutney. Mustn't get any on the Table, though; and better make sure I'd dripped no tea on it either.

I pulled a chair over to his desk, so we were facing each other, and took my first mouthful.

'So what about all these coincidences, Chris?' I asked.

'They still may be coincidences. But,' he added with a sudden smile, 'I'm going to suggest to the Chief Constable that all these incidents ought to be pulled together in a team under one officer. Sadly, and absolutely between you and me,' he said, pausing to make sure I had indeed closed the door, 'I don't think Peter ought to be part of that team. Not with his present problems.'

'He and Harvinder know more about the incidents than anyone else. Apart from you.'

'And you can't pull an Operational Commander out, not when he's got a whole sector to run. What do you suggest?' He sat back wearily.

I scrutinised him for the slightest hint of sarcasm. I found only a face as serious as it was tired, the face of a man approaching middle age sharing problems with a friend.

Who was certainly not approaching middle age.

Putting the sandwich plate on a spare patch of desk, I leant back. Yes, I was tired, too. The temptation to take Luke's advice was stronger than I cared to admit. What about just hopping off on a convenient plane? None of this was my problem.

'I think you have to talk to Peter. Ask Peter what he wants to do. Maybe talk to Sheila—'

'Me!'

'You're his boss,' I said.

'But you're a friend of Peter's. And you know Sheila—'

'I may have met her but I'm certainly not a friend of hers. I'm not even sure I'm a friend of Peter's. Cautious acquaintances, more like.'

'Why should he turn to you if he doesn't think you're a friend?'

'OK. So he's defined me as his friend. Does that endear me

to his wife? No. You've got a team of welfare people ready and eager to do the biz.'

'And you're both college lecturers.'

I read this lovely book by Georgette Heyer when I was younger – not the sort of thing I'd admit to a young constable who knew his Hardy, but a classic in its way. Heyer described a character as 'faint but pursuing'. The phrase summed up Chris wonderfully.

'No. You can't get me to do police work on the cheap. I've got my own, tight schedule. I've no idea what the police support systems are and if you're counselling someone it helps to know what backup you've got. Irresponsible to undertake what I can't follow up.' I reflected on the scene in my kitchen. 'OK,' I said, with extreme reluctance, 'maybe I'd be there for Peter. Maybe. But not for Sheila. Not at all. I don't even like her.'

'You have to like people you counsel!' His eyebrows shot up.

'Of course you don't. But that's irrelevant. I'm not going to counsel her, remember? I'd go so far as to say Peter's better off without her.'

'He doesn't seem to think so,' he said. 'The police are good at this, aren't they? Screwing up relationships?' Dropping his voice, he looked me straight in the eye.

I refused to bite. 'They've certainly got amazingly high divorce figures. Not to mention alcoholism, drugs abuse and suicide.'

'A tough job and getting tougher. All this public campaigning for more officers on the beat presupposes that all the serious crime takes place on the streets. Which, believe me, it doesn't. To put them there, though, means—'

'More police?'

'I wish! No, it means breaking up specialised teams.'

'*Breaking up*? Not redundancy!'

'No. Redistribution. But putting people back in uniform. Taking with them expertise it's taken years to build up . . .'

Just what Harvinder had been saying. I let him talk on. It was better than having him try to resuscitate our relationship. I'd had enough of things ending in tears for one day.

His flow was interrupted by a tap at the door.

'Come!'

God, I hated that abbreviation! Why abandon a perfectly decent preposition?

Harvinder's face appeared round the door. 'Gaffer?'

Chris's smile, even to a junior officer, always transformed his face. 'Help yourself to tea – no, it's not Bridget's brew – and a couple of sarnies and pull up a chair.' His assumption that Harvinder wouldn't mind my presence astonished me. I got to my feet.

'No, you're all right,' Harvinder said, nipping back in with a cup and pouring carefully. 'It's about Peter and since you're a friend of his—'

Chris and I exchanged glances.

'—you might have some ideas. There's this rumour, Gaffer, that he and I are going to be taken off this case.' Balancing the cup and saucer in one hand, he carried a spare chair over with the other.

'Not you, Harvinder. If they set up the city-wide team I'm suggesting they'll want an experienced detective sergeant and I'd say you'd fill the bill admirably.'

Harvinder put down the chair, the better to stand to attention. If the effect was somewhat spoilt by the cup and saucer, neither Chris nor I betrayed the fact. 'That's not right, Gaffer. With respect. Peter ought to be leading the team. He knows everything that's happened so far. It'd smash him up completely if you took him off it.'

Chris smiled again. A serious smile. 'Sit yourself down, Harv. Look, don't you think Peter's got enough on his plate? How many cases in his in-tray? And now this business with Sheila.'

'Sometimes I think your squad's your real family,' Harvinder said. 'We'll all be there for him, Gaffer. You know that. I thought I might go round and see his missus later. Put in a word, like.'

I stared at my hands, blushing. There was no way I'd let Chris catch my eye. No, I'd just pretend to be interested in Harvinder's sudden and unexpected lapse into the local lingo. *Missus*, indeed! But then, why shouldn't he talk Black Country? He lived there, and had almost certainly been to school there. Some time we'd have to talk shared roots.

Then this voice asked, 'Do you want me to come too?' Mine.

'I'd say *you'd* got enough on *your* plate, Sophie. And it's not as if you know her, is it?'

'I met her once,' I conceded. 'Didn't like her any more than she liked me. But I don't want to, I really don't. What I'd really like – and you're not hearing this, Chris! – is for you people to wrap the whole thing up before this new team is formed.'

'What you mean is you don't want a whole lot of strangers coming in on the case. Keeping you where you should be – firmly on the sidelines,' Chris said.

'A possible hit. I want the whole thing done and dusted, that's for sure. I don't like this series of suicides. I don't like my teachers dying in cuts. I don't like vandalism all over the university—'

'What's that?'

'While you were junketing in France some vandals got in and did over some rooms.'

'Any in particular?'

'Funny you should ask that. The post-grad work-room, Tom Bowen's and Carla Pentowski's. Some corridors.'

'Highly selective, for vandals,' Chris said crisply.

'There may have been others. Peter would know,' I said. I risked a grin at Harvinder, who responded in kind.

Raising his eyes heavenward, Chris jabbed buttons on his phone.

*   *   *

'Yes,' Peter said, drawing up a chair. Why we were gathering round Chris's desk, not the Table was anyone's guess. 'Yes, they did do over some other rooms. None quite as thoroughly as Pentowski's, though.'

'They had a head start there. She took untidiness to a new dimension.'

'Funny. Her narrow boat wasn't that bad. In fact, the kitchen was as neat as a pin,' Peter said. 'Have you seen it yet, Sophie?'

'Is that an offer? In which case, yes, please.'

Chris raised eyes and hands heavenwards.

'The thing is,' I continued, 'there's something really strange happened to her. She's disappeared from all the uni records. Even from the payroll.'

There was a most gratifying silence.

Peter had been right about the kitchen – galley, I suppose: had a place for everything and everything was in its place. Another idiom for Lola.

'You know, when you're going away for a bit, how you tidy everything up and run the vac round?' I said.

'That's because you want it to be nice for when you come back,' Harvinder said.

'Some suicides do a spring-clean,' Peter objected. 'To leave it nice for the people who've got to sort out their affairs.'

'All the better for SOCO to check out the carpet,' Chris put in.

'And I presume they've checked this. Or we wouldn't be trampling all over it.'

'You presume right. So, you don't reckon Carla's always as tidy as this?'

'Cast your beadies over the rest of the place, Gaffer.' Harvinder stood aside.

We started with the baby bathroom, complete with loo,

shower, and to my surprise, a tiny vanitory unit. Every square inch of space was being utilised. A doll's bedroom. The sitting room. He was right. The place might not reach the height of chaos of her office, but it wasn't as immaculate as the kitchen. Not nearly.

Harvinder gestured: 'Looks to me like a place someone might have been coming back to.'

'So she might indeed have been going off to do some research, like the note on the door said?' Chris said.

'She'd have told me. Especially as I was supposed to be her guest. She'd have told all her students, come to think of it. A good professional teacher.'

Chris nodded. 'Is that the opinion of her colleagues?' he asked Peter.

'Yes and no. Good teacher, shame about the lack of publications: that was the consensus. But Sheila always reckons – reckoned . . .' He turned away.

'League tables,' I said quickly. 'I gather universities' league tables are based more on research than on students' success. Luke would be able to explain.'

The dimensions of the living room were odd, but it was more than habitable. A television, plus video. A small and very expensive hi-fi. That was the recreation end. The other end was work: bookshelves, a folding desk which opened up to reveal an office in miniature, a folding but apparently ergonomically designed chair.

'Well?' asked Chris, not without irony.

I pointed to the contents of the office: a mobile phone and a state-of-the-art lap-top – more of a palm-top, really.

He nodded. 'I think we should get that along to the IT section, don't you, Peter? Get them on to it.'

'I'm sure SOCO have checked it,' he said stiffly.

'Oh, for fingerprints and everything. But what's more important is inside.'

Peter looked bemused.

I added, 'What we need to know, surely, is when that was last used. Or, more to the point, when the modem was used.'

The boat rose and fell gently in the water. We heard the slap of a wave. Presumably another vessel was passing. We could hear each other's breathing. And then the cold got to us, and with one accord we turned to leave. Peter, slipping the computer and mobile into polythene bags, closed the office and brought up the rear. Chris locked the doors behind us, and we stepped from the boat into the shelter of the polythene tent designed to preserve the scene and keep it from the eyes of curious Smethwickians. And the attentions, come to think of it, of that dog. He exchanged a few quiet words with the poor sod of a constable in for a cold night watching the place – and no doubt watching (provided the audience didn't inhibit her) the toilet activities of the gytrash.

'If I got it wrong,' I said, 'I'd foul up a lot. In any case, all the information you need will be on the hard disk. As you said, your IT people can get anything off the hard disk.'

We were back at Piddock Road. The computer sat on Chris's table. The four of us sat staring at it.

'What do you think you'll find?'

'What I know I'd find,' I said, stressing the *d* slightly; this was definitely the conditional, to Chris's future tense, 'is her last four documents listed, assuming she used Word, of course. But my guess is that it isn't her documents that are important. I'd guess it's what she used the phone and the modem to do.'

'Which is to eliminate herself?' Chris said.

'It's an interesting idea. Especially in view of the tidy boat,' Peter agreed.

'Tidy kitchen,' Harvinder insisted. 'She might just have been cleaning the boat in stages. We don't know how significant that kitchen is.'

Everyone nodded.

'Coming back to what you were saying earlier, Gaffer,' he continued, 'why should someone else eliminate her?'

'Because they didn't know she was going to eliminate herself? Hang on.' I scratched my head. 'There's something her death and the vandalism have got in common, isn't there?' I looked at Peter. 'Remember all that sticky tape?'

'OK, it was sticky tape that was used to hold what we believe was string for her to fall over. But it wasn't the same sort of tape. Something tougher. Something with a stronger adhesive, too,' he said.

I nodded, gloomily. But Chris cocked an eye, and then wrote. 'I wonder if there's any tape in her boat?' he said.

'There's SOCO's list of contents in my office, Gaffer.'

Chris grinned. 'There's also a big whiteboard in your office, as I recall, Peter. It'd give us lots of space to draw all this lot together.'

'Hasn't been fixed to the wall yet. Manpower shortages in Maintenance.'

'When I started here as a cadet,' Harvinder put in, 'there used to be this lovely Irishman. Jim. Technically he was a cleaner. But he'd do anything you asked. And all you had to do was ask. Not like now. Forms in triplicate.'

'We've got policemen in triplicate,' I said. 'If we could find a drill and some rawlplugs . . .'

We stood back admiring our handiwork as if we'd been hanging masterpieces in the Barber Institute. The guy on reception had a brother living down the road who was hot on DIY and had provided the necessary. He'd also brought a dustpan and brush.

So there we were, ready for action.

Except for one thing. Whiteboard pens.

Chapter Twenty-five

It was still horribly dark when the alarm clock summoned me. Not the sort of time to get up. Not after a late-night curry at Peter and Harvinder's favourite Indian restaurant, with copious lager to temper the heat. At least, for the men. I wasn't into macho heat or excess booze, so I'd been deputed to ferry everyone home. We'd deleted shop from the conversational menu, and we'd ended up having the sort of riotous evening that four serious-minded people can have if they set those serious minds on to it. An evening running till about 2 a.m., that is.

Come to think of it, the owner of one of those serious minds was still asleep in my spare room, a circumstance which afforded me no pleasure at all.

Angry with him for having got pissed, angry – no, furious – with myself for not having had the common sense, knowing he was pissed, to drive him to his place and tip him out there, I pulled myself into my dressing gown and headed for the bathroom. Furious. And upset. For both of us. Chris had been sufficiently drunk to be maudlin about our abortive relationship. And to be quite persistent about renewing it. Physically. I'd had to take action. Shit!

At least the bruising to his hand – where I'd had to bend the little finger hard backwards, a technique it gave me some satisfaction but no pleasure to recall he'd taught me himself – wouldn't show. With luck, though, it should be tender enough to remind him of the incident at least until I flew to Australia. Except I didn't want to remind him of anything. I wanted wounds to heal. Ideally we could go back to being friends. In the meantime we had to work together.

Except that was nonsense. He and I shouldn't be working together at all. He shouldn't even be working with Peter and Harvinder. He was the Commander of the whole unit, and should be merely taking an overview, just as he did with Traffic and Community Relations and Domestic Violence and everything else under his eye.

And I should be working on my thesis and for the next assignment.

Dream on, Sophie. You know you could no more drop out of this now than you could fly to Mike without wings.

In the circumstances I thought it better to be showered and dressed before yelling to him – from the bottom of the stairs – that it was time to wake up.

We drove in a silence that was both grumpy and offended to Piddock Road, where he now kept spare shaving gear, toilet things and clothes. Last night's idea – it had seemed so good at the time – was that we should gather before normal working hours in Peter's room, now fully equipped with whiteboard and pens nicked from someone else's office. The four of us were to brainstorm, and the one with the neatest writing was to put the whole lot together on the whiteboard. Chris was the obvious choice. So he was doubly grumpy and no doubt about to pull rank. I kept my head down – I was on sabbatical, for heaven's sake, from such duties! – and found a no doubt illicit fan heater (at least at William Murdock they were illicit!), which simply asked, on a cold morning like this, to be plugged in. What I had to do for everyone's sake was make sure no one could even suspect a problem between Chris and me. I had to be myself. Perhaps me with a hangover (fictitious). Chris's sense of duty and personal dignity would no doubt lead him to a similar conclusion.

If Chris was grumpy with a genuine hangover, not to mention his conscience, Peter – I inferred he'd slept on Harvinder's sofa – was looking downright ill. Harvinder, who'd revealed an amazing repertoire of comic verse, most of it clean, took in what could have been the situation and announced that everyone was dehydrated and should drink at least a litre of the water from the CID chiller, conveniently located just outside Peter's door. Whether it was the prospect of anything ice-cold on this bitter morning, or merely the thought of moving from the fan heater, this suggestion was deafed out. So Harvinder exited to make herbal tea. That's never my favourite tipple, and at six thirty in the morning I wasn't sure if I could stomach it at all. Peter and I peered with gloom at Chris's chart. The centre was small and empty. Chris drew some lines radiating from it. In time he'd add words to the oval satellites he'd drawn at the end of each line.

Peter peered blearily at the board. 'What's that, Gaffer?'

Chris glared. 'Come on, you've seen a sunburst chart before. It's for us to fill in as we brainstorm.'

'A sunburst. So that's what a sunburst looks like. Looks more like one of those blasted spiders to me. Or a daddy-longlegs. You know. Long legs, tiny body.'

'Big feet, whatever it is,' Harvinder said, plonking a tray of mugs on the floor for want of anywhere else flat to put it. Peter ran Carla a close second when it came to office chaos. 'Be very noisy, wouldn't it – one of those clumping over your ceiling?'

'Daddy-longlegs go for windows, not ceilings.'

'Spider, then. Nice spider, Gaffer.'

Chris stepped back in revulsion. Ah, a closet arachnaphobe. I'd often suspected it. And now I suspected he'd never be specially keen on herbal tea again, not now he was standing in a tray clattering with overturned mugs and awash with the stuff. Still quite hot, I'd guess. Blackcurrant, sweetened, by the smell of it, with honey. Would sticky, wet trousers and socks improve the shining hour? Probably not. I was first on my knees, the others restrained by their clanging heads, perhaps. At least Chris'd not broken any of the mugs, just tipped one right over and knocked the other three. But it was a fair guess that neither his trousers nor the carpet would ever be the same again. Not unless quick action were taken.

Quite fun, telling someone on fifty thou to strip off his trousers so you can pour mineral water, icy from the chiller, over them. I poured some over his leg, too, just in case there were any scalding. His socks would have to sit on the radiator, once he'd wrung them out over a Christmas cactus that was failing to live up to its name.

Shaking, and keeping their backs firmly towards Chris, Peter and Harvinder found newspaper to stuff into the soggy shoes and mop the worst of the tea from the carpet, but there was still a very obvious stain.

'Go and find a cleaner's mop and bucket,' I said, still sloshing with mineral water. OK: unnecessarily sloshing with mineral water. But, I confess, beginning to enjoy myself hugely, because Chris quite patently wasn't. And he enjoyed it even less when the cleaner's mop and bucket arrived, accompanied by the cleaner herself, who joined in with gusto when Chris mumbled a suggestion that he should go and dry his trousers under the hand-dryer in the gents'.

'*Hot* air? On *them*? But they're a nice bit of worsted. Don't want them shrinking. You'll have to turn that there heater on to cold, and hold them in front of it. There you go. Hmm, don't often see worsted that quality, not these days. It's all this Terylene, isn't it? No body. Not like these. Very nice.' At the time, however, she was not looking at the trousers.

It was nearly eight o'clock, the time Chris announced he had to head for his desk. We had established a number of action points. The IT experts would be asked to look not only at Carla's computer, but at the UWM system too. Peter would take a role in whatever system were set up to pull together the Eastern deaths: no one had mentioned Chris's original reservations. Meanwhile he was to investigate any premises where young Malaysian and Singaporean women might be found – from the massage parlour to the not especially hallowed portals of the University College of the West Midlands, with their spurious coat of arms.

'There's definitely something – er – *fishy* there,' Chris said, looking at me for the first time. 'But this isn't the moment for you to turn into Superwoman, Sophie.'

'Superwoman Sophie?' Peter ignored the comma. 'Nice one, Gaffer. Or would you rather be SuperSoph?' He grinned a little shamefacedly; he'd once enraged me by abbreviating my name.

'Just at the moment I'd rather be SafeSoph. I'm still worried by that spot of vandalism we had.' I pointed to the words 'CARS – PAINT STRIPPER, ETC.' at the bottom of Chris's sunburst. 'Not to mention that little bomb.' How had we come to forget that? It was not insignificant, after all!

'Bomb!'

Having the grace to look embarrassed, Peter nodded. 'Yes, Gaffer. Except it wasn't, not really. No explosives. Just a tiny little charge of hydrogen sulphide. You know, the stuff they use for stink bombs.'

Chris, whose doctorate had been in astrophysics, might well have known that. But he never, ever, mentioned that part of his life, and I wasn't about to either. If I'd been Peter, I'd have worried about Chris's apparent forbearance. It could presage a bollocking later. For the moment, though, all Chris did was look at me quite hard. 'Nasty stuff, if you happen to be asthmatic.'

'Only the occasional attack.'

229

'One a year's enough. You're still asthmatic.'

'Anyway,' I said, literally pulling my shoulders down, 'I don't want to take any risks, but I really need to spend time at UWM—'

'So who knows about your asthma and would want to capitalise on it? Get you out of the action for a couple of days?'

'Not Bowen – not if she's cooking for him,' Harvinder said.

'Quite,' I agreed, looking round for my coat. I hated talking about my asthma. I hated having it. 'Now, I've got a three-hour evening class tonight, apart from an assignment to finish. Oh, and I'm teaching my English class today – the one with the floating population.' I abandoned the idea of leaving just yet. 'You know, it's funny how the few men seem to be permanent fixtures. Now I come to think of it it's only the women who change.'

Chris added that to the chart. 'Harvinder, I'd like you to take someone over the UWM to check the students' records out. There must be reasons for all these discrepancies. I know they might not be a police matter, so just keep it nice and low-key. That friend of Sophie's sounds bright; have a natter to him.'

I raised a hand. 'If you want to talk to Luke, please may I ask you to exercise the most extreme caution. He's been beaten up once trying to help me – us – and I'd hate anything to happen to him.'

'Come off it! How can anyone be put in danger just by talking to us?' Peter objected.

I shrugged. 'All I know is it happened before. People have seen me with him. If the attack on my car were more than vandalism, maybe someone thinks I know something I certainly don't know—'

'Let us not forget that bomb,' Chris said drily.

'Quite. And nothing must happen to Luke. OK? You may

not look exactly like your classic policeman,' I said, bending the truth, 'but some of your colleagues are still identifiable as plods at thirty paces, however plain their clothes.'

Harvinder nodded. 'I'll talk to him first by phone. Unless you're afraid that may be bugged, Sophie?'

'I don't joke about things like that,' I said. 'Now, just to go back to our massage parlours for a moment. And the University College of the West Midlands. How are you going to talk to the women involved? Not in my class time, by the way, if you don't mind. They need all the practice they can get. And, come to think of it, I don't want to be too closely associated with all this. Just in case.'

'When else do you suggest?'

'Some time when you can organise the interpreter you'll need for your other inquiries to come to them. I keep telling you, their spoken English is minimal.'

'"Spoken"?'

'Some of them write quite well. But orally . . .' I shook my head in despair.

Peter slapped his head. He looked at me meaningfully. 'I suppose you couldn't—'

'You suppose right. Don't you think that if I'd been able to speak their language, if I could even identify it, I'd have tried weeks ago?'

'—find one of your best students to interpret for us?' he concluded.

'That's a job for the university authorities. If they ask me, I'm sure I shall be able to recommend someone. There's something else you should know, Chris. I told you that a fellow student needed information from Carla, and that Mike had offered to get it from her university in Melbourne.'

'What's his name? Jago? And that it wasn't there,' Chris prompted irritably, looking at his watch.

'But *he* was. No, not in Melbourne. Running on the towpath near her narrow boat. That day we had our picnic.' I nearly said, 'I told Peter the other day.' But I'd better remind him without a critical audience.

'I wonder how he is on adhesive tape,' Peter said, catching my eye guiltily. Oh yes, he remembered. 'Not that the two types are the same. Forensic says the Sellotape scattered around at UWM is bog-standard, and the marks on the hull indicate something wider. No rolls of either sort on board the narrow boat.'

'Jago? Tape?'

'Some of his work was tangled up in tape, Chris. In our work-room. He was very distressed. Started asking for extra time to submit work as soon as a tutor appeared.'

'Sounds reasonable. And the tutor was . . . ?'

'Bowen,' I said.

Peter wrote.

'What did you make of Bowen?' I asked. 'I presume he was in his room when you had a look at it?'

He spread his hands. Then grinned. 'Do you remember those Posy Simmonds cartoons in the *Guardian* years ago? The family with the dad who was a poly lecturer? He reminds me of the dad. To look at, anyway. What was his name, now? Wibbly? Wobbly?'

Harvinder stared: had his boss totally blown it?

'Webber,' I supplied.

'I thought that was something to do with carburettors,' Harvinder said.

'No, that's Weber. Harmless old git, anyway,' Peter said eventually. 'Overworked, underpaid, that sort of thing.'

'He may be underpaid, but he's got a lovely house. *Bostin'*, we'd call it in Oldbury. Not far from the soi-disant University College. And as a teacher, he's – lackadaisical.'

'You mean he's not hooked on the work ethic like you masochists at William Murdock,' Chris suggested.

'Or like you people here,' I said sharply. 'I've always believed in a fair day's pay, but I'm happy to do a fair day's work to earn it.' Then I remembered what Seb from the union had said. 'Of course,' I said, trying to sound as if I'd known all the time, 'his value to UWM may lie not in his teaching but in his research.'

'Unlike Carla. Hmm.'

Peter said, 'If he keeps his research work at UWM he won't be a happy bunny. Not after the mess those vandals made of his room.'

'Any news of the vandals? Any sightings?' I asked.

'Someone coming out of that pub – the Chalk and Talk – said he saw some thin kid running away. We're talking to our regulars.'

Chris coughed and looked ostentatiously at his watch. 'Time I wasn't here. Keep me informed. And that includes you, Sophie. In fact . . .' He shook his head and opened the door.

Peter's turn to cough. 'Excuse me, Gaffer. Haven't you forgotten something?'

Oh, he'd been decently be-trousered for the last hour. He'd probably get rheumatism in his ankles, the trousers had been so damp when he'd insisted on putting them back on. But his socks were still baking on the radiator. He grabbed them, scowling, and perching on alternate legs, pulled them on. And then, desperate to add some dignity to his exit, he stuffed his feet hurriedly into his shoes.

Except the toes were still full of crumpled *Sun*. Muttering, he grabbed them and strode out carrying them. Pity it's difficult to do a dignified stocking-foot stride.

Chapter Twenty-six

Call me paranoid – if you can be paranoid on someone else's behalf – but I wanted to remind Luke about his personal safety. And I thought it safer not to phone him from the pay phone in the work-room. Finding an empty-ish bit of road, I parked and fished out my mobile. If I wanted to use it again, I'd better charge the battery tonight.

It seemed to me, as I dialled, that I was still taking risks over my own safety. I'd had the same car for a week now. Time to chase the garage about the repair. Or to change the hired one.

No time to make decisions: the switchboard was quick to take the call. And the young woman who answered first ring in Personnel was quick to tell me that Luke was off sick. I knew there was no point in asking for his phone number – would have been furious if she'd given it to me. But I asked anyway. And then – half relieved, half frustrated by her discretion – I tried Directory Enquiries, to hear the charming plastic voice giving it without hesitation.

What did I want? A bit of pathetic fallacy? Machinery anticipating misery? What I got was a surge of anger: hadn't the silly sod learnt from experience that there are some things best kept private? Had he never thought of being ex-directory? Or was he making a foolhardy attempt to prove to himself that lightning never struck twice?

It was my fault it had struck once.

I counted the rings. Seventeen. Eighteen. Nineteen. If it got to twenty-five I'd go back to Piddock Road and ask Peter to—

'Hello?'

The voice was thick, distorted. A cold or broken nose? Sore throat or shattered teeth?

'Luke! Are you all right?'

'Sophie, my dear, do I sound as if I'm all right? I've got the flu in spades and you get me out of my bed to ask if I'm all right. Oy vey!'

'Are you expecting any visitors today?'

'It should be the Aspirin Fairy?'

'So long as you don't answer the door to anyone else. Promise me, Luke.'

'You sound like my old mother. Are your feet in a mustard bath? Have you rubbed your chest with goose fat? Are you—'

'Someone's after me,' I cut in. 'I'd hate them to be after you too. Here, write down this number, and if you think of anything that could help us both, phone. Peter's OK. He'll listen.'

'With my voice he'll need good ears. Who is this Peter, anyway? Don't I need to know that?'

'He's a senior CID officer, based in Smethwick. I've told him about you. Now, please look after yourself—'

'OK, OK. I'm just going back to bed.'

'Well, for God's sake stay there!'

I knew it would take ages to get through to the garage: they joke I always wait for them to embark on the most difficult two-man job before lifting the phone. Since they don't run to a receptionist, I always have to hang on. And on.

Goodness knows what they'd been lifting; Paul was quite out of breath when he answered. And quite irritated: he'd left three messages with my colleagues (I knew of old that he was allergic to answerphones and I did have the nasty habit of leaving my mobile switched off) to say the car was ready

236

as soon as I'd primed my cheque book to pay the insurance excess. Oh, and a bit of work on one or two other things.

So who had failed to deliver not one but three messages? I was so pissed off, I forgot I ought to be checking behind every lamppost for potential assassins, and charged the short distance into West Bromwich like Boadicea late for battle.

I was greeted by Jago with the sort of smile designed to fetch the ducks off the water. Still sucking pastilles, and, come to think of it, with quite a convincing rasp, which might have been intended to be sexy, he got up, bending his head and striking his chest in a classic *mea culpa*.

'I'm so sorry,' he said. 'I found this. I must have buried it when we were sorting everything out. I hope it hasn't messed you about.'

His script was rather too mannered for my taste, but the message was clear enough. *'YOUR GARAGE CALLED. YOUR CAR IS READY. BRACE YOURSELF FOR THE BILL!'*

'The least you can do is run her over to collect it,' Lola observed.

'No. Don't worry—' No way was I going anywhere with him.

'Where is the garage?' she pursued.

'Selly Oak. Just off Bristol Road.'

'That's excellent. I need to get there for my osteopath's appointment. You could take us both, Jago. It is preferable not to drive after treatment.'

So Jago would have to sit and wait for her. I suppressed a grin and demurred no more. With Lola riding shotgun, surely nothing could happen to me. In fact, I could myself put him to a little extra trouble – I could drop off my hire car on the way.

As I handed over the keys, another little thought path clicked open. Lemon . . . lemon throat pastilles . . . Jago . . . Jago jogging . . .

So, reunited with my Clio and separated from a disconcertingly large amount of money, I set off for West Bromwich. I'd hardly crossed the Birmingham border before I chickened out. I simply couldn't face going back into UWM, not for a bit. I had to be there till nine thirty tonight, after all. I couldn't bear to stick it out that long in the company of a Jago made almost unbearably vivacious after his Sir Galahad act. He'd contrived to flirt with both of us, the stupid pillock.

Irritating little prick . . . Lemon-sucking little prick . . .

I checked the clock on the dashboard. If I did indeed dash I could just nip down to talk to Aggie. No, it wasn't a disinterested visit. I wanted to experiment with some lemony smells. Bowen's lemon-flavoured antacids, Jago's throat lozenges – I wanted to see if she reacted to either of them. It might give some clue about the visitor she'd scared off. Provided the gods were on my side, I should be back in plenty of time for the English Language class in the afternoon.

It wasn't that the Clio wasn't every bit as nippy as the Fiesta. It wasn't that it was tatty – I cherish my cars. It was just it seemed a mite old-fashioned. Well, the model was due for a revamp any day now. I'd have to look into the possibility of turning it in. Fiesta or Clio? And what had Paul said: check every likely model on the market? Well, that could pass some spring days. Depending on my finances, of course.

At least I knew where everything was on this radio. Radio Three or Classic FM? Berg on Three, but Brahms on Classic FM. The sextet I'd heard at the Barber. Lovely. But hardly had the last note died away when the news came on. Then the weather. Finally the announcer declared, as if announcing the end of civilisation, 'And on Classic FM Sports News—' how I hate the way they imply that they've got exclusive coverage! '—England batsman Mike Lowden is set to miss the next Test through injury.'

Mike! Injured! How badly? My God! And I'd been so preoccupied I hadn't even checked Ceefax for God knows how long. Or the sports pages. The announcer chirped on. A pulled thigh muscle. That was all. No need for all those vocal histrionics.

I breathed out. A long, therapeutic sigh. And realised that with my anxiety my speed had increased: better drop that before a passing patrol car noticed. There. I told myself, again and again, repeating it like a mantra. Thigh. That's all. And this time next week I shall be on my way to rub it better. Thigh. That's all . . .

But it was a thigh I'd once rubbed with a tenderness I'd not realised I was capable of feeling. Somehow I felt little comfort.

Aggie was pleased to see me, accepted my rushed explanation with interest and consented to breathe in lemon smells from the tablets I'd brought. Provided – she eyed me with grandparental severity – I had a sandwich with her when I'd finished sucking.

'Or you'll need one of them stomach things for real, won't you? Can't go mucking about with a stomach like that. OK. I'll shut me eyes, shall I?'

I wasn't sure how to do it. Like a wine-tasting? Except it needed both of us to have fresh palates and fresh noses. I started on a throat pastille.

Aggie blew her nose on a voluminous handkerchief that looked as if it might have been one of her late husband's. I breathed out. She sniffed.

'No. I don't reckon it was one of them. Go on, wash your mouth out good and proper and try the other. A good rinse, mind. Like young Ian Dale says.'

I did as I was told, and embarked on the antacid.

She shook her head sadly. 'Couldn't swear to that, either, my love. Not to put a man under suspicion, that is. And, you know, I wonder if the lemony smell wasn't more . . . sort of all over him. I don't know. And there you've driven all this

239

way. I am sorry. Now, you will have a bit of bread and cheese with me, won't you? Only I made a bit of bread the other day, and there's this cheese – they make it round here . . .'

Stinking Bishop! Well, who could resist? Aggie was chuckling even as she passed me the plate.

Fear. That was the smell of my English Language group. Getting back with ten minutes to spare, I'd called the register with clarity and care. Then I'd circulated a sheet of paper for them to sign their names, and I taught exactly what I was supposed to be teaching. The future tense and idioms and vocabulary they'd need if they were ill. But instead of the usual anxious goodwill, I felt this constant tension. What on earth had I stirred up with my visit to the so-called University College of the West Midlands? Christabel, the girl from the university college building, seemed to be avoiding eye contact at all costs. As did the others. Yet I was quite sure that when I was addressing other people, she was staring at me.

The harder I tried to engage their interest, the more I sensed it slipping away from me. The more I smiled and urged, the more withdrawn they became. Was I being fanciful to wonder if it was suspect to engage in conversation with me? That there was someone in the group making sure the others weren't too friendly?

Twaddle, Sophie. You just aren't teaching very well, that's all. And you're boring on and on and all they want to do is head off to the refectory.

Perhaps if I hung around at the end of the class – nothing unusual; I always made it clear to classes that I was happy to give extra help then – Christabel might come and talk to me about whatever was troubling her.

But however much I smiled and looked relaxed, no one stopped behind. Well, after a class with all the charm of an endurance test, I wouldn't have either. But as I sighed with frustration, and prepared to gather all my papers together, I

240

realised I'd not collected in the name list. Hell! I could have sworn I'd picked it up – yes, Tim Yip had passed it to me. So where was it?

In the far corner, on a desk. And it was not alone. Under it, on the back of a spare handout, was a neatly written note. *'Please do not come to the college hall of residence again. But I will try to talk to you. And show you. C.'* The last three words were crossed and recrossed.

So should I try to talk to her in the refectory? No, pointless: she wouldn't approach me in so public a place. Not if she wouldn't risk speaking to me after a class. Perhaps, though, if I could see her around the building, I could persuade her into the comparative safety of a tutorial room.

No. No sign of her anywhere. But as soon as I'd dumped my teaching stuff, I'd scour the place for her.

Jago was looking more than usually smug when I went into the work-room.

'I've just been doing your job,' he said. 'Helping the police.'

It took me a second to remember that on a previous occasion he'd failed to pass a message on. Now he was preening himself as if he'd cornered the market in civic virtue. Oh dear, he'd be a lot less smug, wouldn't he, when they got round to asking him to help them *with their inquiries*. As no doubt Peter would, when he was good and ready.

'That's good,' I said. 'How?'

'They needed someone to translate when they talked to some Malaysian tarts,' he said.

I've never quite been able to call prostitutes 'sex workers', but I didn't like his total lack of sensitivity over the nomenclature. I didn't like the snotty-schoolboy glee with which he spoke, either.

'Prostitutes?'

'Yes. One seems to have topped herself. I suggested Jenny.'

Why Jenny, for goodness' sake? She would speak some sort of Chinese, not Malay.

If he couldn't restrain a coy half-smile, I couldn't hold back my curiosity any more. 'Why on earth did they ask you?' After all, he was, like myself, just a student.

'Oh, someone started to dictate a message for you. I interrupted and offered to help.'

I could almost see the officious straightening of his shoulders, hear the spurious authority in his voice. Why had I ever bothered to try to help this creep? A man who'd volunteered a woman he seemed to be attracted to into what would at best be a harrowing job and at worst a dreadful one. 'Well, that was very kind of you,' I said.

He smiled, modestly, not noticing the flatness of my voice.

I smiled too. I would enjoy telling Peter who'd been so helpful. But I'd also tell him that whoever had spoken to Jago had been in the wrong: they should have gone through official channels.

Right. Time to hunt for Christabel. The refectory? The library? A loo? I scoured the building, only to find her in the corridor nearest our work-room. There she was, assiduously reading the notice board. I went and read it too. The evening's session on Managing the Curriculum had had to be cancelled. Richard Hoffman was ill. He'd reschedule it for next term. Meanwhile there was a set of worksheets in an envelope pinned to the notice board under the note. I wondered if Bowen would have been so conscientious in similar circumstances. Like Christabel, I took a worksheet – actually several sheets stapled together, with exercises to complete at the bottom.

Pointing to the top page, I whispered, 'I'll check if there's anyone using the lavatories. If no one is, I shall stay there, just inside, and you will come in and talk to me. OK?' I pointed lower down the sheet.

242

She turned a page and pointed to something on it. Bless her! She'd followed my ploy. 'OK.'

If only the outer door had had a convenient lock. The best I could do was lean against it. Then, burrowing in my bag for a fat felt-tip and cadging a sheet of plain A4 from Christabel, I wrote

OUT OF ORDER

DO NOT ENTER

'There,' I said. No Blu-tack, of course. So I slipped it between the plate saying WOMENS TOILETS (one day I'd have to do something about that missing apostrophe) and the door itself. It might just hold. Then once again I closed the door and leant against it.

Christabel smiled briefly. But her face was serious, frightened even, when she said, 'You must not come to the hall of residence again. It put – *puts* – us in danger. All the women.'

'Can you tell me how?'

She reached for that tiny pocket inside the front right pocket of her jeans. I've never worked out what it was intended to hold. Tickets? Change? Hers held a scrap of newspaper. She unfurled it and thrust it at me.

I couldn't recognise the language, let alone translate it.

'What does it say?'

'It say – *says* – ah!' She gasped, her eyes widening with fear.

Someone had pushed against the door hard enough even to shift me. I staggered forward.

Christabel shoved the paper into my hand and bolted herself into a cubicle. I pocketed it – same tiny pocket – as a figure erupted into the room.

'Someone should report that door to Maintenance. It could hurt someone, sticking like that.' Lola had clearly benefited from her osteopathy session.

I nodded ambiguously and made my escape.

Yes, there was my impressive notice. Not on the women's loo door. It had fallen from where I had lodged it but someone had thoughtfully given it a new home. Between the name plate and the door of the MENS TOILETS.

Chapter Twenty-seven

So why had Jago asked Jenny Lee to interpret for the police? Of course, he could simply have been trying to help. That was the most obvious explanation. But it took someone as forceful as Lola to persuade Jago to be helpful, although he was keen on ingratiating himself with the staff here. Perhaps he'd somehow thought that this would raise his status with them? But it wouldn't unless people knew he'd done it. Or would it improve his status with Jenny? Here was a manly man getting her useful – and presumably lucrative – work.

Or was it to get power over her?

And what business had Peter accepting the suggestion? He should have known better. He worked in a hierarchical organisation: he should have known there'd be protocol in another. He knew I had suspicions about some of my UWM students; surely he realised this could muddy some waters.

And then, just as I was heading off to the library to photocopy the articles that Hoffman had suggested we read in his absence, another thought struck me. What if Jago had suggested that Jenny interpret so that he would know what was going on? Dim? I was clearly in danger of losing it. I changed direction. I needed a fix of caffeine and the refectory called.

It had called Jago and Jenny too. They were as close as wallpaper and paste when I saw them. I backed out. And trod hard on Harvinder's foot.

I've never transformed an apology into a dressing-down so

quickly all my life. How dare he and Peter involve Jenny? Hell, there were plenty of people capable of interpreting. Why, wouldn't Birmingham's Central Library or Chamber of Commerce have lists of appropriately qualified linguists?

'Come on, now, Sophie,' he said, sounding more like a policeman than I'd ever heard before, 'she's only going to help us question some of her fellow countrywomen. It's no big deal.'

'Have you ever met her?'

'I was assuming someone could point her out to me.'

'Were you indeed? And have you ever met Jago?'

He shook his head.

'Harvinder, this isn't like you. Or Peter. Or even Chris. You're taking short cuts, and this particular one doesn't work.' I took him by the forearm and turned him round. 'You see that balding man over there, the one with the pretty Malaysian girl?'

'The ones all over each other like the proverbial rash?'

'Hmm. Well, she's the woman you've asked to translate. And he's Jago, whom I saw near Carla's boat.'

'Oh. Oh. See what you mean. Oh, shit. And there's Peter just going to have a word with the boss-person of this faculty—'

'The Dean?'

'—and up-date him on the vandalism business.'

'The Dean's a her, but never mind. And the news is?'

'None of our regulars seems to be involved. That's what they say, anyway.'

'And you believe them?'

'To be frank, I got the impression they didn't think trashing a college was particularly exciting. So we're still looking for a small thin person. Hey, Sophie,' he demanded, stepping back a pace and looking me up and down, 'it wasn't you, was it, wreaking revenge on this Bowen character for not being a good tutor?'

'Ve have better vays of dealing wiz him. I'm cooking for

him tomorrow. I could hide all sorts of unpleasant ingredients if I wanted to. Now, my evening class has been postponed so I'm off to do a spot of shopping.'

His face fell comically. 'Chris wanted another meeting this evening.'

'But we had one this morning.'

'To chew over what that fair damsel would have found out.' He nodded in Jenny's direction.

'*Already?*'

'We've got a couple of people lined up for her to help us question. But we'll have to take a rain check on them. Still, with a bit of luck we'll have some news about the computers. And Peter and I have been doing some good old-fashioned detective work too.' He tapped the side of his nose. 'About nine.'

Too bad if my evening class had been running. But it was crazy, their meeting so late: they should be pacing themselves, not trying to work every hour God sent. Except that was partly my fault, hoping out loud that the Piddock Road people could tie it up themselves. Not that they'd needed much urging, of course.

'I've got to nip over to a supermarket. Tell Chris if he has the meeting at his house, I'll be there.' There was no way I was having Chris sleeping over at my place again and this was one way of guaranteeing it.

Harvinder's expression suggested that it was not normal practice to put the words *tell* and *Chris* together as verb and object in the same sentence. But he sighed and nodded.

'If,' I said carefully, 'you'd been able to find another interpreter, I might have something for you.' Yes, the newspaper cutting was still in that tiny pocket. 'But I promised the person who gave it me that no one from UWM would see it. No one.' This was not entirely true to the letter of our conversation, but it certainly was to the spirit.

'Well, who are you going to show it to?'

I shrugged. Then slapped my head. 'A very ex-boyfriend

of mine is Japanese. Not that that as such gets us any further forward. But I bet he'd know a man – or a woman – who could translate it. What we need to do is scan it into a computer and e-mail him.'

Harvinder looked doubtful. 'If it's material evidence, I really should insist that you hand it over,' he said, more in hope than expectation.

'I'm sure you're much too sensible. Look, Harvinder, there's something very dodgy about this place and I for one am not prepared to put anyone's life at risk. Not that much risk.' I held my thumb and forefinger a millimetre apart. 'Now, I'm off home to e-mail Kenji. That's the quickest, as well as the safest, way of getting the info.'

'Home? Are you sure it's safe for you to drive that far on your own?'

'I've got a different car from the one I set out in this morning,' I said blithely. And wished, when I saw how murky the afternoon had turned, that I hadn't.

I got home without incident, and soon my e-mail to Kenji, with the scanned image of the scrap of paper, was winging its way to Japan. Tokyo time's about nine hours ahead of ours, so, even with Kenji's penchant for late nights, it was unlikely I'd hear from him till tomorrow. Unless he were on the move. He was now in an ecstatic relationship with a CNN reporter, whom he accompanied all over the world although he'd once been the most career-minded of men. How he could afford it, I didn't know. Presumably she was earning enough for both of them.

If he could, why couldn't I? Why couldn't I simply drop everything and follow Mike everywhere?

Because that wasn't what we were like. Was it?

I pulled myself together. Now to the rest of my daily routine: closing the curtains – for good measure I popped next door and drew some of Aggie's, too; the post – nothing unexpected; no messages on the machine. No news on Ceefax about Mike.

Right, I'd phone him tonight. A bit to eat, finish the list – surprisingly short – for the supermarket, and check tomorrow's schedule. Meat, cheese, vegetables, bread, flowers from the little nest of shops in Lonsdale Road. All except the flowers already ordered. Malcolm would tell me tomorrow what was best value. Last check on the wine which Ian and I get by the dozen from a mail-order supplier. Tomorrow I must defrost the stuffed squid. I do batches when I can get hold of squid and produce them when necessary. Meanwhile I reached down the tins of devilled cashew and macadamia nuts I'd prepared one wet summer's day and left them ready.

Not a lot to worry about, then: I could go to Harborne Safeway, smaller than the Selly Oak Sainsbury's, but much more convenient for me. More time to talk to Mike. Who promised me that there was a present on the way.

'I don't need a present,' I said. 'I shall be with you this time next week.'

'You need this one,' he said.

I hadn't expected to be greeted by the smell of fish and chips when I arrived at Chris's. His is such an austere sort of house that cheerful food seems out of place. The house was cold, too, since he only heats it when he's there, which is not much, these days. The others were huddled round the kitchen table in their coats. I raised an eyebrow: Chris reached across to the thermostat and put it on to boost. The system roared into action, aided and abetted by the gas rings I also turned on. Before I took off my coat and dug into the chips – I'd already had one tea but that seemed a long time ago and my scales had reassured me this morning that I needn't be dieting – I lit the gasfire in the living room, which was too big for the number of radiators. What was the point of being an old friend if I couldn't bump up his heating bill?

So it was tolerably warm when we adjourned to the living

room, not to the comfort of the easy chairs, however, but to the table. It was already nine thirty.

'Chris, if no one minds I'd like us to treat this as a business meeting, with time allocations to each item. I know this isn't how you like to work, but we all have day jobs. And mine involves catering to quite a tight schedule for Tom Bowen's dinner party.'

'Suits me too, Gaffer,' said Peter. 'I promised I'd meet the wife this evening and I'm already a bit late.'

I caught Chris's eye.

'Reconciliation,' he mouthed carefully. 'The phone's in the kitchen,' he continued aloud. 'Ring her and say we'll be through here by ten – oh, ten fifteen to be realistic. And blame me.'

But whoever Peter had to blame, he would still be late. Had I been Sheila, I'd not have been happy.

'Ten,' I said. 'We've all got to get home. And in any case, we should take Peter's information first. I'll take notes of everything else so he can push off fast.'

Peter flapped a hand and shut himself into the kitchen. We all stared at the table. In silence, Chris leant across to a sideboard, coming up with coasters and pads and pencils. He had to get up to reach glasses to put on the coasters. Then he stopped. Whatever was to go in the glasses was no doubt in the kitchen.

Peter's smile when he emerged was bleak.

'Well?' Harvinder asked, roughly but not unkindly.

'If I'm not back by ten thirty I'm out,' he said. 'Again. And for good.'

Like impending execution, it concentrated the mind wonderfully.

'Very little to report till I get an e-mail back from Kenji,' I began, as Peter sat down. 'Christabel, one of my Malaysian students, is too scared to talk and says it's dangerous if we go sniffing round the so-called University College. She gave me this.' I laid Christabel's scrap of paper in front of him, safe in a little polythene bag. I explained how I'd come by it. 'You will be careful whom you ask to translate this, won't you? Or better still, simply wait for Kenji – it'd be better for your budget,' I grinned. 'Oh, and Aggie sends her love, Chris, but can't be sure that the man who visited me the other day smelt of throat sweets or stomach tablets. Which reminds me,' I said, before he could yell at me for driving to Evesham without his knowledge, 'I still have that cast you took of another visitor's footprint.'

'Shove it in a bag and drop it in at Piddock Road tomorrow, would you?' Chris didn't do casual very well: he'd forgotten about it too. 'Peter: what about you?'

'Harvinder and I have been enjoying ourselves,' he said, with a surprising smile. 'We've been checking out the late Ms Pentowski and her boat. You'll recall she'd been removed from all the college records. Well, on Sophie's advice, you remember, we had her computer checked out, while someone else, on the university's authority, checked their computer systems. We found that she'd been using her mobile phone and her computer at roughly the same time as things went wrong at the university: two separate occasions, in fact. First the Personnel files went down. Then the pay-roll and the teaching timetables lost her. Coincidence? And just in case you think it might be, she's closed down her bank account, removing all her cash. Building society account, too. No sign of any of the money. Or of her passport, her birth certificate or any other documents. If it hadn't been for the adhesive tape and the string, I'd have said she'd done herself in.'

I failed to see the logic. But before I could speak, Harvinder said, 'Sorry, Peter, but I can't see that conclusion. Suicides don't function that way, surely. Leave everything in chaos or tidy compulsively: I've seen both. But taking all your money out and hiding it? That's the action of someone doing a flit. I'd say Carla was intending to scarper but didn't get round

251

to telling the person who got her drunk and pushed her,' Harvinder added, grinning as if he'd made a joke.

At least Chris thought it amusing. 'So we find whoever did that and ask them,' he said, making a note, for all the world as if it were an item on a shopping list. 'What about this Jenny Lee and her activities?'

Peter and Harvinder exchanged a glance. 'First, we thought it was a good idea to ask her to translate. Then we found out the person who recommended her wasn't qualified to do so. And we felt it might put her in an awkward situation – a young lady like that having to talk to young ladies like . . . like that.'

I stared impartially at the table. If that was how they wanted to gloss it, that was up to them.

'So?'

'We – er – aborted the mission, as it were. Thanked her for her trouble and moved on. We discovered the Chamber of Commerce runs an interpreting service. We're meeting their person tomorrow at nine.'

'All these delays . . . These Chamber of Commerce people – you'll check them out first?' Chris asked. A man after my own heart. Except even as I thought it, I realised I could have expressed it better.

Peter looked at his watch.

'You'll have to do without me tomorrow, remember,' I said.

'I'm not sure you should be doing that cooking,' Peter said suddenly. 'Tom Bowen gave you those classes with the changing students. What if he's involved with all this? What if he's at the bottom of it?'

'His room was vandalised too,' Harvinder put in.

'Not very much, come to think of it,' I said slowly. 'Oh, someone had knocked over his geraniums, and they'd messed up his desk. But the strange thing is that the only papers I saw on his floor were exam papers going back ten years. Not the sort of stuff to make or break his academic reputation. And

– here's another strange thing – although all of us had stuff messed up, nothing vital was damaged. All our disks were OK, for instance.'

'And SOCO tells us that though Pentowski's room was a mess, there was no radical damage there. Nor any list of student entry qualifications, either, Sophie,' Peter added.

I gaped.

'Sophie did wonder at the time if the whole vandalism outbreak was just to cover up the fact that someone had searched Pentowski's room,' Peter explained.

Chris looked at his watch. 'Thanks, Peter – now, go! Now. OK?' Chris pointed to the door. 'See you in the morning. And – Peter – good luck!'

The three of us waved him out of the room and listened in silence to the slam of the front door, the slam of the car door. The engine fired immediately. We heard the car pull away.

I was about to remark on the absence of the results print-out when Chris spoke.

'Thank God this isn't Northern Ireland,' he said, 'and we have to listen to every car drive off praying there are no bombs underneath it. It gives a whole new meaning to that Garden of Remembrance they're planting at the nick, doesn't it?'

'Gaffer?' Harvinder probably hadn't seen this side of Chris before: I'd only come across it rarely.

The phone rang. Chris snatched it, listened, anger darkening his face. 'Another assault,' he said, putting down the phone. 'Same locality. A good looking man, according to the victim. Ran off very fast when she screamed. Which reminds me,' he said, with a slight laugh. 'Mike phoned and sent me out shopping, Sophie. Here.'

My present! My present from Mike!

Chris got up and opened his briefcase. He fished out items with a flourish, laying them on the table in front of me. 'One screamer, deterring assailants for the purposes of, and one pager, responding to my phone-calls for the purposes of. When

I try to call you, this vibrates. And if you don't call me back immediately, I have to leap into my car and come and rescue you.' He smiled.

It might have convinced Harvinder. I could only guess at what the smile might be concealing. I glanced down at his hand: yes, I could see the bruise at the base of his little finger from here. And here was Mike asking him to look after me. Poor Chris.

'Thanks,' I said, taking them.

'Mike says you must carry them everywhere – and don't dare switch off that pager!'

'Sir!' I sat up straight and saluted. But my heart wasn't in it.

'Are you going to cancel tomorrow?' Chris asked, sitting down again.

'It would go against the grain, letting people down.' And losing all that money. 'I shall keep my eyes and ears open.'

'And that, Sophie,' said Chris, exaggeratedly covering his face with his hands, 'is exactly what I'm afraid of.'

Chapter Twenty-eight

Two e-mails awaited me when I got up at six thirty on Friday. The first was from Kenji. His partner, Susannah, was pregnant, and he was really looking forward to being an active father. He'd take care of the baby while Susannah was working, i.e., all the time. And wasn't it about time I settled down and did likewise? He'd passed on my message to a friend of his, currently at the Sorbonne studying oriental languages. (What, Kenji, all of them? Well, there were enough to choose from out there – Bahasa Malaysia, Bahasa Indonesia, Iban, whatever. I'd just have to trust his course included whatever that newspaper cutting was written in!) I should be getting my translation any moment.

E-mail two was from Steph. His dad had just, like, joined the twentieth century and Steph thought he'd say, hi! Soon be surfing, OK? Oh, and he'd got this new bike – might drop round on Sat. sometime. OK?

OK by me, I mailed him back. *CU Sat.*

Oh dear, what if they'd got him a more powerful bike than he could safely manage? I wasn't happy about his having a motorbike anyway. Surely they could have bought him a little car – much safer.

I agonised about it all the way down the stairs to switch on the central heating – which I'd forgotten to change from its usual start time, seven – and make the first cup of tea of the day. Then I realised, to my chagrin, and, yes, my guilt, that

255

his parents had no doubt been agonising about Steph and his various adventures – isn't that slide too high for him? What if he falls off his first chopper bike? – for the last twenty years. Scrubbing away tears – self-pity, I told myself crossly – with the heel of my hand, I brewed the tea and slotted bread into the toaster. This would be my first breakfast. I'd have the second when I'd had a shower. And when – hang the expense – I'd phoned Mike. I'd simply thank him for his gifts. There was no way I'd tell him about Chris's likely feelings when buying them or handing them over.

'You know, your voice changes every time you mention Bowen, as if you really don't trust him. Are you sure you have to do that cooking gig for him?' Mike demanded, the tender preliminaries over.

Didn't I trust Bowen? No, I didn't. But I wasn't going to admit it to Mike and worry him. Ignoring his observation, I answered his question. 'I've no reason not to. It'd be horribly unprofessional to drop out now. Anyway, there's nothing to worry about.'

'You're sure?'

I said breezily, hating myself for not being honest with him, 'Even if by the remotest chance he were a villain and he wanted to do me in he wouldn't do it while I was under his roof. Very tactless.'

'Very easy, I'd have thought.'

'Not if he wants his dinner to go with a swing.'

'All his guests may be cannibals too,' Mike said. 'Remember the Roald Dahl story where they ate the murder weapon?'

Meanwhile, his thigh was much better: ready for unspecified action any day now.

If I'd had any moral fibre I'd have taken myself off for a cold shower, but I'm not into that sort of masochism. I'd have to settle for longing for Mike and a warm shower.

By eight thirty, what little cooking equipment I needed to take

– remember that wonderfully equipped kitchen – was ready in its plastic crates. I was off to the shops, next, in the car, despite the short distance. No point in martyring myself carrying too much back home over a principle. In fact, walking there would certainly have been quicker, so solid was the traffic from the pub at the end of my road, the Court Oak, right into Harborne. The shopping didn't take long. Roger and his team had all the meat packed ready for me, and I was just signing my cheque when Jason yelled from the back that the breakfast sandwiches were ready. Seeing me, he disappeared, only to reappear in a moment with, wrapped in a piece of kitchen towel, a fat white bread sandwich frilled with crisp bacon.

'Smoked,' he said. 'Thought you'd need this. With all that cooking you're doing today I'll bet you forget to feed yourself. So I did this extra one for you.'

Manna. I propped up the wall at the far end of the shop and enjoyed it. And the slightly scurrilous conversation about Roger and his aspirations for setting up a Website and selling over the Internet.

Which was nothing compared to the scurrilous conversation with Malcolm, the florist. The vegetables and bread and cheese came with just as much efficiency. No gossip, though. There. I was ready to start.

If life's too short to stuff a mushroom, it's certainly too short to describe how to stuff one, in this case with ripe Dolcelatte. Suffice to say, I stacked each batch of canapés by the crates of utensils – everything unhurried, systematic and ultimately pleasurable. A little voice told me I'd be quite happy doing this every day. I told it that to cater every day would involve VAT, insurance, tax returns and all sorts of other things I didn't like. But it didn't quite shut up, muttering away every time I gave it a chance, singing in time to the bubbling of the vegetable soup.

I was so content I was just about to lock up the house and

drive over to Tom Bowen's when I remembered I hadn't checked the e-mail.

I needn't have bothered. Nothing. So I sent Kenji another one: could he tell his friend just how urgent this was? And could he ask him, since I didn't think I wanted to pick up my e-mail from Tom Bowen's computer, to put the translation on my answerphone? I could page that from anywhere.

Tom was not only at his house to let me in, when I arrived soon after lunch he actually insisted on helping me unload. The only thing he goggled at was the amount of wine he stacked in the hall.

'You have to allow at least half a bottle per person,' I said. 'There in that case there's some you didn't order – but it's nice and light and some people may prefer it to G and T or whatever.'

He slapped his forehead. 'I'd forgotten about drinks before-hand! My God! I must be losing my grip!'

'End-of-termitis, I think it's called,' I said. 'I've just enough time to go and buy supplies.'

'No, you do the creative stuff. Leave the unskilled labouring to me. Anything else you need doing? Peeling all those spuds, for instance? You only have to ask.'

'I'm fine, thanks. Now, I'd like to be able to leave those bottles of red somewhere to come up to room temperature. And later on I'll open them so they can breathe.'

I stood at the sink, peeling the potatoes, my hair tangling in the cluster of potted plants on the windowsill. I almost wished I'd taken Bowen up on his offer, there were so many. I'd brought my own potato peeler, since it was an old friend, but his was better, with a cushioned grip. What a kitchen! Imagine too, the luxury of two pantries, one for spare china and glass, the other for food. And it was good quality china and glass – even if some of the white china was slightly crazed with age. There was so much of everything I wondered if he'd bought it up in a country house – even a hotel – sale. Whatever, it would be a pleasure to serve on to it this evening, and, I hoped, a pleasure for the guests to eat my food from it. You always wonder what the guests will be like. Whether they will match their host and hostess; whether they will match each other. Once or twice I've been invited to bring my coffee and liqueur and join everyone at the table; somehow I didn't expect this tonight.

The pile of potatoes was diminishing, if not fast enough. There were so many I'd slice them in the little food-processor I'd brought – unnecessarily, given the quality of Bowen's. There. Nearly done . . . What I couldn't understand was why I was enveloped in a smell of lemons, which moved with me as I transferred the spuds to the working surface and processed them. It still clung to me as I packed the slices with parsley and finely chopped onion into earthenware casseroles and covered them with stock. A few pats of butter on the top, salt and plenty of pepper . . .

I'd prepared the pork at home, smothering it with mustard and herbs. All I had to do was take the foil off the meat tins I'd brought it in and shove it in the oven. So why did it smell of lemon? Answer: it didn't. I did. I smelt of the lemon geraniums on the windowsill.

I made myself a black coffee and sat down to clear my brain. It was producing thoughts I really didn't like. Making associations I'd have to face.

While I sat, I might as well page my answerphone to see if that translation had come through. Hell! I'd forgotten to charge the mobile! Never mind, there was always Bowen's phone. No, I really didn't want to use it. I'd be uncomfortable if he came back in and found me using it. Particularly if what I was listening to might incriminate him. Might it? Did I *really* think this slightly lazy middle-aged university lecturer was a villain?

I could no more shake off the suspicion than I could shake

off the scent of lemons. Lemon throat lozenges, no; lemon stomach tablets, no. How about testing the scent of lemon geraniums on Aggie? Would that ring any bells? I had a nasty feeling that it just might.

Yes, I'd have to risk the phone. And during the evening, while Bowen and his guests were safely closeted in the dining room, I would search each room of his lovely house, from attics right down to the cellar.

But I wouldn't use his phone. Couldn't, to be more accurate. I could hardly believe my eyes when I saw what he'd done. He'd fitted the phone, the old-fashioned sort with a dial, with a lock! Incoming calls only, unless you had the key! What sort of man was this, denying himself all the advantages of modern phones to save a few pence!

Well, I'd have to nip out to a phone box, wouldn't I? There'd be one at those shops at the end of the road. No reason why I shouldn't go now: everything was safe in the oven and beginning to smell very good indeed.

If I went out, however, I couldn't get back in again. Bowen had forgotten to leave me his house keys. Coincidence or what? I was stuck there. Did I dare start poking round his house now? On the whole, I thought not.

I occupied the dead time by doing what I wasn't actually paid to do: rendering his kitchen as immaculate as it had started out. Not a sliver of sliced spud on the floor, not a leaf of chopped parsley on the work-surface. Spare stock for the potatoes and to make gravy was in a jug: otherwise there was no sign of a main course. I transferred the soup from my containers to a couple of large Circulon saucepans, hardly used by the look of them. The sweets: well, the upside-down cake had better stay in its tin till the last moment and there was nothing more I could do with the nicely thawed raspberries at the moment. Later I would spread a layer of mascarpone over them, sprinkle it with sugar, and flash the dish under the hottest of grills just before serving.

Cheese: yes, I unwrapped that, next – a lovely selection of unusual English cheeses, plus some predictable but good French and Italian ones. I'd serve that not just with biscuits but with some good quality organic bread.

In the dining room, the table looked – yes, elegant. All the china, cutlery, the table linen itself. And Malcolm's flowers. It was so nice to have a table big enough for a floral centre-piece, even though it would sadly inconvenience any guests wishing to talk across the table to each other. I'm sure, in any case, that somewhere there are rules of etiquette expressly forbidding it.

I tweaked the flowers I'd placed in the sitting room, and then remembered the canapés. I could put them on plates now.

But by now I wasn't enjoying myself, and I didn't want to go back to that kitchen, and its smell of lemon.

At one end of the sitting room was a piano. There was no reason not to play that. No, there wasn't any music, but I could make do with what I carried in my head. I'd do the canapés, draw all the curtains to make the place cosy, and then sit down and play. And while I was playing I could no doubt come up with some reason why I had to slip out as soon as Bowen reappeared.

The more I played – I'd moved from the stormiest of the Brahms Intermezzos to a reflective Chopin Nocturne – the less I could rid myself of the notion that I wasn't alone in the house. Crazy. There'd been absolutely no sign of the cat – or cats – that were supposed to wander everywhere: no food, no litter tray, no hairs. No sign, either, of any Mrs Bowen who might have chosen such a wonderful kitchen and worked in it. It might have been Tom himself, of course. But why would anyone want anything as practical as that and not want to cook in it?

I started to fluff notes. No, you couldn't play Chopin without concentrating as hard as on the Brahms. I stopped abruptly.

Get it into your head, I told myself sternly, that there is no Mrs Rochester in the attic, there are no late Mrs Rochesters in the cellar, and that your temporary employer may be a poor tutor and inefficient in the matter of keys, but he is no romantic hero about to be punished for his past misdeeds by being smacked on the head by a burning beam.

Is he?

I settled down to play again. A Bach Prelude. There is no way you can think about anything except each note and its relationship with the others.

There. Complete control. Complete absorption. And at the end complete silence. Only the sound of breathing.

Except it was two people's breathing.

I swung round.

'Why didn't you tell me you were such a fine musician, Sophie?' Bowen asked. He was still in his outdoor clothes, a couple of boxes sprouting the necks of beer and whisky bottles at his feet. He pulled himself up from the door jamb and took a couple of paces towards me.

'It's not something you have on deckles on your essay folders,' I said. I stood up, noting with great irritation that I smoothed my apron as I did so. At least the garment in question was a jolly PVC affair, busy with overweight teddy bears. Nothing Jane Eyreish at all. 'Look, I want to have one last check on the meat, and then I want to pop out for a breath of fresh air.'

'The garden not airy enough for you?'

'The garden doesn't sell tampons. There's a chemist's in those shops along the road, isn't there? I'll be back in fifteen minutes.'

I bought some tampons just in case he should check. When I got back I'd make a point of breaking open the packet and flushing one away. And the purchase meant I got lots of change for the phone, which was mercifully unvandalised.

262

I dialled my own number, and tapped in my code. Hell, why should so many people want to leave messages? But at last I got the one I wanted. This American voice – Kenji hadn't told me his friend was American, had he? – reading at dictation speed his translation of an advert from a Malaysian newspaper. I wrote it down, word by careful word.

University College of the West Midlands
Qualifications for Teaching
Accommodation Provided

There was information about fees – predictably steep – but none about qualifications needed to get on to the course. Nothing about what you'd get at the end of it, either. But an invitation for orphan girls to apply to a special fund for free courses, accommodation and travel. The only stipulation was that they should have no family.

Right: Chris needed to know about this. Now. Predictably his line was engaged. What about Peter's?

He answered first ring.

I told him about the advert.

'Jesus! Are you thinking what I'm thinking?'

'Depends what you're thinking!'

'Christ – is that the time? Look, Sophie, I've got to be off in ten minutes flat. I'm taking Sheila out tonight – you know, to try and patch things up a bit.'

'Well, get Harvinder on to this, then. Or, better still, Chris himself. Just get whoever to listen to this himself.' I gave him my phone number, although I knew he had it already, and the code I'd just tapped in myself. 'I think we're on to something very interesting, Peter.'

'Dead right. Someone gets these kids over to the UK, takes huge fees, and shoves them into a tatty building pretending to be a university but actually no more than a shabby lodging house. So where do they do their classes, Sophie?'

His voice told me he was moving at least as fast as I was.

'In UWM classes?' I said. 'And maybe whoever's organising this gets some poor mutt of a post-grad student to teach them English.'

'That's why you've got students who don't appear on official print-outs, except those provided by someone else. Someone who went to a great deal of trouble to see that you didn't get the original list of students' entry qualifications. So what happens to the women students who seem to come and go?'

'I've no idea yet.'

'I reckon you have. Let's just get this straight. However many classes these kids go to, they won't get a proper degree at the end of it, will they? All that money down the tubes?'

'All that money down the tubes. I dare say they get a bit of paper,' I said, 'probably highly decorated. But quite worthless. Unless of course they not only sit in on UWM classes but do UWM exams.'

'Does that make sense? Shit, I've got to go. I'll brief Chris as I'm on my way home. To hell with not using mobile phones as you drive! You take care of yourself, mind, Sophie. Because you've got to go back and smile at the man behind all this as if there's nothing at all wrong.'

I laughed grimly. 'Peter, you are talking about Tom Bowen, aren't you?'

'Aren't you?'

'I'm very much afraid I am.'

Chapter Twenty-nine

The short walk back calmed me, even though the wind swirled restless and uneasy litter, ominous as in a forties movie. I had time to tell myself that everything was in Chris's hands now. With evidence, not mere suspicion, he could pull in the enormous resources of West Midlands Police. All *I* had to do was act my way through the dinner – not hard, since I'd be behind the scenes. In any case, no one would be dim enough to harm me in his own home, and Tom Bowen was an intelligent man. As soon I could, I'd go home, pulling up the drawbridge as I went in. Oh, and popping a few piranhas into the moat, by way of further deterrent. In truth, my home was better defended than most: I'd had unwelcome attentions before, and a former colleague of Chris's had turned it into a small version of Fort Knox. He'd done the same for Aggie's house lest anyone ever thought of getting access to my place via hers.

So if I left Bowen's before the end of the meal – and I was quite entitled to – I should be all right. I'd better get paid before things got underway, *things* being either his party or the police one to which I suspected he'd soon be invited.

And what about Jago? Was he involved? Jago had managed to talk to Bowen at a time when I'd been locked out. No, that was trivial – they might have met in the loo or the car park. Certainly Jago had failed to pass on that phone message from Chris. But he'd forgotten the garage messages too. Jago had

265

been running near Carla's boat. Jago had wanted information about Carla's Ph.D., but she'd failed to provide it – probably because it didn't exist. Never had existed.

Despite the lack of hard evidence, all in all – and not least because the man was an arrogant little bugger – I'd like him to be involved. It would be a wonderful coincidence if he were on the guest list tonight.

Bowen was all solicitude when I got back. Did I need aspirin or brandy? A hot-water bottle? Assuring him quite truthfully that I was fine, I turned my attention to the food. That was fine too.

'Now,' I began, 'what about—'

'Oh, it's all here. Cash. I thought you'd prefer cash.' He counted it out. It made quite a satisfactory bundle. At moments like that I always forgot that really this was paying for meat and other things I'd bought and already paid for. So not a lot of that fat roll was profit.

'Thanks. But what I was going to say was, what about the serving staff?'

'All sorted out. They're getting changed now. Bless you, you've hardly left them anything to do. All that washing up, laying the table – you could have left that to them. You know, it's like I said over your dissertation: you're too conscientious for your own good.'

Why did such an innocent comment make my flesh creep?

Two neat, smiling Malay women in their early twenties – faces strangely familiar although I could have sworn they weren't currently part of that wretched class – appeared at the top of the stairs as if on cue. They walked down singly. The cliché would have had them graceful; in fact, they both walked in a rather lumpen way, despite their slender, indeed slight, frames. I stood shoulder to shoulder with them as Bowen addressed us.

'Now, Sophie is in charge in the kitchen. You will do

266

whatever she tells you. You will be on duty first in the lounge, where you will circulate with drinks and canapés – circulate? Walk round? OK?'

They nodded as one.

'You will stay there until I usher everyone in to dinner. Then you will go straight to the kitchen. Don't attempt to tidy the lounge at that point. Sophie will give you the soup to serve from those big tureens.' Why, having originally spoken to them as if their English was minimal, did he risk quite complex sentences and unusual vocabulary?

I said nothing, just nodded.

'While the guests have their soup, you will collect the dirty glasses and plates quickly and take them to the kitchen. You will immediately return to the dining room to collect up soup plates. You will then serve the main course. You will remain – one of you at either end of the dining room – to pass more food, more wine, or whatever. You will stand, of course.'

They nodded.

'When I give the signal, you will collect the dirty plates – serve from the right, collect from the left, isn't that right, Sophie? – and take them to the kitchen. You will then bring the sweet—'

'Sweets,' I said. 'There is a choice.'

'Did we agree two sweets?' He didn't change his rather brusque tone, but I'd clearly exceeded my role.

'No. I know I mentioned it when we had the initial discussions, but we never followed it up. But it is usual, these days.' I gave a rueful grin. 'Since nothing was agreed, I didn't invoice you for it.'

He raised an eyebrow. 'I'll settle up in a minute. You offer a choice of desserts. You pour wine. Then you will collect dishes and bring in cheese and biscuits—'

'And bread.' I added.

'And serve that. At last you will serve coffee and liqueurs. Then, her work nobly done, Sophie will pack her gear and go

267

home.' He smiled at me with apparent kindness. The smile left his face as he continued, 'And you two will wash up and put away. From time to time one of you will come in to offer more coffee and more liqueurs.'

They nodded. So did I. What I couldn't fail to notice was that at no time would we women be able to exchange more than the most perfunctory word. Had he intended that?

The good news, though, was that at certain moments I could guarantee that I would be perfectly free to prowl uninterrupted about the house. If Bowen were giving them explicit orders like that, I was damned sure he'd keep an eye on them to make sure they obeyed them.

'Everything OK, Sophie?'

'I'd just like to make one more check – make sure I've got the right number of spoons and forks. Last-minute nerves, Tom.'

He raised an eyebrow but said nothing.

I stopped on the threshold. If I'd been busy in my few minutes away from the house so had he. Or someone acting on his orders. The table had been reduced to two-thirds of the earlier size, with proportionately fewer place settings.

'A few last-minute cancellations,' he said airily.

But not casually.

He'd known about them, hadn't he? So why had he let me go ahead and cater for so many more? All that food left over – enough to keep him in cold roast pork for a week. Or more. I hoped his guests were hungry and that they'd pig themselves.

'How much would the second dessert be?' He dug in a back pocket.

'How about what it cost me? There's no effort involved.'

'So why bother?'

'Because it's delectable and will impress people by its very simplicity.' I did a couple of sums in my head and told him the price.

'Is that all? Are you sure?' Shaking his head, he counted it out in coins.

So what was the key to the man? That he wanted show? Expensive display? Certainly he'd have preferred the wine to come with famous labels. But the rest of the house wasn't ostentatious, just expensive. Furniture, carpets, curtains, piano – all the same good quality as the kitchen. No expense spared, in fact.

So just how did he pay for it all? Not on a lecturer's salary, that was for sure. I'd just have to be thorough when I searched his house.

The first floor of the house was just as well appointed as the parts I'd already seen. A bathroom with new suite and tiles: there was enough room to have separate bath and shower. Then there were three good-sized bedrooms, and another room which was locked. That would repay a further visit, if only I could find a key lying round. Two of the bedrooms were simply but classically furnished: one of them held the unused chairs. The third disconcerted me to say the least. A very low bed, a sunken bath, a Georgian towel-rail laden with thick fluffy towels: fine. Pity about the mixture of mirrors in strange places and sexually explicit Japanese prints. One or two were already slightly foxed – all that steamy heat, no doubt.

Funny, I'd never have imagined Bowen with that sort of sex life. No time to surmise now, however.

Yes! Keys! There in the heap of small change by the modern phone on the bedside table. But there was not time even to pick them up. I should be downstairs, carving the pork.

I'd no idea, of course, who his guests were. I'd been firmly ensconced in the kitchen throughout their arrival. Their voices were a funny mixture, though. There were some of those carrying ones – both sexes – that I associate with public school educated people. A couple of roughish Brummie accents. The

extremely correct tones of someone educated abroad in another
language but very well taught: that was a woman. Not Lola's
contralto, but a much lighter one. Could it be . . . surely it
wasn't Jenny Lee's? But I couldn't pick up anything that
sounded like Jago's. What a pity I'd drawn the curtains: I'd
have been able to sneak a look from outside, like a groundling
goggling at a play. I'd seen dinner parties hosted that way last
time I'd walked through some of the posher parts of Edgbaston.
I fancy Bowen would have preferred that sort of scene – the
public display of fine linen, fine glass and fine company.

As soon as the doors were shut on the waitresses, I was
back upstairs. The attic storey, this time. Still no sign of that
mythical cat. Or was it cats? A couple of cheap beds stood
side by pathetic side. The room was occupied, I guessed by the
students acting as waitresses. God knows what warmth those
thin duvets would provide. And those poor women came from
hot, steamy Malaysia. Two wardrobes – fifties stuff, the sort
you could get cheap anywhere. No dressing-table, no mirror,
no bookcase. The bathroom was spartan – no radiator, even. I
couldn't believe that. No one would be so short-sighted as to
leave unheated an attic bathroom. The bath enamel had long
since been scoured through. The towels were threadbare.

Back to the bedroom. Hardly anything in the wardrobes, and
what there was was cheap. No pictures on the walls, no photos
of families. Two copies of the Koran, however, although the
heads of the girls serving this evening were uncovered. There
was enough for me to conclude they lived here and had not
been hired just for the evening. Bowen had said he'd arrange
the unskilled staff, but he hadn't explained they were already
on the premises.

I'd never have made a decent burglar: terrified of detection,
I was back downstairs in the kitchen long before I needed to
have been. Long enough to make a swift dive into the cellar.
Nothing, absolutely nothing. I sniffed. Was there a sickly smell
in the air? No, it was simply damp. Wasn't it? As I turned

a corner, the smell took me straight back to school. Rotten eggs. Stink bombs. But although there was a wooden bench, and even some test tubes in a wooden rack, there were no chemicals in the ranks of glass bottles on the shelf behind. There were enough stains in the old porcelain sink, however, to make me wonder what sort of cocktail had found its way into Birmingham's sewers.

Back up to turn on the grill, and spread mascarpone and sprinkle sugar on to the shallow bowls of raspberries: thank you, Nigel Slater.

No, I wouldn't leap into action as soon as I heard the dining-room door open. I would give the guests a little time to digest. They'd had a nourishing country soup and a main course designed for hungry peasants. They'd need a breather. And it would give me a moment to speak to the waitresses. In fact, I ladled a couple of bowls of soup and passed them with a smile.

'The grill's not quite hot enough for me to finish the dessert yet,' I said. 'You've got plenty of time.'

They exchanged alarmed glances, but tucked into the soup. If I'd asked them questions, they couldn't have answered them, so quickly were they dispatching it. The first to finish plunged a thin arm into a cupboard. She poured the remaining soup from the tureen into a basin.

She muttered something to her colleague, who put the tureen into the sink and filled it with water.

The latter smiled at me. 'So he not know how much left,' she said.

'Are you only supposed to eat what he gives you?' I asked.

They nodded.

'That meat?'

They nodded.

'But it's pork!' And they had Korans on their beds. I'd have liked to ram the pork bones down his throat, his gratuitous malice made me so wild. He'd deliberately overstated the number of guests so I'd cook extra to feed these women!

'That's what he give us to eat. No eat, go hungry.'

And maybe spend hard-earned money on sandwiches from Marks and Spencer, like the student I'd never managed to speak to. But that didn't make sense. The food was so much cheaper in the refectory. Some of it was even halal.

'Does he pay you properly?' Perhaps the last word was redundant. 'Does he pay you?'

They looked anxiously at me. Then at each other. 'Vouchers. For shops.'

One thing I hadn't mentioned in my lesson on shopping! So poor Shazia had been forced, for one reason or another, to get food that way.

One pointed at my watch. I slid the dishes under the grill. They sighed with relief.

While the sugar bubbled and browned, I tipped the upside-down cakes on to plates. The golden syrup swam enticingly round it. The pineapple smelt good. I had an idea there wouldn't be much left of that for these young women. I ran a finger round the cake-tins and licked the syrup from it. I passed them to them. I had a sense that it was bravery that enabled them to do likewise.

Time to retrieve the dish from the grill. I laid it gently on the table, and handed over the oven gloves. Eyes like a frightened rabbit's, the student I'd offered them to shook her head. At last she folded the napkin at her waist into as thick a pad as possible. Synchronising her movements with those of her colleague, she picked the dish up and set off back into the dining room.

Much as I'd have liked to head straight back up to the study, I stayed put. The dessert was the shortest course. I'd provided a very fine dessert wine which would do equally well with the cheese course, where it would be joined by a visibly expensive port. Yes, they'd linger over the cheese. Which was itself very good – I'd tasted it. Twice to be honest: once, when I'd chosen it, and again this evening. I nibbled enough to keep my own grubs from biting, and then cut enough to ensure that those girls had a little protein today. I put their slices on a couple of plates and covered them with kitchen towel.

Then I finished washing and stacking the last of my boxes and trays: no reason, I supposed, why I shouldn't take them out to the car. It would mean I could make a quicker getaway. And I had a feeling that when I'd checked out that locked room that was exactly what I'd want. Not that I was going to touch, let alone take anything. No, this one I was going to play by the book. Apart from borrowing the set of keys from the master bedroom, of course.

I picked them up using tissues – no jingle of metal, no fingerprints. The third opened the locked room. Yes! Bowen's study!

According to Chris, the instruction to police officers checking out any crime scene is to put their hands into their pockets. If it's good enough for the professionals, it's good enough for me. So I couldn't log on to his computer or go through the floppy disks. Or check out those tempting filing cabinets, one with the enticing label UCWM. No, I had to.

Still holding the keys in a tissue, I selected one that looked as if it might fit the cabinet. It did. I left the keys in the lock, and slipped the tissue between my fingers and the drawer handle.

This man and his love of good quality! Even the files were new – not like some of the scruffy specimens in my own system. Or perhaps they just indicated his scam was recent. I slipped a couple of them out and flicked through them.

If only I had time for a proper read. But what my skim through told me was clear enough, even if I didn't grasp all the details.

He recruited overseas for legitimate, properly qualified students. For UCWM. He helped them get visas, and established them in Handsworth Wood, charging them more or less standard full-time fees. He then inserted them as part-time students at UWM, saying they were UK residents, with the Church Lane address. And pocketed the difference between the full-time overseas student's fee and the much lower UK part-time one. Between three and four thousand a year per student, minus his expenditure on the Church Lane building. Not all that much profit, then.

But then there were the 'bursary' students. All from the sticks, none with much in the way of qualifications. This time his procedure was slightly different. He enrolled them in courses for which they were obviously unsuited. Then somehow he pulled them out of UWM and apparently replaced them. So what . . . ?

Hell! How long had I been engrossed in these? Longer than I ought! I slipped everything back into place and locked the cabinet. On impulse, using a fingernail, I eased the UCWM label out of its holder and slipped it into my jeans pocket. A little bit of paper that might encourage Chris to act more quickly. If he still needed that sort of encouragement.

Time to exit.

Too late! There was a sudden billow of chatter from downstairs, quickly cut off. Out, fast? Or stay put? I locked myself in, switching off the light. Footsteps started up the stairs. Surely Bowen wasn't looking for me? But the footsteps, so muffled by the thick carpet that over the pounding of my heart I could hardly hear them, went past. Of course, the only thing this house lacked was a downstairs loo. I'd have to wait until the process happened in reverse. There! The loo was being flushed. The bathroom door opened and shut. But the feet didn't go back downstairs. They came towards me.

I froze.

The door handle turned. Backwards. Forwards. And then was still. The footsteps went back down the stairs.

Out, now. Back to the master bedroom. And get those keys back where they should be. In my haste I knocked a five-pence piece off the bedside cabinet. I let it roll. And zapped into the bathroom. I slid the bolt. Yes, after that, I needed the loo in good earnest.

Someone rattled the door. My hands barely dry, I opened it.

'Why!' I exclaimed, as if delighted to see her. 'Jenny! I didn't know you'd be here tonight!'

Jenny Lee didn't even bother to feign pleasure. 'What are you doing here?'

'Didn't Tom tell you? I'm the cook. I was just tidying myself up before I left, actually. See you Monday, no doubt.'

'See you Monday.'

Oscar-winning or not? Probably not. And if her work at UWM were anything to go by, Jenny was far too intelligent for anything other than a top-class performance. I would have thought that she'd be too polite not to say something nice about the food, but perhaps it hadn't been to her taste.

Maybe a really quick flit would look suspicious. Perhaps it would be better to see the coffee safely in and then be on my way.

The only question on my mind as I eventually let myself into my car, locking myself firmly in, was whether I should phone Chris or drive straight to his house. Sitting on Bowen's drive while I decided was not, however, an option. Slotting quickly into reverse, and finding a mercifully empty road, I was sure I saw someone open the front door. But I didn't wait to check.

Chapter Thirty

So, like Ivo heading for the safety of his hole, I scuttered for home. Oh, in my head I was brave enough. After all, I'd sailed through the dinner party without so much as a veiled threat. Possibly. Probably. But the rest of me wasn't so brave. If only I hadn't been – almost – caught out. Home was an obvious target for anyone looking for me. But surely even then I had some time on my side. Even if Jenny had told Bowen her suspicions about what I'd been doing upstairs, even if that caused him any anxiety, surely he wouldn't abandon a dinner party he'd paid so much for to give chase on the mere chance I'd seen or taken something. No, nothing to worry about.

Holding the phone, all the same, as if it were a security blanket, I dialled Chris. And got the wretched man's answerphone. The long beep took for ever to sound. My head suppressed what my heart really wanted to say: *Send someone round now! Or preferably ten minutes ago!* Instead, I confined myself to a terse, 'Phone me, Chris, the moment you get in. Whatever time.' And, of course, if I'd decided to flit, he could always page me to find out where I was. I patted the pager in my jeans pocket.

Telling myself I should have a nice milky drink and head for bed, I headed for the kitchen. Hmm, there were all those kitchen utensils to bring in. Later, Sophie. Later.

Except I couldn't, could I? I couldn't even *imagine* going out. Back at Bowen's, someone might be wondering if my

277

quick escape indicated guilt. Hell, I didn't know if they even suspected anything!

But something told me they did.

The drinking chocolate grew an unlovely skin.

'What shall I do, Ivo? Stay put or go to ground?' My voice was wobbly enough for him to regard me with sympathy.

He had a sip from his water bottle, which was not quite empty enough for me to worry about, and scratched his tummy. 'How about a police station?'

'You're right,' I said. Pausing only to drop a handful of food through the top of his aquarium – bother putting it into his food bowl, let him forage! – I headed for the car, clattering cargo of utensils and all. And, yes, I set the alarm and locked the front door.

Rose Road Police Station in Harborne was the obvious place. OK, Chris no longer worked there but enough people would remember him – and probably me, given the amount of time I'd spent there, one way or another – for them to take me seriously.

The police themselves, that is. But first I had to get past the civilian on the reception desk. The middle-aged man behind the desk – not, alas, a man I knew – was trying vainly to make sense of a tumult of noise from four or five well-dressed and well-pissed young men. The tenor of their complaint was that they'd all lost their cars while they'd been at a nightspot. Stolen, every last one. Since they'd parked on double yellows at a notorious bottleneck, it came as no surprise to me – but a great deal to them – to hear that their cars might simply, but expensively, have been towed away. They were not happy.

At last, order only partially restored, it was my turn.

'I've witnessed a serious crime, and I'm afraid the perpetrator may be after me. Can I talk to the duty inspector, please?'

If I ended up with a constable recruited only yesterday, I'd be content – so long as I was safe behind those nice shiny doors.

*   *   *

The police have ways of reaching their colleagues that even their best friends can't use. They promised to contact Chris. Meanwhile I sat, not in the waiting area but to my great surprise in what was once Chris's room. It was now the cheerfully untidy domain of another Sheila, not the prickly wife of Peter, nor even an unspecified Australian woman, but the DCI who'd taken over from Chris on his promotion to Smethwick. Sheila had been working late – didn't these people ever sleep? – on another case, and welcomed me with, if not open arms, an open smile.

'He won't be long,' she said, passing me chilled water. No coffee percolator for her, nor even a kettle and selection of tea bags: things had changed since Chris and Ian's time. Sheila must have caught me looking round the room. She said simply, 'I'm a Mormon.'

She pounced on the phone, first ring, but it was her case, not mine. She scribbled – yes, from where I sat it was a dreadful scrawl – looked serious, replaced the handset and dialled again. The call lasted for ever. How could Chris ever get through?

At this point my jeans started to vibrate. Chris was wondering exactly the same thing.

The problem was, as I should have known all along, that Chris couldn't simply pin on his sheriff's star and go out and arrest Bowen. Until they got a search warrant, and checked for themselves the contents of the filing cabinet – I'd laid the label on Sheila's desk – and indeed of the computer, they had nothing to justify even questioning him. Not, at least, at eleven forty-five on a Friday night. That wasn't to say that Chris wasn't concerned for my safety. Where was I to spend the night? We sat at opposite ends of a phone line, skirting round a problem that could have been quite easily solved had he not still had a bruised little finger to remind us of our most recent night under the same roof.

'Ian,' he said. 'You've stayed there before. Phone Ian. And ring me back.'

Ian's phone rang for ever. If he had an answering machine – and I simply couldn't remember – it wasn't switched on tonight.

I phoned Chris, who picked up the call first ring. By now, it was surely too late to try anyone else, and I didn't fancy the anonymity of a hotel bedroom.

In the end, a compromise appeared. I would – with a little help from my Harborne friends – go home and fasten myself in. Harborne police would pay Balden Road special attention on their routine patrols. Chris – or rather, Peter, since it was his case – would organise a search warrant and while checking out Bowen, would take a look at some of his friends, too. Like Jenny Lee. And Jago? I certainly hadn't heard his voice last night.

Unlike hamsters, gerbils don't go in for wheels. My brain did, though, pounding a treadmill of speculation, as I lay, supposedly trying to catch some sleep. At one point I gave up entirely, donned my dressing gown, roused the central heating, and did my packing. By six everything was ready, bar my flight bag and the ticket still safe in the safe.

I wasn't, of course. But something – the knowledge that I'd soon be safe with Mike, or the thought that daylight would bring police action – allowed me to relax, and I headed once again for bed. And fell into a deep, deep sleep.

It was quite light when I woke, to a thunderous knocking on my front door. Dressing gown, slippers – hell, which was the right foot? – I'd tottered downstairs, my eyes still gluey and only half open. OK, OK! I'd half-slipped the chain before I remembered there were strong reasons for staying locked in.

I peered through my spyhole. Jago? What was Jago doing up at this hour? And what was he doing here? God, I was so dozy. I gave my eyes a scrub.

The letter-flap swung in: 'Sophie? Are you there? For God's sake, Sophie, let me in! Help me, for God's sake.'

I bent down to speak through the flap myself. 'What's the matter?'

'You've got to help!' He turned away, perhaps to check who was behind him, so I missed a couple of words. Then I caught '. . . are after me!'

Time for quick thought. Pity I didn't have any thoughts in my head, quick or otherwise. I didn't like him, but I had nothing concrete to connect him with Bowen, whom I wouldn't have let in, not even with my thick head, not even with all the hounds of hell after him.

He stepped in. Just on to the mat. He couldn't get any further because I was still holding the door.

I don't know how long it took the thought to form itself. *I've made a mistake.* A mistake. Yes, I knew I'd made a mistake. No, there was nothing obviously threatening. But there was something about his posture. And something about the set of his jaw. No, I couldn't put it into words but it meant trouble. I had to get rid of Jago.

So I stepped forward, my hand still on the door knob.

Chris had always dinned into me that controlling a situation meant keeping calm. I must treat Jago as if he was the Betterware man; I mustn't be hostile, nor anxious, just flatly uninterested. Sooner or later he'd notice that I was wafting in gusts of freezing air. It would dawn on him they matched my welcome.

If I was picking up his signals, he wasn't reading mine. He bent down. His face was inches from mine. 'The police. The police say they've got evidence I was near her boat. Carla's boat. Footprints. All the hundreds of people using that towpath and they can pick out *my* footprints!' He bent closer. 'Come on, Sophie, you've got a friend in the police. That man who wanted Jenny to interpret. He said he was a friend of yours.'

I nodded automatically. Where was this going?

'You could talk to him for me.'

In my present state I could scarcely accuse anyone of not

thinking rationally! But would it help my situation to point out to Jago he'd be better off talking to a solicitor than to me?

'How did they know I was there in the first place?' he pursued when I didn't respond.

I shrugged. 'Maybe someone saw you – recognised you.' When would my brain get into gear?

He didn't pick up on that. Fortunately. 'They're going to try and link me with her death, aren't they? All that stuff about Melbourne – they'll think I was trying to find out about her.'

'You were trying to find out about her *thesis*, Jago,' I pointed out. 'I offered to help. Me and Mike. I can tell them that.'

'But how did they find out about my footprints?' He bent closer. 'It must have been when I was running. I . . .' His voiced hardened. 'It was you, wasn't it? The woman on the bridge? It was you that— My God! All your smiling, all your teasing – and it was you who grassed me in.'

He grabbed my dressing gown, between my chin and my breasts. I didn't look down, for fear of giving him ideas. I held on to the door knob as if it were a lifeline.

'I don't know what you're talking about.' My denial was true as far as the teasing was concerned – me? tease? – but I wasn't about to admit I'd snitched on him to the Smethwick police. Not with him in this mood.

'You tart, you bitch. You little prick-tease. You—' He unleashed words I didn't use and some I didn't even know. 'Well,' he yelled, 'this is what prick-teases get!' He grabbed me and shoved. I staggered back. He threw me towards the kitchen door. It gave under my hands as I tried to steady myself. Just as I'd ended on Carla's office floor, I fell hard on my hands and knees.

I scrabbled to my feet. God knows where my slippers were.

He pushed me down. Bare feet aren't much good for kicking. But I kicked all the same. And hooked at his knees, and tried to claw his face. I fought. I clawed. And I yelled. I yelled enough to waken Harborne's Saturday sleepers. To awaken the dead.

He kicked the door shut.

I lashed out with my arms, tipping chairs, grabbing a table leg. The table shifted, bringing the salt mill crashing on to my chest. Then the pepper.

He was fit. He was taller, heavier than I. I didn't have a chance. That wouldn't stop me. Until he banged my head back on to the floor. Not hard, but hard enough to show he meant business. He put his arm across my throat.

All his weight on my thighs now. Hell. He unzipped his flies. I flailed at the arm on my throat. He grabbed both my hands in one of his. I let him. Let him transfer both to the grip of his left hand. Let him think I was going to acquiesce. Then I could make another effort.

I lay still. Quite still.

And he was motionless, too. I tried to read his face. His cold blue eyes. I didn't like what I saw.

What was he doing now? Why was he smiling! Jesus, that smile! He had the salt mill in his hand and was kneeing my thighs apart.

No, no, sweet Jesus, no!

I kicked, writhed – but he was too heavy.

He tugged at the dressing-gown cord. Why was he bothering? Unless he wanted it to—

Which was worse, being raped, or raped and strangled? Maybe if I went limp – let him think I'd fainted . . . Then I'd fight. Really fight.

He released my hands. They flopped to my sides.

No, he didn't stop to check if I was alive. He smashed his left hand flat on my breastbone, using it to lever himself up the better to slam in that bloody salt mill. It took all my will not to scream just at the thought.

And now he was talking. 'One for each orifice. You're a pedant, Sophie. You'll like that word, won't you? Orifice? The salt, the pepper – then we'll see how big your mouth is—'

For a moment I toyed with the idea of enduring everything

until his penis was in my mouth. And biting. Hard. But I didn't trust myself not to be screaming. Couldn't imagine how I'd deal with what he was going to inflict.

So I moved very gently. Very very swiftly. That vulnerable hand on my chest. I put my left hand on top of it, pressed as hard as I could. Then whipped the right up to grab his little finger. Yanked it backwards with all my strength. I heard the crack, felt the joint give.

He flew backwards screaming.

I was on my feet, heading for the door. He'd kill me now, for sure, if he caught me.

The door was open.

Tom Bowen. Two bruisers. One either side of him.

'What are you doing here?' I croaked, pulling the dressing gown together, tying it as tight as I could the way my hands shook.

'What an interesting scenario,' Bowen said, his voice as measured as if he were discussing an assignment. 'Well, let's capitalise on it, shall we, gentlemen? We found our friend here raping poor Sophie. Oh, past tense. He'd raped her – those mills were still in place when we found her, poor girl. Anal and vaginal penetration. And oral sex as well. Shocking. And then he'd strangled the poor woman. In our efforts to pull him off we—'

'No, Gov. He was so upset by what he'd done he went and slit his throat.' This from the heavy to his left. 'What a shame.'

Remind them you're a human being: wasn't that what they said you should do? But all that came into my head was, 'How did you get in?'

Half-laughing, Bowen gestured. 'You'd left your front door open. And when we heard a woman's screams, we clearly had to investigate. OK. Let's deal with her first. And then we'll fix him.'

Jago screamed, but subsided as the right-hand heavy lunged into him. 'Want the other hand broken, do you?'

Did I, did I hear a noise outside?

'There'll be a witness,' I said loudly. 'You won't get away with this. Just give up. Get away while you can.'

'What witness?'

'My lodger.' I staggered to the sink, and poured a cup of water, gulping it down. I think they were laughing. If Bowen let me do that, maybe, just maybe, I could get away with it. I'd told someone – was it Jago? was it Bowen? – that I had a lodger called Ivo to keep me company while Mike was away. I'd never spelt out who or what Ivo was; I'd let whoever it was think it was an adult human. But on Ivo's aquarium was his little name-card, in that lovely italic script.

As if still dazed I lurched towards the aquarium, fishing out the water bottle.

'Empty – can I give her some more? Don't want to hurt her. Don't want her dying of thirst.' My throat sounded as if I was.

The heavies didn't like the idea; Bowen gestured to stop them intervening. 'Can't hurt. Dean: keep an eye on that randy little bastard.' He pointed at Jago, cowering in the corner, his back pressed hard against a cupboard door, holding his injured hand and whimpering at this new attention. 'Dear, dear: and I'd thought he'd been saving himself for Jenny.'

I nodded, spilling more water than I got in the bottle. Back to the cage. As I hooked up the water bottle, I slipped from its holder the little piece of card, rolled it into a cylinder and dropped it an inch from Ivo's nose. He ploughed into it.

'She's my lodger's,' I said. 'He'll be back in a minute. Just went out for a run. Can't be long, now. Do you want to give her her breakfast?' I pushed the food-tin towards the nearer heavy.

'Fucking rat!' He didn't. He looked at Bowen. His mate flexed his fingers, crunching the knuckles. I tried not to wince.

'Look,' I said to Bowen, 'why don't you clear out now? You could take that low-life with you.' I nodded at Jago.

'That trouble-making little shit,' Bowen snorted. 'And if I did, Sophie, what then?'

Bowen wasn't a criminal, was he? Not in his eyes, that is. In his eyes he was just an ordinary man who'd hankered after a bit more money and in getting it overreached himself. The thugs would act on his orders. Maybe. Depended how much he paid them to.

'Think about it,' I gabbled. 'Quite a difference between a bit of fraud and a cold-blooded killing. Fraud – it's not even a crime, officially. What would you get? A couple of years at most. If they bothered to take you to court. Bringing in a few extra students, taking their fees off them and slipping them into the odd class? I doubt if the uni would even complain. It'd be a laughing stock, wouldn't it? Can you see the headline all over the *Times Higher*? "UWM conned!" No, you'd get off scot-free. Maybe the uni would even be grateful.'

My reward was a short bark of laughter.

But I persevered. 'All you have to do is nip back and smash your computer, destroy all your floppy disks, have a bit of bonfire – who could prove anything? Tom, you're a teacher, not a crook. Come on, all those years you've spent helping other people. I'm your tutee, for God's sake. You and I – we've shared jokes. I cooked your food.' God knows what drivel I was talking. I just knew that the longer I talked the longer the chance that something would happen. Please. 'They'd know it wasn't Jago who raped me. DNA. They'd gob swab you and know who did.'

Jago risked getting to his feet. He'd wet himself. I slung the kitchen towel roll at him, but he dropped it, screaming as it hit his hand. I bent to gather the salt and pepper. For all my feigned calm I was shaking so much I couldn't stand them upright on the table. The pepper rolled to my glass fruit bowl. It struck it, not hard enough to break it, but to strike a resounding note.

'You rang, Ms Rivers?' came Chris's voice from the doorway.

Chapter Thirty-one

I must say, having been denied the other day the full armoury of the Bomb Squad, I'd rather have liked the Armed Response Unit now. Despite its absence, though, there were enough police officers with Chris to make Bowen and his friends fold like a prematurely inspected soufflé. Jago was already as prone as a pancake. As for me, I did what I'd wanted to do for some time, which was to throw up. At least I made it to the sink.

'Before you ask,' said Chris, passing me a sheet of kitchen towel, 'it was your pager. You didn't respond. I got sick of the message on your answerphone. And when Peter phoned in to report that his suspects had done the *exeunt, severally* bit, I put two and two together.'

If I replied he wouldn't have heard. My kitchen seethed with uniformed men and women, including a paramedic intent on dealing with Jago's hand. I kept my head down: the last thing I wanted to do was share an ambulance with him.

Peter having officially been the arresting officer – he'd escorted my visitors to either Harborne or Smethwick, I cared not whither – Chris was now technically free. Free to mop Jago's pee from my kitchen floor; to send me upstairs – having established that penetration hadn't taken place – to shower; to insist that in any case my dressing gown had to be bagged as evidence; to become, in fact, so totally efficient as to lure me downstairs with the smell of fresh toast and hot chocolate. And to want to call my GP.

'I'm fine. A bit shaken, a bit bruised. But fine.'

'Have you any idea just how shaken and how bruised you are?'

I shook my head. I didn't want to know about the former, and had some magic ointment to deal with the latter.

He looked at me sternly: I had a fair suspicion he wouldn't give up so easily, that he'd keep an eye on me even if it meant sticking with me all day. However, as if resigned, he said calmly, 'We'll have to tie up all these loose ends later. But Peter and Harvinder can question those – those scrotes – before you have to make your statement.'

I'd never heard Chris use the term before. Police jargon it might be, and not just in Smethwick either, but it wasn't his usual vocabulary. His anger was palpable.

'You wouldn't want to ask them a few questions yourself?'

He shook his head. 'Out of practice, Sophie. I could muck things up. No, I've seen both of them in action and they're as good as you get.'

'You don't think,' I suggested, remembering an encounter I'd once had with Peter, 'that Peter's a bit . . . forceful?'

'Jesus, Sophie, after all you've been through this morning, wouldn't you like him to be forceful?'

It didn't take me long to agree.

'I'd like one of our women officers to take your statement. One trained in such cases. So I'll take you over to Piddock Road as soon as you're ready.'

That would mean talking about this morning. In detail. 'There's one loose end I'd like to tie up first,' I said carefully. 'A very minor one, but—'

'My dear Sophie, the more for the DPP to get its teeth in the better.'

'OK.' I should have told him off about that superior tone, but

I found I couldn't be bothered. 'You know that lemon geranium that scrapes an existence on your kitchen windowsill? I'd like to take it down to Aggie. I'll explain why as we go to collect it. You don't have to come down to Evesham with me,' I said, trying to be offhand but sounding, to my ears, plaintive, 'but it would be useful to have a reliable witness to what I'm sure she's going to say.'

He nodded. He must have thought me off my head – I could no more have driven down the motorway than I could have flown to the moon, and I might well be talking material evidence – but he said nothing. 'OK.'

'And you'd better hand over that cast to whoever should be looking after these things. It's over there somewhere.' I gestured.

He found it. He rooted in my polythene bag store, finding a new bag and a tie. 'It can wait till we get to Smethwick. Are you taking any bets about whose shoe made the print?'

'Too much like taking candy from a baby,' I said.

While he nipped into his house, emerging with a straggly specimen Aggie would no doubt see as a challenge to nurse back to health, I stayed in his car. No special reason – except my legs announced they were too wobbly to walk anywhere they didn't have to. Occasionally I'd shake in a way that alarmed me. When I inspected it, my pulse was all over the place. God, I wasn't about to go down with flu, was I?

'By rights,' said Chris, passing me the geranium and inspecting me closely, 'you should be in A&E being treated for shock. At very least in our Rape Suite being counselled by a couple of experts.'

'Well, I don't want to sit watching a display telling me to hang on for four hours, and I wasn't raped. Though I wouldn't want to get any closer to rape. Just between you and me, Chris, I was as scared as I know how to be. And then some more. In fact, I reckon I've got an Ph.D. in scared.' And now was not the time to fill him in on the event years ago which resulted in Steph.

The poor bugger wouldn't want to pat my hand in a comforting way, lest I see it as a renewed overture. As it happens, I'd have loved to have a hand to grasp. And then I recalled how I'd grasped Jago's and shuddered. I'd never deliberately hurt anyone as badly as that before.

'Jago's finger,' I continued. 'D'you reckon I broke it?'

'With a bit of luck. I should be surprised if he brought a private prosecution for assault, however.'

I managed a grin, and, since Chris wasn't the sort of driver to take his eyes off the road, a bit of a giggle to show I appreciated his efforts. 'Any news of Peter and the reconciliation with his Sheila?'

'His Sheila?'

'As opposed to the Rose Road Sheila currently occupying your old room. She seems to work even longer hours than you did. Without the help of coffee.'

'Poor woman.' Poor Chris: I could hear the restraint in his voice. What he wanted to know was what sort of a fist she was making of his old job. At least, in his position I'd have wanted to.

'I didn't get a chance of a natter with any of your old team, so I've no gossip to purvey. Sorry.'

He grinned. 'The grapevine says she's doing OK.'

'You're a bit of an act to follow, mind, Chris. And she's a woman.'

'So long as she's a good cop. That's what the team'll worry about. Which reminds me: there's a new DI starting next week. African-Caribbean woman. How about that?'

'Great.' I bit back what I was going to say, but to my surprise he said it for me.

'Of course, what will be great is when I don't even need

to comment on something like that. Then we will have *true* equal opportunities.'

I glanced at him: he sounded absolutely sincere, not as if he were parroting something he'd heard on a course somewhere. Perhaps he was embarrassed lest he'd sounded pious. 'But to get back to your question. Peter and his Sheila. Well, I don't hold out much hope. He won't change, you know. Blokes like that never do.'

Blokes like Chris, too. Whoever he had a relationship with would take second place to his job. Was being in the police as addictive as teaching? I'd never seen any of Chris's team shoot off at five o'clock on the dot, any more than my William Murdock colleagues did.

The M5 traffic was surprisingly heavy, and he concentrated on his driving for a while. Lulled by the road noise, full of comfort food, I found I was falling asleep.

And flung myself awake. That way flashbacks lay. This morning had been bad enough once.

'You all right?'

'Trying not to doze.'

'A catnap would probably do you a lot of good. Sophie, if you start getting flashbacks or nightmares, you will ask for professional help. I know you and your *I can cope with anything life throws at me!* routine. But this morning was . . . exceptional. And if you won't listen to me, listen to your stomach. I bet your gastritis will be back on the warpath any minute.'

I couldn't argue. 'Everything that's been a bit strange at UWM – the missing thesis, the students coming and going, the vandalism – then the paint stripper on the car – I've been trying to tell myself I've got an oversuspicious mind, that I'm getting paranoid.'

I knew he wouldn't be able to resist. If I couldn't, why should he? 'Just because you're paranoid doesn't mean they're not out to get you. And I didn't notice much in the way of self-doubt. I'd have said you were certain things were wrong.'

'I didn't want to get involved with anything.'

'Oh yes you did. OK, you're high on civic virtue, but you're like a terrier – get your teeth into something and never let go.'

'I thought all I was doing was a spot of harmless checking up,' I said, not quite truthfully.

'Checking up is rarely harmless. Not if someone wants to hide something. In this case two someones wanting to hide something. I don't know how Carla and Bowen are connected. *If* they're connected, even. But I have a feeling they might be. This – this feeling.'

'I've got the same one, then. Strange, isn't it? Come to think of it, though I've seen them having coffee together, I'd say there was no love lost between them.'

'I'm sure Peter's well on the way to sorting it out. The SOCO people, Fraud, Immigration – there are a lot of threads to tweak. How are you feeling now?'

'Hungry.'

'That's always a good sign, isn't it? Do you want to stop off somewhere or can we rely on Aggie?'

'I'm sure we can rely on Aggie, but why not morning coffee at a posh cake shop in Evesham too? If we can find one.' I might be hungry but I also fancied a treat, a bit of pampering.

'And if we can find somewhere to park. Not many shopping days left till Christmas, remember.'

I smacked the side of my head. 'I haven't bought a single present yet. Or any cards! Oh, my God.'

'You have had a few other things on your mind. Anyway, you can always do what I'm going to do,' he said crisply. 'E-mail Christmas greetings.'

* * *

The best we managed was chocolate bars from a vending machine. But that helped with the hunger, if not the desire for coddling. We'd see what Aggie could come up with.

Lucy was out, so Aggie opened the door herself. We'd not phoned to announce we were on the way, as we probably ought to have done. So the first thing she was aware of, assuming her eyes were as bad as I feared, was the smell of the lemon geranium. Her face stiffened in panic. Chris raised an eyebrow at me. Then there was a chorus of hellos from Chris and me and her anxiety relaxed into a crinkle of beams.

'You really had me worried there,' she said, shuffling back so we could get in. She shut the door. 'I thought you were that man found his way down here,' she said. 'Go on through. Only it was the smell, see. Not as strong as it is now.'

'You're sure, Aggie? I've still got the stomach and the throat tablets in my bag if you'd like to test the smell of them again.'

'They weren't right the other day, so I don't see why they should be right now. Especially as the right one's here.'

'Just to please me,' Chris said, reaching to squeeze her hand.

She squeezed it back, looking up at him as if the sun shone out of his ears. 'Only we could sit down, couldn't we? Come along in. Now, how about that for a telly?' She ushered us into the living room. 'I reckon they must sell that screen by the yard.'

'By the metre, more like,' Chris said. 'Now, that must be your chair.' He helped her down into a wing chair covered with a brightly coloured crochet blanket the sibling of the one she had at home. 'We'll sit over here on this sofa.'

'Come on, then, Sophie, pop one in,' she said. 'Let me have me sniff.'

I obeyed. She screwed her face around in a lovely imitation of Jilly Goolden tasting wine to inhale the smell of antacid tablet. 'Now, that's – that's the stomach one, isn't it? No, not lemony enough. Go and spit it out – you know where the kitchen is, don't you? And put the kettle on while you're on your feet, there's a good girl.'

I did as I was told. Spitting the antacid into the bin, and swilling my mouth out for good measure, I returned to pop the throat lozenge into my mouth.

'Come on,' she cackled, 'you're not supposed to stop breathing. Let's have a good whiff, then. No, nothing like. Now, when you go and spit it out, you might as well make the tea. And there's a big tin in there: there may be some mince-pies left. No, she can manage. You tell me all about the geranium, young Chris. Sit on this chair here, so I can see you. There.'

When, carrying the tray, I stood in the doorway watching, they were still hand in hand, hers with their swollen arthritic joints, his strong, well-shaped. And bruised. I turned quietly back to the kitchen and replaced the tray on the work-surface. There would be a bathroom upstairs where I could sit and have a little weep in peace. Little weep! Me? For what? Not just disappointing Aggie, surely. Not just hurting Chris, emotionally and physically. Not just for myself, scared and a long way from Mike – who didn't even know what had been going on.

My God, I'd forgotten Steph! He was supposed to be bringing his new motorbike to show me today. And I wasn't there. Any more than I had been for the best part of twenty years. Much as I'd have liked to cry in good earnest, I'd better pull myself together and get on the phone to him.

The tea-tray had mysteriously found its way into the living room, and Chris and Aggie were notably tactful about my absence – Chris because he could see I'd been crying and Aggie because she couldn't. Excusing myself again – I felt *de trop* anyway! – I returned to the kitchen with my mobile phone and tapped in Steph's number.

I'd never called him at home, like a mistress not risking

upsetting the wife. But if his mother wanted me to eat with the family, then presumably it was all right to go ahead.

A woman answered the phone third ring.

'You must be Steph's mum,' I said, all brightly sure of my welcome. 'This is Sophie here . . .'

'Sophie? I'm sorry?' She wasn't apologising for mishearing; she was apologising for not recognising the name.

'Sophie,' I repeated, just in case.

'Sophie who?'

When we'd first started to meet, he'd said I should pretend I was someone he knew from college, didn't he?

'Just a friend,' I said. 'He said he might pop over to see me today. Show off his new bike. And I wanted him to know I wouldn't be in, after all. Could you tell him, please?' And I cut the connection.

It could have been worse. She could have told me he'd smashed the bike into a brick wall. She could have told me he was in intensive care, fighting for his life. She could have told me anything, I reminded myself. Pulling my shoulders back, I slipped back into the living room and started on the tea.

'Sophie, what on earth's the matter?' Chris said, cutting across whatever Aggie was saying.

'It's Steph,' I said. 'It's Steph. He told me he'd told his parents – and he hasn't.'

And I threw myself on to my knees by Aggie, and cried my eyes out.

I could hear them arguing over my head. Aggie wanted to pop me in bed with a shot of brandy and a hot-water bottle. Chris favoured popping me into hospital with whatever shots the medics thought appropriate. I favoured neither.

'I just want to go and sort all this mess out,' I said, kneeling up straight and letting Chris haul me to my feet. 'Then I shall sleep until it's time to catch that plane.'

'Plane?' Aggie repeated.

Adopting an apologetic undertone, as if I were a child and couldn't explain for myself, Chris said, 'To Australia. To spend Christmas with Mike.'

'What? But I told Luce I'd be spending Christmas in me own home. I said as I'd be spending it with you two.'

Never apologise, never explain: that was what the man said. I'd take his advice, whoever he was. 'What did Lucy say, when you told her that?' I asked, trying to get my voice under some semblance of control.

'Well, she seemed mightily put out. But I said—'

'I should just think she would be,' I replied. 'Her own gran not wanting to spend Christmas with her. You always spend Christmas with her. You have a meal waiting for when she finishes at the hospital. Always. She says no one can cook a turkey like you do.'

Shit! I'd said the wrong thing – again. What Aggie wasn't prepared to tell Lucy was that she couldn't see to cook the turkey – or maybe she couldn't trust those arthritic hands to lift it out of the oven.

'Actually,' Chris said, 'I was hoping to come down myself. I've got to go into work on Christmas morning, but I shall be free later. And I knew you always left it to the evening to eat. I thought—'

'You've got family,' she interrupted, shocked.

'Long way to Scotland from Smethwick,' he said. 'So I thought—'

'I don't care what you thought—'

'I do. And you thought quite right,' came a voice from the hall. Lucy. *Dea ex machina* if ever there was one. 'I can think of nothing nicer,' she continued, surging into the living room with two bags of shopping which Chris immediately took from her, 'than your joining us, Chris. I'll air the Put-u-up bed so you can drink yourself silly and not have to worry about your licence. Pity you can't join us, Sophie, but you be where you should be. With your man. Now, what's the state of that tea?'

Chapter Thirty-two

We didn't say very much in the car on the way back to Smethwick. I didn't cry any more: someone had pulled a plug somewhere, draining the little energy I had left. Chris had the excuse of the motorway traffic, but with his driving experience that was a pretty thin excuse. He'd never properly come to terms with the arrival of Steph – had typically never quite forgiven me for having had what he would no doubt call an illegitimate child all those years before we'd even met. What he didn't know, of course, was that Steph himself was the result of a rape. Mike was the only person I'd ever told. I'd still got to do what I'd failed to do while I was busying myself sniffing out fraud: not only to tell Steph who his father was, but also to break to the father the information I'd so long suppressed. And now Steph had suppressed information. Why, why had he lied to me? Because he'd intended to tell his parents and never quite found the moment. Why? No, I could make no sense of it.

I was glad when Chris turned to me at last. 'We'll get a bite in the canteen before you make your statement – OK?'

'Fine.'

Though he was perhaps expecting me to, I wouldn't thank him for stepping in to rescue Aggie's Christmas. It was his own choice, and he'd probably have a better time there than with anyone else. I did permit myself a gentle speculation about him and Lucy. They'd met several times before, notably when

Aggie had been hospitalised with a broken hip and Chris had been a conscientious visitor. She'd always looked at him with interest and seemed like a woman who would get her own way. Well, a good festive bonk never did anyone any harm. And, who knows, it might lead to something more long term.

As far as I was concerned, if someone had told me I could stay with Mike in Oz not just for Christmas but for ever, never coming back to the godforsaken dump that was the Black Country I normally loved, I would have showered him with blessings. What was the matter with me? Here were my people, my roots. My home.

No, it wasn't the place I wanted to get away from, it was the feelings that were inside me.

After a larger portion of the police canteen's home-made chicken pie and chips than I would have believed possible, I felt much better. Well enough to dredge through my bag to see what it held in the way of make-up. I came up with lipstick and powder. Tickets for a long-gone concert. A couple of pound coins. A further delve produced some eye-shadow I thought I'd lost months ago. But no mascara. Tough. There. Ready for action.

Except I needed them all over again after I'd made my statement. In the past I've been really irritated that it should take a police officer so long to transcribe my words on to paper – and transform what I thought were quite cogent, shapely sentences into a mess of sprawling words. The WPC, a woman of about my age, who took me through the process this time was incredibly efficient at writing things down accurately. But her sympathetic silences – my head found time to admire her technique and wonder where she'd been trained – allowed my feelings to keep spilling out in tears.

It must have been about four thirty when we gathered in Chris's office – Peter and Harvinder, both clutching sheaves of paper,

Chris and I. Chris had acquired two flip charts from somewhere – nothing like as convenient as the big whiteboard in Peter's office, but then, that room didn't have the Table. Someone – Bridget, at a guess – had found some beer mats (Beamish Stout, to be precise) so that no drinks would stain the surface.

'Right: we're all clear that this isn't an official police meeting,' Chris said. 'Otherwise Sophie wouldn't be here, and the rest of the team would.'

'Just think of all that overtime, Gaffer,' Peter said.

Wasn't he supposed to be spending more time with his wife? And here he was, making jokes.

'The rest of the team would be mightily pissed off, I should think,' I pointed out, 'since the Baggies are at home this afternoon.'

Harvinder snorted. 'A lot of us get to see matches at the Hawthorns whether we like it or not. And not all policemen – or women – like football. Or the so-called supporters. Especially some of the visitors.'

So what had got up his nose? He wasn't usually so ratty. I intercepted a glance between Chris and Peter. They looked as taken aback as I was. He slung himself into a seat at the far end.

'You sure you're all right, Sophie?' Peter asked, putting an arm round my shoulders and hugging me. Perhaps it was easier to be nice to someone you weren't really close to. 'Shouldn't you be in hospital or something?'

'The only place I want to be right now is Australia,' I said. 'With or without Mike. But since I can't be, and since I can't be sorting out my future at UWM till Monday—'

'Future?' He pressed me gently into a chair.

'How – indeed, whether – I can complete this course. There'll be considerable disruption to it, I should imagine, with two lecturers . . . unavailable. And I really can't afford another year without pay.'

'Since you've stopped two bits of fraud – we think it's two

– they ought to give you next year for free if you need it. *Ex gratia*, or something,' Peter said.

Harvinder looked up. 'And refund this year's fees.'

'But another year *without salary*? Sorry, this is neither the time nor the place for this. Let's get on.'

'When I talk to the vice chancellor,' Chris said quietly, 'on Monday, I shall point out that they owe you rather more than a free year. There was something in the papers about a man who gave up his job to go to some other university for some specialist course and they failed to deliver it. He's just got £100,000 out of them in compensation. I'd have thought the VC might like to think about that.'

'It's hardly comparable,' I began.

'But well worth a try. I might throw a few words around like "duty of care", and so on.'

'It should tighten up their staff recruitment procedures,' Peter said. 'Checking qualifications and references and so on.'

I smiled. 'Thanks, Chris.' I didn't know at the moment if I'd ever want to complete the course, but it was good to have someone else trying to keep my options open. I straightened my shoulders. 'So what news of Bowen? Bowen and friends?'

'Well,' Peter began, 'he's got more friends than we thought. Given that it was a fair cop, he and his solicitor thought it might look better if he got everything off his chest. Unfortunately that everything doesn't involve all the Carla business. Most but not all. Or Jago. So shall we start with him? Or with her?' He looked at Chris.

Chris glanced at me. He couldn't fail to notice the puffiness of my eyes. Perhaps he thought I'd be better having a respite, however brief, from Jago.

'Carla. Fire away.' He prepared to write down the salient points; no doubt Peter would eventually be compiling an enormously long and detailed report, but Chris would want to keep his own notes.

'As soon as we found her body, and it became a murder inquiry,' Peter began, 'we moved in on all aspects of her life that could give us an ID on her. As you know, she'd erased everything at UWM, and emptied her bank and building society accounts.'

'It was definitely Carla's doing?' Chris put in.

'That's what the IT people think.' He patted a file. 'Shall I read it out now or would you prefer to look at it later?'

'Later!'

'So,' Peter continued, 'there's a lot of cash somewhere, with her passport, assuming she ever had one. There was never a British one issued in that name, incidentally. Sorry, we still don't know where everything is. But we soon will, I'm sure. We've got a slot on *Crimewatch* coming up – hang on, Sophie, you'd be surprised at the amount of information something like that throws up! Now, the result of our cut-dragging is—'

'I didn't know you were doing that!' I said.

'Once we had the suggestion that someone might have tripped her, of course we did. We've come up with a piece of string! The forensic people assure us it's the right length, and may well have had something adhesive attached to it. I don't think a jury would be overimpressed by all the ifs and buts, but it may be if it's taken in conjunction with something else. Bowen's explanation.'

'What!'

'Bowen tells us he went to remonstrate with her. His word.'

'Did "remonstrating" involve a couple of heavies?' I asked.

Peter shook his head. 'Not according to his statement. He saved them for tougher stuff, Sophie! He'd suspected for some time she didn't have the qualifications she claimed, and had tackled her. She didn't admit anything, but hinted that she knew something of his activities. They had a tacit pact. Armed truce. Whatever. Then he realised that if Mike found no thesis in Oz, people like Jago might start rocking the boat.' He paused as everyone groaned. 'Sorry. Bowen was afraid that if Jago asked other people the questions he was asking him, this would attract attention to the faculty. This, of course, was the last thing Bowen wanted. He says she was already drinking when he arrived and was quietly wrapping up a big parcel. That's true: a box of books, wrapped in brown paper. But not sealed with tape. Or, more's the pity, addressed. When he, er, 'remonstrated' she became quite wild but, realising she was losing it, went to get some fresh air. In the end he stormed out after her, stumbled but kept his feet and made for his car. Then, as she pursued him, yelling at him, she too tripped. One ankle caught in the thick string that had caught him. And that, alas, tallies with the PM report. But she went over. The boat rocked and crushed her immediately. Well, that tallies with the PM report too. Scared as hell, he left her where she was and drove off.'

Could all that be plausible? I narrowed my eyes. 'Hang on. They'd both been drinking. All the prints were hers . . .'

'We suspect he went back on board and cleaned up a bit. Remember that kitchen? How tidy it was compared with the rest of the place? Perhaps he cleaned up too well. He's an amateur, isn't he? Anyway, it'll take some explaining to a jury why he came to eliminate all traces of himself.'

'All?'

'Not quite all.' Harvinder grinned. 'That notice you retrieved from the bin, Sophie. It had his prints on it, and the experts say they can show he held it to feed his printer, held it as it came out, and then held it to pin it to Carla's door. Very decent of him to save you poor students wasting your time trying to see a woman who was lying dead in the cut.' He curled his lip ironically and took a deep breath. 'On the boat itself, he'd removed all but a couple of hairs and a thread from his jacket. But since he admits having been there earlier in the evening – unless he confesses to pushing her . . . And remember, the post mortem showed no sign of bruising to her back.'

'Through layers of clothing?' I said scathingly. 'Can't you charge him with – with leaving her there? A decent woman. Well,' I conceded, as they laughed ironically, 'a decent teacher.'

'You are supposed to report bodies when you find them,' Peter confirmed drily. 'But we've plenty of other things to pass on to the DPP. Including,' he paused, with the air of someone pulling a rabbit from a hat, 'a statement from our Geordie friend.'

'Eric the Red,' Harvinder said.

'Eric Bloodaxe,' I said simultaneously.

Peter stared. 'Eric Conrad. Now, he'd already said, remember, that there'd been partying on the boat. We pressed him on this again, in the cold, sober light of day. He insists that there was no one hanging around. And SOCO haven't been able to pinpoint anything at all to suggest anyone else's presence.'

'Hang on! Jago's footprint! That was why he turned up at my place this morning. Because you were on to him!'

'Can I come back to him? Let's finish with Bowen first,' Peter said, shuffling through the pile of papers in front of him. 'Where was I? Yes. So – much as I hate to accept it, and believe me I'll be talking to him till we're sick of the sight of each other – I'm inclined to accept what he says.'

'As much sinned against as sinning,' Chris ruminated. 'Hmm. After his performance this morning I hate to leave it there. Well, let's move on to Jago. Or Carla.'

Harvinder picked up his notes. 'Maybe Carla was a decent teacher.' Harvinder nodded in my direction. 'But she was a very complex person. Or at least a very healthy one. She wasn't registered with any doctor or dentist, had never any dealings with a hospital . . .'

'But she must have paid tax and national insurance! I mean, she was a member of UWM staff.'

'That's Monday's job, Sophie,' Harvinder said. 'She's dead,

now. It'd be nice to put all the pieces together, but it'll keep till then.'

'Overtime,' Chris said, his eyes twinkling. 'More to the point, staff welfare. Everyone's put in very long hours: I want everyone who can to have tomorrow off. Including you, Peter.'

I clapped my hand to my head. 'Kathryn refused point-blank to leave me alone with the student files, as if someone else had messed them up. Have you talked to her?'

Peter raised his eyes heavenwards. 'Sophie, of course we've talked to her. And to Luke—'

'Luke!' I yelled. I'd forgotten about Luke!

'What about Luke?' Peter looked at me as if I'd flipped.

'She's got this crazy notion that just because Luke got beaten up once, everyone else is after him,' Chris said. 'Sophie – he's peripheral. No one would need to get at him.'

'Just check,' I said. 'Just bloody check that he's all right.'

Chris nodded at Harvinder, who pushed away from the table and picked up the phone. 'What's his phone number, Sophie?'

'Oh, phone him yourself, Sophie,' Chris said. 'I'll get the kettle on. Harv, just get her an outside line.'

'I told you he'd be all right,' Chris said, pushing Bridget's rock cakes at me. 'Here, have another. This titchy amount's my iron rations for the weekend.' He smiled ironically, joggling an old-fashioned biscuit tin full to the brim.

I rubbed my nose ruefully. 'Sorry, Gaffer. That paranoia thing again.'

He nodded. By common consent, the four of us returned to the Table. Chris looked meaningfully at the mats.

'The thing is, I nearly walked into a Saab when I was down at the Oldbury campus,' I said, my mouth not quite empty. 'And Bowen drives a Saab. So it might have been him messing round with the staff records.'

'Could have been,' Peter began. 'But wasn't. He was at some meeting, so his alibi is watertight. On the other hand, Carla was down there earlier in the week. The more we know, the better it looks for him, the worse for her.'

'Harvinder, do *you* think Bowen killed her?'

He looked straight at me. 'Funnily enough, I don't. I'm sure he's all kinds of shit, but I don't actually see him as a killer. He's the sort of man who might drive young women to their deaths, but I don't see him getting his hands soiled. No, if he wanted someone wiped out, he'd pay someone else. He says he kept his heavies off you this morning.'

'That's certainly an interesting interpretation of what I overheard,' Chris said drily.

'But what brought him to my place at all? Just how far did he intend to "remonstrate" with me?'

'He *says* he just wanted to tell you to fuck off to Australia and stay there. And he was going to smash up your place to encourage you. And if that didn't work, he'd have had you roughed up a bit to reinforce the message.'

'And when Sophie turned up in Australia black and blue, Mike wouldn't have been on the phone to Chris before you could say "no-ball"?' Peter asked.

'I would say Bowen seemed quite keen on a bit of rape,' I said, trying to keep my voice mild. 'Three bits.'

Harvinder smiled kindly at me, as if to show he understood how much effort I was making. 'Only because someone else gave him the idea, he says. And he assured us, hand on tender heart, that he would never have done it.'

'Or let his heavies do it? OK,' I said, 'so what does he actually admit to?'

'Prostitution, illegal detention, fraudulently depriving UWM of student fees.' He counted off the items on his fingers with considerable relish. 'The scam seems to be this. He advertises, as you know, for students for University *College* of the West Midlands, gets them student visas, pops them into a lodging house – a pretty naff lodging house. We might be able to get him on fire regs, too, Gaffer.'

Peter made a note.

'So he's got a few thousand pounds off them. Then he enrols them at UWM on a much cheaper basis, as part-time students. Just how legal that is we'll have to discuss with Immigration.'

Peter took up the thread again. 'Those students who can cope with the course, continue with it. Those who can't – especially those orphaned young women on those special bursaries – they have a special treat. And this is where he gets his real money from. They get siphoned off into what my gran would have called domestic service. Domestic slavery to you and me. He's given us addresses already. Other girls – well, those heavies might have given you a clue . . .'

'Prostitution?'

'Hostessing in clubs, officially. And massage parlours. Like that one you spotted.'

'And some of them can't stand it and top themselves,' Harvinder said. 'Some so-called employers – owners, more like – are already answering questions. Respectable men and women treating kids like slaves. Jesus Christ!'

I raised my eyebrows at this expletive from a Hindu, but no one else seemed to find it unusual. So I said, wishing I didn't have to, 'Is there any news yet of Shazia Nazir?'

Harvinder smiled. 'There could just be a happy ending there. A young woman turned up in a terrible state at that mosque down in Highgate. Hypothermia, malnutrition, the lot. And not talking. She's in Intensive Care in the Queen Elizabeth at the moment. The prognosis is good. And no, Sophie,' he continued, holding a hand up to silence me, 'you do *not* have to dash over there. There's a Malay interpreter standing by. OK? From the Malaysian High Commission, before you ask. They're very interested in the whole case.'

'I bet they are. So my floating population of students . . .'

'Waste not, want not. Bowen's already paid fees to UWM for their education. So he simply gets other women to take on the identities of their predecessors. God knows what sort of a line he spins them.'

'He thinks on his feet, that bugger,' Harvinder said. 'He'd come up with something plausible. In any case, their English isn't up to much, remember. Perhaps they think it's normal in England.'

'More likely he tells them that if they don't play ball he'll have them deported,' Peter said. 'After all, you'd have thought they'd be pleased to see me and Sophie when we turned up at that so-called hall of theirs – British Bobby to the rescue and all that. But they were scared. Yes, Bowen would have put the mockers on them.'

'But why all that business with the print-out showing entry qualifications?' I said. 'If he'd got this lot sussed out, why bother with – presumably – making up his own convincing list?'

'You tell us! You taught them!' Chris said.

I held my head. Grey matter or grey cotton wool? 'I suppose he was using my invaluable teaching skills to help some poor women to grasp enough English to make them useful in whatever trade he'd chosen for them.'

'Eh?'

'Well, if he's got some with really dodgy English, he might not think it worth while to slot them through his other channel. Waste of money, rather. So he just slips them into English Language classes until he considers they're ready for – for—'

'What about Security?' Chris asked.

'May have one guard at least in his pocket. Like the one that found me in Carla's office.'

'Wouldn't they need proper ID to use the library?' he pursued.

Harvinder laughed. 'Come off it, Gaffer. You only need

libraries if you want books. And to want books you must be able to read. Poor kids,' he ended.

There was a little silence.

'I suppose Jenny Lee must feature somewhere in this.' I wouldn't remind them they'd been ready to use her translation services. 'She didn't like the way I was using Bowen's bathroom.'

'Eh?' Chris said. As well he might.

'Well, she must have realised there was a time-lapse between my going upstairs and going into the bathroom. She's a very bright woman – excellent grades in all her assignments.' I added, more slowly, 'She's also very thin, very tiny . . .'

Peter grinned. 'Just the right size for our vandal. I mean, a lot of mess was made, but no serious damage – and if she was a very good student, she'd know the amount of work people were putting into the course.'

'Very good intellectually or morally?' Chris asked.

'Point taken, Gaffer. I shall enjoy talking to her about that. No, we haven't interviewed her yet. She's waiting for her solicitor. We think that effectively she was the madam. She and Bowen are like this.' Peter crossed his fingers.

None of us spoke for a few minutes.

'You know what really gets to me,' I said. 'Oh, I know that compared with the suicides this must seem trivial. But those two skivvies at Bowen's. Muslims. And he deliberately gets me to cook extra pork, which will be on their menu – and nothing else – until he sees fit to change it. Waste not, want not,' I echoed Harvinder, but in my case in homage to Lola.

'But Muslims don't eat pork, any more than Jews,' said Chris.

'Exactly,' I said.

'I think we need some more tea,' Chris said, suiting the word to the deed.

'So what about Jago?' I asked, comforted by two more fine

cakes bulging with dried fruit and knowing I had to ask sooner or later.

'Fucking little scrote!' Chris exploded. This man, who rarely swore.

Peter, registering it, flicked a glance at Harvinder. 'He's still groggy from the anaesthetic – you did a good job on that hand of his, Sophie! – so we can't question him yet. Try as we might, we can't find anything more than a footprint to link him with Carla's narrow boat. What I'd like him to admit – when he's stopped gibbering with fear – is that he went to the boat to confront her and thus started the whole avalanche that followed. But even that isn't a crime. Attempted rape, however, is. And grievous bodily harm. He said when we arrested him he'd come to you desperate for advice. But you were so provocative in your dressing gown he lost his head.'

Chris smiled at me with great affection. 'That's the "provocative" garment that even Aggie would find a bit respectable, isn't it? Will Bowen's solicitor be trying some sort of bargain – if they snitch on Jago, the DPP reduce the charges against them?'

I stared at my hands, which seemed all of a sudden to have taken on a life of their own. Peter reached across and clasped one of them.

'It's OK, kid,' he said.

I took a mouthful of tea. 'He should never, ever teach again,' I said, loud as if I were at a public meeting. It was the only way to keep my voice steady. 'He's got problems with women. Real problems. Maybe jail isn't the right place. But he sure as hell needs some sort of therapy.' As I might. I had to admit it, the thought of rape and buggery by cruet set might be blackly comic, but I didn't just at the moment find it amusing – especially if I'd been forced into oral sex as well.

I was almost relieved when Chris's phone rang.

He got up, swearing in disbelief. No doubt he'd asked for

no incoming calls. He barked once, then settled into silence, making occasional notes. I watched my shaking hands, tried to steady my heart beat. Then I caught a familiar name. Jago.

A last Chris cut the call, returning to the table with a grim but satisfied smile. 'The woman who was assualted the other night,' he said, 'has just remembered that her assailant had one irregular tooth in an otherwise perfect set. Apparently he smiled at her when he accosted her first. She claims she could identify him in a parade by that tooth alone. I think we should give her a chance. When Jago's up to it,' he added considerately. 'Meanwhile SOCO are going to ask a forensic odontologist—'

'A what?' I managed to ask. It felt as if great areas of my brian were closing down.

'A dentist specialising in criminal work. They want one to look at an apple they found at the scene – some very nice toothmarks in it, they say. I suspect,' he said, smiling grimly, 'with a conviction for sexual offences, he might find it difficult to continue teaching.'

'And the bonus is,' added Peter with relish, 'that a prison sentence for sexual assault is much longer than one for fraud. Yeah!'

To my amazement, he and Chris exchanged a triumphant five.

'Where are you staying tonight?' Harvinder asked me suddenly. 'Because I don't think you should be on your own. I've only got the one bedroom at my place—'

'Don't risk his settee, for Christ's sake,' Peter said, rubbing his shoulders as if they still hurt.

Harvinder looked irritated by his jokiness. 'But there's my mum – she'd—'

'Ian Dale's away, isn't he?' Chris said. 'I could run you down to Lucy's. Aggie would love to look after you.'

I shook my head. 'I need to make that house my own again.'

*　　*　　*

Chris pulled up outside my house. We got out stiffly, not speaking. For all my fine words, I dreaded going in on my own. Chris was no doubt working out how he could suggest coming in with me. I'd bet it would be something along the lines of being there to pick me up if I fell on the frosty path. If he did I wouldn't point out there wouldn't be any frost, not inside.

We laughed at nothing, on edge.

'I'd better go in and feed Ivo,' I said. 'And organise his transfer to Shahida's for Christmas.'

'If she can't have him, I will. I'll take him down to Evesham with me.'

I gaped.

'Sophie, I shouldn't have done what I did the other night. You know. After that meal,' he said, locking the car. We walked up the path. He had to take my keys from me to open the front door. Would my hands ever be steady again? 'But I did. I can't blame the alcohol. And I'm sorry.'

We stepped into the hall. I switched off the alarm. The house felt safe. I pushed through into the kitchen. It still smelt of the disinfectant Chris had used on my floor.

'You see,' he said, feeding Ivo a peanut, so he didn't have to face me, 'I know – you and me – it didn't work out before. And it may never . . . And I wish you and Mike every happiness. But if – if . . .' He gave up, at last turning to face me. 'Anyway, if you want to reclaim your kitchen, I'll lay my notebook on the table like a drawn sword between a knight and his lady, and we'll cook up a meal together.'

'Done,' I said. But my voice wasn't as steady as it should have been, either.

It's a long flight, whichever route you take to Australia. Half of me couldn't wait to be in Mike's arms again. The other half was busy editing bits of my narrative, and working out how to explain away the bruises that had blossomed all over me.

For the team's sake, I wanted to protect him from knowing all I'd been through. In the end, though, as we lay in the over-airconditioned bedroom, I told him everything. He had a right to know.

Most of his reaction was entirely predictable. One part wasn't.

'You do realise,' he said, 'that this means I shall have to get myself picked for the One Day series? The three-way competition against Sri Lanka and Australia?'

I shook my head, confused.

'If I don't, I should have to fly back to the UK with the others who aren't selected. And I want to make damned sure I don't go home yet.'

'Why?' It was one of the things we'd spoken about with dread, those extra weeks of separation.

'Because if I'm in the team I stay over here another six weeks, don't I? And you're staying with me. Right? Your tutor's in jail, you're – what was the term you used? intermitted? – and your course is postponed till next year. Aggie's safe with her granddaughter. You've nothing to go home for.'

'Except Ivo. Shahida thinks he's giving her daughter an allergy.'

'What a good job Dave's got that stress fracture and will be flying home this weekend. He can look after his own rodent. And we, Sophie, will stay in Oz. Together. And we won't be spending our time hunting for non-existent Ph.D.s. OK?' said Mike.

'OK,' said I.

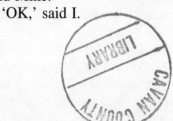